FATHERLESS

Fatherless is the first volume of a trilogy by Brian J. Gail
Volume 2: Motherless
Volume 3: Childless

FATHERLESS

REVISED 2ND EDITION

THE CRITICALLY ACCLAIMED NOVEL BY

BRIAN J. GAIL

EMMAUS
ROAD
PUBLISHING

Steubenville, Ohio

The first edition of *Fatherless* was published in 2008 by Human Life International in Front Royal, Virginia. This new edition contains modifications to the original and is published by Emmaus Road Publishing.

Emmaus Road Publishing
827 North Fourth Street
Steubenville, Ohio 43952
www.emmausroad.org

ISBN: 978-1-931018-73-9

Cover design by
Devin Schadt

Layout by
Theresa Westling

For our priests
in the Year for Priests
June 19, 2009 – June 19, 2010

1

Father John Sweeney raised the Host and slowed his pace. He had promised his mother on ordination day that he would always conduct the Consecration of the Mass, the most sacred moment in what the Roman Catholic Church has always regarded as its most solemn prayer, with manifest reverence.

As he knelt, Host in hand, he couldn't rid his mind of Margaret Kealey's voice. She called just before he left the rectory to tell him that chronic migraine pain was engulfing her in a fire of unbearable torment and that she thought she was close to death.

"Father," she whispered, "I think I'm dying. Bill's in New York. Please help me."

"I'll come, Maggie," he promised. "Right after Mass. And I'll be praying for you."

As he reached for the chalice that held what he believed was about to become the very real Blood of humanity's Savior, he did a quick scan of the men and women in the pews. There were eleven of them, three of whom were men. All were regulars, daily communicants—the "gray warriors," as he referred to them.

John greatly admired them. He couldn't always relate to their fervor or, for that matter, to their death grip on every particle of the Faith—including the so-called "hard sayings." Some of those hard sayings he found quite hard indeed. His problem, he often told himself, was that he knew the men who ran the Church, at least in the United States, and he knew them to be among the most fallible of God's fallen creatures. In fact, he knew a number of them no longer believed all of what these simple souls in front of him held as gospel truth.

Chalice in hand, he settled his gaze on Rose O'Rourke. She was recently widowed after raising nine children, including five notorious sons who had alternately scandalized and terrorized the small community. She was now working part-time as a nurse's assistant at Lower Merwood Hospital. He often found himself avoiding her gaze while saying Mass . . . such was its beatific quality.

He would ask Rose to go with him, he decided.

After Mass, John removed his vestments quickly and hurried to catch her in the vestibule where she was wrestling with an umbrella. She nodded immediately upon hearing the request. Today they would drive the short distance to the Kealey home. On a good day it was a short and splendid walk, with only the hill over the bridge on South Narbrook Avenue as a bit of an obstacle. This morning, however, was wet and blustery, as it often was along the mid-Atlantic seaboard in the middle of November.

The borough of Narbrook was something of a Brigadoon for middle-income families in the middle and latter decades of the twentieth century. The town itself was first settled in the early 1800s by European immigrants who came to America to work as domestics and tradesmen in the homes of the Main Line aristocracy. It was staunchly Calvinist and Lutheran, which made it a very good place for Catholics, particularly Irish Catholics. They arrived in waves, along with their counterparts from Italy, Poland, and Germany. They were good, decent, hardworking people who brought with them their faith, their work ethic, and the immigrant's deep, abiding hope for a better life.

The town was split roughly in half by the rail line, which connected the wealthier outreaches of the fabled Main Line with the business, cultural, and historic centers of Philadelphia. On the north side lay the town's center—its churches, shops, restaurants, movie house, and saloons. There were three of the latter, in addition to a well-appointed liquor store in the single block that comprised the downtown "shopping district," proof enough the Irish had arrived.

The north side of town was hilly and crowned on its perimeter with decorous Victorian homes made of stucco and clapboard, boasting large, wraparound porches that functioned as neighborhood gathering places in pleasant weather. Classic working-class turn-of-the-century twin homes dotted the interior. The entirely residential south side was a mirror image from the Rockport Avenue Bridge all the way down to Wyncote Road. In the 1950s and '60s these homes were filled with large Catholic families, somewhat smaller Christian denominational families, and a smattering of empty nesters who had long ago finished life's central task and now simply enjoyed watching their younger neighbors suffer the sweet burdens of parenthood.

As they drove up the hill and over the bridge, Rose O'Rourke turned slightly in her seat and asked her young assistant pastor, "Father John, why can't the doctors do something for this poor woman? I've never seen such suffering."

They turned right onto Winchester Lane, and John Sweeney counted the homes on the left side of the street until they arrived at the fourth house. It was an old Victorian home, with an oversized wraparound porch, a shared driveway, and a small patch of grass in the back. The front yard and the driveway were littered with balls, bikes, and other toys.

"I don't know, Rose; I wish I had an answer for you," he said as he edged his four-year-old black Acura parallel to the curb. They entered the home through the back door. The front door was locked and, not that it particularly mattered to John, pretty well-covered with what looked like strawberry jam. All six of Margaret Kealey's children were in the kitchen, the oldest two girls trying to make breakfast and pack lunches at the same time.

The boys, aged two and three, were sitting on the floor eating cereal without bowls or spoons, which drew a lecture from one of the older girls in a language the little fellows seemed neither to hear nor understand. Father Sweeney shuddered and wondered why—even now, in the 1980s—some Catholic couples still hadn't gotten the message about regulating the size of their families. "You don't have to do this to yourselves anymore," he wanted to shout. But at . . . to . . . whom?

Moia, who was tall, fair, and the oldest at thirteen, approached the visitors with a spatula in her hand. "Father, my mom's sick again. I don't know who will watch Sean and Andrew when we leave for school."

Rose O'Rourke quietly took the spatula and headed for the range to ladle scrambled eggs onto six assembled plates arranged on a small table in the corner of the kitchen.

"Where's your mom, Moia?" the priest asked.

"She's upstairs in her room," the child answered. "I'll show you."

As John Sweeney followed Maggie Kealey's firstborn up the narrow stairs to the second floor, he reflected on what the future might hold for a youngster who was forced to assume such a heavy responsibility so early in life. He observed that she gave no visible indication of resentment at having her childhood shortened by her mother's unfortunate condition. On the contrary, she seemed to rise to the occasion with an effortless grace that put others, even awkward clerics, at ease.

Moia led him to a large room in the back of the house. The eerie, dark coldness that greeted him as he entered was immediately unsettling. The shades were drawn, as were the drapes, which swallowed any light attempting to steal into the room. Light, he quickly recognized, was clearly the enemy, although sound too was apparently an unwelcome intruder. The only noise that penetrated the stillness was a low groaning coming from the dark figure in the bed.

Moia rushed to her mother's bed and gently removed a damp washcloth from her forehead. She went into the adjoining bathroom and opened the tap in the sink, letting it run, barely audible, as if hoping the gentle sound of running water might bring relief to her stricken mother. With each step toward the bed, John was filled with a growing dread. Intuitively, he knew that he was in no way prepared to dispense relief or hope to this poor soul, and yet he summoned the will to draw closer and offer . . . something.

Once bedside he was startled by what he saw. Maggie Kealey, raven-haired and doe-eyed, ever poised and trim, was among the most beautiful of women—always the most striking woman in any room she entered. Still more winsome, she wore her beauty with an ease and humility that drew even other women to her.

She was also a woman of accomplishment both before and after her much-heralded wedding to Bill Kealey. She was an honors graduate of Springton College, a small, elite women's college on Philadelphia's storied Main Line. She was also a classically trained cellist who had briefly held a chair with the internationally renowned Philadelphia Orchestra. She yielded that chair with great reluctance, to a half lifetime of regret, at the persistent entreaties of one Bill Kealey and, ultimately, the presence of their daughter Moia, who arrived precisely nine months to the day, or perhaps evening, of their wedding.

All the beauty, however, had vanished from Maggie Kealey's face on this November morning. Father John Sweeney saw instead a grotesque distortion of her features and a limp resignation in her contorted body, as though all her physical and emotional reserves were entirely spent. She lay in bed as if awaiting the relief of death. "Maggie," he whispered, "it's Father John. I offered Mass for you this morning."

She nodded her gratitude. "Did you bring the oils?" she asked through gritted teeth.

"Yes, Maggie, I brought the oils," he replied softly.

Moia was back with two cold, damp washcloths that she applied to her mother's forehead and neck. "Mom, I'm going to take the girls to school; Mrs. O'Rourke will watch Sean and Andrew."

This drew a groan from her mother that John thought reflected her embarrassment, not to mention guilt, at having another woman assume her burdens.

John Sweeney opened his black carrying case and removed his slender stole, a candle, a small green prayer book, and one tiny jar of blessed oil. Within several moments, without so much as a word of introduction, he launched into what his Church once referred to as the "Last Rites" but now called the "Anointing of the Sick."

As he did so, he recalled the old priest professor in the seminary droning on about the ritual. John and his classmates had hoped uncharitably that the professor's next anointing would be his own, but both the classroom and the faintly unsettling smell of the hospital rooms where John Sweeney typically performed this ritual were now a world removed from this quiet room and its tormented occupant.

The Catholic Church corrected the widespread belief that a baptized soul had to be in death's vestibule to receive an anointing. A chronic and enervating illness or even advanced age was now sufficient to summon the Church's sacramental intervention—which, to the surprise of at least some, occasionally provided a measure of relief that seemed otherwise beyond the reach of modern medicine.

As John Sweeney prayed, he anointed, and as he anointed, he invoked his deceased father's intercession on behalf of this faithful wife and mother. He finished, closed the book, and began packing his carrying case. There was simply nothing more he could do for Margaret Kealey. She reached for his hand. He clasped it with both of his and whispered, "God loves you, Maggie. The Church thanks you for the gift of your suffering." Then, under his breath, "The good Lord knows we have never needed it more."

2

John Sweeney sat in a green Adirondack chair on the front porch of St. Martha's rectory. He was praying. His prayer was a prayer of thanksgiving for the strangely remarkable journey that returned him, at age thirty-five, to his native parish in the summer of 1985—and even more remarkably, as its assistant pastor. It was a warm, early summer evening, and the only sound on this moonlit night came from the cicadas droning high in the towering oak trees above him. It was somewhat late, perhaps slightly after 10:00 p.m., when a figure emerged from the darkened street in front of the rectory. It was Michael Burns.

The two men could have passed for brothers. Each was round shouldered and slightly stooped with dark, untamable hair and pale Celtic skin that never quite tans. John was several years older, but Michael Burns carried himself with a poise and confidence—some said cockiness—that suggested that he was either older . . . or wanted others to think he was.

"Michael, me lad, to what do I owe the honor?" he said, standing to greet his guest.

"Ach, fadder," Burns mimicked, "I've a wee bit of problem, and I thought maybe yourself might give me a listen."

"Come, sit . . . sit," John Sweeney replied, pointing to the rocker next to his. "First tell me how Carol and the kids are."

John considered the Burns family among his best parishioners. Michael and Carol were daily communicants—Michael at the 7:00 a.m. Mass and Carol at the 8:00 a.m. Mass—after dropping off the couple's three girls at the parish school. Both were active in the parish: coaching youth teams, organizing and giving Pre-Cana conferences to engaged couples, chaperoning young adult dances, and generally making themselves available whenever their pastor or his assistant needed help.

"Father, I need some advice," Michael Burns began slowly. "I'm feeling dead-ended at Slattery, and I've got an opportunity to go to New York and work for a major firm with offices all over the world. Carol and I don't want to leave Narbrook, but I'm worried that if I don't do something now, my career will stall within the next few years, and I'll be trapped with no out."

Slattery and Associates was a small advertising firm with a somewhat unusual mix of industrial and packaged goods clients. Michael Burns started as a copywriter, preparing mostly press releases and brochures for the firm's public relations division. He was promoted twice in his first four years and was tasked with writing television commercials for a packaged goods company headquartered in Chicago. When he realized soon after he could make more money on the business side of the firm, he asked to be reassigned and returned to school for an MBA.

He was named vice president in his seventh year, but Slattery wasn't attracting the kind of clients that provided the intellectual challenge or the visibility within the advertising community that Michael Burns knew he needed at this stage of his career. As a consequence, he began to shift his focus north to Mecca, as America's advertising community commonly referred to New York.

At first Carol resisted, but after considerable discussion and prayer, they emerged with a unity of intent that they believed was a sign of the grace of the Sacrament of Marriage at work. They trusted that their decision, whatever it was, would have God's blessing. Michael contacted several headhunters in the City and began using commercial broadcast production trips to New York as opportunities to conduct interviews with major advertising firms.

He was surprised at the reception he received. Within a month he had offers from the first three companies with whom he interviewed—one from the vaunted General Foods, in their Coffee Division. Two were with global packaged goods advertising firms; one working on the Hershey business at Parsons, Kling, and Herbert; and the other on General Mills products with the Ashmere Group. But the opportunity that interested Michael Burns the most was the chance to work for the Hal Ross agency to launch a new cable network called the Cable Movie Network, or CMN, as it would come to be known.

The prospect of an offer to work as an account director on the national launch of the country's first pay television service brought Michael Burns to Father John Sweeney's porch on this seasonably warm summer night.

"Well . . . I command you to cease and desist from all such thoughts. Be advised you would leave this town and parish under pain of excommunication," Father John Sweeney said with mock sincerity.

"Well, that makes it easy," Michael replied with a smile. "Carol is gonna miss you."

Father Sweeney grinned. "How does she feel about this?"

"Like me, she has reservations. But we both prayed about it, and we've found some peace. So if something comes through, and it seems right, we'll probably be inclined to do this."

"Well then . . . what brings you to my door on this fine summer evening?"

Michael Burns hesitated. "Father, there's a problem, or at least a potential problem. I've got a few things working right now. The one opportunity that most interests me is working on the launch of a new cable television service. It'll offer Hollywood movies for a monthly fee. Some of those movies will be R-rated and, I'm sure, borderline soft porn. Can a practicing Catholic be involved in something like that?"

"Sure," John Sweeney said reflexively. "The Church encourages her sons and daughters to leaven society. Jesus referred to it as being 'the salt.' How can we affect the culture if our people aren't involved in it?"

This gave Michael pause. He had hoped he would hear this from his confessor. Now that he had, he didn't fully trust it. "Father, I don't suspect these people will listen to me about the content of their product. I'll just be a contractor helping them sell more of it so they make more money and keep their shareholders happy."

"My understanding of what you advertising executives do, Michael, is a little different from that. Don't you help your clients determine which markets to enter and exit and how best to package a product to sell more of it?"

"Yes, Father . . . we do, and, yes, sometimes our recommendations involve potential product modifications or even new products. But CMN's product is essentially Hollywood movies, and they don't control the production." Michael paused. "I guess what I'm asking you is this: Can I take that job, if it's offered, knowing that at least some of the current product will be objectionable?"

Now it was Father Sweeney who paused. "Michael," he began slowly, "the very fact that you're here, seeking the Church's blessing on a decision reached in prayer with your wife, is itself a confirmation that the Holy Spirit has been guiding you on this journey. Be assured that as long as you remain faithful in prayer, you and Carol will continue to be guided. And Michael, I want you to listen to me; if this thing comes through, you take it, and know I'll be praying for you."

3

Father Sweeney closed his breviary, turned out the light in the confessional, and parted the window drape ever so slightly to see whether he was alone in the church. He was. It was an ungodly hot summer afternoon in late July. Many of his parishioners were somewhere down at the South Jersey shore or up in the mountains, or at the very least sitting in air-conditioned comfort watching their beloved and accursed Phillies extend their latest losing streak.

John believed the confessional was an anachronism. In his parents' day, people generally went to Confession on Saturday evening so they could present themselves for Holy Communion on Sunday morning. He was discovering that his generation, by and large, was not overly preoccupied with either.

When the pre-Vatican II types—an ever-dwindling number—came to him for absolution, he only half listened. He knew their sins, or what they regarded as their sins. John thought of them as human imperfections and told them so. But this only disturbed his senior penitents, so he gave them light penance, conferred absolution, and sent them on their way with repeated assurances that God loved them just as they were.

Still, they came. John wondered what would happen to his Church when the older parishioners slipped the veil, as the Irish referred to death. What happens to a religion when even the remnant is no more? There were now comparatively fewer, and decidedly much smaller, young families attending Mass weekly and only an aging consort of priests to attend them. He believed it was only a matter of time before the Church was forced to acknowledge reality, changing its policy on married priests and perhaps, in time, women priests.

Three times in the past five years the pastor at St. Martha's, Monsignor Grogan, had reduced the Saturday afternoon and evening hours for weekly confessions. Initially, he cut evening hours out entirely. There was no protest. Did anyone notice? Then he cut the afternoon hours in half—from 3:00 to 5:00 p.m. to 4:00 to 5:00 p.m. Finally, at the beginning of the year, he halved the hours again, reducing them to only half an hour, 4:00 to 4:30 p.m. He did all of this with nary a protest from the faithful.

John entered the confessional late. It was now 4:20 p.m. He thought about closing shop and heading back to his air-conditioned suite to catch the tail end of the Phillies game. Then he heard a sound. Someone entered the darkened church. He knew from the groaning sound coming from the pew that it was a man, and a rather large man at that. In what seemed like mere seconds the groans painfully signaled that a priest-seeking, bunker-busting human missile was homing in on his confessional.

There were now two ways to confess sins, a relatively recent development. The traditional way was through a screened window that most of his elderly parishioners preferred; the other way was face-to-face, which involved sitting in a chair opposite the priest. This alternative was intended to help draw younger Catholics back to the Sacrament. It hadn't.

John heard the Bunker Buster approaching and wondered which door he would open. Traditional, he guessed. He guessed wrong. In walked Joe Delgado, former college football star at Princeton University, now an oversized teddy bear breathing far too heavily. He sat down immediately, filling the chair and eliciting its defiant rebuke.

"Bless me, Father . . . it's been awhile," he began.

"Joe, how are you and Fran doing?" the priest responded, throwing protocol to the wind.

"Uh . . . OK . . . I guess," he replied hesitantly. John recognized the man's discomfort, noted that it was more than physical, and sought to put him at ease.

"Joe, I'm glad you're here. Just relax. We'll begin when you're ready."

Joe Delgado exhaled. "Father, I do need to confess my sins, but I also need . . . a little help."

John shrugged his shoulders and opened his palms. "Good. That's what we're here for . . . just a little bit of help," he offered, smiling.

Joe hesitated, "Father . . . I've . . . I've got a dilemma."

"What kind of dilemma?"

Joe stared at the floor for a long moment before answering. "A moral dilemma, Father. Is there any other kind?" He shrugged his shoulders. "I've got a choice between my career and my family."

"Well, Joe . . . that wouldn't appear to be a hard choice, would it?"

Joe settled his gaze somewhere in the back of John Sweeney's eyes and said evenly, "In this case, it will be, Father. It will be."

Father Sweeney was struck by the transformation that had just taken place in the man sitting opposite him. It was all the more striking because it happened in a matter of moments. The once formidable lineman was now a portly, prematurely aging corporate "suit." But in this instant, he showed a gravitas that greatly surprised John, who thought that perhaps he'd caught just a glimpse of why smart, serious men would entrust him with a portfolio of financial assets that measured in the billions.

"Joe, why don't you tell me about it? I don't think all those people waiting in line will mind."

Joe smiled, looked at his feet, and tried to shift in his chair but found no room to do so and abandoned the effort. He began, "Father, Pittman Labs is being investigated by the U.S. Attorney's Office. They are alleging that there were irregularities in the way we collected and reported data on our biggest beta blocker, Alphasint. They believe we knew before we launched it that some of those deaths you've been reading about would occur. They want our files."

Now it was John Sweeney who tried to shift weight in his chair. "Joe, that would indeed be a serious matter."

"Our CEO asked me . . . and our General Counsel . . . to retrieve the documents, review them, and then report our findings to him directly . . . with recommendations."

"What have you found?"

"Nothing yet with respect to that particular matter. But while rummaging through the archives, I uncovered something far more troubling."

"More troubling than cooking the books for a beta blocker?" John Sweeney was now leaning forward in his chair.

"Father, I found files with studies dating back almost twenty years. They reveal that hormonal contraceptives are actually abortifacients, extremely carcinogenic abortifacients."

John Sweeney's eyes widened. "Who conducted the studies?"

"Father . . . my company was the lead sponsor. We organized the project and provided the seed money. Then we solicited the participation of four other pharmaceutical houses—all of them now major players in the oral contraceptives sector of the industry. The papers were sealed and marked 'Highly Confidential' and directed to the attention of those who at the time were the senior officers of the sponsoring companies, including Pittman Labs."

"And you broke the seal?"

"Yes, Father, I broke the seal."

John dropped his head for several moments, then raised it and said, "Joe, you don't have to worry about me breaking this seal. What is said here remains here, by the Seal of Confession. It's a matter of canon law."

"I appreciate that, Father."

John had arrived at a fork in the road. He could either probe for more information about the studies, or he could guide his penitent to the moral issue in play and provide some guidance. He decided to probe. "Joe, how credible, in your opinion, are these studies and their conclusions?"

"They are extremely credible, Father."

"How do you know that?"

"Because what they proposed to do . . . they did."

"And what exactly did they do?"

"They proposed commissioning leading medical researchers to publish white papers in influential medical journals to change the terms of the debate on the beginning of life."

John Sweeney was incredulous, "How did they accomplish that!?"

"They stipulated that the beginning of life is an issue best decided by ethicists. They argued that, as men of science, only they could define when pregnancy begins. Pregnancy, they pointed out, begins not with the fertilization of an egg, the embryo, but with the implantation of the embryo in the uterine wall."

John Sweeney thought he understood, but he wasn't certain. "Joe . . . isn't that a distinction without a difference?"

"Father . . . they're saying, no pregnancy, no life."

"So they're claiming the embryo is . . . what?"

"A nonperson. What they call a 'pre-embryo.'"

Father Sweeney inhaled audibly and said, "And the role of the . . . the contraceptive . . . in all this?"

"It's decisive, Father. Contraceptives don't just suppress ovulation. They don't just interrupt the pairing of sperm and egg. They have other 'actions.' They also can, and do, interrupt the implantation of embryos. They do that by destroying the adhesiveness of the uterine wall so that the embryos can't find a natural home. These embryos end up getting flushed out . . ."

"You're saying that oral contraceptives prevent pregnancy, not conception?"

Joe Delgado was nothing if not patient. "No, Father, I'm saying they do both."

John was suddenly feeling out of his element. His heart began to race. How could he provide moral guidance to this man in front of him if he couldn't even follow the basic issues involved in his dilemma?

"So these oral contraceptives," he began again, "They . . . kill off . . . these embryos by not letting them . . . what, again?"

Joe paused briefly, then said evenly, "Implant themselves, Father. Implant themselves within their mothers' uterine walls."

"Effectively killing them?"

"Yes, Father—killing the embryos."

"And the embryo is a person."

"Yes, Father, the embryo is a person."

"Oh, my." John made no attempt to hide his incredulity. Twelve years of Catholic school, five years in the seminary, and six years as a priest, and he was hearing this . . . this . . . scientific fact . . . for the first time only now, and on the other side of the confessional? *Why?*

It was left for Joe Delgado to guide the discussion back to the matter at hand. "Father, if I blow the whistle, I blow up my career and my family. Our eldest child will start college next year, and the other two are coming up right behind her." He paused briefly. "Father, what does God want from me?"

Father John Sweeney exhaled slowly and began to pray.

4

John Sweeney's vacation had officially started two hours ago. His first year of priestly ministry had been a nonstop litany of baptisms, weddings, liturgies, home visits, hospital visits, teacher conferences, coaches' meetings, parents' nights, student discussions, choir practices, food collections, clothing pickups, ecumenical outreaches, and of course, a weekly lecture from his boss, the parish pastor, on how John might improve his "overall productivity."

He sat at his desk in the rectory with perhaps another two hours or so of paperwork—Mass schedules, altar boy assignments, baptismal records, wedding notices, and parish bulletin edits—when Trudy, the parish secretary, walked in to chase him on his way.

"C'mon, Father John," she said, with feigned reproach. "Haven't you done enough damage for one week?"

John loved Trudy Magnuson. Everyone in St. Martha's parish loved Trudy Magnuson. She was the mother of eight grown children, and when Tim, the youngest of them, moved out to take a job with the Secret Service, she arrived unannounced at the rectory one day and told her pastor, "Big Jim" Grogan, that it was time he "put his house in order." That day had now been over eighteen years ago, and John knew that Monsignor Grogan would be the first to concede that the affairs of his house and his parish were indeed now in order.

"Just finishing up, Trudy," John replied lamely. "You know how the boss hates surprises."

"Not to worry, Father. I'll handle the monsignor. You be on your way now. C'mon . . . go, go, go!"

He went. His bags were already packed and stored in the trunk of his black Acura, which he had purchased with the generous help of a parishioner who owned a local dealership. All he had to do now was change out of his clerical garb and into a pair of worn Bermuda shorts and a Phillies jersey with his name on the back—a gift from his parishioners. This he did with great haste.

He was in the car and out of the driveway in moments, heading over back roads and onto the I-76 Expressway to the Walt Whitman Bridge, and from there to the Atlantic City Expressway, where he would pick up the Garden State Parkway south to Sea Isle for a reunion with his classmates from St. John Chrysostom Seminary.

As John Sweeney drove over the Walt Whitman Bridge into New Jersey, he felt some of the tension in his neck and shoulders begin to ease. On the eve of their ordination, the men had pledged they would regroup once a year somewhere, as close to their anniversary as schedules would permit. For this their first year, they would gather along the South Jersey shore at the home of one of their classmate's parents. They were grateful. Exotic it wasn't, but it was close, it was familiar, and it was practically free. His father would have approved, John thought, as he exited the bridge and followed the signs to the Atlantic City Expressway.

His four years in the "Upper School" at St. John Chrysostom Seminary in Philadelphia passed with a swiftness that bordered on the surreal. He remembered his first day, when despite his protesting, his mother and brothers and sisters had accompanied him right through the heavy, bronze doors, down the corridor, and up the stairs to his room, more clearly than he remembered the last day, which seemed at the time, seemed even now, to be a blur.

. . .

As he edged his car off the Atlantic City Expressway and onto Exit 7 and the Garden State Parkway, he thought of the sheer joy his ordination day had brought to so many. He'd never seen his mother so euphoric, like a school girl on her first date. She'd repeatedly grabbed his arm and rushed to present him to yet another McFadden, McCluskey, Fogerty, Sweeney, Stockman, Wren, Kealey, Mueller, Burke, Murray, Timoney, Rooney, Mullen, and McCurry. There had been over a hundred in all, some thirty of whom had come over from both the North and South of Ireland.

John permitted himself to bask in their joy. In that moment he thought he understood something of the Faith's singular hold on the Irish. When all else was taken from them—their land, their homes, their crops—and their very families scattered about the hillsides, it was the Faith alone that was always there to offer hope and provide identity. It was an identity the Irish clutched with a death grip, which they refused to relinquish under the most fearsome and systematic oppression. It was the Faith—*their* Faith—that was the pearl of great price.

To be sure, the "keeping" of that Faith was arguably somewhat easier now for those who remained behind in Ireland. Their own culture lagged behind the quickened pace of global trade in the 1970s and '80s, and it would not be until the '90s, the decade of the "Celtic Miracle," that a notable decay began to appear. It was coincident, unfortunately, with the first tremors of clerical pederasty. Their American cousins, John thought, faced a much more frontal assault; their culture had been shaken at its very foundations by the sexual revolution in the sixties and had responded with a general relaxation—perhaps suspension—of its moral norms almost immediately.

Still, he was of the opinion the second generation had, on the whole, adhered to the core tenets of the Faith. It was the third generation, his generation, that gave every evidence of having been wholly seduced by the promise of pleasure and possession in the "new world." He knew he was not invulnerable to these seductions and feared their power to complicate his own priestly ministry. What he did not know on this summer afternoon was how his response to these complications would provoke the first great crisis of his priesthood.

John took Exit 17 off the Parkway, heading east toward Sea Isle. Moments later he ascended the bridge over the marshlands, which afforded him a glimpse of the sea. He lowered his windows to feel the cool ocean breeze and smell the salt air, which immediately summoned the happiest memories of his childhood. He suddenly felt the emptiness of a son longing for a lost father. He missed his dad terribly.

Jack Sweeney was an American original in John's opinion—larger than life in every way. He died the night John Sweeney had led the Scarlet Knights of Rutgers to their first, and only, win as a sophomore quarterback against Boston College, which hadn't recruited him. He had dropped out of college immediately and gone to work to support his mother and five brothers and two sisters. The family had never really recovered, he realized for perhaps the first time. John missed the completion his dad brought his mother. He missed the family they had been. He missed the sweet innocence of the family's own youth, its shared dreams and struggles. He missed its goodness and its dysfunctions. He missed the simple, joyous sharing of all things new, fresh, and blessed.

John turned right onto Landis Avenue off 42nd and headed south to 61st Street, beach block. He determined the house's location before he saw it, the cars of his classmates spilling out of the driveway and onto the street. As he approached, he saw Rick Stuart tossing a football with Jim Cafano. They waved and feigned fright at the sight of him behind the wheel, affirming that his reputation for impatience would always precede him.

It was early evening, just before sunset in the first week of July. The little town, numbering about three thousand residents in winter, had already swelled to thirty thousand—a good many having already commenced the rite of midsummer celebration. They were young, and many were his age, but there were also families—mostly larger, Irish Catholic families—who tended to cluster in the southern end of town. Everywhere he turned there were memories. He was at ease here and quietly he gave thanks to God.

His former classmates had rented the second-floor unit of a duplex that offered central air, a wraparound balcony, three bedrooms, and a small loft. John entered and, unbidden, claimed the loft by tossing his overnight gear over the railing and onto its floor—from the floor below. This drew the predictable catcalls from his fellow priests, "You can always tell the ones from the big families, they have to have their own rooms." And, "Sweeney, should we just send the meals up?"

"I don't think that's going to work because Sweeney's going to have kitchen duty most nights," said Bill Bradford, pointing to the refrigerator flow chart that presented the household assignments for the week.

John looked at the chart, winced, and said, "If I had known I was going to have this much fun, I'd have stayed home and painted the rectory for Jim Grogan."

5

They fell into a welcome pattern of laid-back seashore living. The early risers walked on the beach, got the morning papers, and made the coffee. The others, of whom John was one, slept in and awakened to the smell of the coffee, asking when their eggs Benedict would be ready. After breakfast, some read, others played cards, and still others chatted about anything and everything, save work.

In the afternoons they went to the beach, usually in twos and threes. Once there, they body surfed, threw Frisbees, read escapist summer novels, walked the beach to the inlet, searched out and caught up with other friends, and did their best to avoid parishioners. This was their vacation, and they needed their space.

Late afternoons, after the men returned from the beach and as the sun began to set, they gathered quietly to concelebrate Mass in the living room. They wore only shorts, sandals, tee shirts and stoles—those ancient symbols of sacramental authenticity—and each took his turn with the various liturgical functions. After Mass, no one spoke for the better part of an hour, such was their reverence for what had just transpired in their presence. John felt in those moments as close to these men as he did to his own family. The bond that had formed among them was at the deepest part of the human mystery.

If they didn't feel like cooking or eating what John might prepare for them, they went to restaurants, usually off the island. Their tastes ran from northern Italian, which John loved, to Tex-Mex, which he barely tolerated—and even then only for reasons of solidarity. The other dinner patrons never seemed able to get a handle on this mannerly group of single men dressed simply in dark slacks and polo shirts. They were asked if they were some sort of Christian rock band, or if they were IRS men in town to investigate local businessmen, or—John's favorite—if they were the famous Tri-State Honda Dealers.

After dinner they read, watched ballgames, or—because there were two bikes at the house—took turns riding up and down the island. They almost never talked shop, each sensing the others' need for distance from the enormous pressures of pastoral ministry. To a man, each felt that he had not been properly prepared for the sheer crush of human need they routinely encountered; none of them, however, directed any blame toward the seminary. On the contrary, they were grateful they'd been granted a brief, four-year sanctuary where their formation could be gently guided by a divinizing Spirit.

On their first day at the beach, the men were approached by a group of kids between ten and twelve years old. They needed a steady quarterback for a touch football game, having an even number of players. The men were quick to volunteer John, who had been a high-profile football and baseball star in high school and whose athletic prowess was still legendary in the seminary. With some reluctance, he closed his Updike novel and gathered himself to join them.

On the first play John told one of his young charges to "go long" and watched in astonishment as the boy ran down the beach a good seventy yards without so much as even glancing behind him. Finally he stopped, turned toward John and began yelling, "I'm open! I'm open!" As much to quiet the little guy as anything else, John pivoted and, with a short, violent snap of his wrist sent the ball on its way—over beach umbrellas, over the lifeguard stand, over ice cream vendors, over beach tag girls, and ultimately over the little head of his wide-open receiver, the ball eventually finding open sand five or six yards beyond the boy.

The astonishing feat did not escape notice. First came the kids, then a few of their parents, then one of the lifeguards, then a number of the twenty-somethings who were clustered near the water, all convinced there'd been a sighting of an NFL quarterback. John was embarrassed by the attention and greatly annoyed that his classmates were now goading the small crowd to "get his autograph."

So dismayed was he by their refusal to accept that he was a "nobody," as he kept referring to himself, that he finally turned and began to jog down the beach to the inlet, only to find a small army of youngsters scurrying after him. It was the highlight of the week for his classmates.

6

On their final night together, John cooked a big pot of pasta with all manner of garlic and seasonings, which he served with a Florentine wine sauce and cold Michelob. The men were sufficiently grateful that they actually toasted him, "Here's to Sweeney," Bradford said hoisting his bottle, "who would've made some lucky girl a helluva live-in cook."

After dinner, once the dishes were done, the young priests settled in for the night, each alone with his thoughts. John broke the silence, saying—to no one in particular—"Well, it took a week with you fellows to make me realize how much I miss Grogan." A few chuckles, some grunts. After another period of extended silence, Rick Stuart said what everyone else was thinking, "It's all pretty overwhelming, isn't it?"

An uneasy silence descended. Then Jim Cafano said, "What's scary is that these families depend on us for answers to questions we don't really even understand."

More silence.

Paul Krueger broke the silence again, "The Faith is losing its relevance for too many of our people, and quite frankly, I don't know what to do about it."

Joe McManus was the youngest among them and looked it. When the rector at the seminary first saw him, he mistook McManus for a high school senior, not the college senior he was at LaSalle University in the Germantown section of Philadelphia. He was wise beyond his years, however, and when he spoke the others listened. "The central issue is the Church's position on contraception. We lost most of our people on that one. They either don't understand it or they don't accept it—or perhaps both."

This led to a spirited debate on the issue, and everyone, including John, weighed in with opinions. The subject had almost never been discussed in their classes at the seminary. Their moral theology professors explained the Church's teaching on what they referred to as "the Sacred Transmission of Human Life," a topic once quaintly referred to as "responsible parenthood," and pretty much left it at that. There was very little discussion or debate, formal or informal.

Now, however, they were in the trenches, the Church's front lines, so to speak. Their mission was to call souls to holiness and accompany those individuals and whole families on every leg of their earthly journey, or at least until such time as a family moved, at which point they became the responsibility of another pastor . . . and associate pastor.

"Well, I gave it a try one Sunday, and I didn't make out too well," said Jim Cafano.

"Whadd'ya mean, gave it a try?" asked Rick Stuart.

"It was the 'hard sayings' Gospel, and I tried to weave the contraceptive thing in, but either I didn't explain it right or our people weren't ready to hear it."

"What happened?"

"They nailed me after Mass."

"Who did? What did they say to you?"

"One young couple with three children told me that the pastor had told them they could in fact, should—use birth control;

another couple in their late thirties or early forties told me, and I quote, 'The Church flat-out got it wrong on this one.' Then a single older woman whom I always considered one of those quiet saints—she had to be in her sixties—told me, 'Stay out of our bedrooms, Father. You don't belong there.'"

At this John laughed and said, "I would have said to her, 'Ma'am, you can rest assured your bedroom is one I will never enter.'"

Bill Bradford said, "I just never go there. There's just too many other issues, not to mention all the Vatican II reforms . . . which I'm still trying to explain."

"I agree with that," Joe McManus said. "But I do think this will become a bigger issue in the years ahead. It's just too central to the Church's mission of being countercultural."

John then surprised them all by recalling a conversation he had with a young professional couple in their early thirties, "They were married about ten years and had three children; they were convinced they'd have another three children during the next ten years if they didn't 'do something.' So I asked them what they did, and they told me they both were sterilized. I asked them if they consulted a priest before they made their decision. They said they did and that he was . . . supportive . . . I believe was the way they put it."

Silence.

Finally, Jim Cafano asked the question on everyone's mind, "Did you ask them, John, who the priest was?"

"I didn't have to. They volunteered it."

No one asked the identity of the priest in question. No one wanted to put him in the position of betraying a confidence, even outside the confessional, or tempt him to slander another priest.

Bill Bradford broke this brief silence, "I think a lot of our men, particularly the older ones, have just been ground down. We shouldn't be disappointed if we don't get a lot of leadership on these issues."

"How about some leadership on at least some issues?" said Jim Cafano.

"It's up to the Bishop," said Joe McManus. "It all starts at the top. I'll begin addressing these issues when I see him doing it."

"Don't hold your breath," Rick Stuart suggested. "That one's too smart to get caught in that trap. He's not going to have the archdiocese go bankrupt on his watch. He knows better than any of us what would happen to weekly Mass attendance and collections if he committed to detonating this ticking time bomb."

"Do you really believe that, Rick?" John asked, somewhat startled.

"I do, John. How else to explain the silence?"

"I don't know . . . I don't know," John said. "I think the jury's out on this one. I hear what the Church says, but I know firsthand what my mother went through after my dad died; what she is still going through. I think there's gotta be some give there."

Paul Krueger, who had been relatively quiet, said, "I didn't get into this business to sow dissension. I want to help build a community of believers. If I start proselytizing on the evils of contraception, the only people I won't offend are the extreme conservatives—who are pretty much offended by everything else."

"You're right about that," Joe McManus jumped in. "Remember what happened to Milford."

Peter Milford was a controversial priest whom the archbishop had transferred twice before assigning him a hospital chaplaincy somewhere in the outer regions of the archdiocese. He was ordained about ten years before John and his classmates, and he'd taken Our Lady of Mount Carmel parish in Dalesford by storm. Within three months of his arrival he'd taken stock of the sorry state of affairs—plummeting Mass attendance, liturgical abuse, feminist nuns, modernist catechetics, a borderline heretical pastor—and had decided that what was most needed was a new sheriff. He'd also decided that he was just the man for the job.

Within six months he was gone, having managed to offend everyone, including his initial supporters. He'd found an old catechism of St. John Vianney and taken to reading excerpts from his sermons at Sunday Masses. Unfortunately, the sermons were written in the nineteenth century for a poor, rural people in central-eastern France, who were still reeling from the aftershocks of the French Revolution. The late twentieth-century parishioners in Dalesford approved of neither the content nor its presentation and made their objections known by boycotting Father Milford's Sunday Masses.

This left the seventy-one-year-old pastor, a gentleman by the name of Matthew Miller, whose mother had been a colorful woman wrestler in the 1940s, in a bit of a predicament. He did not take personal exception to Father Milford's rants, even when they were directed toward his stewardship, but he was not about to say two more Masses every Sunday morning. If anything, he had been hoping to cut back to one Mass when this unfortunate mess landed on his desk.

Miller did what he had to do. He flipped the issue to the cardinal, who arranged a transfer for Milford, and, to show his displeasure with Miller for adding to his burden, delayed sending a replacement priest for six months. These actions were not lost on any of the priests in the archdiocese. Milford became something of an urban legend in the seminary, a classic case study in how not to exercise priestly ministry, particularly in your first year after Ordination.

"Yes, well, that approach certainly didn't work," Jim Cafano said soberly. "Frankly, I don't know how you even broach any of these contentious moral issues, let alone the matter of contraception. Certainly none of it can be done from the pulpit. We'd have a run on the bank."

Several of the men nodded at this, and John sensed that each of these priests was feeling the same ambiguity he was experiencing. They were all young and idealistic; none of them wanted to slide gradually into the calcified cynicism evident in their older, perhaps wiser, pastors. They wanted to be popular and able to influence others; they wanted to build, not divide, their communities.

7

ig Jim" Grogan was in his twelfth year as pastor of St. Martha's. In that time he'd gone through clerical assistants the way the New York Yankees' owner, George Steinbrenner, went through managers. There were some six in all, which was believed to be an unofficial archdiocesan record. Monsignor Grogan didn't think much of the way the new men were being trained. They were lazy, in his opinion, and deficient in pastoral formation. Most egregious, they lacked even a rudimentary business sense.

He was constantly training and retraining men who, in his eyes, "just didn't have it." And so, one by one, he would simply get rid of them without so much as an explanation to either the men or his parishioners. He would call the men in, tell them they were history, and ask them to pack their things and leave immediately.

Jim Grogan's reputation as a high-powered "parishioners' pastor" was sufficiently secure enough that he was never called on any of this by his superiors. One additional reason may have been that he had taken St. Martha's out of quasi-receivership and established an operating surplus in his first year, as well as a parish investment portfolio worth an estimated two million dollars. It was to Grogan that the archbishop, Cardinal Alphonso Porreica, turned first when he had a question about a financial matter—or, more frequently, when he needed cash to cover a shortfall somewhere else in the sprawling 250-parish archdiocese.

So Grogan always got his replacements. And he always got the replacements for his replacements. Then one wintry day Father John Sweeney showed up at his front door, bags in hand. Grogan had requested Sweeney, then in his second year of ministry. Initially, the archdiocese balked at assigning a priest to his family parish—there to hear the confessions of those who "knew him when," but they relented under the persuasive powers of Jim Grogan.

John Sweeney was not anxious to leave St. John's in Roxborough, where he'd quickly made a connection with his parishioners. They were sturdy blue-collar stock—mostly Polish, Irish, and Italian—who reminded him a great deal of his semi-pro football teammates. They were honest, fearless, hard working, and unpretentious. They liked John, and saying goodbye was extremely difficult for him, but diocesan priests make promises—one of them the promise of obedience—and when you were reassigned, you went.

John liked Grogan, though from a safe distance. When the young man announced his decision to enter St. John Chrysostom, Grogan had dropped by the house to tell him what to expect in his first year, and to give him some advice regarding certain professors he would encounter. On the whole, John found the advice helpful, and their interaction grew more frequent in subsequent years, particularly during holidays, when John, home from the seminary, volunteered to assist with liturgical and devotional activities.

Grogan came to his ordination and presented him with a surprisingly generous gift—a check for five hundred dollars. John immediately gave it to his mother, as he suspected Grogan knew

—

he would. He also offered some poignant comments about John's mother at the post-ordination party and led the crowd in a rousing chorus of "Jackie Boy" in honor of his deceased father.

So when John rang the doorbell at St. Martha's, it was Big Jim Grogan himself who opened the door. He made no attempt to hide his obvious delight. "Sweeney!" he bellowed. "I've been waiting for you for six years. What took you so long?"

The past five years had been difficult, and Grogan proved himself to be every bit the martinet John anticipated. They were also rewarding years. He slowly won the trust of his parishioners—one after another confiding their innermost hopes, fears, and to John's everlasting surprise, moral lapses. Much of this took place outside the confessional, the value of that sacrament having been substantially diminished in the eyes of many of the laity in the aftermath of the Council. John found it interesting, however, that at least some people still had a need to tell a priest when and how they'd fallen. He gently reminded them that if they could sacramentalize these discussions, he could grant them absolution.

There were few takers. The older parishioners, with the fewest sins, came regularly and edified John with their simple humility and their constant striving to live a holier life.

He had his favorites, of course. All priests do. He was especially fond of Michael and Carol Burns, and another couple, Bill and Maggie Kealey. The Kealeys, very much like the Burnses, were involved in virtually every aspect of parish life and modeled a witness of humble and faithful service to the entire parish, including their parish priests. So when John was told by Trudy Magnuson that Maggie Kealey was on the phone, he immediately dropped what he was doing and took the call.

"Father John, may I come see you? I need some advice."

"Of course, Maggie," he said, somewhat surprised. "Do you want me to drop by the house?"

"No, no. I'd rather come to the rectory. Are you available tonight?"

"Of course, of course," John replied not even bothering to check his calendar. If there was a conflict, he'd move it. "Anytime after dinner."

"And Father," Maggie Kealey said in a whisper, "will there be anyone else there?"

John, taken aback, said, "Not likely, Maggie. Monsignor Grogan will be out to dinner with some friends. And I'm not expecting anybody."

"Good," said Maggie Kealey. "I'll see you at seven thirty."

8

Michael Burns was a man with an agenda. At thirty-
five, he was trim and athletic, six feet tall, with dark
hair and eyes and an impulsive, somewhat combat-
ive, nature. When "on mission" he was, in a figurative sense,
quite accustomed to barging into doors already open. The job
offer from the new Cable Movie Network came through, and
he immediately gave notice at Slattery and Associates. Old man
Slattery did not take it particularly well. "I have plans to make
you the president of this company within three years," he told
Michael. When Michael told him that he wouldn't want to work
for an advertising firm that employed him as its president, Slattery turned a bit cranky and said, "This is a mistake, Michael,
and you'll regret it."

Leaving Narbrook was much harder for the Burnses. Though
raised in West Chester, some thirty miles west of the city, the
blonde, spirited, and cover-girl pretty Carol Burns had grown
to love the little borough and considered it an idyllic place to
raise a family. Of their three children, the oldest daughter,

Carole, took the news the hardest. She was in high school at Bishop McCauley and had a boyfriend—something her parents didn't know. She assailed her father, telling him that he was "ruining her life forever." Their other two daughters, Kate and Elizabeth, both in grade school, seemed to take the news with a measure of excitement and embraced the move as a family adventure.

They settled in a little bedroom community in North Jersey, about twenty-five miles west of Manhattan. The town, Mountview, reminded them somewhat of Narbrook. It boasted a three-block main street and a commuter rail line running through its heart that divided the town into northern and southern sections.

The Burns family bought a post-Revolutionary War farmhouse on the north side of town. The home was set on a bluff overlooking a spring-fed pond stocked with bass, perch, and bluegill. It had a barn with a hayloft constructed with wooden pegs from the period, and it was set on the edge of a small apple orchard where the younger girls loved to play with their friends after school.

Mike commuted by train into Manhattan, which took some getting used to—during his seven years with Slattery & Associates he'd driven the family car to a small office complex on the outskirts of the city not more than five minutes from his home. He eventually settled into the familiar pattern of the other commuters, reading the *New York Times* on the way into work and catching up on his work-related reading on the way home.

The first few months were quite difficult. He frequently found himself sitting in his office on the thirtieth floor of a midtown high-rise, looking out the floor to ceiling length window at the canyons below and wondering what he was doing in New York. He missed his home in Narbrook. He missed his family and his friends, and most of all he missed the familiar faces and streets of his beloved little town.

His professional life presented immediate challenges. The launch of the new pay cable network was proceeding at a turbocharged pace, and he simply couldn't staff the account quickly enough to avoid drowning in a sea of loosely related projects all of which seemed of life-or-death importance to his individual clients and their respective divisions and departments.

His management at Hal Ross/NY was of little help. The firm had built its reputation largely on its ability to move packaged goods clients from a number-three share of market position in their product categories to a number-two or—occasionally—a lead share position. They were less comfortable with "novelty" products or services, as they regarded CMN. Michael realized very quickly that this meant it was going to be an additional challenge for him to get the resources required to feed and grow the business. He suspected that this would also prove to be a problem for a client with enormous expectations.

Michael liked his clients individually and believed them to be among the best and brightest young men and women in the country. CMN was owned by National Publishing, which had about a dozen print magazines in circulation and possessed a reputation for hiring only elites. Cable Movie Network made a practice of limiting its hiring to MBA's from Wharton, Harvard, and Stanford, though some high achievers from Yale and Princeton found their way into a number of management positions.

The mean age of the CMN's staff was thirty-two when Michael started in the business, with the CEO and COO each being thirty-seven, and the president thirty-six. The young company's vitality was all but palpable, even from the lobby of their Sixth Avenue headquarters. To Michael, the building seemed chock-a-block full of high-energy kids, mostly twenty-somethings who believed they were going to rock the world. All they needed was a stage, and now they'd found one. They were going to change the face of America's entertainment industry, radically altering the very nature of network television in the process. Their success would be the next great Harvard Business School case study.

CMN's business model was predicated on the predatory leasing of rights to original theatrical releases from Hollywood studios and major independents. These films ran on CMN after a nine-month window following their initial release in America's movie theaters. The network was distributed to individual homes through cable operators, or what those in the industry called MSOs—Multiple System Operators.

These companies, licensed by local municipalities, would create what they called a "pay tier" around CMN, hoping it would drive up household penetration for their "basic" cable service, which consisted of news, sports, and a wide variety of narrowly cast special-interest channels.

The MSOs would charge their customers about ten dollars a month for the new "pay tier" in addition to the roughly eight dollar monthly fee for the basic cable service. The revenues from the pay tier would be evenly split with CMN. In return, CMN promised to market the new service aggressively to the families who lived in areas served by the cable operators. This marketing assignment was awarded to Hal Ross/NY and placed in the hands of Michael Burns.

What might have been a moderately profitable enterprise turned out to be enormously profitable—some said obscenely so— as a result of a stroke of good fortune that none of the brilliant businessmen at National Publishing had anticipated. The business model for the major movie studios sought only to "break even" through theatrical distribution in the U.S. They expected to realize profits for most releases through licensing distribution rights to network television and overseas distributors. They regarded this new distribution outlet—what they called the "pay window"—as a minor ancillary revenue stream. It was "found money," good to have, but not something that would greatly impact their financial statements. As a consequence, they assigned what could only be fairly characterized as the "third team" to the negotiating table with the CMN bull sharks. Together they developed a cents-per-household pricing model based on pay tier penetration. It wasn't long before the studios discovered they had been devoured whole.

In very short order CMN was plowing those considerable profits back into their own original productions—made-for-television movies, concerts, sporting events, docudramas, and other unique properties. Soon they were dominating industry award shows, including the Oscars and Emmys, which served only to fuel even greater consumer demand. This in turn generated even more enormous profits for the network and its owners at National Publishing. In fact, within its first five years of existence CMN came to account for almost 25 percent of National Publishing's revenues and a staggering 50 percent of its profits. A certain swagger began to set in among the young elites on the fifteenth to twentieth floors of the National Publishing building in midtown Manhattan. They and their careers were launched, and were now on an appropriate trajectory.

CMN's success ultimately depended on one key philosophical tenet in their business model. They would offer their product in its original form, "uncut," and would market that "unique selling proposition" very aggressively. "Uncut" of course meant their product, largely movies and concerts, would not be subject to the review or standards of broadcast network censors. This meant that for the first time in the nation's history, Hollywood had direct and uncensored access to American living rooms.

In the early 1980s the broadcast networks began to see their collective share of prime-time viewing beginning to soften, slip, and then plummet. They lobbied the FCC for regulatory relief, citing their business interests, and when that failed they lobbied for the "general welfare" of America's communities, communities that were now "being polluted" by the rancid sewer of uncensored media flowing into their living rooms. And when this failed, ever resourceful, they took to "counter-programming" CMN. This meant creating increasingly salacious movies and sitcoms.

War had been declared. An important front was opened in what would become America's broader "culture wars" of the late twentieth century. It was not a war Michael Burns had signed on to wage, much less to help lead. But this was precisely where he now found himself. And for him and his family it would prove to be even more problematic than he feared on that summer evening when he went to pay a visit to his parish priest, Father John Sweeney.

9

―――――

Rumply, unshaven Joe Delgado eased his black BMW 750 sedan into the Lower Merwood shopping center, found a spot in the virtually empty lot behind the shops, parked and locked his car, and headed for a popular coffee shop on the corner.

He entered at 6:45 a.m., a full fifteen minutes before his scheduled rendezvous with Steve Dalkowitz, general counsel for Pittman Labs. Joe took great satisfaction in being first to arrive for scheduled business meetings. He believed it sent a signal, and in the corporate world signals were important.

As he entered the shop he squinted into a blinding glare created by the brilliant, crisp, fall sunshine. He saw no one and felt relieved. Then, "Hey, Delgado, back here. I got your coffee." It was Dalkowitz.

Steve Dalkowitz was a bright, energetic, thirty-nine-year-old lawyer from the western suburbs of Philadelphia. He graduated at the top of his class at Penn and edited the law review at Columbia. His father had been a pharmacist in the Northeast for over forty years and his mother had been an elementary school teacher in the inner city for almost as long. Both were now retired and living in Boca Raton, Florida.

Joe liked Dalkowitz, who was direct and unpretentious. The two of them watched each other's back as they navigated their way through the corporate maze at Pittman Labs. Both men were charter members of "The Carney Boys," named in honor of one of their contemporaries, the ferociously driven salesman Bill Carney, who had made it all the way to the top and was now Pittman's CEO.

Theirs was a bumpy ride, but the perks more than compensated. The mid-six-figure salary, the enormous end-of-year bonus, the outsized stock options carefully "backdated," the choice of an imported automobile every two years, the exclusive country club, the corporate apartment in New York—available for personal use—the controversial pension program that would allow twenty-year men to receive up to eighty percent of their top annual salary for life, the quarterly executive team meetings lavishly staged in the finest European and Caribbean locations—yes, the perks made the bumps and bruises from the intramural skirmishes quite tolerable.

The Carney Boys also included John Terrell, Pittman's chief information officer; Peter Halifax, executive vice president of sales and marketing; Ryan Winters, executive vice president of research and development; and Robert Avenel, executive vice president of human resources. The seven men worked together on one project or another for the better part of fifteen years, and their collective rise in the ranks bonded them at a very deep level. They looked out for one another, particularly for Carney. Anything that might even potentially embarrass him in the eyes of their corporate parent, National Health Products, was immediately spotted, analyzed, and resolved, often without his knowledge.

Joe made his way to Dalkowitz's table in the back and plopped down on one of two chairs facing the general counsel. Dalkowitz slowly slid a coffee, black with no sugar and the lid still on, in

Joe's direction. "So, what's up?" he asked as Joe reached for the hot plastic cup.

"You pull that stuff together for Carney yet?" Joe replied, removing the lid and cradling the cup in his hands.

Dalkowitz narrowed his eyes and peered intently at his colleague. "Joe, I sent you a copy of the file at the end of last week with a rough draft of a proposed memo to Bill for our signatures. Didn't you read it?"

Delgado was immediately on the defensive. He hadn't read the file, hadn't even opened it. And despite what his younger colleague assumed, he had not called this little meeting to discuss the Alphasint files and the status of the U.S. Attorney's investigation.

"No, Steve, I didn't read it. Sorry, I should have. I've been deeply disturbed by some other files I discovered in the archives and I haven't been able to get a handle on what, if anything, I should do."

"What files?"

"The 'OC' files."

"What 'OC' files? What the hell are you talking about?"

"When I was rummaging about looking for the Alphasint stuff, I came across an unmarked box which was double-sealed with masking tape—"

"—and you opened it, why?"

"I thought it might contain something relevant to our search."

"Did it?"

"No."

"Joe. Where are we going with this? Do I need to know what you're about to tell me? Because if I don't, I don't want you telling me, understood?"

"Steve, the stuff I found all happened on Heyworth's watch, after we arrived. What I need to know is what kind of accountability we would have if it ever surfaced."

Al Heyworth was Bill Carney's predecessor and a legendary figure in the pharmaceutical industry. He ruled Pittman Labs for twenty-six years in an autocratic "command and control" style that was a vestige of another era. He was known to be ruthless and was widely feared by many of his own people. But he was also respected as the man who "never missed a quarter," and during his last eighteen years with the company, he had established a performance standard that none of his peers had approached—seventy-two consecutive quarters of double-digit, top- and bottom-line growth.

Heyworth was lionized by industry and general business publications in the U.S. and Europe. He became a cover boy, cultivated by politicians, statesmen, and other elites in the business and entertainment community. As a rising young executive, Joe Delgado had marveled at Al Heyworth's legend and at the sheer length of the shadow he cast across American enterprise.

But now he understood how Al Heyworth had achieved what he achieved. And he had every intention of sharing that story, or at least its outline, with his younger colleague across the table.

Steve Dalkowitz buried his head in his hands and stared into his coffee cup. "All right, Joe," he said, slowly, in a near-whisper. "Because you're obviously going to tell me about it, why don't you just tell me about it?"

10

At 7:34 p.m. the doorbell rang inside the rectory. Father Sweeney was alone upstairs. He glanced at the clock in his sitting room, smiled, and bounded down the steps to open the door. "Maggie, come in, come in," he said, opening the door and motioning his guest inside.

"Father, it's so good of you to make time for me."

"Come, sit . . . please," he said, leading her into the small receiving room just off the center hallway. She took the chair farthest from the door—all but completely obscured from any unexpected visitors.

John studied her face as she removed a light housecoat that she wore to take some of the edge off the early autumn chill. She laid the coat over the back of an adjoining chair. My God, this woman is beautiful, he thought to himself. No one meeting her for the first time would ever suspect her to be in her early forties, the mother of six children, and a victim of chronic migraine pain.

"Maggie . . . how's Bill?" he began, as much to take his mind off her physical beauty as to find a safety zone for their discussion.

"Grinding away, Father," she answered, shaking her head slightly. "He's on track to bill over three thousand hours again this year. He thinks if he can do it for two more years he might make managing partner. I've told him, either way, he'll make managing widower."

John laughed and said, in dialect, "Ach, Maggie Kealey, you'll not be escapin' this vale o' tears that easily."

Maggie smiled, looked down at the hands on her lap, paused, and then looked up and said, "Father, I'm very concerned about our Moia."

John felt a slight tremor run up and then back down his spine. There was talk—and he'd heard it—that Moia, a strikingly attractive young lady who was now seventeen, had been behaving oddly. His own recent interactions with her were strained. Whenever he encountered her in town, he found her distant, directing a certain coolness his way.

"School problems, boy problems, Mom-and-Dad problems?" John asked.

"All of the above. But it's deeper, Father." Maggie looked at the priest, and for a moment he thought she might break down. "She talks constantly about taking her own life. The other morning before school I found her in my medicine cabinet and confronted her. She started screaming at me in the vilest language. I thought she might actually attack me. It was frightening."

John immediately felt out of his depth. He had absolutely no idea what to say to comfort or advise this woman. "What does Bill think, Maggie?"

"He thinks it's just a stage she's going through. He reminds me that he grew up with four older sisters. But when I press him, he admits that none of them ever threatened his parents with suicide."

"What do you think is driving it? Is she having problems with her boyfriend?"

"Father, Moia is having problems with everybody. She's just not the same person anymore. I don't know what's come over her."

"How long has this been going on?"

"I'd say over a year, and it's just getting worse. I'm afraid she's on the verge of spinning out of control."

"Have you talked to any of her teachers?"

"Yes, and they're mystified too. She was third in her class through her sophomore year. Last year she slipped to the middle of the pack. Now I'm worried she might not even graduate. She cuts class, Father. She doesn't hand in homework assignments. She's no longer playing lacrosse. She's cut herself off from most of her friends. Her own brothers and sisters are afraid of her. I don't know what . . ." she broke off, crying.

John began to pray. He asked for wisdom he knew he did not possess. His visitor was now staring at him through her tears. She needed answers. He had none.

"Father, she seems to have a genius for inflicting pain," she said. "She knows where all the wires are, and she trips them one by one without remorse. She pits one child against the other, even Bill against me. The whole house is roiling."

John looked at Maggie Kealey with genuine concern and said to her, "Maggie, how can I help? I'll do anything I can for you and Bill." It was moments like these, he realized, that led him into prayer of deep gratitude for his own vocation. He simply couldn't imagine having to deal with problems like this, in addition to everything else parents routinely shouldered in the feeding, clothing, sheltering, educating, and socializing of their children.

"Father, I think we need professional help. But the last thing I want to do is turn Moia over to some atheistic psychiatrist. Do you know any good Catholics in the field?"

"I do—I do," he said, instantly relieved. Maybe that's all she wanted, he hoped. If that was indeed it, he could be of some help after all, thanks be to God. He would send her to Jim McNeeley, and he would add the girl to his prayer list. He would ask to be kept in the loop on all developments. Nothing more, thanks be to God.

"Maggie, I'm going to make a phone call for you tomorrow

morning. There's a fellow who was three years ahead of me in the seminary. He dropped out and became a psychiatrist. His name is Jim McNeeley, and he's developed a little niche for himself with Catholic families and—you didn't hear this from me—a number of priests in the archdiocese. He's a very strong Catholic, and I do believe he'll see you and Moia. He's got a woman partner by the name of Karen Wright, and I've heard good things about her, too. After the initial visit I'd be very surprised if he didn't get Karen involved with Moia right away."

Maggie Kealey smiled again, and John thought he was staring into the face of an angel incarnate. She radiated such a natural beauty that John was actually taken aback.

"Oh, Father, you're so wonderful," she said, coming forward with arms outstretched.

He adroitly grabbed the hands at the end of those arms and brought them, and his own, to their sides. "Maggie, I'll be praying for you and Bill . . . and especially for Moia."

"Thank you, Father. Thank you. I came in despair. I leave with hope. What a good priest you are!"

John Sweeney led his guest to the door, and when she departed he decided he'd better make a visit to the church next to the rectory. In the darkness, he would ask his Lord for grace sufficient to be worthy of his calling.

11

Michael Burns slid his lean body between two buxom women and angled toward the large mahogany bar in the southeast corner of Windows on the World. CMN was hosting an extravagant reception for their cable operators who were in town for the annual cable convention. They had rented the entire 105th floor of Tower One at World Trade Center in New York.

Michael was running late. He found himself trapped in a conversation about cable marketing with two operators from Texas. They wanted help with their advertising, but like many of their colleagues from other parts of the country, they didn't want to pay. "Maybe CMN would pay," one of them suggested. "Yeah, maybe," Michael replied, smiling—and seeing an opportunity, he excused himself.

Rick Reynolds was scheduled to address the CMN staff, and Michael didn't want to miss it. Reynolds was a former all-Ivy tailback at Princeton, and his rise at National Publishing had been nothing short of meteoric. He was running *America*, an iconic high-gloss photo magazine published biweekly, by the time he was twenty-eight. At thirty-four he was running National Publishing's print division. He was handpicked by Pete Stallard, National Publishing's charismatic chairman and CEO, to run CMN two years later. It was like getting the keys to a brand new Maserati, Reynolds told friends at the time.

Michael liked Reynolds, and Reynolds gave every indication of liking Michael Burns. He even got personally involved in recruiting Michael, telling him that he would be a good fit with CMN's young team of pedigreed achievers. "They've got the paper and the expectations," he told him. "You've got the talent and know-how. It'll be my job to make sure the gears mesh. And I'll make sure they do," he promised.

At the bar, Michael lowered his voice and ordered a Coke. He'd always been careful about alcohol. He had been a very good prep school athlete, and he had seen too many of his friends blow college scholarships by getting wasted on weekends, even during the season. And although he was not big enough, at barely 6'0", to play Division I basketball, he found a niche at St. Francis in New Hampshire, a Division II school, where he was a 2,000-point scorer, earning All-American honors in his senior year.

Michael took the Coke from the bartender, a handsome young man who held onto the glass a little too long for Michael's comfort, and edged his way to the floor to ceiling windows in the corner. The view of Lower Manhattan from the 105th floor of Tower One was breathtaking. It was a week before Christmas, and the city below—so far below it seemed surreal—was lit like a scene from a Frank Capra film. Michael made a mental note to be sure to bring Carol and the kids to the city for dinner and some shopping and sightseeing.

"All this is yours if you but fall down and worship me." The voice was familiar, and Michael turned to see Ron Zimmer approaching with a drink in his hand. Zimmer was the president of the New York office of Hal Ross Worldwide, the third largest advertising firm in the world. He was brilliant, falldown funny, and completely amoral. Burns' presence seemed to trip wires from Zimmer's upbringing in a strict Calvinist household in Connecticut, and he was forever needling Michael about the paradox of his being a practicing Catholic working in the heart of the evil media empire.

"How'd you get past security?" Michael said, smiling.

"I didn't. I bilocate just like some of you Catholics. I'm also at my desk calculating your year-end bonus."

"In that case," Michael said, "Reynolds just told me they're going out at fifty million dollars, half of it network TV."

Zimmer never wore profit accountability particularly well. He often told new employees, "I've been fired three times, but I only deserved it twice." He was in fact fired twice for violating company policy on substance abuse and sexual harassment, but he so skillfully insinuated himself into the favor of HRW's chairman and CEO, Bob Meyers, that he was reinstated each time and, quite improbably, promoted into the top job a short time thereafter.

Meyers was a controversial figure in the advertising industry—tough, driven, and quite outspoken. It was well-known that he packed a pearl-handled Colt .45, and he liked to tell intimates that he was undercover CIA. Indeed, he did file briefs on what he saw and suspected while on his overseas trips, and did in fact send them off to the Agency, but it was unknown whether they were ever opened, much less read and circulated.

Meyers was denied entry into the U.S. military after his Harvard graduation because at 5'1" he didn't meet the height requirement. This hadn't settled well, and he channeled this ferocious drive into a highly successful business career. Whenever and wherever obstacles arose, he simply climbed over the strewn bodies of larger men whose legs he fastidiously severed.

Meyers liked and trusted no one, save Ron Zimmer. At 5'4" Zimmer was an eyeball-to-eyeball peer of Meyers, who typically wore platform shoes custom made by Bruno Mali. Zimmer understood the strange mix of forces that drove men who were brighter and more resourceful than their peers but also less popular. Many people in the industry assumed that Zimmer's rise was accompanied by pictures of Meyers in compromising positions, and indeed Meyers once had a coke addiction that Zimmer serviced. But Zimmer, with his disarming candor, always said to those who needled him, "No. No pictures. I just make it a practice of kissing every ass in town until I find the right one."

"Fifty million? Well, I'd say that small investment you've made in lighting candles in every church in Manhattan is paying off," Zimmer replied.

He just can't help himself, Michael thought. "Ron, Reynolds is going to address the troops in the Winthrop suite in two minutes. I can't promise I can get you in—they've got a minimum height requirement—but I'll try, by God, I'll try."

Zimmer winced involuntarily. He was, for all his bluster, openly sensitive about his height. "Oh, good. And I'll try to forget you said that when I review salaries next week."

· · ·

Rick Reynolds stood at the podium looking composed and alert. He waited patiently for the room to quiet. He let himself absorb the enormous energy and prodigious aspiration coursing through the room's occupants. He looked at his audience of some seventy-five young men and women in their late twenties and early thirties—all from the best families, the best schools, and the best country clubs—and wondered whether the National Publishing hiring model that worked so well in the magazine business would work as well in the cable industry.

He knew well firsthand that the decision makers in America's corporate advertising departments and within the media departments of the largest advertising firms were, for the most part, former classmates at Ivy League universities. This was not the case with the small-town entrepreneurs who tended to own and operate America's cable systems. These men—and they were all men—distrusted pedigree. They looked upon "those kids," as they referred to the CMN staff, as dilettantes incapable of creating wealth, or much else, on their own.

Reynolds knew his central task was to productively channel the energy in the room, making sure the business model—bringing uncut first-run movies into the country's living rooms at fractional cost—was given a chance to work. He knew it would be a challenge. Entitlement always was. "Could I have your attention for just a moment, please?" he began evenly. The room grew quieter by stages.

"Thank you," he continued, as something approaching quiet settled within the room. "I promise not to keep you from your customers for more than a few minutes."

"That's all right, Rick. They're already wasted." Raucous laughter. It was Burt Camfy from the back of the room. Camfy had been one of Reynolds' classmates at Princeton. It was well known that he had blocked for Reynolds as starting right guard on the Tigers' Ivy League championship team in their senior year. He liked to tell people that he was still blocking for Rick Reynolds at National Publishing.

Camfy was a double-edged sword for Reynolds. He was, by any standard, Reynolds' top producer at every publication Rick had managed. But he was also his biggest headache, having bedded—by his own count—nearly a third of the single women at National Publishing. To be fair, there were surprisingly few complaints, and those few came from ladies who for some reason had actually believed Camfy's promises of job advancements.

"If Burt's right," Rick replied, "then get the hell out of here. Go. Write business." This drew the expected laughter. When it died down, Rick continued. "But if he isn't—and there's a first time for everything"—more laughter—"then let me assure all of you that these folks will be taking our measure with, dare I say, great sobriety this evening."

The room grew quiet. "They are here representing their own customers and the municipalities who have licensed them. You will find them understandably skeptical of our claims that we can broaden and deepen their relationship with their customers and make them rich while we're at it. Many of them are from small towns in the South and Midwest, which means they'll have concerns about product content, which they will not—I repeat, will not—voice . . . at least directly.

"These are good, decent folk who have placed a very large wager—for most of them, everything they own—on this new industry. Their business model is based almost entirely on cash flow, and most of them couldn't give a rat's ass about debt. They're in it up to their eyeballs, and they sleep quite well at night, thank you. As long as they're awash in cash, and most of them already are, they can continue to borrow and expand, which most are doing." Pause. "You're not going to find too many unhappy campers in there.

"Our mission is not to present ourselves as the cure for cancer. Their businesses aren't broke, but they know there's a lot of room for growth. They're here because they're curious. They've heard about this new thing called 'pay cable,' and they want to know what it'll mean for their customers. They'll want to know what kind of movies and concerts we'll be paying them to carry. They'll want to know what we're going to do to crank up market demand—I see Michael Burns from Ross is here; Michael, we're going to put you and our launch plan front and center on that one—and they're going to want to know how the financial model will be structured. The large, multiple-system operators are going to want deep discounts. And the smaller ones will claim discrimination if they feel they're being treated unfairly . . . ."

"Sounds like a perfect job for Camfy, Rick," Jim Sutter shouted. "He won't discriminate. He's an equal opportunity fornicator."

Bedlam.

Rick Reynolds held up his right hand at the podium to restore some semblance of order. "The point I want to make is this, we're here to listen. So ask questions. And ask questions about their answers to those questions. We're not selling, we're solving. And we won't know what we're solving unless we understand what their needs and wants are.

"I'll also say this to you, we are going to change the way America consumes entertainment. I've promised corporate that we're going to be in ten million homes in three years. This is going to be a revolution, not an evolution. You're on the front lines of cultural history in the making. I can't think of a more exciting place to be. This is our moment. Let's make the most of it."

The immediate applause was loud and long. Like an oversized and overstimulated beehive, the swarm of energy and sound made its way to and through the walnut double doors of the Winthrop suite and out onto the floor of the restaurant on the 105th floor of Tower One. The hyperactive hive was in search of alcohol, customers, and, most of all, personal fulfillment.

Michael Burns lingered behind. He wanted to thank Rick Reynolds for the plug and assure him that the Hall Ross Agency was up to the task they'd been given. He would speak from conviction. The launch presentation was finished and the TV storyboards were being "comped" for the road show. He had every confidence that the pitch he'd make directly to the cable operators would be compelling.

"Introduce me to your client, Shamrock," Zimmer said as he caught up to Michael, who was headed to the podium. Michael merely nodded.

"Michael . . . like the plug?" Reynolds asked as Michael approached, Zimmer in tow.

"Yeah, thanks, Rick. We're already good to go." A pause. "Rick, I want to introduce you to Ron Zimmer, head of our New York office."

Reynolds immediately walked from behind the podium and extended his hand. "Good to meet you, Ron. Thanks for putting your A-Team on our business," he said, nodding his head in Michael's direction. Ever gracious, Michael thought. These guys at the top are very good indeed. They've got more fire in their belly, and disguise it better, than any of their counterparts.

"Good to meet you, Rick," Zimmer said with a broad smile. "I want you to know that we searched the entire country to find the most brilliant marketing strategist, the most dynamic team builder, the most charismatic pitchman . . . we never found that guy. So we hired Burns. But we'll keep looking. You have my word on that."

Reynolds convulsed in laughter. Michael marveled at Zimmer's ability to charm anyone, thinking it entirely novel that here the snake was actually charming its handler. But his client was laughing, and even if it was at his expense, that was never a bad thing. Reynolds put his hand on Michael's shoulder, turned to Zimmer and said, "Just keep this fellow happy, Ron. We've got a lot riding on him."

Rick Reynolds exited through the double doors shaking his head and laughing.

12

Maggie Kealey was trying to manage the end of one day and prepare for the beginning of another. Dinner was over, dishes were being washed, lunches were being packed, and homework was being supervised. There was only one other chore on the list; Maggie had to get Moia properly dressed and in the car so she could escort her to their first appointment with Dr. McNeeley.

Moia was in high-maintenance mode. "I'm not going, and don't try to bribe me into it," she yelled down to her mother from her bedroom.

"You're going, or you won't be going anywhere else for a good long time," her mother yelled from the kitchen. "Now get down here. I want you in that car in two minutes."

Six carefully calibrated minutes later, Moia opened the passenger side door and slid into the car, having made her statement. It would be the only statement she would make that evening. About ten minutes later, Maggie pulled into the parking lot of a small commercial center of shops, restaurants, and small office buildings. She parked the car, and without a word to her daughter headed for a seven-story office building that housed the offices of Jim McNeeley and Karen Wright.

She entered the elevator with her daughter trailing sullenly. They got off together at the sixth floor and headed down the well-lit corridor, looking for the McNeeley office. When they found it, the door was ajar. They entered to find Jim McNeeley waiting for them. They were his final appointment of the day, and they were twelve minutes late.

"Must be Maggie . . . and Moia," he said, smiling graciously and extending his hand to Maggie.

Maggie took his hand and said, "Dr. McNeeley, we're very pleased to meet you. Thank you for making time in your busy schedule to see us. Sorry we're a bit late. Dinner hours are quite hectic in the Kealey home."

"I'm sure they are. Father Sweeney said you have six children. Honestly, I don't know how you do it." Turning to Moia, "And I understand you're the first child, Moia. I'm a first child, too. Not always easy, right?"

Moia responded with silence to McNeeley's efforts to make an initial connection. He looked at Maggie, who shrugged her shoulders and said, "I'm afraid we're not talking tonight, Doctor."

Jim McNeeley smiled and said, "That's all right. There are a lot of people who come through my door who don't feel very much like talking." He led Maggie and Moia to his office, which was richly appointed with dark leather chairs and couches, a large cherry desk, and a number of attractively framed diplomas and citations adorning the walls. "Please sit. Make yourselves comfortable," he said, pointing to the seating area opposite a large picture window that presented views of the city silhouetted in the distance.

As soon as they were all comfortably seated, McNeeley took off his glasses, and leaned back in his chair and said, "Moia, there's only one reason for me to be here. And that's to help people remove barriers to happiness so they can lead productive lives.

God has given us all certain gifts and aptitudes. He expects us to develop those into talents and skills, putting them at the service of others. This is how we find meaning—a sense of fulfillment—in our lives. But none of us can get beyond square one if there are things blocking us, whether emotionally or spiritually. I got into this line of work because I want to help people identify those impediments and then work with them to help remove barriers. My greatest joy is seeing people conquer their problems and live productive lives."

Nothing.

Jim looked at Maggie, who felt compelled to end the awkward silence. "Thank you, Doctor. That's why we've come. Moia is a very special young lady. God has blessed her with many gifts, as you said. But we're struggling right now. We know we have a problem. We just don't know how to fix it."

"Well, maybe Moia could tell us a little bit about what's been bothering her. I understand you're a senior at Bishop McCauley. Sometimes we get to a certain point in our lives, and we need more freedom than parents really want to give us."

Moia sat in a sullen silence that seemed to drop the room's temperature ten degrees.

"Moia's been given all the freedom any young woman still living in her parents' home should have, Doctor," Maggie responded a bit defensively. "We've had to gradually reduce some of that freedom when she has acted in ways that are destructive to herself and the family."

"What kind of destructive behavior?" McNeeley asked, looking at Moia but directing his question to Maggie. He didn't make a practice of asking questions of anyone other than a patient. It was a white flag, he believed. But he needed to know symptoms so he could decide whether to pass this "hard case" off immediately to Karen Wright or to redirect this young lady and her mother to an intervention unit downtown.

"About two years ago, Doctor, everything began to change," Maggie answered haltingly. She wanted to respond to McNeeley's question, but she didn't want to set Moia off and create a scene in the office. "Moia just started rebelling against everything. We've talked to her teachers, her coaches, even—though with great reluctance—her friends . . ."

"Have you talked to Moia?" McNeeley interrupted, hoping again to establish a connection with the young lady sitting passively on the other side of the coffee table.

"Of course we've talked to her, Doctor," Maggie said, irritated. "Bill and I do nothing but talk to her, and we get back what you've gotten here tonight, which is to say—nothing."

McNeeley decided to go for broke. He was willing to risk the parent, at least in the short term, if he could establish something, anything, with the daughter. If he couldn't, he wouldn't bother Karen with another Mission Impossible. Neither needed another impossible case.

"I'm sure you have, Mrs. Kealey. But my question is a little different. I want to know whether you've talked *with* Moia . . . or merely *at* her."

Maggie exploded. "*At* her! *At* her? I don't talk *at* anyone, Dr. McNeeley. And neither does my husband, who is a senior partner at Flynn and O'Hara. We have five other children, and not a one of them has given us a moment of trouble. We don't create problems, Doctor McNeeley, and I resent the implication that my husband and I are somehow to blame for Moia's problems."

Jim McNeeley was studying Moia's face as Maggie Kealey shouted. Now she turned and looked at him impassively. He couldn't read the look itself, but the fact that she was looking at him for the first time was itself a source of small encouragement. He chose to interpret her unblinking stare as a "now you get it" signal.

"I apologize, Mrs. Kealey," he said, now turning to the mother. "I didn't mean to upset you. Father Sweeney told me you and your husband are exemplary parents and parishioners. I wasn't being critical. We always probe the family dynamic up front. In good families like yours, it allows us to move on to other areas quickly."

Maggie, feeling affirmed and vindicated, accepted the apology and calmed herself. When she regained her composure, she looked at McNeeley evenly and said, "OK, Doctor. Where do we go from here?"

McNeeley stood up abruptly, looked at Moia and said, "I think Karen Wright will be a big help to Moia. She lost a daughter about Moia's age a little over a year ago, and she loves young people. They're her therapy." And to Moia, softly, "You'll like Karen. She's a great listener, and she's got a big heart."

Moia Kealey stood up, turned away from McNeeley without saying anything, and headed toward the door. Her mother stood, looked at the doctor, and said, "I'm sorry we didn't give you more to work with. Maybe she'll be better with . . . a woman."

Doctor McNeeley looked for a hint of malice in Maggie Kealey's eyes and, finding none, put his hand lightly on her back, guiding her in the direction of the door. "I'm sure she will, Maggie. I'll have Phyllis, our administrator, call tomorrow to set up an appointment."

"Thank you, Doctor."

"And Maggie, would you tell Father Sweeney I was asking for him?"

"I will indeed, Doctor McNeeley."

13

Karen Wright took the call from Phyllis McKinney informing her that the Kealeys, mother and daughter, had arrived. She'd been looking forward for almost two weeks to this appointment. She'd done her homework—calling the principal at Bishop McCauley, the head coach of its lacrosse team, even Father Sweeney at St. Martha's in Narbrook.

Karen's practice had evolved slowly over the years into one that was now almost exclusively comprised of women clients. She worked hard behind the scenes to create an apparently effortless, open, low-key environment in which her clients would feel entirely tension-free.

The walls were painted in pale island hues; the furniture was casual Dutch Indies; the music was early Rod Stewart and David Bowie, muted but audible. Karen was acutely aware that she was regarded as a formidable woman, big-boned with somewhat oversized hands and feet. She dressed in loose-fitting one-piece outfits of neutral colors and spoke in modulated tones in an attempt to soften her presence.

On the whole, it seemed to be working. In a profession that was almost entirely dependent on referrals, some 90 percent of her schedule in any given month was booked solid. This permitted her to take on a few new clients periodically—clients with problems in her areas of demonstrable expertise or in areas she considered interesting. She believed Moia Kealey would prove to be a combination of both.

She rose from behind her desk to greet the mother and daughter. "Welcome, Maggie. Welcome, Moia. I'm so happy you're here. I've been looking forward to meeting you."

Mother smiled, daughter glared. "Where do you want us?" Maggie asked, looking around the room.

"Oh . . . right here, Maggie," Karen responded quickly, leading them to the other side of the large room and to an oversized couch set against a wall adorned with pictures of Karen's extended family. Lots of nieces and nephews, lots of fun, lots of love. Nothing to distrust here.

Maggie sat down, sinking a good three inches into the couch. Moia pointedly walked to the open chair farthest from the couch and sat down in silence. Karen grabbed the back of the nearest wing chair with both hands and walked it closer to her guests, inching it to a point equidistant from the warring factions.

Karen walked around from behind the chair and sat in it, never taking her eyes off Moia. She'd seen this look before, a cold fury fueled by feelings of guilt, shame, and fear. This little one, she thought, is at sea. She doesn't know how she ended up in this bottomless black hole. And her biggest fear is that there's no way out. Karen knew intuitively that she would have to jump this one quickly or she would never get any traction with this frightened little girl.

"Moia," she said, engaging the pain evident in her client's eyes with great kindness, "I want to talk with you about relationships. And I don't need you to say anything. I just want you to feel whatever you feel. To just be conscious that almost all of our relationships bring a measure of pain, even the best ones. The ones that cause the most pain are the ones we need to focus on. Those are the ones that are sending us signals that something's wrong. Something needs to be fixed. We're here to fix what's wrong, Moia . . . so that the pain goes away and you can get back to being you, which from everything I've heard is someone pretty terrific."

Moia's expression did not change. She was staring at a point on a distant wall, appearing oblivious to whatever was happening around her. However, Karen knew that Moia was hearing and processing everything. Karen wasn't expecting a miracle. She just needed something to work with, even the tiniest of breaches in that impenetrable wall. Perhaps that was why she was unprepared for the sheer magnitude of the breach she uncovered—and the torrent it unleashed.

"Moia," Karen resumed, "I just want you to relax and to let pictures form in your mind. Don't fight them; just let them come in whatever form they want to take. I'm going to go through a short list of people in your life. We're going to focus today on whether those relationships have brought you peace or pain.

"Let's begin with your mother, Moia. Peace or pain? Take a few moments. What kind of picture is forming in your mind's eye? Are the people in the picture smiling or are they angry?"

Though there was no voluntary response from Moia, Karen could observe her jaw stiffen at the sound of her mother's name. She took this to signal that Moia regarded her mother as an implacable foe to whom she would never submit, regardless of consequence.

"OK, Moia, I want you to think of your father. What pictures do you see now?"

Blank stare. Karen read it as indifference. The father was a somewhat remote figure in her life who hadn't been there for her. In her truncated world, he simply ceased to exist.

Karen waited patiently. Then in a soft, hushed tone, "Moia, I want you to think of your best friend. The one girl you've had more fun with, maybe got into more trouble with, than all the others."

Tears formed in Moia's beautiful, blue eyes. They welled and gently rolled down her lovely face and onto her cheeks, which were flushed with embarrassment. She said nothing. Karen regarded this as a relatively fresh wound. This friend was indispensible, yet was dispensed—for not comprehending the incomprehensible. Her departure had created a vacuum in Moia's life that was filled with only additional, unwanted pain.

"There's not a one of us who hasn't had a best friend disappoint us, Moia. And it always hurts worse than we can ever imagine. How about a favorite boyfriend?"

No visible reaction. Karen felt Moia grow distant. Whatever happened there was now buried, and in a moment of impulsivity Moia had thrown the key into a large, deep body of water. There would be no going back.

"Now, Moia, I'd like you to think about your relationship with your favorite teacher."

Nothing. It was evident that Moia had effectively walled off the authority figures in her life. Karen decided to pick up the pace, get through this part of her list quickly and double back to family and siblings.

"Coaches, Moia. I want you to concentrate on your lacrosse coach and her assistants."

Nothing. They, too, ceased to exist. They didn't cause pain, but they'd done nothing to relieve it, either. They'd been evicted.

"How about your principal, Sister Joseph Mary?"

Nothing.

"Father Sweeney."

A clenching of the jaw. Karen read this as Moia now linking this priest with her mother. He would never be an honest broker in her eyes.

"Your pastor, Monsignor Grogan."

Nothing.

"Any other religious figure who might come to mind—maybe a former pastor or parish priest?"

Suddenly, Moia's hands began to shake. In moments she was

convulsing in torment, shaking and crying, shriveling in her chair, her eyes glassy and wide with fear.

Karen rushed to her side and held her, burying Moia's head on her ample bosom. Her mother was kneeling at her side, one hand on her child's head, the other on her own. "Moia, what happened?" she pleaded, repeating it over and over.

Karen cut her off. "It doesn't matter today what happened," she said as she continued to stroke Moia. "This precious little one has been hurt. She feels great pain. This is where our work will begin."

They would learn in the years to come that the pain in Moia's deeply troubled mind was caused by Monsignor Grogan's predecessor, Monsignor Munger, now deceased. The process of unraveling this mystery would bring fresh torments every step of the way.

14

Joe Delgado turned left off Broad Street onto Catherine Street, heading east toward the river and Fortunato's, a popular South Philly saloon patronized by athletes, entertainers, and mobsters. He thought it an interesting place for what he regarded as an important meeting, but, then again, his colleague Steve Dalkowitz, who chose it, was a master of symbolism.

As he made his way through the narrow, cluttered streets, Joe couldn't help but marvel at the enduring character of the neighborhood. The Italians, his own family among them, had famously settled this part of the city in the late nineteenth century, building its Romanesque cathedrals and Art Deco theaters and shops, creating its beautiful small parks and open markets and popularizing a culture that now reached well beyond the city's limits.

The Irish had arrived sometime later. After them came the Polish and Germans. Then the blacks and Hispanics. Finally there was an influx of Asians, who arrived after the end of the Vietnam War. Lose a war; gain a restaurant, as Joe's boss and former Navy Seal Bill Carney was fond of saying. Each ethnic group soon made their presence felt both within and beyond the borders of their enclaves. None of them, however, had succeeded in materially changing the character and culture of this authentically Italian neighborhood. On this pleasant early summer evening, the men, as they had for six generations, were clustered on corners smoking and ribbing and ogling. The women, too, huddled on their stoops, laughing at each other's complaints about the men in their lives.

Joe slowed to take in all the sounds, sights, and smells of real city living, where people actually had to work at getting along, so intimately did they share space, time, and parking spots. Up ahead, he saw Fortunato's. Too late, he started looking for a parking spot. It took him almost five minutes to find one, and when he did, he ended up having to walk almost four blocks to the restaurant.

Along the way he began mentally preparing himself for the meeting. Dalkowitz didn't buy his argument that Pittman Labs, and by extension the "Carney Boys," would have legal exposure if the "OC" files he uncovered in the archives surfaced in an untimely manner. "Bull!" he'd characterized Joe's handicapping of its likelihood. Nonetheless, Dalkowitz was sufficiently unsettled that he suggested they get Pete Halifax on board for an objective "threat assessment."

Halifax was widely considered Joe's only rival for the top job, when and if Bill Carney moved up to corporate. Indeed, there were "rumors" being circulated that such a move was in the offing. Joe suspected the rumors were initiated by Carney. He eventually decided the decision to get Halifax involved was just Dalkowitz being Dalkowitz. He knew that Joe would never accept his judgment alone on what was shaping up as more of an ethical issue than a legal one. So he'd pull in Halifax, a rival and fellow Christian, and he'd let Joe make his case. Halifax would see it for what it was—that distinctive alchemy of Catholic guilt and moralizing, and would say as much. That would end the matter, Joe ultimately realizing that his "going nuclear" on the "OC" files would greatly advantage his rival in the foot race for the top spot.

Joe also understood as he walked through the highly aromatic side streets that this meeting would provide Dalkowitz with cover if the subject ever came up in Bill Carney's presence. Carney would see clearly that, by bringing Delgado's only rival into the discussion early on, Dalkowitz did everything he could, everything within the bounds of confidentiality and prudence, to arrest the files' likelihood of gaining exposure. Carney would be grateful to Dalkowitz for that deft interception. Who knows, maybe he'd even pull him along and appoint him general counsel of National Health Products when he assumed the top job.

Joe entered the restaurant to find Dalkowitz already seated in a booth facing the door in the back room. Joe waved and made his way back, stopping to say hello to a couple of friends from the neighborhood. As he neared the table, Steve rose to greet him and said, "Halifax just called. He's running late. He told me to have a drink and order him the veal piccata."

Joe took a seat in the booth and watched Steve summon an extremely short waiter with an earring in each ear. "Whadd'ya drinkin', mate?" he asked, handing a menu to Joe. When Joe ordered his dry martini, Steve nodded and told the waiter, "Make that two."

Over the next fifteen minutes they caught up on family and mutual friends. Joe liked Dalkowitz—liked his intelligence, liked his candor, and especially liked his wit. He didn't want his growing concerns over the files he'd uncovered to damage their relationship. He was now beginning to view getting Halifax involved as a plus. He saw Halifax, Pittman's EVP of Sales and Marketing, as a smart, tough straight-shooter with a moral compass.

Joe did think he would make the better CEO if Carney moved on—he was much more familiar with Pittman's complex financial issues—but he'd long ago decided he'd have no trouble reporting to Peter Halifax if he got the nod. He both trusted and admired him.

Halifax suddenly arrived and sat down, placing his suit coat on the back of the chair next to their table. He loosened his bright Hermès tie and opened his collar and sleeves, rolling the latter to his forearms. Peter Halifax was about average height with a slim, wiry build. He'd been an All-American golfer at Duke University and still carried a low single-digit handicap. His humility and prodigious work ethic helped him earn the respect of Pittman's four hundred-person sales force, but it was his smooth, effortless golf stroke that won him the admiration of every high-profile doctor that Pittman routinely targeted for its products. He offered the docs entry into the best clubs in the U.S., and after a couple rounds of golf with him even the most resistant high-volume docs were persuaded to write scripts for Pittman's latest entry into the beta blocker category . . . or the oral contraceptives category.

The diminutive waiter returned with drinks, riffled through the specials, fetched his pad, and took the orders, carrying on a very funny conversation with Dalkowitz about his earrings all the while. Joe ordered the linguine with clam sauce, Steve the manicotti, and Peter the veal. They also ordered a white California table wine and some light appetizers. After the waiter collected the menus, took a parting shot at Dalkowitz, and departed, Peter turned to Joe and said, "Steve tells me you've uncovered some stuff in the archives. What's up?"

Joe always appreciated Halifax's directness. Everything was short and sweet, like his golf swing. "Well, I'm not sure, Pete. That's why Steve thought we should talk." At this, Peter and Steve exchanged glances, which did not escape Joe's attention.

"So whadd'ya got?" Peter asked again.

"Pete, I stumbled across these files in the archives while helping Steve research the Alphasint investigation." He wanted it clear from the outset he wasn't on a witch hunt. He was "on assignment"—an assignment that originated with their mutual boss, Bill Carney. He was as surprised as anyone, as indeed perhaps Peter Halifax himself might be, to discover what he did.

Halifax stared blankly and said, "Got it. Now . . . what did you find, Joe?"

Joe momentarily stumbled. "I found something labeled the 'OC' files . . . ah, 'oral contraceptive' files . . . from about twenty-five years ago. You know, why and how we should get into the business and . . . ah . . . some of the . . . the obstacles . . . we might face, and some . . . recommendations on how to deal with those . . ."

Halifax interrupted as though Joe were a junior staffer. "Joe, not hearing a problem. Is there one?"

"Well . . . yes." The verbal backhander helped Joe find his voice, "The files give evidence"—it was a poor choice of words, he immediately realized—"of an effort on the part of Pittman Labs and, well . . . let's call them some 'friends,' to cover up—"

"Who are the friends?" Halifax interrupted again, a bit testily.

"A consortium of pharmaceutical manufacturers, researchers, and medical journals," Joe replied evenly. "The files reveal a plan to conceal the significant and lasting damage oral contraceptives do to women who use them."

Halifax nodded. "Yeah, that's what Steve said." He tilted his head slightly in Dalkowitz's direction. "Can you break some of that down for me, Joe?"

Joe nodded. "The files reveal that back in the early 1960s our patriarch Al Heyworth commissioned some highly credentialed medical researchers to study the way oral contraceptives worked in women. They returned two years later with their findings. I'll outline them for you as best I can . . ."

Halifax looked at Dalkowitz and interrupted again, "Have you read any of this stuff?"

Dalkowitz stole a look at Joe and shook his head.

Joe continued. "The researchers found that oral contraceptives generally have three mechanisms of action. Two of these are purely contraceptive in nature, meaning they prevent fertilization. As we know, they do this by preventing ovulation and by initiating changes in the cervical mucus that prevents or delays migration of the sperm into the uterus, the womb—"

"Thanks for that important clarification," Dalkowitz interrupted, dryly.

Joe ignored him. "There is a third action, however. It's not something most people know about. I dare say very few, if any, of our own people know about it. Yet this third action occurs, by the researchers' own estimates, during some 10 to 20 percent of a woman's monthly cycles.

"This is what happens in these instances. The oral contraceptives alter the cell adhesion molecules, called integrins, which act like chemical receptors preparing the uterus to receive the embryo and help facilitate its reception. Put plainly, the adhesions lose their adhesiveness. In other words, after the sperm has fertilized the egg and a child has been conceived, the third action of oral contraceptives is to block the embryo's implantation in the womb. Ultimately, the embryo just gets flushed away. End of child. The child's mother is none the wiser."

Dead silence.

He continued. "Then there are the anti-progesterones. They prevent the embryo, the child, from getting the progesterone it needs from its mother, causing the placenta to wither and ultimately be expelled. One of these anti-progesterones is called Mifepristone. It works to cause severe contractions that help expel the child from its mother's womb with about 88 percent effectiveness, or so it claims. This one is made by one of our competitors, Boedke-Tongsin. They bought the German company that originally developed it. The files reveal that the name of that company is Bosche AG, a spinoff of IG Farben. You may recall Farben produced the 'final solution' . . . Zyklon B gas for the Third Reich."

Peter Halifax now gave every appearance of a man who wished he were somewhere else.

Joe soldiered on. "The report also concluded that oral contraceptive manufacturers should expect to contend with five associated risks to which the women who use their products would be exposed—in no particular order, a sharp increase in sexually transmitted disease, a rise in pelvic inflammatory disease, considerably higher levels of infertility, a dramatic rise in cervical cancer, and, finally, what would be nothing less than a pandemic of breast cancer."

Peter glanced nervously at Steve Dalkowitz, then back to Joe. "Tell me again. How did Heyworth and Pittman Labs figure into all of this?"

Joe paused for effect before answering. "Heyworth was the project's patriarch. He fronted the money for the study and pulled together four other manufacturers whom he hand-picked to share the results with. He saw not just a huge and growing market for a new product category; he saw an industry within an industry—with its own product cycle, so to speak, and its own sales and profits trajectory, completely independent of everything else going on in the industry. He referred to it as his "corporate whole-life policy"—providing him with both an insurance policy against downturns in Pittman's product portfolio and an annuity to guarantee him immunity from unhappy directors."

"You're saying Heyworth purposely created his own competition?" Dalkowitz asked incredulously.

"Sure," Joe answered, "because he didn't see the other houses as competitors. He saw them as a cloak of respectability. He also saw them as category-building pistons in his earnings engine that would help prime the pump for the all-important job of raising investment capital. Finally, and perhaps most importantly, he saw them as potential co-defendants if the industry ever faced a class-action suit."

Peter Halifax whistled and said, "Clever guy. Do the files reveal the identities of the original companies?"

"They do," Joe said, and nodded. "Pearce-Faber, Ranger Labs, AR Wentworth, and American Günter."

Peter's eyes widened. "They're all sister subsidiaries at NHP."

"Bingo," Joe replied.

A hush fell upon the table. The appetizers arrived, warm oversized plates of calamari and bruschetta.

When the waiter departed, Steve Dalkowitz looked at Joe and asked, "How big a piece of the NHP portfolio do the oral contraceptives represent today?"

"Over 30 percent," Joe answered. "We're talking about five billion dollars on a sixteen-billion-dollar base."

"What about the other classes of contraceptives?" Peter asked.

"The oral contraceptives represent about 70 percent of the category. There are also progestins like Depo-Provera, from Framingham Labs, whom Heyworth used to call the 'Merchant of Death'—a bit enviously, I'm sure. Their little task is to fundamentally change the consistency of the cervical mucus to prevent migration of the sperm, and, should that fail, to alter the basic character of the endometrium, which renders implantation of the embryo all but impossible.

"We also of course have the progestin called Norplant, which involves implanting six one inch polymeric capsules under the skin in the woman's arm. Sounds like fun, right? They expect problems with this one. Apparently in early tests, women started growing facial hair and bleeding heavily."

Peter Halifax looked ashen. "Tell me about the longer-term . . . uh . . . issues."

Joe nodded, reached for a bruschetta, and continued, "Let's start with the worst. The studies revealed that the risk of breast cancer among American women will double from 6 percent today to almost 12 percent by the year 2000. Those are our mothers, sisters, and daughters, gentlemen."

"Why?" Dalkowitz asked.

"Well, because women, very young women, are starting on these things . . . ah . . . sooner and sooner. According to the research, women are most vulnerable when they're young. The time between their first period and their first baby is the worst because their breast tissue just isn't mature enough to absorb all the estrogen that contraceptives deliver. The estrogen makes the breast lobules in these young women multiply, and that's how and when cancer starts."

"What's the scale—the magnitude—of the problem we're looking at here?" Peter interrupted.

"By 2000, they—meaning the professionals Heyworth

commissioned to analyze the studies and make recommendations—projected that abortifacient contraceptives would cause somewhere between five to seven 'hidden abortions' for every abortion performed through surgical procedure. By my calculations that would come to about two hundred fifty million abortions, one way or another, by 2000. That's roughly one for every one of us expected to be alive in the U.S. by then. Add to that some thirty to forty million women projected to have breast cancer and you can understand what this pope means when he talks about a 'culture of death' in America."

Peter and Steve fell silent and looked down at their plates. Joe immediately knew he'd made a mistake . . . a big mistake. He had taken an ethical issue and made it a moral issue. Worse, he had made it a Catholic moral issue. To these men, the whole matter had just become a combination Inquisition and Crusade. No place for businessmen.

"I think I've heard enough," Peter Halifax said, looking visibly uneasy.

Dinner arrived. Joe, though hungry, couldn't eat. He had spent the better part of the past week studying the files in preparation for this meeting. There was more to say, whether anybody wanted to hear it or not. And while his colleagues were eating, he decided, they were going to hear it. Then, Steve Dalkowitz surprised him by providing an opening.

"I want to hear about these . . . these recommendations . . . you mentioned earlier," Dalkowitz said, breaking the awkward silence. "You didn't tell me there was an actual agenda in the files."

"When I met with you, Steve, I didn't know there were recommendations," Joe said evenly.

Dalkowitz reached for his platter, took a huge gulp of wine, looked at Halifax, and said sardonically, "Well, since we're now talking about a ten billion dollar industry on its way to doubling by 2000, I can't wait to hear how these guys accomplished all this."

"Essentially there were three recommendations," Joe resumed, happy to continue the tutorial. His colleagues were nibbling at their food again. "The first proposed the commissioning of a well-credentialed, highly influential cadre of physicians to begin publishing carefully annotated opinions suggesting that conception actually occurs at implantation, not fertilization . . ."

"Because?" Halifax interrupted.

"Because the contraceptives are better at preventing implantation than they are at preventing fertilization," Dalkowitz answered, looking at Joe for affirmation.

"Yes, that's correct," Joe said. "Once an egg is fertilized and is an embryo, the action of many of these compounds is that of an abortifacient, not a contraceptive. And if it were labeled as such, it would raise a hue and cry from all kinds of special-interest groups, which would have killed the business at the outset, or—at minimum—significantly altered its projected growth trajectory."

Joe saw that his colleagues were now listening again. "Change the definition of when life begins, and you change the debate. It becomes a debate about which compounds and methods are more effective at preventing pregnancy, not aborting tiny children in the form of embryos."

"What kind of special-interest groups?" asked Dalkowitz.

Joe paused. He needed to proceed delicately. "I brought the actual recommendations with me—I'll show you," he said fumbling for the manila folder on the chair next to him.

"No," Halifax said, abruptly. "No need to see them, Joe. Just top-line it for us, OK?"

Plausible deniability, Joe realized immediately. Neither one of his colleagues wanted to admit to seeing any part of the file. Not a good sign.

"OK. I don't want to make you guys uncomfortable . . ."

"Oh, that's clear," Dalkowitz interrupted.

"These fellows identified 'the Catholic Church as the most likely and most significant impediment'—and I'm quoting here—to the growth of the oral contraceptives industry. And they proposed a strategy to neutralize it."

"OK, what else?" Halifax said impatiently, making it clear

he did not want to hear any more about the presumed moral superiority of the Catholic Church, an institution he did not hold in particularly high regard.

"All right," Joe resumed, tentatively. He thought it a real blind spot that otherwise open-minded people would turn away from objective fact simply because the Catholic Church also recognized it as objective fact. That, however, was not a battle he intended to fight. He merely wanted his colleagues to see the elaborate strategy these pioneers had developed to neutralize the moral authority of what they presumed would be their arch nemesis. That the Catholic Church's opposition never materialized should have been as curious to them as it was to him.

"The final recommendation dealt with the expected backlash from medical science itself. They identified all the side effects the studies revealed and proposed an elaborate method of scientific obfuscation to blunt what they feared would be a ruinous attack in influential medical journals.

"In the so-called clinical trials they went down to Puerto Rico, where the government was focused on controlling population growth. They gave the compounds away to any woman who would take them. They figured the free distribution of the contraceptives through these 'make-shift' health clinics would yield an enormous public relations coup. Once the clinics were set up in rural areas, away from a blind government and a mute press, an army of clinical researchers descended on the little villages. It was their job to document the effectiveness of the oral contraceptives—and here's where it gets incriminating. They were also asked to document their safety."

Joe paused to let this settle, then reiterated, "Note that we're not talking here about the *question* of their safety, but the *fact* of their safety.

"Now, I'm sure it will come as no surprise to either of you that initially these folks had monumental problems getting the dosage right. Eventually, they course-corrected their way into a mainstream dosage that had wide application—but not until an alarming, but still unknown, number of the natives died from complications. Whole villages lost mothers and daughters out of all proportion to the general population. This presented certain problems with respect to the finished report, as you might imagine. Heyworth was quite resourceful here . . ." Joe looked at Halifax and stopped abruptly.

Peter Halifax was not happy. Dalkowitz had led him to believe this whole matter would be easily dismissible. Clearly, it was not. He didn't want any part of it. He wished he hadn't agreed to this meeting. He sensed that how he responded at this moment would forever alter his relationship with his rival and maybe even Dalkowitz. For one of the few times in his life, Peter Halifax did not know what to say . . . or do.

"Joe," he said finally, "I need some time to digest all of this."

"Of course," Joe replied. "I didn't expect to reach any decisions tonight. And by the way, I haven't reached any decisions on what, if anything, should be done with this file. I'm as much at sea as you guys."

"Oh, I wouldn't go that far, Delgado," Dalkowitz said. "Think of us as floating on a melting ice cap somewhere in the Antarctic."

For the first and only time all evening, the three men laughed together.

15

Michael Burns was going home. Carol had the girls dressed and the car packed and was gently suggesting it was time to get this "show on the road." But Michael remembered that he'd forgotten one very important item, his basketball sneakers. One of the real joys of going home, he would tell anyone who would listen, was the chance to plug back in to his favorite pickup game at the Narbrook courts.

The courts, the players, and the games themselves were the stuff of urban legend. Sports Illustrated had once published a lengthy piece on the top pickup games in the U.S. and had listed Michael's home court as among the country's best. This drew local press coverage and even a public television documentary crew. This, in turn, drew more and better players, many of whom left after their first day or weekend, never to return.

The game itself was extremely physical. The crew of over forty regulars included a number of former NFL and college football players, several ex–NBA players, and a number of former college basketball players. But the essential character of the game was forever defined by its motley mix of lawyers and dock workers, corporate executives and carpenters, doctors and construction workers. Winning, or "holding court," as it was called, was the one goal of every man who stepped onto the court on any given Saturday or Sunday. Tie games were settled by a "next basket" overtime that ratcheted the sheer brutality to a whole other level.

Yet there were almost no fights. The men bonded over time and each shared a tacit understanding that the other man had the same need to release the week's buildup of work and family frustrations. So they came with the intention of both using and sacrificing their own bodies, granting the other men the right to punish them in pursuit of their own sanity. Somehow it all worked, and after years of playing with and against each other, the men had come to consider the core group as extended family. When one suffered a reversal in his family or work life, the others rushed to help.

Michael threw his sneakers in the back of the station wagon, jumped in the car, and turned on the already running ignition, earning a wince from his wife and a chorus of catcalls from his children in the back. "Last call for bathroom," he yelled, smiling. "There'll be no stops, so don't ask."

Michael pulled the car onto Route 24 and headed west to Route 287 South. They were heading home, this time for a wedding in Carol's family—one of her brothers—and he felt at peace. His CMN road trip had gone extremely well, and he intended to use the time on the highway to put into perspective what he'd learned in the twelve cities he had visited in the last ten days.

The purpose of the trip was to urge cable distributors to carry CMN by demonstrating the sheer "throw weight" of the fifty-million-dollar media campaign and the pretested efficacy of the advertising itself. His road partner was Jim Concini, the network's number-two programming executive. It was his job to tell the assembled cable executives in each city what the network had planned for its viewers in the coming year.

Concini was an atypical National Publishing executive, in a sense. Though he had graduated summa cum laude from Princeton

University and earned a scholarship to Harvard Business School—where he also graduated with honors—his family was proudly blue-collar. He had been raised in an Italian neighborhood on the west side of Providence, Rhode Island. His father was a plumber, and his mother was an administrator with the municipal government. Jim Concini was a smart, tough, earthy guy filled with confidence and career expectation, and Michael greatly enjoyed his company.

The format for the one-hour presentation that typically took place in each city's best hotel—itself a statement—was evenly split between the network's plans to buy and create feature programming and the massive advertising campaign that would accompany it. Michael followed Concini not simply because the network's top executives thought it was the proper order of things, but because they also thought Michael to be the better "closer." And, indeed, "asking for the order," even in a gathering of one hundred to two hundred assembled cable executives, was an intrinsic feature of Michael's DNA.

The presentation was followed by a question-and-answer session that usually ran about a half-hour. This was followed by an open-bar reception featuring exquisitely fashioned and presented hors d'oeuvres. This was the time when the CMN field marketing types were expected to circulate and write business. After the reception, they were generally gathered in an adjacent suite to give an accounting for each and every contact they'd made . . . or not made.

The feedback from both the cable executives and the network's field marketers for Michael's work was uniformly positive. His presentation was built around the scope of the marketing opportunity, a top-line preview of the media schedule, and, of course, a viewing of the TV commercials that would air in the operators' cities, creating what Michael promised would be an insatiable demand.

The combination of previewing upcoming feature programming and the television commercials that would promote it served to create a buzz about the network among the local press and city officials. This, in turn, created certain expectations, if not pressure, on the cable executives to "carry" CMN. Because cable systems were municipally licensed monopolies, their executives tended to be responsive to such expectations.

The road show was judged to be quite successful, exceeding the ambitious projections that CMN's senior executives promised their corporate bosses at National Publishing. The national launch could now proceed and, it was presumed, begin to drive much-needed cash into National Publishing coffers, somewhat depleted at the moment by the costly failures of three new publishing ventures.

All things considered, life was OK, Michael reckoned as he veered the family station wagon onto the exit for 202 South. And yet there had been a couple of red flags waved in his direction by cable operators in Southern and Midwestern cities. Generally, the cable executives in these cities were more skeptical of CMN's programming model. They asked questions about the "uncut" movies. Just what would be shown in the living rooms of their customers' homes? As one particularly colorful operator from Texas put it, "You know, *our* kind don't cotton to *your* kind."

Perhaps the most memorable moment had occurred after the presentation in Atlanta, when one crusty old operator—worth hundreds of millions, someone later pointed out—stood and directed a question to Michael. "I've heard about some of those movies y'all are plannin' to run, as is, into our homes, and I can tell y'all, that stuff just ain't fit for a livin' room."

A crackling tension filled the room. All eyes were now on him. The gentleman, seeing he had an audience, decided to seize the moment, "Y'all got people ain't married havin' sex right there on the screen. That kind of programmin' ain't got no place in a home, and I'm just tellin' you what every other operator here is thinkin.'" He sat down, his eyes never leaving Michael's chest.

A hush fell over the crowd. All eyes reverted to Michael. He glanced at Jim Concini, who smiled at him as if to say—it may be my question, but hey, it's all yours. Michael intuitively sensed the anticipation shared by the CMN marketing executives who were primed to pounce, this having been the putative last question. He took pride in being cool under pressure. He understood he'd been given a gift to move people, particularly large audiences, in the general direction he intended. But he also knew that the source and secret of that power was his willingness to be refreshingly— some would say brutally—candid in all circumstances. His power to persuade was born of conviction. Put simply, if he didn't believe it, he couldn't sell it.

Michael looked at the gentleman, then panned the crowd, looked back again to the gentleman, and said, "My friend is right. Programming that's unfit for family consumption has no place in the home. And I think, and trust, CMN knows that."

The audience response was audible, a collective exhaling of bated breath, then, slowly, a smattering of applause that built into a solid and somewhat sustained applause that acknowledged, at least in Michael's mind, the level of concern in the room about CMN's programming model.

Afterward, even as the reception was just beginning, he was besieged by CMN marketing executives congratulating him for "stepping up big-time," as several put it. "You completely defused the situation," another said, to the nodding approval of colleagues. "I've never seen anything quite like that. That could have been a disaster." The young man was all of thirty, Michael reasoned, so he hadn't seen a whole hell of a lot. Instead of pointing this out, he said, instead, "I meant what I said."

They appeared so euphoric at the clear and present danger that had been at least temporarily averted that his simple statement of belief seemed to go unregistered—but not to Concini. He had approached Michael with his hand out, saying, "Nice job. Bet you didn't know when you signed on we'd have you goin' one-on-one with crackers, did ya?"

"All things considered, it's better than being back in New York hanging out with Zimmer," Michael replied.

This drew the expected laugh, as the mere mention of his boss' name always did in not-so-polite company.

As he pulled off 202 South and onto 611 South, heading for the Pennsylvania Turnpike, Michael was still mildly uncomfortable with that question from the floor in Atlanta. Were they, all of them, mere cogs in a wealth-creation engine that was a seminal force unto itself? The municipal authorities who licensed the cable companies were in business to use tax revenue collected from wealth-creating businesses to promote civil society. The cable operators were in business to create as much wealth as they could and retain as much of it as they could. CMN was in business to meet the profit expectations of its corporate parent, National Publishing, which in turn was in business to meet the earnings expectations of its shareholders. The Hal Ross advertising firm, which was privately held, was in business to make as much money for its senior partners as it could from its contracts with corporate clients like CMN.

And as Michael conceded to himself—he, too, wanted to get a fair share of that money for his own family.

He had no problem with the free enterprise system itself. He entered it with the same dreams as pretty much everyone else. He wanted to be able to buy a home and raise a family, get his kids through as much schooling as they could handle, and achieve a measure of financial independence. This would enable him to launch a second career, an "act two" if you will, which no less an authority than F. Scott Fitzgerald had said was beyond the reach of American mortals.

His present concern, he thought, was perhaps best expressed in a single question: would those most fundamental of needs—the very embodiment of the American Dream shared so universally by all the parties involved—prove so enticing that they would lead all of them to compromise the common good? And in compromising the common good, might they jeopardize the American Dream for future generations?

He had no answer.

16

Michael and Carol Burns made their way through the line waiting to greet Father John Sweeney, who was standing atop the church steps after celebrating the ten o'clock Mass. As he saw them approach, John stepped to his left to signal he wanted to catch up with the Burns family.

"Don't you know you can't go home again?" he asked, putting a big body hug on Michael and a discrete peck on Carol's cheek.

"There's no distance we wouldn't drive to hear a sermon like that," Michael needled back. "*God loves us.* Bet you spent all night on that one."

"Michael!" Carol shrieked.

"That's all right, Carol," John soothed. "We've never listened to a word he's said. As long as he drops those C-notes in the collection basket, we let him back in."

"Somebody took up a collection? For who? For what?" Michael feigned.

"How long you in town, Big Time?" John asked.

"We'll head back after dinner," Michael replied. "Unless we get a better offer."

"How about droppin' by for a cold one after your run at the courts?"

"Will do."

"I wasn't talking to you. I was talking to Carol."

. . .

Michael toweled himself off and plopped himself down on the first row of aluminum stands that adjoined the main courts at Narbrook Park. He was done for the day. Not a particularly good day on the court, he was forced to concede. He had been a first-round pick, as he nearly always was, but the wind kicked up during the second game, and that pretty much closed him down. He was a shooter, and in the autumn wind, there were no shooters. Still, it was a rush being on the court with his buddies again. The trash talking, the barely disguised muggings, the negotiated settlements over disputed calls at game point, all were tonic for his overwrought psyche.

Stretched out now over several rows of stands, he luxuriated in the mid-afternoon sun and occasionally contributed to the ritual heckling of the players still on the court. He missed this, he reminded himself. New York would not be an ultimate destination—merely a way station and a finishing school, something that would prepare him to open his own firm back here in Philadelphia.

When the last of the games ended, he bade his farewells, promising he would return, and pledged to his teammates this day that he would shoot much better next time. This drew the expected onset of ridicule, which greatly pleased him.

He got the station wagon pointed in the right direction,

wincing when he shifted his weight. He felt the usual assortment of welts and bruises from a day on the courts. Now he was ready for that cold beer with his former confessor.

Michael genuinely loved Father Sweeney. He saw in him everything he aspired to be as a Christian. He admired Sweeney's generosity of spirit, his willingness to put the needs—even the interests—of others ahead of his own. And he particularly respected his ability to "be all things to all people." This priest had gears, and he could shift swiftly and effortlessly into a persona appropriate to the task without in any way diminishing his authenticity.

This made conversations with him quick and productive. He was on whatever page you were on in no time, and without you even realizing it, he was gently guiding the discussion in the proper direction. *And* he knew how to stay in touch. The small note, the quick phone call, and the unexpected visit if he was in the vicinity were all trademarks of the John Sweeney pastoral touch.

Michael pulled the car close to the curb and saw that his host was already on the rectory porch with two beers. "Hey, Padre," he called out before he was even out of the car.

John responded with a smile and a beckon.

When Michael scaled the steps to the porch, John stood and welcomed him. "Here," he said handing him a Heineken. Then, pointing to Michael's feet and one of the Adirondacks, "Go sit and rest those puppies."

"How in hell are ya, Father?" Michael asked, seating himself.

"I'm good. Carol looks good. When's her due date?"

"About three months, middle of January."

"Any complications with this one?"

"Not so far, thank God," Michael replied. There had been problems with all three of his wife's other deliveries, each of which had been Caesarian. He was happy to see that Father Sweeney shared his own deep concerns because it meant that he was praying for the same thing Michael prayed for every morning at Mass—the safe delivery of a normal child.

"How goes the job?" Father Sweeney asked.

"Great. I love it. It's everything I needed but never could've gotten if I stayed in town," Michael gushed. "I really feel like I'm in the big time, Father. These guys are good. They're smart, they're aggressive, and they're all about winning. I really feel at home up there."

"How about that matter we discussed, the programming content. Any problems with that?"

Michael paused, he hoped not too long, and said, "So far, so good, Father."

17

Maggie Kealey turned left onto Lancaster Avenue and headed east to Lower Merwood Hospital in Wynncoate. It was rush hour, and she was rushing, driving in excess of sixty miles per hour in a thirty-five m.p.h. zone. In the back seat were two of her children, tossed about with every turn and lane change.

Grace held her big sister Moia tightly in her arms and yelled to her mother, "Hurry, Mom—she's barely breathing!" Twenty minutes earlier, Moia had slipped into her parents' bathroom, opened the medicine cabinet, reached into a plastic bottle of generic pain medicine, and emptied its contents, swallowing over forty pills in a series of swift, continuous gulps.

She was discovered by her younger sister, now sixteen, who wrested the remaining pills from her hands and screamed in panic, arresting the attention of her mother, who was downstairs preparing breakfast for the other children. When Maggie arrived and saw Moia on the floor in a fetal position with the empty bottle on the floor beside her, her primal scream gave full voice to her worst nightmare in a single sound—a sound that reverberated through-out the house, bringing the other children running up the steps and into the bathroom.

Maggie was now angry at herself for panicking the other children, and, as she neared the hospital, she began to direct that anger toward her husband. *Why, why, why, am I left to fight with demons while he pursues only his career? How can I be expected to do this alone? Who will help me, Lord? Must my child die before I get help? Where are the men? . . . Where are the men?*

Maggie turned right into the hospital's main entrance from the left lane, setting off a symphony of horns behind her. In the back seat Moia, without lifting her head, raised her right hand and responded with a digital salute visible to all through the rear window—all save her mother, who did not take notice. Halfway up the long and winding entrance the glare of the sun over the roof of the hospital became so great that it forced her to pull off the road.

"Mother!" screamed Grace from the back seat.

"I can't see!" Maggie screamed back. When she grasped the full symbolism of her simple statement, she laid her head on the steering wheel and began to sob. It was then that she remembered Bill having to pull off this same entrance road the morning he'd driven her to this hospital to deliver the child who now lay dying in her back seat. She began sobbing uncontrollably. Neither of them was able to see that morning.

Suddenly, the driver's side door was being jerked open and Maggie felt herself being shoved into the passenger seat. It was Grace. "Move over!" she shouted at her mother, shifting the car from its parked position into drive and steering it back onto the main entrance way. She was a good four inches shorter than her mother, and the glare was perhaps not as significant a problem. She was also a good bit more resolute than her mother in this instance; nothing was going to bring this car to a stop until it arrived at the entrance to this hospital's emergency room.

The attendants were waiting at the curb with a wheelchair, Grace having had the presence of mind to call 911 and have the police alert the hospital's emergency room to expect them in minutes.

Once inside, experienced hands and feet moved with dispatch to meet the wheelchair and lift Moia from the chair and onto a gurney with large aluminum side rails. The head emergency room nurse approached Maggie and said, "Mrs. Kealey, can our administrator get some information while your daughter's stomach is being pumped?" Maggie nodded as she watched Moia being rushed through automatic double doors. There was nothing for her to do now except sit and wait . . . and ponder and pray.

18

Bill and Maggie Kealey drove in silence. The days since Moia's admission to the psychiatric unit at Methodist Memorial Hospital in Center City had been especially difficult. Each of them withdrew into a private space that they managed to fill with generous doses of guilt, doubt, and fear. The children, taking their cue from their parents, were unnaturally quiet in the home. The home itself now gave evidence of an absence of joy, even of hope. The family was listing on its keel and badly in need of a strong gust of wind to right it.

Bill Kealey parked the car and walked around to the passenger side to assist his wife. "C'mon, dear," he prodded gently, as Maggie sat disconsolate and unmoving.

"I don't want to go in," she said without looking at her husband. Bill understood. He sensed there was only more pain awaiting them within the padded walls beyond. He felt a deep guilt that no words of consolation from his own family, friends, and colleagues at the law firm were able to assuage.

This would not have happened, he told himself over and

over, if he hadn't pursued his career with such single-mindedness. He should have seen the warning signs. The landscape had been littered with bright red flags over the past two or more years. Why did he ignore them, all of them? He simply looked the other way and allowed the entire burden to fall on the slender shoulders of this beautiful woman whom he loved, who now sat before him motionless. "Maggie, let me help you," he said, reaching for her hand. She looked at him without recrimination, took his hand, and got out of the car without saying a word.

Once inside, they were directed by the woman at the front desk to the elevators in the east wing of the hospital. They entered the oversized lift, which was packed with poor people of color. They were all heading, Bill suspected, to a shared destination—the same psychiatric unit where they would visit their children for thirty minutes and have a consultation with a therapist for fifteen—all in what he knew would be a futile attempt to untangle the nightmare that had been visited upon their families.

Taking stock of the others in the elevator, he wondered how they did it. How did they work all day, many of them through the early evening hours as well at second jobs, only to come home to the nightmare of an emotionally crippled child who was menacing their family? How did they deal with the turmoil and dysfunction? How did they manage to carve out a dimension of quasi-normalcy for their other children? How did they pay their bills? Where did they go for help, or for hope?

They stepped off the elevator in waves, Bill and Maggie among the first to depart. They approached the desk, and Bill asked the relatively young black woman behind it for Moia's room number. "Ain't gonna happen," she said, looking at the crowd forming a line behind them. Then, to no one in particular, "Sign here and take a seat. Your doctor will be with you as soon as he can." Bill signed for himself and for Maggie, repressed an urge to bang his head against a wall, and took a seat. He had decided not to bring any legal briefs with him, figuring it might set Maggie off. Instead, he began taking a mental inventory of what he saw around him.

He was roughly halfway through the task of determining the central animating force in the life of each employee and visitor when a smallish wiry fellow with disheveled gray hair and black bifocals approached him, hand outstretched, and said, "Dr. Kirschner." Bill rose from his seat, shook the proffered hand, and reached for Maggie. Maggie rose quickly and asked, "Can we see Moia?"

Dr. Kirschner looked at Maggie and smiled. Then, with a twinkle in his eyes, he replied, "Do you think I would bring you all the way down here and not let you see your child, Mrs. Kealey? How would I explain that to my own mother, to whom I must give a full accounting every Sunday?"

Bill Kealey laughed and said, "We all have bosses, don't we Doctor?"

"No," Dr. Kirschner replied, twinkle intact. "Some of us have bosses. Others of us have Jewish mothers."

He led Bill and Maggie into his office, which was small and littered with textbooks, files, and folders. He motioned them to two chairs opposite his desk. When they were seated, he said, "Before I bring Moia in, I thought we might chat about what's been going on at home."

Bill looked at Maggie, then back to Kirschner, and said, "Sure. What can we tell you?"

"Well that would be my question to you, Mr. Kealey."

"Of course, of course. Well, she and her mother have not been getting along—"

"She and her mother!" Maggie half-shouted indignantly. "Is that what you think this is all about?"

Bill moved to soothe his wife but was rebuffed. He turned to Kirschner, who was observing the dynamic—and, Bill presumed, already making a mental note to the effect that the source of the "patient's problem" was no doubt a tension between her parents, rooted in a clueless father. "I think I may have oversimplified . . ." he began again.

"Yes, yes. By all means, let's try that again," Kirschner interrupted, seeming to enjoy his discomfort.

"Look, Doctor, I'm not quite sure what to tell you. Moia began having problems about two-and-a-half years ago, when she was a sophomore."

"How old?" Kirschner wanted to know.

"She was fifteen," Bill replied looking to Maggie for confirmation. None was forthcoming. "Her grades began to slip. Her teachers reported she wasn't completing tests and handing in papers. She started missing lacrosse practice, even skipping games. Her relationships with her friends grew strained. She had a boyfriend, but thankfully that went nowhere . . ."

"Thankfully?"

"Well, Maggie and I didn't approve, Doctor. We thought she was too young to be going steady. She was sixteen, seventeen, at the time. We discouraged it."

"How?"

Bill Kealey squirmed a bit, which did not escape the attention of Dr. Kirschner. "We sat her down and told her she ought to be spending her free time with girl friends; and we told her that if she were to date boys, we wanted her dating several at once and not limiting herself to one boy."

"And your reasoning?"

Bill didn't like this line of questioning. As an attorney, he was used to asking the questions. He didn't like being cross-examined in this manner by what he considered an outsider and was on the verge of saying so when he heard Maggie's voice, "Our reasoning was and is this, sixteen-year-old girls don't belong in cars alone at night with seventeen-year-old boys. That's an accident waiting to happen. We don't want that for our children. And we couldn't care less what their friends' parents permit."

Kirschner nodded thoughtfully. "Did this cause tension between you and your daughter, Mrs. Kealey?"

"Of course it did!" Maggie responded defiantly. "My husband and I prefer the presence of tension and the absence of a baby to the opposite, Doctor Kirschner."

Formidable, the aging psychiatrist thought to himself. This

daughter would not win many battles against this mother. Nor, he mused, would this husband. "OK. Perhaps it's time we include Moia," he said, rising from his chair. He left the office, leaving Bill and Maggie in unsettled silence. He returned shortly with Moia. She was ashen, her clothing stained, her eyes vacant. Maggie shrieked at the sight of her. Then, turning to the doctor, "What's going on in here? Have you no nurses?"

"We do, Mrs. Kealey. Your daughter chooses to refuse their simple requests to bathe her and wash her clothes."

Maggie attempted to put her arms around Moia, who shrugged her off and went to the farthest corner of the office, half turning to the wall. Her body language confirmed Kirschner's conviction that a fierce and pervasive sexual repression within the family was the root cause of this child's estrangement from family and friends. State law mandated that any child who attempted suicide must remain in the unit for a minimum of seventy-two hours, after which those who had reached the age of eighteen were permitted to leave. He would propose she be admitted to the thirty-day counseling program that she was eligible for, and for which he believed her to be a prime candidate.

"Moia," her mother called softly. "I've brought you some clothes, and a cake that Grace baked for you, and some cards from Noreen and Shannon . . . and . . . Billy and Tommy."

Nothing.

Dr. Kirschner broke the silence, turning to the child's mother, "I propose Moia be admitted to our post-treatment counseling program. I would ask you and Mr. Kealey to please give it thoughtful consideration. In my opinion, Moia would benefit greatly from it."

Maggie said nothing in response. Bill looked at his daughter, then said to her doctor, "We will do whatever is best for Moia." Upon hearing her father's voice, Moia turned the remaining portion of her body to the wall so that her back was now fully facing both her parents. Her mother slowly exhaled and laid the carry bag with the clothing and cards on her chair, then placed the cake she had wrapped in cellophane on Dr. Kirschner's desk. She then turned and walked out the door, offering neither a goodbye nor waiting for her husband to follow.

19

Father John Sweeney registered surprise when the door to the confessional opened and Maggie Kealey entered. He'd been hearing confessions for seven years now at St. Martha's, and as best he could recollect, she had never opted for a face-to-face sacramental encounter. Not that he blamed her. He couldn't imagine doing it himself, were he not a priest. The act of publicly confessing one's sins was difficult enough, he reasoned, requiring no small measure of humility. Why add to the burden by sitting at your confessor's knee and having him peer into your soul?

"Hello, Maggie," he welcomed, sotto voce.

"Hello, Father John," she replied as she seated herself opposite him. They were roughly the same age, she being perhaps two or so years older. He knew of her when he was in high school. Her great beauty and bearing, her effortless charm and high achievement set her apart, earning her near-iconic status among that generation's Catholic high school students in the western suburbs of Philadelphia.

Christened Margaret Anne Timoney two weeks after birth, she was the first of Bill and Anne Timoney's eight children. Her mother had been the Philadelphia Orchestra's first woman cellist. Her father was still a practicing attorney with Mullen, Rooney, and Timoney, a sixty-lawyer firm specializing in medical malpractice and headquartered in Center City.

Maggie met Bill Kealey when he was a junior at St. Joseph's Prep in North Philadelphia. He quarterbacked the Prep's championship football team in his senior year and graduated first in his class, scoring over 1500 on his SATs. It was just enough to earn him a full scholarship to Harvard, something that was, although not unheard-of, nonetheless exceedingly rare for a Catholic school student. As expected, Bill excelled at Harvard—in his senior year earning all-Ivy honors as a free safety on the football team, landing the lead in the Drama Club's presentation of *A Midsummer Night's Dream*, ranking fourth in his class academically, and earning a scholarship to Harvard Law.

Many a young Catholic school boy dreamed of squiring Maggie Timoney around town, and quite a number of girls went to often hilarious lengths to arrest the attention of Bill Kealey, some even canvassing his neighborhood in Dixon Hill all hours of the night hoping for a "sighting." To many, however, Bill Kealey and Maggie Timoney "going together," in the parlance of the day, was merely the right order of things. They were a perfect fit, two apex achievers destined to slip the bonds of Catholic middle-class life and take their rightful place among the forefront of Philadelphia's surging meritocracy.

John Sweeney studied Maggie's face as she blessed herself and beseeched his sacramental blessing. What he saw did not surprise him. This one, he thought to himself, has had a rough go of it. Her face was drawn and sallow, and her eyes gave evidence of a fear and an overall weariness he hadn't observed before. That she was sitting opposite him was in itself a signal of distress. She was burdened, overburdened, and she was here seeking relief. He prayed that he could provide it, or he corrected himself, that he might be an instrument through which the Lord Himself would minister to this dear soul.

"Father, Bill and I . . . are struggling," she began haltingly. Oh no, he immediately thought to himself. Not this marriage. This can't be happening. Not on my watch. As he attempted to peer into her eyes, her expression changed, and she looked up at him as though she could read his thoughts. "I don't mean to suggest we're contemplating divorce, Father." He felt a sudden wave of relief flow through his body, relaxing him.

"What's the problem, Maggie?" he said, gently trying to help her get started.

"It's all too much, Father. These terrible migraines. The open warfare between Moia and the other five children. The anguish about finding someone, somewhere, who can help her. The growing tension between Bill and me. I just . . . I just . . . don't know what to do anymore."

John had never seen Maggie Kealey look so vulnerable. It took every ounce of self-mastery he possessed to resist leaning over and hugging her, holding her tightly and promising her that he would make it right, all of it. "Maggie," he said with ever greater gentleness, "tell me about Moia." He was convinced the problems in the family began and ended with that child, and he was perplexed that Jim McNeeley and Karen Wright weren't able to make a dent in the case.

"She's threatening to run away now. She says everybody in the family hates her. She's stopped going to school, just dropped out. All she does is watch TV, eat, and wait for her sisters to come home so she can agitate and terrorize them."

"Do you think Moia will run away, Maggie?" he asked, not thinking it likely. It was his experience that when one of these problem children threatened some dire action they seldom followed through on it. It was when they didn't threaten . . .

"Oh yes, Father, I do. If she says she will do something, she does it. And just the thought of it, of her being alone at night on a street in some city, exposed to all the dangers . . . is a horror,

Father. An absolute horror, just beyond my ability to endure. I can't sleep from the sheer terror of it."

"Who is seeing her now, Maggie?" he asked, hoping that some clinical professional was at work on the problem but suspecting otherwise.

"No one, Father. We've taken her to eight different clinical psychiatrists or psychologists over the last two-and-a-half years. Men, women. Old, young. Confrontational, conciliatory. None helped. She refused to speak to any of them. They all promised us that they'd get her to open up. None did. We took her to every scheduled appointment, paid our hundred dollars for every visit, and after the third visit with each one of them, either they'd give up on her or we'd give up on them."

John winced. He simply couldn't imagine trying to navigate such a tortuous journey. "So she's basically on her own?" he asked, thinking of Moia as not unlike a malignant cancer, growing unimpeded on one of the family's most vital organs, the very heart of its mother.

"What do you mean on her own? I'm with her every second of every day," she responded defensively.

John saw a flash of that Irish temper Maggie was never able to hide from him entirely. He masked a smile and said, "Of course you are. And without you in her life, that child would have already entered eternity. You, Maggie—your love—is all that binds Moia's tortured soul to this paradise lost."

She instantly welled up and appeared on the verge of crying, then, abruptly, pulled herself together and, remembering why she had come, said to him, "Father, I've gone on the Pill . . ." She stopped to assess his reaction and, when he didn't visibly react, continued, "The rhythm method doesn't work for me. My menstrual cycle is too irregular. Some months the 'safe' period is only a week or so, and that's just too hard for Bill."

John sat in a daze. He couldn't believe he was a party to a discussion, no, a sacramental confession primarily focused on Maggie Kealey's menstrual cycle. It was nothing less than surreal.

He was simply unable to say anything. Sensing this, she continued. "Father, Bill says we'll have another six children, maybe more, if I don't do this. And he thinks even one more will make him a widower. He doesn't want that. And I don't want it either, Father. I don't want it for Bill, and I don't want it for my children." She stopped and looked at him, waiting for a rebuke.

She knew well that, at least "objectively," she was contravening the teachings of her Church. Whether or not "subjective" factors would mitigate her guilt she did not presume to know. So she understood the price she would in all likelihood have to pay. There would be no reception of Holy Communion on Sunday with her family. There would be no absolution in this very sacrament, because she would be unwilling to "amend her life." She also knew she might well be "living in sin," the worst of all dark fates for a practicing Catholic. Yet she was willing to pay that price if it delivered her from this region of hell in which she now found herself.

Maggie told her husband that the birth control pill was not a magic bullet that would cure all ills. But they both hoped it would allow for the intimacy that would ensure they remained yoked to their covenant. Short of that, she feared, there was no hope. The very foundation of their marriage would be rent asunder and the whole family, all eight of them, would find themselves in a freefall into the blackest of bottomless holes.

She entered the confessional because she desperately wanted to remain in the sacraments. She knew her only chance to do so rested with this young contemporary who sat opposite her with a stole around his thick neck. It was her experience, and that of other couples in their mid-twenties to mid-forties, that Father John Sweeney was an "understanding" confessor. He listened, he probed the doubt and pain, he offered some light counsel, and he absolved. What more could any penitent want, particularly in times like these?

"Maggie, just let me be clear," John said after he was certain she had finished speaking. He had noted that she most assuredly hadn't confessed a sin with any discernable remorse. She had really delivered an advisory of, strictly speaking, illicit intent and provided a justification. Nevertheless, what she was asking of him was certainly manifestly clear. "Are you saying Bill is convinced you will die if you have another child?"

"I think that's what he thinks, Father," she said tentatively.

"And did he say why he thought that? Is there some medical condition I'm not aware of?"

"No, Father," she answered, her eyes downcast, her voice demonstrably lowered. "It's just that he thinks I can't take any more, and he's afraid of what'll happen to me and the family if we have more kids."

"Well, that's certainly a reasonable concern. I share it. What does Bill think about this decision?" He needed to know before he could offer guidance.

"He wanted me on the Pill after Noreen, our third child, Father. But I wouldn't do it because I thought it was wrong, and I didn't like what I was reading about the side effects. But after the next three—and these blasted migraines—and now all the problems with Moia . . . and Bill and I growing apart . . ."

She started crying, and it struck him how much like children adults were. We try to be good, most of us, and we hold on as best we can in the midst of great trials, but ultimately it's all too much for many of us and we grind down, slowly, until all that's left is our shame and our guilt. And that reduces more than a few of us to tears.

"Maggie, you're a very special treasure in the eyes of God. It's important that you know that. Do you know that?" he halted, momentarily wanting to engage her.

She simply nodded without looking up.

"God knows better than any of us what you're going through. And He knows how courageous you have been in opening yourself to life, how generous you've been in receiving the gift of new life. He would never ask more of you than He knows you can handle."

He paused, aching to reach over and take her hand.

"Objectively, yes, the Church opposes contraception. She knows most couples use it to justify fewer children and more earthly possessions and, in my judgment, the Church is correct in opposing it on those grounds alone. But most of the priests I know, including a good many of the older ones, believe we have to include subjective factors, conditions that 'modify' personal responsibility when weighing a penitent's absolution. The penitent's lived experience and her own conscience are primary among them. Clearly you have made every attempt to follow the Church's teachings. And, as I understand it, her normative method for regulating births hasn't worked for you, for reasons entirely beyond your control.

"I simply don't believe God wants you holed up in some asylum, Maggie, with your husband and children visiting you on weekends. He's a God of Love, and He sent His Son to earth to ransom us from our sins so that we may, as He said, 'have life and have it abundantly.' He wants you to be happy. He wants your whole family to be happy. And, in His time, He will heal Moia. Nothing is impossible for Him, Maggie. We all just have to remember that."

John stopped and waited for Maggie to raise her gaze to meet his. She did so slowly and deliberately, as though waiting for a "but." When her eyes finally came to rest in his, he couldn't help but think yet again of how lovely she was and how extraordinary it was that their God could create such beauty in mere mortals. "I . . . we . . . can do this, Father?" she asked timorously. "We can . . . I can . . . go . . . stay . . . on the Pill and still receive Holy Communion with my family?"

"As far as I'm concerned, yes, Maggie," he replied with his trademark smile, which lit up even a small, dark confessional. "You're a good and faithful Catholic, and I would not—*could* not— in good conscience refuse you absolution. Now I want you to say your act of contrition, and I will grant you, in Jesus' name, the forgiveness you seek."

John thought Maggie left the confessional looking a good five to ten years younger than when she entered. He hadn't told her of course that he knew from personal and all too painful experience that the Pill was indeed no magic bullet. He knew there were times when it worked, and there were also times when it didn't. But the woman had entered his confessional bereft of hope and left with what she sought. And wasn't that the fundamental meaning of Christ's life and death—that fallen mankind might have the hope of eternal salvation? And wasn't his personal mission, as an *alter Christus*, to bring the Good News of that hope of eternal salvation to every soul?

When Maggie departed, John Sweeney checked his watch. It was almost 5:00 p.m., so he assumed there would be no other parishioners waiting in line. But when he switched off the light and opened the door to the confessional, he saw the solitary figure of the widow, Mrs. Sara McKinney, standing alone in the darkened church with a pair of black rosary beads in her hands. Her lips were moving in silent prayer. He immediately wondered if she'd heard any portion of his discussion with Maggie. Given her age and the deeply serene, mystical nature of her prayer, he thought it unlikely.

He smiled and waved her into the box. One more, he thought, and this one should be hearing my confession.

20

They filed into the large and impressively appointed boardroom in twos and threes, arbitrarily taking seats around an elliptical forty-foot mahogany table that was reputed to be New York's largest, one that the Hal Ross agency boasted was constructed on-site.

They were the men and women of National Publishing's elite video unit, the now astonishingly successful Cable Movie Network. There were sixteen in all, only four of them women. They were no ordinary women, however, and some of the men liked to boast that these women were entirely capable of castrating, without remorse, any man who attempted to derail their career progress before that man even knew his trousers had been removed.

They came this day to screen the new network television commercials the Ross creative team had produced for the next phase of CMN's marketing plan. The launch had exceeded everyone's expectations, driving a significant incremental penetration of their distributors' basic cable service with the highly profitable pay "tier"—CMN. The post-launch campaign in year two was equally effective, lifting both basic cable and pay cable penetration of what the industry called "homes passed" to levels not anticipated until year three. Everyone was happy, or so Michael Burns thought.

The large boardroom seemed to vibrate with animated discussion of business, sports, and the sexual exploits of senior vice president Burt Camfy, who ran the network's sales and marketing operation. Camfy, for his part, sat smiling, neither affirming nor denying anything, skillfully lending credence to his mystique. Michael thought it fascinating that the pressure to set oneself apart, to brand oneself in industry terms, was so strong in this city that some men, even some women, would choose to do so on the basis of their individual weaknesses rather than their strengths.

He certainly didn't think of himself as particularly virtuous, but he did believe in the binding nature of sacred vows. Almost all of these men and women were married or had been married. He was surprised to discover just how many were divorced. When one of them, Todd Milgrim, who ran the cable affiliate marketing program, once told him that the best client/agency relationships were like a marriage, he responded by saying, "Yeah . . . but most of you guys are divorced."

Michael looked at his wristwatch and saw that it was now 9:27 a.m. He'd told Zimmer that the 9:00 meeting would begin, in typical CMN fashion, around 9:30, and he now saw Zimmer enter the boardroom to waves and catcalls. One of these digs was so scatological that Zimmer turned, and seeking out Burt Camfy, flipped him the bird. It was good being in the big time, Michael thought ruefully.

Zimmer took the open seat next to Michael and said loudly, "What's the matter, Shamrock? What—did you run out of Irish Spring?" This drew the usual guffaws. Michael waited until they subsided and said, "Not exactly, Zimmy. These guys said they'd add another ten million dollars to the spend if I sat you over here, away from them." More laughter. When it trailed off, Michael added, "I want you to know I held out for fifteen million . . . and got it." The room resounded in laughter, and Michael sensed this was the perfect time to get the meeting started. He stood to speak, but Burt Camfy immediately raised a hand to stop him, "Michael, I think we should wait for Richard."

"Richard" was Richard Kloss, the mercurial and imperious head of programming for CMN. Michael wasn't expecting him. A Kloss "sighting" was a rare event, and word of his intention to attend the screening caught Michael momentarily off guard. "OK, Burt . . . when do you think Richard might arrive?"

"Oh, sometime before noon," Camfy replied to much laughter. "He usually gets hungry around then and starts looking for a meeting to drop in on." More laughter. Michael sat down and looked at Zimmer, who simply shrugged his shoulders as if to say, "Hey, it's your client."

Richard Kloss arrived at precisely 10:12 that morning. He pointed to Nancy Beck, CMN's corporate attorney, who was seated in a position that might loosely be described as the head of the table, and signaled for her to vacate the chair. She did so immediately. So much for CMN women's toughness, Michael mused. As Kloss seated himself he said to no one in particular, "Coffee, black." Two of the women and one of the men rose to attend him. Without looking at anyone, he turned to the large-screen TV monitor and said, "Whadd'ya got for me today?"

It was Burt Camfy who answered. "Richard, the agency has some new commercials to show us. We told them we wanted more sizzle for the post-launch campaign. I've seen the work, and I think they've responded well to the direction."

Kloss merely grunted. In another life he had been an extremely aggressive and successful talent agent with the New York office of the William Morris agency. He had a law degree from Columbia and had quickly earned the trust of his Hollywood clients by showing them entirely novel but thoroughly legitimate ways of avoiding confiscatory taxes.

His clients' dependence on him grew so complete that when he left William Morris for CMN, a number of them pleaded with him to continue reviewing scripts and deals for them. He declined in every case but promised instead to create original "entertainment properties" that would highlight their unique creative gifts. He kept his promise. His original CMN films and specials were the buzz of the entertainment world and its capitals in New York and Los Angeles. He'd become a "player," gracing the covers of not only the entertainment trade magazines but even several mass-market titles in the National Publishing portfolio.

It was in Hollywood, at the knee of his famous clients, that Kloss first observed that real players must act the part. The act must at all times cloak the fear, and in more than a few cases, he learned, it must also cloak the absence of authentic talent. So he mastered the act. And his colleagues at CMN accepted him as he presented himself, believing that his front, even if a bit contrived, held real currency in the salons of New York and Los Angeles. But they were very careful to keep him away from their largely rural cable operators, understanding that the mix of tinsel and tractor would likely be combustible.

Michael realized instantly that all the pre-mumble they'd so laboriously scripted and rehearsed would have to be discarded. Richard Kloss, it was eminently clear, would sit through none of it. He glanced quickly at his team of writers and art directors, media planners and buyers, researchers and account managers, and shrugged his shoulders. And looking at the agency producer assigned to the CMN account, he nodded and said, "OK, Tony. Let's show Mr. Camfy, Mr. Kloss, and their colleagues the "sizzle."

Tony Bancone took his cue from Michael and, without a word, directed the remote in his right hand to the large monitor and clicked twice to initiate the screening of the commercials that were pre-synched to begin within three seconds. As the tape rolled, Michael scanned the faces of his clients. Most were seeing the new work for the first time, and they were smiling. Camfy, who'd seen the new spots the day before, was nodding in affirmation. Michael couldn't see Kloss' face—his back was turned—but he sensed his reaction would be the only one that mattered.

There were five thirty-second spots, or commercials, in the

new "pool," advertising jargon for a body of broadcast creative work. There were also five sixty-second "lifts" for use as radio commercials. The package cost over three million dollars to produce, a number Michael still found a bit numbing. His clients, however, never complained. They reasoned, he supposed, that they spent more than that on one of their cable operator shows, which often featured name bands and high-profile athletes and celebrities.

When the screen went dark and the lights went up, one of the CMN marketing executives took a giant leap into an abyss by saying to all assembled, "I think the agency is to be complimented. These new spots are hot. I'm pumped, and I know our operators will be, too." His name was Ron Ashley, and he was a difficult guy for Michael to get a handle on. He was extremely bright and altogether calculating, but at the oddest moments he would display a misplaced bravado that undermined all the capital he'd so painstakingly built with senior executives.

Michael knew enough not to respond. Unfortunately, Zimmer didn't. "Good," he said summarily. "Why don't you all come up to my office. My secretary has drawn a line of coke for each of you. Then, Burnsie will take you over to St. Patrick's where you can all confess."

The only sound in the large boardroom was that of Michael choking. All eyes were now on Kloss. Ashley looked at Michael and made a sweeping gesture with his right index finger under his throat. Michael thought this was probably not a good sign.

Kloss leaned forward in his chair and laid his forearms on the table. He removed his glasses and folded his hands. With a measured theatricality, he began, "The problem I have with the Hal Ross agency is that your work does nothing to reinforce the viewing experience of our customer. That's the fundamental task of good advertising. When a customer has consumed your product, they're supposed to feel better about consuming our product. I don't see that in your work."

Michael read it cleanly. The network's "churn rate"—the percentage of people who disconnected CMN after buying it—

was about 4.6 percent a month, which meant that the network's entire customer base would turn over every two years. This, of course, was a prohibitively costly way to do business. Eventually, the network would run out of "first-time triers" and would have to go back to those who had disconnected, somehow convincing them to return. But how—and at what cost?

Michael understood that Richard Kloss was staking out an early position. He was suggesting that the network's unacceptably high disconnect rate was a function of poor advertising. On its face, this was, of course, absurd, and he knew Kloss understood this. Yet he also knew that no one would challenge him on it. In fact, he'd learned that Kloss could say pretty much whatever he chose to say with total impunity. There would be no challenge—not in Hollywood, not here in New York, not within the corporate offices of the Cable Movie Network, and certainly not here in the boardroom of a supplicant advertising firm.

Michael felt the eyes of his colleagues. He knew that he had to challenge the thesis without appearing to challenge the man. This was not his strong suit. He had risen in the corporate world on his unique ability to say sometimes difficult, even controversial, things with what was generally considered an excusable passion. That, he knew, would not work here.

"Richard, what you say is correct, of course," he heard himself begin. A hush fell over the room. "But our assignment was very clear. We were directed to create advertising for the 'homes passed' segment, the nonbuyers. Our central task, as we understand it, is to convince these families in ever greater numbers that they're missing out on something very special and that they ought to reconsider their decision to pass on CMN."

"Who the hell gave you that assignment?" Kloss demanded, sensing he'd been boxed in.

Michael waited in silence for Camfy to acknowledge his accountability as head of Marketing. "I did, Richard," he said after a slightly painful pause. "Our overall penetration of 'homes passed' is 27 percent. There's one helluva lot of homes we still need to sign up. Reynolds and the corporate folk are counting on us doubling that. We're pursuing an acquisition strategy, not a retention strategy. We're still building a franchise, not just trying to maintain one."

"Good advertising can't do both?" Kloss said, looking at Michael.

"Good advertising can do one thing at a time. It's a matter of focus. We'll be happy to build you a retention campaign, if that's what you want," Michael replied. He had overplayed his hand with that last comment, he knew. Both Camfy and Kloss would take exception to his exacerbating their differences. No one was saying anything, and Michael grew increasingly uncomfortable at what the others might be thinking.

Ron Ashley broke the silence. "I agree with what Burt and Michael have said. The time will come when we have twenty million homes, and our biggest challenge will be holding on to them. But we have less than five million now. We've got to build this sucker first."

Richard Kloss stared at Burt Camfy. Michael read the look as a rebuke, "You surround yourself with the likes of that? You're not a serious rival. You're not going anywhere. We both know that."

Kloss looked at Michael and said, "You may think that work is acceptable. It isn't. And I know plenty of agencies that can do better."

With that, Richard Kloss gathered his things and left.

21

The moment of truth had arrived. Carol Burns tapped her husband on the arm and said, "Michael, it's time." He awoke with a start, blinking his eyes several times and wondering where he was. He had been dreaming, he instantly realized, relieved. There was no anaconda with Richard Kloss' face around his neck.

He jumped out of bed and said to his wife, "I'll get the car running."

"Michael," she replied sharply. "Put your pants on."

Once in the car Michael hit the accelerator. "Easy, Mr. Andretti," Carol cautioned. "I want to live long enough to deliver these children."

When they received the news that the baby they were expecting was actually two babies, they reacted with unrestrained joy. To Michael's thinking, two babies roughly doubled the chances of his finally having a son. He loved his three daughters. Loved to teach them and coach them and, most of all, to tease them, which he did unrelentingly. He teased them about their hair, their clothing, their music, their friends, pretty much anything and everything that was important to them.

But he wanted a son in the worst way. And knowing his intentions, his friends told him he *did* in fact want a son in the worst sort of way. "You think you're gonna get this stud two guard, a consensus D-1 All-American and a Lottery pick," they loved telling him. "You're gonna get a scorekeeper. That's what you're gonna get."

They didn't know, he told himself. They didn't know about the covenant.

. . .

It was a warm August evening four years earlier, and Michael and Carol Burns sat on the floor of the overseas terminal at Philadelphia International Airport. The plane that was to take them to Shannon Airport in Ireland had just been decommissioned, and they were waiting for another plane to be flown in from Phoenix.

Seven months earlier Carol delivered their third child, Elizabeth, and it was a difficult pregnancy. Michael was in the operating room, as he had been for the birth of their other daughters, Carole and Kate. The extraordinary mystery of new life emerging from what appeared to be certain death rendered him, for once, speechless. He thought his wife was the best and bravest person he knew and repledged himself there and then to be a better husband and father.

They each had large families in Ireland and had decided that the following summer would be an opportune time to visit them. The Burns family didn't have much money, but they pooled what they did have and cobbled together a loose itinerary entirely reliant on what they presumed would be an abundance of relatively inexpensive bed and breakfast lodgings. They would start in the south, visiting with Carol's family in Galway, and proceed into the north to spend time with Michael's family in Derry. Then they would finish with a weekend in Dublin. Their shared sense of anticipation was like that of their children on Christmas morning.

They were scheduled to leave Philly International at 6:20 on a Wednesday evening. The plane from Phoenix arrived sometime after midnight. The passengers were none too pleased. Then came the announcement. The flight from Phoenix placed the pilot over his maximum FAA allowable monthly flying time. He would not, could not, pilot the plane across the Atlantic. The airline promised to have a pilot "on the ground" by 2:00 a.m. "I'd settle for a pilot 'in the air' by 3:00 a.m.," Michael said to Carol, who was fast asleep on the ground, head resting on her carry-on bag.

By 5:00 a.m., they were airborne. At roughly half past six they made an unscheduled stop in Nova Scotia. The plane needed to be refueled, they were told. "I don't think I can do this," Michael said to Carol when they were on the ground. "The plane sits for five hours in Philadelphia while they search for a pilot. They finally find one at a McDonald's and by the time they get him cleaned up, strapped in, and airborne, he checks the fuel gauge and discovers it's . . . empty?"

"What are you suggesting?" Carol said evenly.

"Let's just go home. We've already lost a day. How do we know this clown will even find Ireland? It may be dark by the time we get there."

"Go sit down and don't think about it. Put it out of your mind," she lectured him. He did need to be lectured from time to time, he conceded. He went and took a seat.

The pilot found the Island, and the plane touched down at roughly 2:00 p.m. Philadelphia time. Their twenty-two-hour odyssey was over. Carol reached across the seat and gave Michael a big hug. "This will be special," she promised. This simple statement proved to be unusually prescient, although it would be four years before they realized it.

On their third day in the country they were driving along the northwestern tip of County Galway when they came upon a rather large mountain range, at least by Irish standards. Michael stopped the car and asked a young man on a bike about the mountains. "Ach, sure, that'd be Croagh Patrick," he answered. "Would you be knowin' the legend of Croagh Patrick, now?"

Michael shook his head.

"Well, now, I'll tell ya. Legend has it that this is where St. Patrick went to pray and fast for forty days and forty nights to rid the land of its snakes."

"Snakes?" Carol shrieked out the passenger side window.

"Ach, snakes, to be sure," he replied. "But not to worry, other than a few politicians in Dublin, the entire Island is long rid of them."

Michael jumped back in the rental car and drove into what appeared to be a base camp at the foot of the range. It was a weekday, and fairly warm for coastal Ireland. There was only a handful of people ascending and descending. "What are we doing?" Carol wanted to know.

"We're climbing. Follow me," he answered.

"Michael, have you lost the little bit of sense you were born with? I just delivered a baby six months ago. I can't climb a ten thousand–foot mountain."

Michael paused and eyed the mountain. Then he turned and said, "Ah, come on . . . it's only about four thousand feet."

Some four hours later they reached the top. On all fours. The last hour was slow going. They were crawling more than climbing; the rocks were large and jagged, and it was easy to get a foot caught or an ankle twisted. Michael found it difficult to believe that many of the more than one hundred thousand people who climbed Croagh Patrick at midnight on the last Saturday night in July every year did so barefoot to atone for sin. He did recall, however, an old Italian priest once telling him of a recent pope's observation after meeting with a group of Irish bishops, "Isn't Irish Catholicism a terrifying thing?" he reportedly remarked.

The vista from the peak was breathtaking. The whole of

Connaught was visible on this fine day. He thought he could see Benbulben, the mountain at whose foot rested the great Irish poet W. B. Yeats. He also thought he could make out the legendary Aran Islands in the distant summer haze. Michael suddenly felt a profound peace settle on him. He looked at Carol, who looked young, alive, and very, very happy. Then he did something he'd never done before or since. He knelt and prayed and made a covenant with the God of the Saint whose name this mountain bore.

"God of Saint Patrick," he began in the silence of his heart. "I know you exist because I feel your love whole and unconditional through this woman you have given me. I want her to feel your love whole and unconditional through me. If you would please, allow me to give her a son, I will pledge to you here and now that I will name him after this Patrick, who found your favor on this very mountain."

He rose and led his wife down the mountain. It would be more than four years before Michael would answer his wife's question about what he was doing on his knees at the top of that mountain.

• • •

It was pitch black when Michael and Carol left for St. Theresa's Hospital in Dennison, New Jersey, about forty miles west of Manhattan. The early light of morning greeted them as Michael pulled into the lot and a parking spot opposite the front door, some fifty yards away. "Michael," his wife said to him with a sharpness that penetrated the predawn fog.

"Yes dear?"

"Would you please drive me to the entrance of the emergency room?"

"Oh. Ohhh . . . sure."

This, too, had been a difficult pregnancy. Sometime in its third month they were shocked to learn that she was carrying two little souls within her. During the last month of the pregnancy, Carol was consigned to her bed on the second floor of their farmhouse. She added over eighty pounds to her thin frame, a good portion of the weight being fluid, and suffered from a cracked rib that could not be medicated because of concerns over potential damage to the unborn children. She suffered in silence, as she always did. Michael did not. His impotence in not being able to relieve, even temporarily, his wife's acute pain so angered him that he launched into a virulent tirade against God, calling Him the vilest of names and even, at one point, challenging Him physically. This only caused Carol more pain, of course, and through an intermittent stream of sobs she begged him to stop, which he eventually did.

Carol's response to the horror of Michael's abusive rant was to quietly consecrate the new life in her womb to the Virgin Mary. "I give them to you, dear Mother," she silently prayed. "We're not fit to raise them." She then offered her great suffering to God and asked Him to forgive her husband, reminding Him that, for better or worse, He had created Michael, too.

Michael parked in front of the emergency room double doors and rushed inside, looking for a wheelchair for his wife. He emerged with one, but to Carol's horror, another patient was still in it. He was followed, however, by a large black man in a white top pushing an empty wheel chair and yelling at him frantically.

Once Carol was safely inside, Michael went to the desk and asked to see her doctor. Told he was "en route," Michael asked for writing paper. He wanted to reiterate the instructions he'd given, that only Carol was to tell him whether the children were boys or girls, or, as he said, something else—meaning a combination—though that distinction was temporarily lost on the doctor.

Before he finished, Carol was gently relieved from his custody by a gracious head nurse, who also gave him something to read. It was a popular magazine, and in it he found a story on why, in the opinion of one noted physician, former athletes disproportionately tend to sire girls. He promptly tossed the magazine in a nearby receptacle.

The wait was painful. Michael found his heart racing and his palms moist when the attending nurse came out periodically to tell him his wife was in labor and "doing fine." He would ask, "How long?" And she would smile and say, "Not long." After about six hours of this, Michael had convinced himself the babies were girls. Boys would be here by now, he reasoned. This recognition sent a dagger through his heart. It surprised and disappointed him to rediscover just how important gender was to him, despite his fierce attempts to bury it deep within his subconscious. Indeed, he'd never spoken of the children's gender to his wife, or she to him. They both understood. Only their youngest daughter, Elizabeth, broached the subject when after dinner last night she approached her mother, patted her tummy, and said, "Bring home boys."

Michael was falling into a familiar black hole. He was cursed by God for past sins. He was impotent. He was worthless. Carol had made a mistake in marrying him. He should never have been born. These poor children deserved a better father. He . . . he was being summoned. The doctor, Carol's doctor, was now stand-ing in front of him with a smile. His cap was askew, his green gown was stained, he appeared exhausted, but here he was, and it was immediately clear he understood the instructions. All he kept repeating with a heavy East European accent was, "Everything good. Wife, babies, good." This was followed only by a slightly rueful, lopsided smile.

Michael trailed him into the operating room. He was aston-ished at how large the room was, almost a full half court, he reck-oned. Where was the basket? In the corner stood six nurses and what looked to be two physicians, perhaps interns. The nurses were crying. Not a good sign. Carol lay on the operating table with a large white sheet covering her body, but her struggle must have disturbed it, because a portion of the right side of her body was uncovered, up to her thigh. He resisted the urge to cover her up.

The sight of her sobbing, in obvious distress—no doubt disappointment—now moved Michael to tears. He rushed to her side, inadvertently jostling the doctor. He leaned in, kissed and hugged her, and said, "It's all right, sweetheart. We're going to love these ladies as if they were the last kids on earth. They're angels. Pure gifts from God." He was crying.

Carol looked up at him and said through her tears, "Did they tell you?"

"Tell me what?"

"Tell you what they were?"

"Two more girls, right?"

Carol shook her head. Michael's heart leapt into forbidden territory. "We've got a boy? We've got a boy!" He shouted, turning to the nurses, whose eyes were fixed on his wife. He turned back to Carol. She was shaking her head. His heart plummeted. "Two girls," he said again. Again, she shook her head and sobbed convulsively.

Michael turned to the nurses again. This time they were smiling. He was palpitating visibly. Just what had happened here? It was clear Carol hadn't delivered two girls. It was also clear she hadn't delivered the son they had longed to present to each other. What other mathematical possibilities remained?

It struck him like a thunderbolt. His mind immediately slipped its mooring. His heart catapulted into the vacuum created by his mind's strange voyage into a world of pure awe and wonder. The unthinkable, the unimaginable, had just happened. He was now aware that everything was changed. His life, their life together, would now have a completely different trajectory. Nothing was impossible now. Everything was in play. There was a God. He had heard Michael's prayer on that mountain in Ireland. And He delivered. Delivered beyond anything Michael himself dared to dream. And now it was Michael's turn. He, too, would deliver. He vowed in that instant that whatever this God of abundant blessing asked of him, he would do. *Anything,* he promised from the depth of his utter and boundless joy.

He leaned close to Carol and said through his tears, "We have two boys! Two boys!" She nodded and sobbed and grabbed him by the front of his windbreaker. She pulled herself closer to him. He thought she was about to kiss him when she stopped, fixed him with a stare, and said, "Check it."

There was no need. The nurses rushed forward to kiss, hug, and congratulate him. And to confirm that, yes, his wife had indeed just delivered two healthy baby boys.

22

Fran Delgado sat across the kitchen table from her husband, studying him closely as he wolfed down a late supper of comfort food—meatloaf with mashed potatoes and gravy. She'd taken to substituting water for beer at dinner in an attempt to diminish her husband's caloric intake and reduce his cholesterol. She was worried about him. He'd gained weight. His breathing was increasingly labored, particularly if he was forced to walk long distances or up a hill. He never exercised. He only worked, ate, and slept. On Friday night they would make love, at least when she was on the Pill, and in her experience this was like wrestling with a panda. In all these things, his mind seemed perpetually elsewhere. He was grinding down. She must do something, she told herself.

"Joe, how's work?" she inquired with a seeming nonchalance.

"OK," he responded guardedly.

"What are you working on?"

He looked up. She had never asked him that before. "Nothing special," he replied.

"Honey . . . you seem so preoccupied. Are you worried about your mother?" His mother had recently been diagnosed with ovarian cancer, and it was a source of constant worry. Joe's father had passed into eternity four years ago, and though he wanted a joyous and eternal reunion for them in heaven, he didn't want to lose her. His mother understood him in a way no one else could—even his wife. Her love was unconditional, as only a mother's love was. In his scholastic years he'd been a source of disappointment, and he knew his father had ultimately given up on him. Not his mother. She always believed in him—believed in him so much she actually convinced him he was a better person than he knew himself to be.

"Yes," he answered. "I do worry about her."

"Joe, it's in the hands of the doctors now."

And God, he thought, but did not say. He didn't like talking to his wife about religion. Although she was raised in a traditional Catholic home, she had a different view of the Faith, believing the clergy to be out of touch and the Church itself something of an anachronism. She attended Mass on Sunday, though not always on holy days, and allowed Joe to enroll the children in Catholic schools. But she made it a point of openly criticizing Monsignor Grogan and Father Sweeney in front of the children, which Joe did not think proper.

"Honey, I'm worried about you," she said, breaking the brief silence. "What's going on? I'm feeling shut out."

He knew better than to attempt to evade her. She could be relentless when she was on the hunt. He saw it with the children, particularly their eldest child. If their daughter Theresa, who was a high school senior, tried to dodge or dismiss her mother's probing into her social calendar, Fran Delgado became a pit bull. She would strip and extract what she sought in a manner not unlike her father, who was once a federal prosecutor, before becoming a banker. All of them, including Joe, eventually learned it was better to answer Fran's questions sooner rather than later.

"Well," he began tentatively. "I do feel under a little pressure at work. I just didn't want to bother you with it." He knew immediately that he was toast. He conjured a vision of himself in a rural precinct, holed up in a small room with a single light bulb dangling by a cord from the ceiling. He saw his wife grabbing him by his tie, lifting him out of his seat, and shoving him against a wall, the impact from his head loosening the plaster and leaving a small indenture.

"Honey," she said demurely. "We're husband and wife. If you can't share these things with me, who can you share them with?"

He told her everything, even his confession with Father Sweeney, which she dismissed out of hand as lacking in relevance. What he had to say visibly unsettled her.

"Honey, I think you should talk to Dad," she said after a long pause when he feared she might elect to "straighten this mess out" herself. Her father, John Canuso, was perhaps the most influential "money guy" in town. He had never been much of a Joe Delgado fan.

"No, dear," he said firmly. "I'm not going to speak to anyone else about this."

Fran grew pensive. "What do you think will happen?"

"I don't know," he answered simply.

"Will you be fired?"

"Honey, why would they fire me? I was asked to search the archives for files relating to a federal investigation. I uncovered other files relating to the inception of one of their major classes of therapeutic drugs. I've done absolutely nothing—*nothing*—with those files."

"Well, you did unseal them."

"Yes, I unsealed them," he said, his tone conceding nothing.

"And you did share their contents with two senior executives of the company."

He was annoyed. He had done nothing wrong. He knew it, and she should know it. He really didn't need this cross-examination at nine o'clock in the evening after a twelve-hour workday. "Look," he said, struggling to stay composed. "I don't believe it's in the interests of either Peter Halifax or Steve Dalkowitz to turn state's evidence." He regretted the sarcasm immediately.

"Well, honey, clearly something is going on. Neither one of those men has said a word to you after your dinner. What's up with that?"

She had found a soft spot and thrust her lance through it. She was right, of course. Both Halifax and Dalkowitz had done everything possible to avoid him for the last two weeks, and that did in fact concern him greatly. He had left terse voicemails with each of them, simply saying he was available for a follow-up discussion of their dinner meeting. No response. They had been together only once, to review a marketing presentation for one of their major drugs that was about to go generic. He even sat next to Halifax, who greeted him as though their dinner discussion never took place.

It was the same with Dalkowitz. Joe had given him his comments on the draft memo he had prepared for CEO Bill Carney on the Alphasint investigation. They had even gotten together briefly to discuss the final draft of the memo. Joe waited for him to make some reference to their dinner or for any subsequent thoughts he may have had about their discussion. Nothing.

He concluded that neither of his colleagues wanted to discuss the matter further; this both puzzled and angered him. He resisted the impulse to confront them, but given his wife's line of questioning it was now obvious that he must do so, and do so soon. "I don't know what's up with that," he mimicked. "I will speak to them about it, and I will tell you what they have to say. Now, end of discussion." He stood, lifted his plate and glass, and placed them in the sink the way his mother had taught him. Then he left the kitchen, climbed the steps to his bedroom, undressed, and got into bed.

23

Joe was at his desk at 7:00 a.m. the next morning. He decided to greet his colleagues when they arrived. There would be no escape.

Steve Dalkowitz arrived within ten minutes and was surprised that Joe's office door was open and the lights were on. He peeked his head in the door and waved a silent hello, careful to discourage conversation. Joe, however, was immediately on his feet and out the door, following Dalkowitz into his office. Dalkowitz was hanging his overcoat and suit coat on the back of the door to his office when he saw Joe cross the threshold. "What's up?" he said, looking at Joe as though Delgado was about to give him the scores from last night's NBA games.

"We need to talk, Steve," Joe said as he made his way to one of the four chairs in the sitting area of the office. Dalkowitz followed him and took a seat opposite Joe. "Let me guess," said Dalkowitz. "Fran's pregnant and you want me to be the child's godfather."

"No, Steve. Franny wants to be pregnant, and we want you to be the father."

Steve laughed and said, "Sorry. That would be against my religion."

Joe paused, looked at his colleague, and said, "Steve, what am I not getting? Did we not agree over dinner several weeks ago that each of us would give some thought to the matter we were discussing and get together again to share our thoughts?"

"I don't remember any such agreement, Joe," Steve replied soberly.

"You do acknowledge we did have dinner together and that you had the manicotti," Joe said with evident sarcasm.

"Look Joe, I will not be part of your witch hunt."

"One and done?"

Steve's forehead creased, and he squinted in puzzlement. "One and done?"

"Meaning I'm already involved in one witch hunt, initiated by those reptiles in the U.S. Attorney's Office, and I don't have time for another one?" Joe wanted to impale him on his own petard.

Steve grimaced. "Yeah, something like that."

"So you'll leave the next one to your successor. Some poor kid not ten years out of law school. Only this one won't be a federal investigation, it'll be a class-action suit brought by some women's group. And your wife will be leading it." He intuitively realized his intemperance had just cost him the offensive position in this conversation. "I'm sorry Steve; I didn't intend to make it personal."

"Hell, I don't mind Susan leading that charge; I just want to be her group's outside counsel," Steve replied, hoping to defuse the tension and appear gracious at what he hoped was the conclusion of this conversation.

"You really believe there's no exposure here?" Joe persisted, back on message.

"Oh, there's potential exposure, I suppose. I view its likelihood at about a one on a ten-point scale. And you're right. I've got my hands full with a ten right now. This Alphasint thing ain't going away. And it's going to own me for the next twelve to eighteen months."

Joe could not determine a basis to continue their discussion on. "And Peter?" he probed.

"Peter will have to speak for himself," Steve replied. "I have enough problems speaking for myself. Did I ever tell you I was mute until I was fourteen? That's when I lost my virginity. All I said was 'WOW!' Haven't stopped talking since."

Joe laughed in spite of himself. He rose from his chair, shook his head in bemusement, and made his exit. Steve's eyes never left Joe's back. Mission accomplished, he thought.

At 8:00 a.m. Joe headed across the floor to the other end of the executive suite, looking for Peter Halifax. His secretary, Phyllis Hanson, a late middle-aged woman whom Joe liked very much, intercepted him, saying, "Joe, Peter's in Boston for most of the day. He's due back late afternoon. He'll be calling in. Anything urgent?"

Joe thought for a moment before answering. "No, Phyl. It can wait. Call me when he arrives."

. . .

It was shortly after 3:00 p.m. when the phone on the credenza behind his desk buzzed. It was Helen, his secretary. Joe had "inherited" Helen from his predecessor, Bradford Shillcock, Al Heyworth's chief financial officer. Joe never thought much of Shillcock, finding him more concerned about the location and identification of his parking spot at the Merion Cricket Club than the business. But he did like Helen Hurd, who had been a classmate of Fran's at a convent school just outside the city, and whom he regarded as both competent and discreet. When he was promoted upon Shillcock's retirement, he asked her to stay on. He had never once regretted doing so.

Joe assumed this was the call he'd been waiting for from

Phyllis Hanson, alerting him that Peter Halifax had returned from Boston. He hit the buzzer with his left index finger, "Yes, Helen?"

"Joe, Sharon called. Bill wants to see you." Sharon Williamson was Bill Carney's secretary. Joe was more intrigued than surprised. He presumed that Carney wanted an update on the acquisition discussions he'd been having with his counterpart from a large Swiss pharmaceutical house. Still, he realized, Carney's office usually scheduled those meetings in regular weekly intervals.

When Joe entered Bill Carney's large and well-appointed office, he found his boss not behind his desk but sitting on his couch, awaiting Joe's arrival. He was in his shirt sleeves, and his tie was loosened. His enormous neck, which had made no small contribution to his career rushing record at Georgia Tech, was bulging, and he was rubbing the back of it with his right hand.

Joe liked Carney. Nearly everyone at Pittman Labs did. He arrived as the anti-Heyworth and instituted a number of popular reforms, including year-end bonuses, contributions to 401(k) retirement funds, and Friday afternoons off in the summer. It was all aboard when the train left the station, and pulled by its indefatigable locomotive, the improvement in the company's overall performance was dramatic. Detractors said that Carney was an empty suit, or, as they put it—an empty helmet—but Joe saw something different.

Carney had what Joe regarded as the "x factor." He could size people up better than anyone he knew. Carney understood intuitively what people wanted, sometimes even before they themselves knew. And he knew how to manipulate that central animating force to get people to do things they might not want to do—with people they might not want to do them with—all to the benefit of Pittman, now NHP, shareholders. He was extremely hard-working, a veritable bull of a man who never met a wall he wasn't convinced he could breach.

Carney turned the upper half of his body toward the door at the sound of Joe's approach. Joe immediately noticed the pain on his boss' face and said, "Bad muscle day?"

Carney grunted and said, "Too many stingers."

Thinking he meant too many nightcaps the prior evening, Joe laughed and said, "I've had a few 'day afters' like that."

Carney looked at him blankly, and Joe, embarrassed, realized that Carney was talking football-speak for pinched nerves—usually a consequence of sticking your head in places it ought not be.

Carney signaled Sharon to close the office door and motioned Joe to an expensively upholstered wing chair opposite him. Joe immediately felt a chill in the room and a slight feeling of nausea in the pit of his stomach. The cold, planned efficiency of this encounter tripped wires from his childhood, when he was routinely summoned by his father and asked to give an accounting for some misbehavior or deficiency in his academic performance. He began to feel extremely uncomfortable.

Carney picked up on his discomfort quickly and sought to put Joe at ease. "How are Fran and the kids? Has Theresa decided where she's going to college yet?"

Joe wanted to relax but couldn't. "Not yet, Bill."

"Plenty of time yet. Plenty of time. Hell, my daughter decided on Vanderbilt after we moved her into the dorm at Tulane. Just looked at her mother and said, 'Get me out of here.' And we did. Next day we drove her up to Nashville." He paused to read Joe's face and then continued. "Anyway, I appreciate you making time for me."

Joe, sensing his boss' discomfort, now knew where this was going. He felt a hot flash, a mixture of panic and anger. "What did you want to see me about, Bill?" he said guardedly.

Carney hunched forward, and for a brief instant Joe could imagine what it must have felt like to be an opposing linebacker moments before impact. "Joe let me get right to it. I don't want you dickin' around with those OC files. I need your head in this Swiss thing, 24/7."

Joe was stung by the simple bluntness of the admonition. "Bill, I'm not spending any, I repeat any, time on what you're calling 'OC' files."

Carney paused and slowly pulled back until his own back was resting against the couch. "Joe, I didn't mean for it to come out like that."

Sensing an opening, Joe pounced. "Let me tell you what I have a problem with, and it's a big problem, Bill. I think it's unconscionable that Dalkowitz would come to you with this thing. I found those files by accident when I was looking for the Alphasint files for you—"

"Joe," Carney interrupted, "it wasn't Dalkowitz who brought the matter to my attention." He said this matter-of-factly and with equanimity that Joe found totally convincing. Joe felt his anger rising swiftly. He wanted to confront Halifax immediately. Catch him when he got out of his chauffeured town car in front of the lobby and just cold-cock him. No explanations.

"Joe," Carney continued, throttling back a bit, "you're an important guy here. We got a lot to get done. It ain't gonna happen without you. Those files you found have nothing to do with this company's future—only its past."

Joe met Bill Carney's muted stare and said, "How can you be absolutely sure of that? How do you know you won't be sending Steve and me back into the archives in three to five years, asking us to prepare a strategy to defend a class-action suit?"

"I think that's very unlikely, Joe. But if it were to happen, we would do whatever we had to do . . . then. Not now, *then*. We have a make-or-break bet on this Swiss acquisition. That's a *now*. Let's focus on the now, Joe."

Joe felt cornered. How could he argue with any of that? Still, something gnawed at him and he couldn't quite bring himself to just let it go. "I guess the basic problem I have, Bill, is that this isn't simply a matter of 'then.' The OC business is still very much a part of our 'now.' And those little hummers are doing one helluva lot of damage to women throughout this country. And we know it. Yet we're not prepared to do anything about it?"

Bill Carney hunched forward, a clear sign he was losing patience. "And what—just what in hell—would you propose we do about it, Joe?"

"Well, J&J recalled Tylenol for a lot less damage, Bill."

"Product recall! Are you seriously suggesting we recall whole classes of OCs, IDs, and anti-progesterones?"

"No, Bill. Not whole classes. Just our compounds."

Bill Carney paused to consider the sheer magnitude of the consequences of such an action. First of all, he imagined it would be like putting a .357 Magnum in his own mouth. The announcement alone would implode Pittman Labs, perhaps even bringing down the entire NHP conglomerate with it.

The aftershocks would decimate one of the truly significant industries in America, and the entire world for that matter. The recalls would trigger an avalanche of class-action suits that would cause a meltdown in the public markets, perhaps even the temporary closure of the Big Board. Whole pension trust funds such as CALPERS would teeter on the brink of insolvency, causing a meltdown of public confidence in government-backed bonds and treasury bills.

Pure chaos.

On balance, Bill Carney didn't favor the idea. "You are a dangerous man, Joe Delgado," he said, fixing Joe with a hard stare.

Joe hadn't intended to make such a suggestion. He hadn't even contemplated it. In fact, he was surprised when he heard it coming out of his mouth. But having said it, he now believed it was the only ethical thing to do. All hormonal contraceptives should be recalled, he thought, until such time as definitive studies could be conducted to assess not their "potential" impact on the reproductive systems of women but their "actual" impact on the lives of countless millions of women. That data was now available.

"No, Bill. I'm not dangerous. Some of the products we make and distribute are dangerous. You're the CEO, and I think you should do something about that."

"Joe, let me be clear. You need to go home and have a conversation with Franny. If you're prepared to get your head back into our mission, this conversation never took place. Your dinner with Steve and Peter never took place. We will all move forward together. We'll make those boys over at NHP even fatter, dumber, and happier, if that's possible. And in about five years, all of us will retire to our own islands somewhere in the Caribbean with more money than we'll know what to do with."

"And if I'm not, Bill?"

Bill Carney did not hesitate. He pointed the gun at Joe's heart and pulled the trigger.

"If not, Joe . . . Pittman Labs will be looking for a new CFO."

Joe pulled himself out of his chair and nodded at his CEO. "Clarity is a good thing. Always admired your candor, Bill."

As he reached for the door, Joe heard Carney call his name. He turned around to see Bill Carney on his feet, heading toward him. "Joe, I want you to know that I need you here," he said, putting his large hand on Joe's forearm and gripping it tightly.

Joe waited for him to release his grip. Then he smiled and left.

24

It was a Currier and Ives tableaux. The snow was falling, and the billowing wind from the northeast was piling large drifts of snow at the foot of the Marian shrine just outside the rectory dining room. The statue itself was magnificently lit by two floodlights set in large oak trees on either side of the cove. Inside, a fire visible from the large picture window lent the room warmth, and a glow that caught the attention of commuters returning home from the train.

The rectory's cook, a widow by the name of Mary Kennedy, whom Monsignor Jim Grogan had hired after her husband died, laid a plate of freshly carved turkey in the middle of the table. She returned moments later with hot dishes of mashed potatoes, homemade stuffing, peas, corn, and gravy.

"Mary, you're spoiling us again," Jim Grogan said with a broad smile. He looked at his young associate and said, "John, why don't you call your mother and have her bring the kids up? Who's left over there?"

"Just Mary Eileen, Jim. And she pretty much does the

cooking for Mom." John had grown very protective of his mother. Peter was in New York working for an investment firm named Canter Fitzgerald, whose offices were in the World Trade Center. Bill was working for Fidelity in Boston. Jim was in Chicago working on the Commodity Exchange. And Tom was working for the FBI in D.C. He was proud of his brothers and prouder still of his sister, who had chosen to return home to care for their mother after earning bachelor's and master's degrees from Fairfield University in Connecticut.

Mary Kate Sweeney was still working the night shift at the hospital, and John thought it was time she should begin winding down. He worried about her, dropping in at home every couple of days and gently prodding her every now and again to slow down. What his mother did to hold the family together after Jack Sweeney's death was nothing short of heroic, in his estimation. True, her brother-in-law Joe Stockman was good to his word in taking care of the family—mostly medical bills and high school tuitions—but it was their mother who put the food on the table and the clothes on their backs. And, most importantly, it was their mother who provided a living witness for the theological virtues of faith, hope, and charity.

John was extremely proud of her, and he found himself drawing more and more on her as a model of fortitude in his own priestly ministry. It was easy, certainly easier than he'd imagined, to grow disillusioned with the Church. The politics, the incompetence, the cynicism that, when he'd first encountered it, actually shocked him—these were all too common, and difficult to overlook. But he was happy and still felt privileged to be a priest. He believed he had been called to this work and had responded as fully as grace permitted. He loved the core mission of his priestly ministry—the accompaniment of souls through this "vale of tears," as his grandmother, Bridget McCluskey, liked to refer to life on earth. He once read that the great Spanish reformer St. Teresa of Avila had likened life on earth to "a night in a second-rate inn." The older John grew, the more he observed the assorted sufferings and afflictions of his parishioners, and the more he thought the saint had gotten it precisely right.

Monsignor Jim Grogan was in an expansive mood, something that happened about once every full moon. Perhaps it was the realization that the heavy snow would in all likelihood bring with it a cancellation of school and the morning Masses. Perhaps it was the new assignment from Cardinal Porreica to study the overall financial health of the archdiocesan school system and propose remedial or corrective action. Or perhaps he just likes his company, John Sweeney thought to himself, and smiled. Whatever the cause, Jim Grogan was talking, and when the Monsignor was talking, there really wasn't much for anyone else to do but listen.

John guessed that most parishioners would find it surprising that priests didn't talk much shop in the rectory. There were very few, if any, discussions on Church doctrine or policy. There were even fewer discussions of individual parishioners and their difficulties. If there were conversations—and in many rectories there were shockingly few—and if those conversations touched on parish life, they tended to focus on school problems, social activities, and liturgical or devotional schedules, usually in that order.

John, then, was caught somewhat off guard when he heard Jim Grogan talking about the fiscal and spiritual vitality of the archdiocese. Grogan thought it scandalous that the school system was on the brink of insolvency. And he appeared to blame it on ecclesial leadership that had done little or nothing, in his estimation, to stop the steep decline in weekly Mass attendance.

John was enjoying Mary Kennedy's culinary art, and he chose to interrupt neither the good Monsignor nor the even better sensation of rich, warm food on a bitterly cold winter night. But he made a mental note to double back on this topic if the opportunity presented itself. Who knew where this was going and whether he would even be awake, when and if it reached a conclusion?

There was a pause. John waited while Jim Grogan attempted to better synchronize his consumption and conversation. When the physical exertion of chewing several forkfuls of turkey and stuffing manifested itself in the pastor's features, John saw an opportunity to redirect the conversation and seized upon it, "Jim, what really did happen? Where did all the Catholics go?" He had his own ideas, of course, but he was interested in knowing what this aging veteran of the culture wars thought.

Jim Grogan paused to allow his windpipe to clear. It was slow going, and John wondered about his pastor's health for the first time. He had always given the appearance of being invincible to his parishioners and curates, but there were signs that he was finally beginning to slow down now that he had turned seventy-five. John watched him carefully and now regretted having asked a question.

"The Pill . . ." Jim Grogan said with belabored effort. John thought he was asking for medication and promptly summoned Mary Kennedy who, to his distress, had left for her home next door. His first thought, to his everlasting shame, was, "Hey, who's going to do the dishes?" He rushed into the kitchen and returned with a glass of ice water, only to find his pastor sitting serenely, having resumed his meal. "Who's that for?" Jim Grogan wanted to know, pointing his fork at the glass in John's hand. Embarrassed, John sat down and said, "Me."

"The Pill, Johnny-boy. It changed everything." The pastor was back on point. "Didn't they teach you anything at that seminary?"

"They taught us that contraception was wrong and that every marital act had to remain open to the possibility of new life," John responded, slightly irritated. "They also taught that the Church has always held this to be true and that the teaching would never change," John added evenly. He didn't much care for Grogan's attempt to belittle his formation, the clear implication being that he would never measure up to his pastor's exacting standards. John accepted that Grogan knew more, would always know more, than he did. He thought, however, that the capacity to effectively accompany souls depended less on intellect and more on will— the pure willingness to absorb a portion of a parishioner's cross, regardless of its weight or intractability. In this core aspect of pastoral ministry, John did not regard himself deficient.

Grogan simply ignored the response. "Holy Mother Church fought the good fight. She lost. Simple as that."

"Could you break that down for me, Jim?" John asked. "When, and how, was the battle lost?"

"Well . . ." the Monsignor paused, looking at his plate for the answer to the question, searching his mind for a place to begin. "I suppose most would say we lost that battle when the papal encyclical *Humanae Vitae* was published in 1968 to a firestorm of criticism from both secular and clerical sources.

"The you-know-what really hit the fan on that one."

John nodded. He knew the encyclical had not been well received.

"The reality was that we lost that battle long before 1968," Grogan continued. He put his knife and fork down, took a considerable gulp of wine, sat back in his chair, and fixed John with a look he knew all too well. The tutorial was about to begin.

"The immigrant Church of your grandparents was far from perfect, but it did not question. If the Church said it, they accepted it, and tried to live it the best they could. They loved the Church. It was the Church that preserved their memory and gave them identity when they arrived from Europe. It was their faith that gave them meaning and hope. No, they weren't going to question. They accepted.

"Their Church was clear on contraception. It was wrong, grievously wrong. Marriage was their best opportunity for heaven," Grogan paused and smiled. "After all, has a better way of getting to heaven ever been devised than raising children? And if you want to be saints . . . raise a whole baseball team of them."

Grogan paused and fixed John with a hard stare. "They got the fact that the sex act must remain open to life. They were Catholics . . . and Catholics didn't use condoms. Those who did were told they couldn't present themselves for Holy Communion until they went to confession, pledged to amend their lives, and received absolution. Otherwise they 'ate and drank unworthily.' That, they understood, was sacrilege. Something akin to spitting in our Divine Lord's face. You just didn't go there. And besides, the last thing you wanted was to be the one sitting in your pew alone while the rest of the congregation was heading for the communion rail.

"Things began to change after the war. Wars always leave a bitter aftertaste in the mouths of those who fight and survive them. The world loses whatever innocence it appeared to have. A certain cynicism settles into the heart of men, and it takes root in the soil of human interaction. Man suddenly seems much more fallible. Priests, even bishops, are not exempt from this observation. The gap between what is preached and what is lived is duly noted; it draws suspicion on what is taught . . . and why.

"Still, by and large, your parents' generation held firm. They knew the Anglicans broke ranks on contraception at the Lambeth Conference in 1930, but they didn't give it much thought. They assumed all Protestants were going to hell anyway." Grogan paused and laughed.

John winced at the painful reminder of old formulas that even the Church conceded during the Council had no basis in reason.

"They also heard that demonic eugenicist, Margaret Sanger, taunt them by telling them they now had a choice between 'birth control' or 'church control.'"

"The Planned Parenthood lady?" John asked, wide-eyed.

Grogan smiled. "The same. And by the way, she objected to the euphemism Planned Parenthood. She called what she founded the Birth Control League. She was very much for truth in labeling." He shook his head, half in apparent admiration. "It would be hard to understate her influence. She opened birth control clinics in most big cities and promised Catholics, in particular, they no longer had to practice 'Catholic roulette,' as she called it.

"Our people heard her. She did begin to create some doubt about a new discovery at the time—the so-called rhythm method—asking why it was even necessary, particularly for women whose cycle was irregular and who had husbands who couldn't limit their . . . ah . . . need for intimacy to three or four nights a month. Here the Church experienced its first division. Some of our bishops came out and opposed the rhythm method—or at least its unrestricted use. They attempted to distinguish between intent and method. They said married couples were permitted to use the rhythm method to space children . . . but not to avoid having children."

"How did that go over?" John asked.

Another wry smile. "About as you might expect," Grogan grunted, adding, "though we both know they were on solid ground theologically. They were fighting what we now know is a 'contraceptive mentality'—sex is just for pleasure—but some of the subtleties got lost in the heat of battle. It sounded to a lot of people like the Church was once again in opposition to scientific discovery. You know how it is; people hear what they want to hear."

John thought that a bit cynical. "So . . . division in the ranks. How'd that get resolved?"

Grogan laughed loudly. "It didn't, John boy! That division in the ranks ultimately settled into a venomous, protracted battle between Church progressives and Church traditionalists. It ain't over yet. Won't be over until the Lord returns and settles it Himself." He paused reflectively. "I won't see it. You might."

John suddenly felt warm.

Grogan took another gulp of wine. "Anyway, John boy . . . the progressives argued individual conscience was preeminent and choice therefore was subjectively defensible; the traditionalists argued individuals have a responsibility to form conscience in conformity with magisterial truth and that all moral choice, though subjective, was nevertheless grounded in objective moral truth—either its acceptance or its rejection."

John thought he understood the essence of what he was hearing. That was enough, he told himself. Why ask questions and offer his boss the joy of condescension?

"Then cometh the Pill . . ."

Long pause. Into the silence, ever the minimalist, John leapt, "And . . .?"

Grogan shrugged and shook his head sadly. "And . . . the long, slow, terrible decline and fall of the world's only indispensible institution began."

John thought he was now seeing something in Big Jim Grogan he had never seen before. A slight but detectable film appeared covering his eyes.

"The Pill's initial promise was that it could help women regulate their cycle and therefore expand the 'safe period.' It was a simple matter of science aiding nature. What's not to like . . . right?"

From the edge of his chair, John nodded.

"Well, we broke ranks. Our theologians saw the arrival of the Pill as a gift from heaven, a platform to demonstrate the Church's openness to scientific discovery. Look, they were signaling the elites that we're not as reactionary as you think. OK, we got the Galileo thing wrong . . . and sorry about the Crusades . . . and that Inquisition thing was our mistake, but hey, our Neanderthals get it now. Treat us like equals . . . in fact like partners.

"Our bishops, on the other hand . . . at least here in the U.S. . . . thought the theologians delusional. Most of them read Chesterton and accepted his premise that life in this vale of tears was nothing, more or less, than a battle between good and evil. That in the final analysis everything ultimately comes down to a struggle between the Church and her enemies. Think Augustine . . . City of God, City of Man. The Christian is called to have a foot in each. The elites were strictly City of Man people . . . enemies . . . and our bishops believed attempting to appease evil by compromising truth risked damnation. Not only that of their flocks . . . but their own, as well."

John had read some Chesterton and Augustine. He decided perhaps he hadn't fully absorbed what he read.

"The result was great confusion," Grogan said softly. The swagger was gone . . . but not the certitude. "The Church no longer spoke with one voice. The issue grew so contentious Paul

VI formed a commission to study it. That, too, proved to be a disaster."

"Why!?" John heard himself exclaim.

"The commission ignored the question he asked it to answer; instead, they posed their own question, answered that question . . . and got it wrong!" Grogan flashed anger. "The Church simply wanted to know whether the essential nature of the Pill was contraceptive. She had never been faced with a contraceptive act taking place before the conjugal act. The commission ignored that question and instead posed an entirely different question, in light of this extraordinary new discovery, should the Church change her teaching on contraception. They decided that she should.

"Paul VI thanked them and sent them packing. Then he went to his desk and began writing *Humanae Vitae*. By the way, he had some help from a little-known bishop in Kracow."

It came flooding back. The dinner table conversations, the discussions with visiting priests, the extended family reunions—it had been the burning issue of the day. Would the Church change her teaching? He remembered great hope in the voices he heard. There was an air of . . . what? . . . quiet assurance, particularly among the priests.

The long-awaited answer finally arrived near the end of the decade. John remembered the encyclical was received in America like the confiscatory act of a treasonous king who was demanding fealty from all subjects. It was a tax on personal freedom. A sin tax. A sin tax on those few moments of transcendent physical pleasure that married couples are able to steal for themselves amidst the drudgery of their earthly existence.

John recalled his mother's anguish upon hearing the news . . . then her quiet resignation. He recalled what he believed was his father's anger . . . then his untimely death. He recalled his own latent doubt about the Church's wisdom and her right to intrude into the bedrooms of good people like his parents . . . people in whose shoes she would never walk.

He gave voice to none of this.

"Jim, what did you think of that encyclical when it was released?"

Grogan answered abruptly, almost dismissively. "*Humanae Vitae*? Too little, too late." He paused. "It came out in July of 1968. At the time our people regarded it a settled issue. They had already moved on. Understand . . . it was entirely prophetic. The pope warned that whole societies would suffer from a sharp rise in conjugal infidelity, a general lowering of morality, a widespread disrespect for women, and a massive effort to impose contraception on the world's poor by insidious governments." He paused for effect, "Bingo!"

This astonished John. He'd always thought the infamous encyclical was the beginning of the seemingly irreconcilable fissure in the Church. "Then why all the fuss when it was released?"

"Pride," Grogan shrugged. "The progressives had promised the people . . . relief . . . in their words. This was to be their moment. They would take their rightful place in positions of influence. Then they would take a closer look at all the other things they thought the Church had gotten wrong through the centuries. Now, the Church was once again officially on record that she is not free to change what she regards as divine Law. She was reaffirming . . . maybe *updating* is a better word . . . a papal encyclical issued by Pius XI in the 1930s named *Casti Conubii*. She was saying nothing has changed. Right is still right . . . and wrong is still wrong. The marital act is clearly designed for babies and bonding. That is the natural order of things as all people of good will can plainly see—and as Vatican II had just affirmed. To reduce it to a biological act simply to satisfy a desire for momentary physical gratification denies the transcendent nature of not only the act . . . but of man himself. Clearly not what the Creator intended when He granted man this primordial privilege."

"How did the progressives voice their dissent?" John asked.

Grogan smiled wearily. "With a paid advertisement! They ran it in the *New York Times* the day after the encyclical was released. I imagine it had been sitting there for weeks, if not months, just

waiting. It was signed by over two hundred religious."
Then . . . softly, "We've never recovered."

John pondered the magnitude of loss. "It's a different priesthood, isn't it, Jim?" he asked softly.

"We're little more than sacramental mechanics," Grogan
grunted. "We have very little credibility on the important issues
in our people's lives. When's the last time someone came to you
for spiritual counsel? Hell, they don't even come to confession.
And why should they? They're convinced they can determine for
themselves what's sinful. They don't need or want the Church to
tell them anything."

Jim Grogan got up and went into the kitchen. He returned
with another bottle of wine and proceeded to pour John a glass,
despite his best efforts to wave him off. He poured himself a half
goblet and sat down. John studied his pastor and felt for the first
time a twinge of sympathy. This was a good priest. The world,
his world, had changed around him. It was no longer the same
covenant he'd signed on for. And he wasn't bitter, just somewhat
disaffected. He was now too old to rock any boats. He would do
whatever his superiors asked of him. And he would keep his parish
solvent and far from any controversy.

The last thing John was prepared to do was tell his boss that
parishioners were in fact coming to him for counsel in matters
of great import to their marriages and families. He did not want
Jim Grogan feeling any worse than he already did. Nor did he
want him scrutinizing the counsel he was offering these people,
suspecting that the advice he was giving might not be the same
advice Jim Grogan would give under the same circumstances. So
he sipped his wine and kept his silence.

The long, somewhat awkward silence was broken by Mary
Kennedy's return. "Well now, will you look at the two of you?
And not a care in the world. How can I clean up if you two won't
get up?"

"Mary, Mary," Jim Grogan broke in with a smile. "You busy

yourself with too much. Only one thing is important. John has chosen the better part, and it will not be denied him."

Mary Kennedy looked at her pastor as though he had been drinking too much, which was not entirely untrue. "Ah, you're daft, Monsignor James Grogan," she replied with a shake of her head. She began clearing the table. Jim Grogan looked upon his cook with great kindness. This woman, he believed, and women like her, were the salt of the earth. What are their lives if not one long, unbroken act of self-donation? And in return, they ask nothing. He had come to believe that they and they alone were the saints among them.

"Mary, leave the dishes," Grogan admonished. "We'll clean up. We're not finished here. You go home. Do you need help getting through the snow?"

"Do I need help now getting through the snow?" she replied. "And if I did you'd certainly be the last one I'd ask. You'd be pulling me down into the drifts with you."

John laughed at the thought of the two of these icons of decorum thrashing about on the ground, cussing each other.

Grogan chuckled and said, firmly, "Good night, Mary."

"Good night, Monsignor. Good night, Father Sweeney. I'll see you both in the morning."

When Grogan heard the front door close, he turned to John and said somewhat philosophically, "The older I get, my son, the more treacherous I find the arc and the slipperiness of the slope to be."

John simply nodded. "Jim, the thing I don't get is why our bishops haven't taken this contraception thing on if it's the linchpin of this whole 'culture of death,' as the pope is calling it?"

"Oh, but they did," Grogan shot back so quickly that John was momentarily taken aback. "Look it up. The archbishop of Washington, Cardinal O'Boyle, suspended thirty-nine priests for signing a local protest in response to the publication of *Humanae Vitae*. Wouldn't let them preach or hear confessions until they retracted their signature on the statement. They refused and petitioned Rome for relief. A year later there were only nineteen dissenters left. The others either left the priesthood—which should tell you something right there—or relented. The pope ultimately bucked the case to the Sacred Congregation for the Clergy, and one of O'Boyle's supporters was running it, an American cardinal named Wright. But Wright backed the dissenters. He pretty much ordered O'Boyle to reinstate those bad boys."

"Why?" John found this particularly difficult to believe, and were it not coming from a man he knew to be completely truthful—sometimes to a fault—he would simply dismiss it.

"Good question—to which Wright gave the wrong answer, in my opinion. He said conscience was preeminent. That no man, priests included, should be forced to act against his own conscience. He said the whole of the Church's moral tradition upheld this fundamental principle."

"We were taught in the seminary that we all have a duty to form a right conscience," John interjected.

"Well, yes. That one seems to have gotten lost somewhere along the line."

"Did it stand? Did the archbishop have to reinstate them all?" John asked.

"Every one of them."

John fell silent.

"So, Johnny-boy, when your young priest friends ask why we old-timers have fallen silent in the face of this growing disaster, this near-total decimation of our families—now you know. Nobody wants to be O'Boyled."

"Nobody's asking that question, Jim," John said quietly. "We all pretty much accept this as a settled issue."

"Well, looks like your buddy the pope is trying to open it up again with those weekly addresses of his."

John smiled. "Yeah, well, he's Polish. What do you expect?"

"I don't understand a word he says. Do you?"

John shook his head. He had tried to read each address as soon as it was published but ultimately he'd given up, understanding little if any of it.

"And if we don't understand, how in hell is the laity supposed to understand?"

John nodded.

"You know, I think more and more about what Christ said in Luke. 'When the Son of Man returns, will he find any faith upon the earth?'"

John looked at his superior for a long moment, thought to himself, Why not? and said, "I must say, Grogan, you are one morbid son of a gun. No wonder you don't get invited to more parties."

Jim Grogan blinked and paused for what to John seemed like an eternity. Then he began laughing. And the more he laughed, the harder he laughed.

John got up to clear the rest of the table, but Grogan waved him off, still laughing. "You go to bed, young man. Rose O'Rourke will be waiting for you at 7:00 a.m., snow or no snow. And I don't want to have to come looking for you."

John obeyed. He didn't want his pastor to come looking for him either.

25

There was no note. The missing money, empty drawers, and empty closet were the only clues. Grace was the first to notice, and when she told her mother that Moia was missing, Maggie screamed like a woman in childbirth. It frightened Grace. It frightened the other children, too.

It was Trudy Magnuson who brought the news to John Sweeney, who was seated at his desk preparing the altar boy schedule for the following month. He received the news with a forced equanimity. His mind, however, was racing. Where had the child gone? Who might have been consulted? How might her movements be traced?

He decided to walk to the Kealey home. It was a cool, clear spring morning, and he wanted both the exercise and the time to think. He passed the post office and the movie theater, stopped at the light at Haverhill Avenue to wave on an elderly couple in a Ford Taurus, and then proceeded up the hill, crossing the bridge that spanned the train tracks. Moments later, he angled onto Walnut

Lane and walked directly to the front door of the Kealey home on the left side of the street.

The front door was open. Maggie was alone. She was sitting with her back to the door and did not so much as stir when John entered, closing the outer door behind him. He walked around the chair in the middle of the living room and stood before her. She was in what appeared to be a catatonic state, her eyes fixed on some distant object.

"Maggie," he whispered. "It's John. How can I help?"

There was no response.

Alarmed, John went into the kitchen and searched for the family directory. He found it next to the toaster and looked up Bill's work number. He punched in the number and got Bill's secretary, Jane Sammons. "Jane, this is Father Sweeney. Is Bill available?"

"Father, he's in conference. Is it important?"

John momentarily hesitated, then upbraided himself for doing so. "Yes, Jane, it's important," he said firmly.

"I'll get him, Father. Please hold."

Five minutes later he was still holding, having lost his patience roughly four minutes ago. When Bill finally came on, John was fully prepared to rip into him, but the gentleman was profusely apologetic, so much so that to his great amazement John heard himself say, "Don't worry about it, Bill."

"Father, what can I do for you?" Bill Kealey immediately asked.

"Bill . . . Moia appears to have run away. And Maggie is awake and conscious but totally unresponsive."

"That little devil! God damn her to hell. She won't be happy till we bury her mother. I hope to God she's dead."

John was stunned. "Bill, that's your daughter you're talking about. Get hold of yourself."

There was an awkward silence into which Bill Kealey timorously crept. "Sorry, Father. I'll be right home."

"No! Bill—wait! Bill . . . are you still on?"

"Yes, Father, I'm still here."

"Don't come straight home. Go to the bus station at 11th and Filbert and the train station at 30th and Market. See if Moia bought a bus or a train ticket and get all the trip information you can. I've got Trudy checking the airlines."

"Father, Moia has no money. She can't be traveling on public transportation."

"Bill, Grace told Trudy that over eight hundred dollars is missing, much of it from Grace, apparently."

"Oh, Christ! Christ!"

John restrained himself with great effort. He said softly, "Exactly right, Bill. Christ is the answer. I need you to remember that in the days ahead."

John Sweeney hung up the phone, refusing to come to judgment on the child's father. He learned early in his young life that a man never fully knows what it's like to walk in another man's shoes. He had made very serious mistakes in his youth, and he believed it was a sign of God's great mercy that he had been called to offer forgiveness in Christ's name to those who also fell.

John checked Maggie and found her still unresponsive. He went back into the kitchen and called Rose O'Rourke. She answered the phone with that ethereal serenity that made John alternately envious and solicitous. "Rose, Father John. Could I trouble you to come over and take a look at Maggie Kealey? Moia has run away, and I'm concerned about her."

"Father, I'll be right over. Don't you worry about a thing. God love you."

John felt his eyes misting. He'd known this woman most of his life. She was one of his mother's best friends. And she never failed to deliver a brief glimpse of eternity in every meeting, every conversation. "Thank you, Lord. Thank you for Rose," he prayed aloud. He took a seat in the living room opposite Maggie, pulled his rosary from his left pants pocket, and began to pray.

• • •

It was a little after 7:30 that same evening when the phone rang in the rectory. John was alone and answered it. "Father, it's Bill Kealey. Moia bought a ticket for a bus to Las Vegas. It left at 8:20 this morning. It's due to arrive around dinnertime Thursday evening."

"Bill, I'm going to go get her."

"No, Father. She won't respond to you any more than she would to her mother or me. We've got people in Las Vegas who are going to tail her for us and keep us updated on her whereabouts."

"Bill, she can get into some serious trouble out there."

"We're not going to let that happen, Father."

"Why can't we just go get her?"

"Because she's twenty-one and can't be forced to do anything against her will. She'd have strong legal standing if we abducted her. And that's all I need right now—to have a court rule against me and in favor of my own daughter. Can you imagine the headlines in the local papers?" Bill laughed at the thought. "Daughter sues chump lawyer dad—and wins!"

John thought it a good sign that Bill Kealey was laughing rather than cursing. He decided against pushing any further. "Bill, how's Maggie?"

"She's resting comfortably, Father. It's a very traumatic time for her. She blames herself. She's convinced Moia's problems are God's way of punishing her for her own sins—though for the life of me I don't know what sins she could be thinking of. I've never seen anyone suffer like that woman. She's always been the best wife, the best mother, the best Catholic. She's a saint, Father, a living saint. Maybe you could help me convince her of that."

"St. Thomas Aquinas once famously said there are only two kinds of people in the world, Bill, sinners who think they're saints; and saints who think they're sinners."

"That's good, Father. Tell Maggie that."

"You tell her, Bill. It'll mean more to her coming from you."

"I will, Father."

26

It was shortly before noon when Jane Sammons walked into Bill Kealey's office, folder in hand. "Well, Bill, what do you want first—the good news or the bad news?"

Jane Sammons was an attractive blonde perhaps four years older than Bill. Her husband had been an attorney with Mullen, Rooney, and Timoney when he'd run off with his secretary, leaving her with three school-aged children. She was forced to return to the workforce. Jim Timoney, Maggie's father, approached Bill directly with an appeal to find work for her. His own secretary was on maternity leave at the time, and he'd hired Jane as a temp. She proved to be an exceptionally good hire; equally at ease with clients and colleagues, and superbly intuitive and discreet. When his own secretary informed him she would not be returning to work, he offered Jane a full-time position.

Bill looked up from the brief he was reviewing and fixed his secretary with a hard stare. He didn't like pop quizzes, particularly when he thought he knew the topic—a topic where there were never any right answers. "I'll let you make that call, Jane."

Jane realized that she had misread her boss' mood and re-treated slightly. "We just got an update on Moia, Bill. She left Las Vegas this morning on an early bus for Hollywood."

"And the good news?"

Jane shrank visibly. "We know where she's going?"

Bill Kealey lost it. He grabbed a paperweight from his desk and hurled it with such savagery that it hit a lamp on the end table next to his couch, knocking it to the floor and breaking it. This greatly frightened his secretary. It also further unnerved him. He sat back down, his hands shaking badly.

The reports at first were hopeful. Moia had taken a room at a youth hostel on the edge of town. She'd apparently connected with another of the young ladies there and accompanied her to a job fair at the Las Vegas Convention Center. She spent a consider-able amount of time at a trade booth for cocktail waitresses and another for lounge hostesses, filling out forms at each. She had two interviews, each at casinos apparently hiring for waitresses. She spent a lot of time in her room, even returning there with her fast food lunches and dinners.

Then, suddenly, she was gone. Had she sensed that she was being tracked? Had she been rejected for both jobs? Had someone, perhaps a young man in the hostel, come on to her? Bill felt a fresh wave of fear and grief wash over him. He saw her again as a little child, so beautiful and vibrant and innocent. So huggable, so kiss-able. When they were all just starting out together, he had lived for the return home each evening. Maggie would be waiting at the train station with Moia. At the sight of her approaching father she would jump up and down in the passenger seat, point to her dad, and shriek in pure joy.

How he loved that child. Even when the others came, so many, so quickly, he'd never lost that special bond with his first-born. Despite his prodigious work commitments, he tried to take her everywhere—ballgames, plays and recitals, shopping malls—he loved being with her, and more significantly, he loved that she loved being with him.

She had matured into the finest of young ladies, precocious and virtuous. She became an indispensable gift to her longsuffering mother—helping to organize the house, caring for the younger ones, and handling the interactions with teachers and neighbors. Bill saw her mid-stride in the process of becoming . . . anything. *Anything* was possible for this one.

The full realization of the chasm between his daughter's promise and her present torment so deeply anguished him that Bill Kealey did something he had never, ever, done before. He began to cry in public. Ashamed, he laid his head on his desk and tried to muffle the wrenching sounds in his thick arms, to no avail.

Jane Sammons laid the folder on her boss' desk and made her way to the other side. She hesitated momentarily, then put her arms around Bill Kealey's head, gently lifting it. In one long, slow movement, she pulled the distraught father to her bosom. She lightly stroked his thick, black hair and kissed the top of his head. Bill Kealey placed his hands on her forearms and squeezed. He looked up at her through his tears. She put her palm on his cheek, turned his head slightly, bent down, and kissed him on the lips.

27

John Sweeney pulled into the Kealey driveway and honked the horn. Maggie appeared at the front door, yelled something, and disappeared. Moments later she reappeared with a small white box and descended the porch steps with an effortless athleticism. "Thank you, Father, for doing this. I'm so nervous."

"Relax, Maggie," John replied when she'd fastened her seat belt. "I assure you, she may not be prepared to show it, but she'll be very glad to see you."

Three days after arriving in Hollywood and holing up in a particularly seedy motel on the Sunset Strip, Moia sent a telegram to her parents demanding that they wire a thousand dollars in cash immediately and threatened to "walk in front of a bus" if they didn't. That little missive touched off quite a row on Walnut Lane. Maggie pleaded with Bill to wire the money. Bill refused. Maggie threatened to go back into the workforce to earn the money and wire it herself. Bill invited her to do so. Maggie told her husband she would go to her father and borrow the money. Bill remained adamant, saying through clenched teeth that he would never submit to blackmail, especially from his own child.

The following morning Bill awoke early, having slept poorly. He showered, dressed, and before he departed for work, prepared a short note for his wife. It read, "Maggie—I'll purchase a one-way first-class ticket home for Moia that she can pick up at the American Airlines counter at LAX. I'll wire her this morning with the details and have Jane call you with the flight information. I'll be in court all day—xxxxx, Bill"

Maggie was euphoric upon discovering the note on the kitchen table. Grace saw it too, and shared the news of Moia's probable return with the other children, who did not share their older sister's unrestrained joy. Maggie convinced herself that Moia would accept the offer, believing she was rational enough to understand that she had no other options. So when Jane Sammons called confirming that the ticket was picked up at the American Airlines counter and that the party in possession of the ticket had boarded the plane, all Maggie needed to hear was the scheduled arrival time. She would be at the gate when her baby came off the plane.

As she began to think about the moment of arrival, however, Maggie grew nervous at the possibility of a scene in the terminal. She knew what Moia was capable of, and thought it likely she would blame her mother for her ignominious return. On impulse, she picked up the phone and called the rectory to see if Father Sweeney would accompany her to the airport, convinced that his presence would deter any physical attack or abusive tirade.

Approximately twenty-five minutes after pulling out of the Kealey driveway, John Sweeney pulled his black Acura into the short term lot at Terminal D. He and Maggie rode the escalator to the American Airlines gates in silence. Maggie went straight to gate D24, and John went into a PGA golf shop in the strip between terminals. It was still thirty-five minutes until scheduled arrival. He picked up the newest edition of Callaway's popular Big Bertha.

He ran his left hand along the smooth graphite shaft. Probably a week's salary, he told himself. John played the game seldom and poorly. However, he was delighted to discover that he could drive the ball off the tee great distances and do so with surprising consistency. His friends marveled at the sight of the ball sailing off in a near-perfect trajectory before disappearing in the distance, and advised him that he had what they referred to as "tour length."

He wanted to take the game up, thinking it would be a good release from the constant and growing tension of his ministry, but he didn't really have anyone to play with on a regular basis. None of his band of brothers played the game, and the few younger men he knew in the parish only played on weekends, which were typically a very busy time for him. He placed the mammoth-headed driver back on its display and looked at his watch. He thought it best that he start heading to the gate.

As he drew within fifty feet of gate D24 he saw Maggie standing across the aisle, rosary beads partially visible in her folded hands. She was clearly nervous, and John approached determined to put her at ease. "Maggie," he whispered, "I have a strong sense she's going to get off that plane with her face painted half white and half Eagles green."

Maggie laughed, thinking that her daughter wouldn't know the difference between the football team and the rock band. "If she does, Father, she's going home as your daughter, not mine."

Moments later, the door opened, and people began to stream into the terminal, looking for familiar faces. Moia wasn't the last to depart. There were at least three others behind her, but by the time she did emerge Maggie and John had lost much of their sense of anticipatory hope. Everything about her—her look, her clothing, her body language—said, "I'd rather be in hell than here."

Maggie approached tentatively. She tried to hand Moia the small box that she'd brought from home. Inside the box was a cake that she'd baked for her prodigal daughter. Maggie opened the top so Moia could peer inside and see it was her favorite homemade chocolate cake.

As Maggie drew closer, now moving in parallel with her daughter, who'd steadfastly refused to acknowledge her and was striding with a quickened pace in the direction of the terminal, she extended the cake for Moia to see. The daughter glanced into the box, shifted her carry-on bag to her left shoulder, extended her right arm, and blasted the cake out of the box and onto a woman pushing a stroller with a small child in it.

Maggie froze, her face sealed in horror. She turned to John, who was now moving swiftly toward Moia in an attempt to overtake her. When he got within a stride, he reached out with his left hand and placed it on her right shoulder. Using her momentum and his natural strength, he spun her around till she was facing him. He was about to lecture her, his right index finger already raised, when he became fixated on the look in the young lady's eyes. It was, he thought, a look unknown to him—at once revulsion, fury, and fear. For a moment he was completely unsettled. He opened his mouth to speak and found no words.

Moia was under no such disadvantage, however. She opened her mouth and bellowed at the top of her lungs, the sheer bellicosity of the sound arresting the attention of all within a hundred feet. "Get your filthy hands off me, you worthless priest!" she rasped. Then, leaning forward she spat in his face, grinning in a way he would later characterize as demonic. She then turned away from him and in high dudgeon resumed her forced march to the terminal.

John stood transfixed, disbelieving that what had just occurred had actually happened. His face was crimson with anger and shame. His insides were churning. His mind was racing, wondering whose eyes were now on him, thinking what thoughts, forming what opinions of him and the priesthood. The collar around his neck suddenly felt like a scalding bath towel. He wanted to rip it off and run clear out of the terminal and onto the highway, not stopping until he was safe again in the privacy of the rectory.

He felt a trembling hand on his back. He turned to see Maggie. She was crying. "Oh, Father, forgive me. I'm so ashamed. I never should have asked you to come. Please forgive me, Father."

He swallowed hard, put his arm around her shoulders, and said to her, "Maggie, I need you to forgive me. I am useless. You needed me to help. Instead, I made this whole thing worse. May God forgive my worthlessness."

Slowly, on unsteady legs, he led her from the gate and in the direction of the terminal, lost in his own misery and completely oblivious to the eyes of all upon him.

28

It was a beautiful early summer morning and John Sweeney was on the steps greeting parishioners after the nine o'clock Sunday Mass. He felt a hand on his arm and turned to see Joe Delgado. "Hey, Father, how you doin'?"

"Good, Joe. How bout you?"

"Good. Good. Listen, Father . . . I need a few minutes. When's a good time?"

"How 'bout now? I'm sure Mary's got some coffee on. Hey, where's Fran?"

"Oh, she and the kids went to the early Mass," he lied. There was only so much he was prepared to disclose on the church steps.

"OK, you head on over. I'll be there in two minutes."

Joe walked around to the back of the rectory so he wouldn't be observed. He entered through the kitchen door and happened upon Mary Kennedy, who was preparing an omelet for Father Sweeney. When she saw him she brightened and said, "Joseph Delgado, as I live and breathe. What brings you to our door this fine morning?"

"Just dropping in to see Father John for a bit, Mary. How have you been?"

"Ah, Joseph, what's the use of complainin', now? And who'd listen? Do you think Monsignor Grogan pays me any mind?"

Joe laughed easily. "Ask him for a raise, Mary. That'll get his attention."

"I'd have an easier time getting the Devil himself to hear confessions. Come to think of it, the old boy might like that."

Joe smiled and thought perhaps Mary Kennedy might be right.

"How about a ham-and-cheese omelet, Joe? I can make you one in no time."

"No thanks, Mary, but I will have a cup of coffee, black, if you have it."

"Oh, I do, I do. You go sit now in the dining room, and I'll be right in with it."

He'd just started his second cup when John Sweeney entered the dining room through the door from the kitchen. "Sorry, Joe. I got tied up with a young Pre-Cana couple. Can I have Mary cook you up something?"

"No, Father. She offered. Thank you."

John nodded, waiting for Joe to tee up the conversation.

"Father, may I bring you up to date on that matter we discussed a few weeks ago?"

"Certainly," John fidgeted uneasily. "Listen Joe, I have to say this. Canon law requires that I, personally, make no reference to that discussion because it's under a perpetual 'seal.'"

Joe nodded. Not an issue for him. "Well, Father, things came to a head, and I need a little counsel."

"Joe, I'm confident that no priest anywhere will give you as little counsel as I will."

They both laughed at his unashamed use of a tired old formula.

"Father, I've given the matter a lot of thought, as you suggested. I understand, as you said at the time, that this is a matter of individual conscience. But I really don't know what I should do, and I was hoping you could give me at least some moral principles to guide me."

John tensed immediately, hoping his discomfort wasn't manifest in his facial expression. He nodded for Joe to continue.

"Father, I confronted my boss, our CEO. Actually, he confronted me. One of the two men I had taken into my confidence ratted me out."

John winced.

"I told him that I thought it was unconscionable that Pittman Labs was trafficking in abortifacient contraceptives that they knew were not only killing babies but killing their mothers through breast and cervical cancer as well."

John immediately saw where this was going and grew alarmed. "How did he respond, Joe?"

"Not well, Father. And it got worse when I suggested that Pittman Labs should order a recall of its own compounds until further study could either validate or invalidate these . . . uh . . . concerns."

"No, I don't suppose that went over very well."

"Father, he told me to go home and talk to Franny and to make a decision about whether I wanted to continue as Pittman's chief financial officer. He told me to let him know the next day."

"And?"

"Well, I did have the conversation with Franny."

John brightened. "Joe, we know God speaks to married couples in a very special way through the Sacrament. What did Fran advise?"

"She said she'd leave me and take the kids with her if I lost my job."

"Mother of God," John gasped. He was appalled. There were times when he wanted to get down on his knees, even in public, and give thanks to God for his vocation. This was one of them. "Joe, what did you say to your boss?"

"Nothing, Father. I went in the next day as though the whole thing never happened. I didn't say anything to him, and he didn't say anything to me."

"How's he been when you're around him? Do you sense a tension?"

"Oh, no. Bill's not like that. If he's got something on his mind, he'll let you know it. I think in his mind the whole thing's blown over."

"But you're still troubled?"

"Yes, Father. I don't feel I've done the right thing. But I don't really know what the right thing is."

John felt inadequate to the task. He knew the Church did in fact have moral principles to guide its sons and daughters through difficult dilemmas like this, but he neither knew what they were nor trusted their application when a family and career were hanging in the balance.

"Joe, I can tell you this with great certainty. The God we worship does not want you doing anything to jeopardize your family. That is your primary responsibility in life. You are a husband and father first. If your wife won't support you on this, you don't go there. It's that simple."

"Yes, Father. I wish it were that simple. But every day when I go to work I can't stop thinking about all the damage these pills are doing to innocent young women and their babies . . . and I start to think that maybe I'm just taking the easy way out. The whole thing just gnaws at me."

"Have you had any subsequent discussions with Fran about your reservations?"

"No, Father . . . mainly because she's not talking to me. She thinks I've effectively eliminated myself from consideration for the top job, and she's not too happy about it. She kind of had her heart set on me getting that chair. I didn't realize just how important it was to her."

John felt a great wave of sympathy for the man in front of him. He was wonderfully raised by devout parents. The Catholic school system had obviously succeeded in reinforcing those values. His military service in Vietnam added another layer of insulation, further solidifying the timeless virtues of courage and honesty.

And yet life demanded difficult choices. Too often, it seemed, life pitted those same values and virtues against an individual's basic needs and wants.

"Joe, I want you to put the whole thing out of your mind. You go home and hug Fran and tell her you love her. Take her out to dinner. Get away for a long weekend. I'll see if I can even get Monsignor Grogan to babysit the kids, OK?"

Joe Delgado laughed. He got up and extended his hand in thanks. "Thanks so much, Father. You have no idea how good it is to have the Church in your corner."

"The Church will always be in your corner, Joe."

29

Michael Burns loved many things about the advertising business, but entertaining clients was not one of them. He particularly did not like entertaining the Cable Movie Network clients because, truth be told, they were far better at entertaining themselves.

Nonetheless, the idea to take Burt and Louise Camfy to dinner and the theater was his, and the dinner at LaVerda, an Upper East Side haunt popular with politicians and entertainment types, had gone smoothly enough. Carol got on well with Louise Camfy, who was a delightfully engaging woman of proud and noble bearing. Michael found he preferred Louise to Burt, and therefore had to work extra hard to attend Burt's stream of consciousness commentary on the sexual predilections of other diners, none of whom he appeared to know.

The cab ride to the theater was interesting simply because it was quite clear that the Nigerian driver understood English, and he made a point of glaring at Michael in the rear view mirror after several of Camfy's rants on the genetic lineage and intellectual capacities of West African immigrants. But he'd been tipped lavishly, as he no doubt anticipated, and therefore the party of Burns departed the cab at the entrance to the Wintergreen Theater without an international incident.

The evening's entertainment came courtesy of an Italian-American playwright from South Philadelphia whose script permitted him to both explore and display his own childhood neurosis, now writ large on a Broadway stage—neurosis that evidently was carefully cultivated at the heel of a domineering father. For reasons that were not readily apparent, at least to Michael and Carol Burns, the price of such submissiveness in formative years was a vengeful homoeroticism in adult years that was not only of great personal embarrassment to the protagonist's father, as scripted, but clearly to a good portion of the audience as well.

Michael squirmed and Carol writhed through the first act, promising themselves they would be good hosts and not run from the theater as if they had been asked to play a cameo in the second act. At intermission, however, Louise sensed their discomfort and graciously offered an out—coffee and desert at a café around the corner. Burt Camfy was initially resistant—he reportedly had determined "where this thing was going" and was planning to enhance the second act by introducing an unscripted audience participation element. But Louise gently yet firmly insisted, much to Michael and Carol's everlasting gratitude.

It was therefore with no small amount of relief that the Burns family pulled into the long and sinuous driveway leading to their 175-year-old farmhouse some twenty-five miles west of Manhattan, hoping to intimately celebrate a surprisingly early night. When they entered their home through the garage, however, it was immediately evident that something was wrong. Their fourteen-year-old daughter, Carole, had her arms around the two younger girls—Kate, who was eleven, and Elizabeth, now eight—both of whom were crying. At the sound, rather than sight, of their parents' return, the youngest rushed to her mother, reaching her in the kitchen, and buried her little head in her mother's coat, which served to largely muffle the sound of her torment.

"Mommy, the man was very mean. He was bad to the girl," she said, which started her older sister crying again.

"Who? What happened?" asked Carol alarmed, turning to her eldest daughter for an explanation.

Carole looked at her mother and looked at the floor. She wished she could dematerialize. Her mother was prepared to give her neither space nor time to fulfill her fantasy. "I'm waiting for an explanation, Carole. Why are your sisters crying? And why aren't they in bed? It's almost eleven o'clock."

Carole dove in. "I was watching television down here, but not Cable Movie."

"Yes, you were too," countered Elizabeth. "She was too, Mommy. You can even ask Kate."

As a middle child, Kate knew from careful observation that only three things could happen when you opened your mouth in situations like these, and two of them were bad. First, you could indict yourself by telling the truth. Second, you could exculpate yourself while incriminating others, which brought on retribution generally meted out in forthcoming embarrassments both personal and public. And third, you could exculpate yourself without in-criminating others, which required a deftness that Kate was just beginning to master.

Kate chose not to accept the opening her younger sister had so graciously provided.

Her mother correctly interpreted the silence and turned again to her oldest daughter. "So they weren't in bed! Why?"

"I put them to bed, Mom. They snuck out and went into your room and turned on Cable Movie."

"And what happened?"

"They saw a bad movie. Some guy hurt a little girl."

"He didn't have any clothes on Mommy, and he made the girl scream and cry really loud for a long time and it scared us,"

Elizabeth interjected, her eyes welling again with tears. The verbal reenactment drew a similar reaction in Kate.

Carol looked at Michael, who'd been sorting his mail and half paying attention until he heard Elizabeth's description of the rape scene. He instantly felt the gas furnace heat of that Irish flame that can ignite so suddenly in the stomach of its choleric victims. Damn them all, he quietly raged. *Damn the childless Kloss for putting that monstrosity in a prime-time slot. Damn Camfy for hiring him to market it. And while I'm on the subject, damn me for being dumb enough to say yes.*

He fixed the steel of his gaze on Carol and without a word went into the bedroom and ripped the cable wires from the wall. He saw the channel box resting on the top of the twenty-seven-inch Sony television and ripped its connection from the back of the set, opened the window, and hurled it from his second floor bedroom onto the front lawn. He slammed the window shut so hard a neighbor's porch light came on momentarily. He stripped to his boxers, rolling his clothes in a ball, and threw them in a cold fury in the direction of the bathroom. They landed on Carol's dresser. He groaned and got into bed, vowing he would give his notice on Monday morning.

30

R on Zimmer was idling behind his large desk, feet propped on half a dozen newspapers. He was reading the *Times* business section, which on Mondays posted noteworthy acquisitions and divestitures, promotions and terminations. It was always hard to divine which provided Zimmer with the most pleasure, because he was a notoriously equal opportunity offender. He had a penchant for directing gleeful insults to those whom he knew, often in the form of penned notes, without regard for mood or moment.

Arlene Hammond entered the spacious corner office with the breathtaking views of both the Upper and Lower West Side of Manhattan with a T&E reimbursement form. Zimmer glanced over the top of his newspaper and, seeing his former long-term temp approaching for a signature, turned back to the paper and remarked casually, "Arlene, get lucky this weekend?"

Arlene Hammond knew Zimmer long enough and therefore well enough to be neither surprised nor offended. She ignored him and laid the form on his desk. Without looking at it, Zimmer doubled his paper on his lap and asked, "So who you temping for today, my lovely?"

No one had ever referred to Arlene as lovely. Not her father. Not her mother. Not the young man they furtively paid to escort her to her senior prom. "Michael Burns," she replied with a smile, knowing that the mere mention of the name would divert Zimmer's attention. "Michael Burns! Arlene, I want you to go home right away and double up on your birth control pills."

"Ronald," she winked coyly, "with that one, if anything happened it would be an immaculate conception."

"That's what he wants! That's what he wants!"

Arlene laughed. "No, what he wants is a word with you."

"A word with me. Is that how he put it?"

"Yes, as a matter of fact."

"I wonder what the word is. You don't suppose it's a four letter word, do you Ar—?"

"Not in his vocabulary, Ronald."

"Well, there are plenty of words that aren't in his vocabulary, but that doesn't stop him from using them."

"Can I send him up?"

"Sure, what the hell. The day's already ruined."

Michael took the elevator to the executive floor and promptly sank into the thickly matted Persian rug set into the floor of the foyer. The walls were deeply muted grains said to have been imported from the Dutch West Indies, where the firm's chairman had built a getaway compound several years ago. "Is the eunuch in today, Sheri?" Michael asked the receptionist.

Sheri Rosatto was an attractive brunette in her early forties whom Michael liked despite the widely circulated rumor that she was sleeping with the chairman. "Of course he's in, Michael," she twinkled. "You, of all people, know how hard Ron works."

Michael snorted. "If he's in, that means the chairman's in."

Sheri threw her head back and laughed. "Oh you're bad. You're bad. You two deserve each other."

"Ah, the unkindest cut of all," Michael said over his shoulder as he headed for the northwest corner of the building. Seeing the office door open and his boss at his desk, Michael entered and strode across the room diagonally. Zimmer looked up from his reading and said, "I see you had our client out to dinner Saturday night. Make him pick up the check as usual?"

Despite himself, Michael laughed. "No, I followed your instructions. Took them to the cocaine den first, then to the whorehouse. Put the whole thing on our corporate card."

Zimmer didn't so much as blink. "Camfy have his clothes on when you left?"

Against his better instincts, Michael sat down. "Ron, I got a problem."

"Good, Shamrock. Now the next eleven steps will be much easier."

"I'm pulling CMN out of our home. That butthead Kloss ran Lipstick in prime time Saturday night and the two little ones snuck out of their room and saw it on the TV in our room."

Zimmer winced. "Pure, unbridled arrogance."

"I thought long and hard over the weekend about resigning. I didn't sign on for this."

Zimmer's eyes widened. "What the hell did you think you were signing on for, the Discovery Channel? Did you think Kloss would overhaul the programming model when he heard we found a nice Catholic boy from Philadelphia to run the account?"

Michael was at the net waiting to pounce on the lob. "That stupid S.O.B. turns his base over every two years. Guess what? He ain't got a business. He's got a peep show, and it ain't playin' in Peoria. And who do you think is gonna be left holdin' the bag when it bottoms out?"

Zimmer sat back and trained his heavy machinery on the problem at hand. He knew the toxic bile in his account director's throat had a half-life, and those enzymes had a nasty way of manifesting themselves in oh-so-many insidious ways when the opportunity presented itself—which it invariably did at the most inopportune of times. What he didn't need was a fifty-million-dollar account walking. What he also didn't need was a search for a new Top Gun. They were easy to screw up. He knew. He'd been both the initiator and the designee in several of those now-classic searches.

"Let me handle this one, Shamrock. I don't want you saying anything."

Michael looked at his boss, who was now very serious indeed. He nodded in silent affirmation.

31

Michael was at his desk early the next morning when the phone rang. It was Zimmer. "All right Shamrock, get that righteous red ass of yours up here."

"Right up," Michael replied, already half out of his chair.

Zimmer was waiting on the couch in his reception area when he arrived. "Why don't you just lie down now and tell the good doctor all about it," Michael baited.

"Face down? Not with you in the room." Zimmer countered.

"What's up?" Michael asked when he was seated on the couch opposite Zimmer.

"Talked to Camfy last night for over an hour," Zimmer began deliberately. Michael noted that length of time was a staple of New York client speak—it suggested the measure of an ad man's capacity to arrest and retain client attention—as if spending fifty million dollars of their money wasn't itself sufficient incentive. "He's a big fan of yours. He doesn't want you going anywhere."

So Zimmer had disclosed the severity of Michael's reservations about the assignment. He didn't get that. How could that possibly advantage the agency? But he knew that in the high-liquidity labyrinth that was Zimmer's mind, no disclosure was without purpose. He would just have to stay alert and eventually all, or most, would become clear.

"He's no fan of Kloss. Says he's an insufferable cretin. But he acknowledges that Kloss is smart, tough, and in the driver's seat right now. He'll ascend to the top spot within two years unless Camfy can figure out a way to derail him."

"Kloss will do that himself," Michael offered.

"I wouldn't be so sure. Camfy's convinced that Kloss got pictures of Reynolds doing things the Catholic Church wouldn't approve of with barnyard animals."

"So you told him about your Church?"

Zimmer, uncharacteristically, did not rise, or sink, to the baiting. "Camfy wants you to know the industry is working on a parental lock that would prevent a reoccurrence of the kind of thing that happened at your house last weekend. Apparently it's being pushed by the cable operators, who are getting a lot of heat about CMN's prime-time content. It's becoming a cause célèbre in the industry, and Camfy's going to mount it internally."

Michael was fascinated to observe how the corporate world operated in its Mecca. It wasn't enough to demonstrate mastery over your own affairs; you had to be equally adept at exploiting the real or perceived weaknesses of rivals, and yet do so without ever appearing to jeopardize either the illusion of collegiality or the success of the venture. It was only the most skilled of these "three-tool players" who rose to the top chairs, whereupon they immediately vanquished rivals, elevated allies, maxed net worth, and, in more than a few cases, set their sights on bigger game— generally a governorship, a Senate seat, or a cabinet position in a future administration.

Michael was not a betting man, but if he were, he reckoned his money would go down on the horse named Kloss. All the leverage in the business model was being driven by the programming side. The ability to buy finished product in bulk from major

studios—who regarded the ancillary revenues as found money—
and then to turn around and resell it for a premium to cash-flushed
cable operators under the form of what amounted to a monthly
annuity, left Kloss as a king who had only subjects, not serious
rivals.

Still, Michael saw a vulnerability that Camfy apparently
didn't yet see, and he believed it was Camfy's ticket to the top job
he so desperately sought. Yes, in the short run the business was a
pure purchasing play, but in time—and this time Michael believed
was fast approaching—the "wiring" of America would reach a
tipping point, whereupon it would become necessary to stabilize
the continuously eroding customer base to ensure projectable cash
flows. And this would provide Camfy with his opportunity to put
his imprint on the business, because that stabilization would largely
be a function of sound marketing—beginning with an "outside in"
approach to buying or creating programming for targeted audience segments. Simply put, sooner or later, CMN would have to
understand the "end customer"—which tended to be a family of
discrete viewers with both individual and collective needs and
wants. Knowing that customer, Michael knew, would ultimately
prove more valuable than knowing the Hollywood starlet who
wanted CMN to create a vehicle for her. He believed he was
uniquely qualified to help Camfy begin that process.

"Ron, I think we ought to get Camfy out to dinner. Just the
three of us," he suggested abruptly.

Zimmer's eyes widened. "And the agenda?"

"How the Hal Ross agency can help make him king. We're
going to lay it all out for him."

Zimmer looked hesitant. Michael immediately realized he
hadn't defined a role for his boss. "Let me share with you what I'm
thinking and get your input. Then you can lay the whole thing
out for Burt, and I'll provide the detail."

Zimmer brightened perceptibly. "Good. Let me get on his
calendar right away," he was already up and moving toward his
credenza. Watching him speed dial, Michael marveled at the pace

that self-interest induced. He couldn't imagine making that call without knowing what it was he was proposing, but that didn't stop Zimmer, and hey, he was the president of the agency. "Camf, Zimmy. You free for dinner tonight?" Zimmer put the conversation on speaker phone.

"Only if you supply the babes," Camfy retorted.

"Better. Michael and I have a play for you that I think you're going to like."

Camfy's mood changed quickly. He knew underneath the Don Rickles veneer that Zimmer was flat-out brilliant, and he knew firsthand that Burns, though quirky, was an authentic marketing talent. If they had a track for him to run on, hell, he was all ears. "Where and when?" he asked.

"Titania's. Upper East Side. Seven o'clock."

Camfy confirmed and Zimmer hit the conference button on the phone. "OK, Shamrock. Cut me in on this thing."

32

Burt Camfy arrived twenty minutes late for dinner and saw no reason to fashion an excuse. He sat down, smiled, and began singing, sotto voce, the immensely popular track from *Fiddler on the Roof*, inserting the word "sedition" for "tradition."

Zimmer ordered a three-hundred-dollar bottle of French Lafitte, which arrived presently. Camfy pushed his glass in the direction of the steward to indicate he expected to be the designated taster. Zimmer promptly called him on it, "Oh, no, you don't. This is altar wine. Burnsie's the connoisseur."

Burt Camfy grinned delightedly and turned toward Michael. "Zimmy tells me you used to serve High Mass—or wait, I'm wrong . . . he said you served Mass high," Camfy needled.

"Yes, the experience was deeply mystical for me, even then," Michael responded evenly. Some things were off limits, faith and family among them, and he wasn't the least bit reluctant to send clear, strong signals to that effect, even if they weren't always well-received.

"Zimmy told me about the problem with the kids. That shouldn't happen," Camfy said, recovering nicely.

Michael nodded. He didn't want this conversation to be about him, or his family. "What's the monthly churn now, Burt?" he asked, knowing the answer.

Camfy smiled. He understood. "Oh, about what it was last month when you reminded me we'd better start to address it."

Michael turned to Zimmer, signaling this was the time to get into it. Zimmer thought differently. No foreplay, he lamented. This kid was going to have to develop that gear if he was going to get to the top. "Did Michael tell you we hired that playwright and assigned him to your account?" Zimmer began instead. "He's going to write Kloss into the commercials with him in bed."

Camfy laughed uproariously. "Did Burnsie here tell you I had my own script that I was prepared to introduce from the audience during the second act?"

This time it was Zimmer who laughed. So this is the big windup, Michael realized. Like wine, no business before its time. "Listen," Zimmer said composing himself. "I wouldn't have taken you to a play like that, but then again, I'm not an intimate friend of the playwright."

Camfy couldn't get enough of Zimmer. Their turn of mind was of a pattern, each reading the other's intent as though it were his own. The waiter arrived, imperious and very much "out of the closet." Camfy immediately looked at Zimmer and guffawed, apparently assuming it was a send-up. "I'll have the foie gras, for starters," he announced with exaggerated affectation, looking at Zimmer for affirmation and finding none.

Zimmer reddened. He had made a practice of bringing only his best clients here, and he enjoyed a reputation as a good if somewhat obscene sport—judiciously nonhomophobic—and an excessively generous patron. Camfy's wanton mockery, he immediately calculated, would probably cost him roughly half the goodwill he'd built over the past fifteen years. How to recover?

"Make that two," Michael chimed in, clearly enjoying his boss' discomfort.

"Victor, do we have a trough in the back where the pigs might feed?" Zimmer inquired of the waiter, struggling to recover.

The waiter merely grunted, "May I take a drink order, please?"

Michael looked at Camfy, who was now a schoolboy, crouching behind his menu like the class clown behind his desktop lifted at a forty-five degree angle. He was prepared to carry out his guerilla war until forced to come out with his hands up and his pants down. Michael decided right then and there that he too liked this Burt Camfy fellow. "I'll have the Liza Minnelli splattered on the rocks like her worthless hetero husbands," Michael said with only slightly less affectation, "and you can give the cherry to my friend," nodding toward Zimmer.

Camfy made no attempt to suppress. The sound reverberated off the walls of the smallish room, arresting the attention of the other patrons and chasing the waiter back into the kitchen, apparently for good. Zimmer was now irretrievably shamed. Camfy and Burns were bonded. And Michael was forced to concede that maybe his boss was right about this client foreplay thing.

Presently the owner himself, the regal and courtly Giovanni Titani, appeared to take the drink and dinner orders, adding further rebuke to their host. Michael felt what he thought might be the beginnings of an extremely remote twinge of sympathy for Ron Zimmer, but he noted it required surprisingly little effort to dismiss.

When the orders were in, Ron Zimmer, acting as though none of what just took place had actually taken place, turned to Burt Camfy, whom Michael now envisioned sitting with his tie rolled up and in his mouth, and said, "Burt, Michael and I are convinced your end customer is saying something important that is not being heard. We've got some ideas on how to ferret some of that out and package it so you can get everyone at CMN on the same page."

Good, Michael thought. Just the right touch. Zimmer neither overstated the significance of the premise nor over-promised on its intended result. Camfy was nothing if not extremely shrewd. He knew precisely what was being proposed—a tool to get him off the defensive about CMN's marketing performance and onto the offensive with respect to the network's product performance.

"Fun, food, and ideas too?" Burt Camfy knew there was a reason he hired this agency. "This isn't going to cost me more money, is it?"

"No," Zimmer protested. "Like all our clients, we work for free."

Michael was glad Zimmer was back in form. He would need him to close this deal, which he believed would cement the client/agency relationship for years to come, on the basis of pure performance. Call me naïve, he thought to himself, but at the end of the day, as the Brits like to say, performance must count for something.

Camfy turned to Michael and said, "You have my full attention."

Michael looked at Zimmer, who nodded, then back to Camfy, and plunged in, "Today we have a product concept, not a product. That won't become apparent until the pace of cable 'wiring' slows. When it does and the customer disconnect rate runs the business model aground, the pressure from corporate to shut the back door will be white hot. Contrary to what Kloss will allege, that door can't be slammed shut simply by better marketing. Its rate of closure can only be slowed—and that will require a greatly refined programming model marketed with far more precision."

Camfy nodded. He hadn't heard anything new yet.

"We can't do any part of that without input from our end customer," Michael continued. "Not the cable operator—I'm talking about the family he's selling to."

Camfy brightened, "What kind of family do you think Victor has waiting for him at home?" he inquired, referring to their waiter.

Point taken, Michael conceded. "OK, individual or family."

Camfy nodded and cleared his throat. "Michael, as you well know, we do constant research on our customer base. Are you asking me to propose more?"

"Yes. To begin with, we need to put a face on that data so it gets a serious hearing."

"Why are you assuming it's ignored?"

"Because it is," Michael stated flatly. "Look at your TSS scores, then look at Kloss's Original Production calendar. Do you think they're talking to each other?"

Camfy nodded. Kloss had an obvious disdain for the customer. He was pumping huge sums of money into original films and specials with no regard for either cost or appeal. If an "original property" made one of his Hollywood friends forever indebted, well, that was sufficient reason to get the project funded and produced. Its success sure as hell wasn't going to be measured in box-office receipts, and besides, he had a 24/7 hole to fill—and there were only so many "high-concepts" out there.

"TSS refers to total sexual satisfaction?" Zimmer asked hopefully.

This delighted Camfy. "See what we've done to your altar boy?"

Michael cut in, "Total Satisfaction Scores, Ron. CMN multiplies the percentage of their customer base who watches a particular show with the overall percentage of satisfaction they report. So if fifty percent of their viewers watch a particular movie over its three- or four-week run on the network and they rate it, say, a fifty on a hundred-point satisfaction scale, the Total Satisfaction Score is a twenty-five."

Zimmer got it immediately. "What categories of product tend to produce the highest scores?"

Michael looked directly at Camfy, "The family stuff. Movies everyone can watch. You know, happy endings, stuff like that."

"Why do you assume Kloss' production schedule won't include those kinds of films?" Camfy challenged.

"Because I've studied it, as you would expect me to do,"

Michael replied evenly. "Jimmy Stewart and Bette Davis in an end-of-life suicide pact? What do you think the TSS on that little hummer's gonna be? Think it'll hit double digits?"

Zimmer chortled. "Are you kidding me?"

"No," Michael replied, looking at Camfy. "He's kidding himself."

"He's got some pretty big specials and concerts lined up, Michael," Camfy added a bit lamely.

Michael nodded. "Eddie Murphy Uncensored. Bet the operators will love that one. Think he'll run that baby in prime time?"

Zimmer erupted. He was enjoying his client's obvious discomfort. "Hey, Camfy, you're screwed," he concluded. "Go ask Reynolds if you can have your old job back."

"It's all fixable," Michael said pointedly. "Let me sketch it out."

Camfy said nothing, but he was listening.

"We've got to segment your base. It's not nearly as monolithic as your audience research would suggest. We've got to look at the homes that have passed on CMN and understand why. We've got to look at the homes that have disconnected CMN and understand why. We've got to look at the homes that are currently paying for CMN and find out who among them are not fully committed to retain the service . . . and why. And, of course, we need to have the data cut for age and gender, income and occupation, education and geography.

"Then we've got to match this data with the satisfied buyer profile from your audience data and probe for convergence/divergence. Once we get a handle on what kind of programming is helping you attract and retain customers and what kind is causing you to pass and lose customers, we'll spell out the implications for both the programming model and the marketing plan."

Camfy was clearly uncomfortable. He understood the mere commissioning of this research would be a declaration of war, drawing the full retaliatory energies of a most formidable Richard Kloss. He also knew it had to be done.

"How long . . . and how much?" he asked guardedly.

"We could be in the field with the survey work within a month and have a first cut inside another six weeks, eight weeks tops, with a finished report in twelve weeks."

"How much?"

"Figure about four hundred thousand dollars. Then we'd run some focus groups off the field study to put a face and a voice on the data—in and out with a full report in another month for about a hundred thousand dollars. So, all in, you're probably looking at five, maybe six months and about five hundred thousand dollars."

"You guys at least picking up the check for dinner?" Camfy asked, turning to Zimmer.

"Yes, but only because you were so well-behaved," Zimmer retorted.

"Burt, a couple of housekeeping notes," Michael amended. "First, the Hal Ross agency can't field this study for obvious reasons. Have Rick pick one of National Publishing's house suppliers. That way when, not if, Kloss does a dump on the research, it'll be clear to all that he's crapping on his boss, not a rival. And secondly, when we do the groups we'll pack the full swarm—your programming as well as marketing people—behind the glass in every city, so nobody can legitimately dispute what the customer is saying."

Camfy was impressed. "You could present the findings and conclusions tomorrow morning, couldn't you?"

"Would I propose it if I couldn't?" Michael replied, making no attempt to mask his adroitness. He had learned early in his career that peers on the client side greatly resented their consultants showing them up in front of their bosses. But their bosses often encouraged it, knowing it would prod their own executives to work harder. It was always a balancing act, and Michael had discovered that he was prone to occasional clumsiness in this regard. This was why he preferred one-on-ones with the top decision maker when he could get them, though his client peers would often discourage him or even occasionally block him from doing so. That was precisely why he had Zimmer schedule this dinner meeting. The Ron Ashleys of the world might not like it, but they understood they would never have much influence on their boss' calendar.

"Michael, this can't be a witch hunt," Camfy said pointedly.

"Nor can it be a god hunt," Michael replied. "The battle over the final questionnaire will prove decisive. Kloss will want the questions slanted to confirm that all is well in paradise. If you think he'll prevail, my advice to you, our advice to you, is don't field the study."

Clumsy, he thought. He would put Zimmer in short pants, and his long pants were short enough.

Camfy didn't let it slip. At this level, every point was played. "You sure Ron agrees?" he smiled.

Michael knew better than to look at Zimmer. He tried to recover, "Lapsis linguae est non lapsis mentis."

Camfy looked at Zimmer, who returned a blank stare and said, "He's praying you'll pay for dinner. He didn't bring enough cash . . . again."

33

After dropping Camfy off at the National Publishing building, Michael rode in silence with Ron Zimmer to the Hal Ross building just off Times Square. The city always looked more seductive and more vibrant in the evening, Michael thought. It seemed to attract people with an inexhaustible energy, people who regarded the work day as a mere prelude to the serious business of bacchanal, often in pursuit of an edge in business. These were the "full court players" who set the bar for whatever-it-takes commitment. If they didn't get to the very top it wasn't going to be because they didn't leave a piece of themselves in the office . . . or in the right watering hole.

Of course those 24/7 campaigns weren't altogether conducive to the marital state, as born out in the divorce rate among corporate executives in Manhattan—which Michael guessed was probably the highest in the United States. The price was indeed steep, and was accepted as such, but to the "players" the rewards were all but unimaginable, and that of course was what ignited the superbly crafted engines of all the life forms now darting hither and yon about his cab.

He knew he would never be one of them. It simply wasn't in him. He was entirely willing to outrun, outthink, and out hustle anyone during the day, but when darkness fell, he needed to be home with Carol and the kids. All the more so, now that the boys had arrived. He lived to see those little guys every night, and he thought that the balance gave him an edge, or at the least allowed him to perform at his highest level. And he hadn't done badly, he reasoned—three promotions in three years—and now there was talk of a fourth, which would make him the youngest executive vice president in Hal Ross' forty-year history. Already there was a buzz in the corridors that he was presidential timbre.

"Shamrock, you done good tonight." It was Zimmer, gently reminding him he was boss.

"Thanks for setting that up, Ron," he replied graciously. "Had I attempted it, I would have caught more heat than I care to wear right now." Pause. "Think he'll do it?"

"Oh, he'll do it. What choice does he have?" Zimmer replied as he exited the cab and reached in his pocket for his wallet. "Kloss has him cornered, and he knows it. He can fight him now, or he can fight him later."

"Shame it has to be that way. Seems like there's more than enough of everything for everybody."

Zimmer looked at Michael Burns with a mixture of surprise and reproach. "It's the law of the jungle, Philly. Welcome to the Big City."

Zimmer paid the cabbie and headed for the bar on the corner. "How about a quick one?"

"No thanks. Gotta get home."

"OK. But no sex. You've already done more than your share to propagate the race."

Michael laughed and watched Zimmer disappear into the crowd, wondering if he would run into Camfy again before dawn broke over the city that claimed never to sleep.

34

———

Sounds like a classic Borderline to me." Hal Schwartz was ladling the cream cheese onto his sesame seed bagel, never taking his eyes off Father John Sweeney, who sat opposite him in the back booth at Artie's sipping coffee. Schwartz, a high school teacher and coach, had been John's semi-pro baseball coach; he'd become something of a mentor since his father's death. John was drawn to the older man's gentle, self-deprecating humor and profound wisdom.

"Not familiar with the term, Coach."

"Borderline Personality Disorder is a relatively new diagnosis, maybe forty to fifty years old," Hal offered. "Its manifestations cluster on the border between psychosis and neurosis. Very tough to treat. Most clinical professionals won't accept them. It's two steps forward, one step back, all the way home."

Hal Schwartz never ceased to amaze John. If he didn't know something, he knew somebody who knew everything there was to know about it. He'd called in desperation. Bill and Maggie Kealey were suffering mightily, trying to keep home and hearth intact in the wake of Moia's most recent difficulties.

Moia had come home from the airport that day and gone straight to her room, locking the door behind her. That was now almost fourteen months ago. Her sister Grace brought food and books, placing them on the floor outside her door. Initially she also left small notes offering information about friends and so forth, but they were not well received. Moia left bitter and profane rants on the other side, and left them on the tray with the dirty dishes and unread books.

Her older sister's rebuffs deeply wounded Grace, who wanted nothing more than to see her, talk to her, and help her. She began eating less and less and sleeping more and more. Bill told Maggie that he thought Grace was anorexic, but Maggie was protective. Bill suspected that Maggie was in denial, and she resisted his efforts to get Grace professional attention. Bill was now more concerned about Grace believing Moia was beyond help, though he did not share any of this with Maggie.

John felt a dark, smoldering presence in the home whenever he entered. He thought the family was hanging onto a ledge by its collective finger tips. He saw them losing hope. He knew that once hope was lost, faith followed. So he had taken it upon himself to stay involved, though he knew he was well beyond his field of competence. Clearly, Moia had a serious and still undiagnosed mental illness that a full complement of mental health professionals had not been able to address, for whatever reasons. But within the depth of his own prayer and discernment, he concluded that he just might know one person who could possibly shed light on the mystery that Moia Kealey had become.

"They're very difficult to diagnose," Hal added.

"Why?"

"No blood tests. No brain scans. Kids won't talk. The psychiatrists are left to make judgments based on the symptoms presented by their parents and maybe a teacher or coach. It's pretty much guesswork."

"So how do you really know for certain?"

"There is no such thing as 'certain' when you're dealing with the disordered mind. There are often other factors present too. That's why you often hear two, sometimes even three, diagnoses for the same condition. It's all but impossible to be certain."

"How did you come to be acquainted with the disorder, Coach?"

"We see them at school. Maybe once every two years. I've had several in my classes over the past ten years or so. Really can't do much with them, or for them. They just won't let you."

"What are the symptoms?" John asked.

Hal Schwartz blew gently on his coffee cup, momentarily fogging up his bifocals. "Unstable self image. Self-destructive impulsivity. Intense mood swings. Fear of abandonment. No enduring relationships. Frequent emotional overreactions. Long-term depression. Recurring suicidal impulses."

"Coach . . . I think this child has pieces of all those things."

"Any five and she's a BPD."

"BPD?"

"Borderline Personality Disorder."

"What happens to them?"

"One of two things; they either grow out of it . . . or," Hal fell silent.

"Or they don't make it," John completed the thought.

Hal nodded and stared into his coffee.

John envisioned the scene. The church filled. The casket closed. The mother collapsing in grief. The other children looking to the father. The father looking at him in silent rebuke, wordlessly demanding an answer to the great unanswerable. And he, John, beginning the invocation in the name of Christ, wondering where in the name of Christ his Lord had been as this unmitigated tragedy was playing itself out.

"That can't happen," John asserted. "Not on my watch."

"Careful, my friend," his old coach cautioned, laying a meaty hand on his forearm. "This is not child's play. We are talking about a very serious mental illness here. Highly trained professionals steer clear of these cases."

"Hal, there must be something that can be done. This girl is decimating an extraordinarily strong, loving family. We can't just sit back, do nothing, and watch them all go under. That could eviscerate the entire deposit of faith in that single family for a full generation or more."

"Or not," Hal said and smiled.

John felt at once shamed and blessed. This good and wise man had a living faith stronger than his own. Elder brothers and sisters in the Faith, wasn't that how John Paul II referred to the Jews? John accepted his friend's gentle rebuke. He was right. Nothing, he knew, was impervious to prayer.

35

——————

Bill Kealey waited in the pew until the last penitent left the church. It was quarter to five, and he would be Father Sweeney's last confession on this wintry Saturday afternoon. He got up quickly and a bit noisily, so his confessor would know he still had some unfinished work. He headed for the door with the screen. What he would confess would not be confessed face to face.

As the door opened John immediately sensed it was Bill Kealey without knowing why he sensed it. Maybe it was his physical presence, palpable even in the darkness. Then again, John reflected, maybe it was the sound of prematurely aging knees creaking from too many arthroscopic surgeries—a consequence of too many football collisions. Bill Kealey had retained the sturdy bearing and rugged good looks of his youth into early middle age. He still possessed that alpha male power to turn the heads of both men and women in a public gathering place. As he settled into the small box, John waited for confirmation that his intuition was correct.

"Bless me, Father, for I have sinned. It's been about two months since my last confession and these are my sins."

Right down the middle of the fairway, John thought. No greeting. No acknowledgment of any kind. This must be serious.

Not waiting for a response, Bill Kealey continued, "Father, I committed a mortal sin against the sixth commandment."

The Pill, John assumed. He's here to reconcile himself to the Church's most unpopular teaching. He wants his conscience clear and his immortal soul spotless when he receives the precious Body and Blood of his Lord and Savior tomorrow morning at Mass. Good for him. Good for Bill Kealey.

"What were the circumstances, my brother in Christ?" John inquired with supreme gentleness.

Long pause. John repeated the question in precisely the same tone.

"Father, I've had an affair with my secretary."

A bomb detonated inside John Sweeney's head. His heart began to race in a way he instantly understood to be unhealthy. His entire body tensed. His hands moved in the darkness as though fending off an unwanted attack. It was several moments before he could speak, the very silence that Bill Kealey had dreaded when he envisioned this moment in the box with this priest. It was the singular reason he'd resisted going to Confession for the past two months. He simply couldn't bear to hear this silence, and the judgments it portended.

"Bill . . . How?" John couldn't help himself. He had grown too close to this family. He immediately saw that his childhood infatuation with Maggie Timoney now posed sacramental challenges. How wise of Holy Mother Church to require a year of total and complete abstinence before admitting him to one of its seminaries. During that year, he had ever so gradually come to understand that, contrary to what he'd previously thought, his Church understood the transcendent power and mystery of sexual intimacy.

"How?" Bill Kealey seemed startled by the question. "I fell, Father. I sinned. I've come for absolution."

For some reason this angered John Sweeney. How had Jim Grogan referred to priestly ministry in the current age? They were "sacramental mechanics?" He wouldn't submit. He knew he was well within his rights—no, his duty—to complete his inquiry, though canon law required he do it respectfully, with prudence and discretion. He was taught in the seminary that the circumstances surrounding what the Church regarded as a mortal sin, a grievous wound, were important because they could mitigate culpability. No, he would not do this in anger. To do that, he knew, would be to invite the demonic into the booth, profaning the sacramental rite and its divine initiator.

"Bill, I need to ask a few questions in order to provide proper guidance," he said evenly, well-aware that Bill Kealey had not entered the confessional in search of guidance.

So it'll come down to a negotiation, Bill immediately surmised. He didn't see this as a problem. He certainly had far more experience with negotiations than his friend on the other side of the screen. "Anything, Father," he replied, offering nothing.

John Sweeney hesitated. He wanted to get both the questions and the tone canonically right. "First, how long has this been going on, Bill? Is your wife aware of it? And most importantly, are you prepared to end it?"

Bill Kealey was uncharacteristically unprepared for this line of inquiry. He had built his career on never having permitted himself to be caught with his pants down, so to speak. This priest, this friend, had boxed him in, and his finely tuned and exquisitely calibrated mind was not presenting him with the usual escape routes.

He decided against trying to put too much spin on it. "Father, I guess it was a gradual thing. She's attractive and lonely. She's divorced—her husband left her—and she has problems with her kids, which she's shared with me. And of course, she's all too familiar with the problems in our family. She screens and makes a lot of calls for me."

He slowed to a stop and John sensed this was going to be a tractor pull. He decided, against his better judgment, to ask a question he knew that he had no right as a confessor to ask. "When did this thing actually begin?"

"About a year and a half ago."

"Where?"

"In the Marriott downtown."

"Oh my!" John gasped, despite himself. He knew he was now in danger of profaning the Sacrament. The penitent had entered the seat of mercy and John Sweeney's intrusive questioning and all too personal responses were violating the sacredness of the penitent's sacramental encounter with Christ Himself. But all he could think of in this moment was Maggie Kealey, migraines burning the inside of her head, making dinner for six children and hearing homework at the same time, while her husband was rolling in the sack with his secretary. The image of it very nearly overwhelmed him.

"It began in the office, Father," Bill Kealey added matter-of-factly. "It was innocent enough at first, but we continued it after work that same evening."

"How often do the two of you meet?"

"Usually about once or twice a week."

"For the past year and a half?"

"Yes."

"Maggie knows nothing?"

"She knows nothing, Father."

"Not even a suspicion? She's an exceptionally intuitive woman, Bill."

"Yes, she is that. But no, I haven't gotten a sense that she suspects anything."

"Bill, I must point out the obvious. Your wife is a very beautiful woman. She's uniquely accomplished and virtuous. From all appearances, she's an absolutely wonderful wife and mother."

"She is . . . Father. She is . . . all those things . . . and more," Bill Kealey was suddenly struggling. The thought of his wife's heroic witness, amidst great emotional trials and physical torments, and his own feckless dalliance clearly unsettled him. It seemed to ignite a dying ember of his love for her, and in this moment he found himself deeply ashamed.

John Sweeney sensed his penitent hadn't quite exhausted his treasury of surprises.

Bill Kealey coughed somewhat nervously. "Ah, Father . . . about a year ago, I got a vasectomy," he volunteered. "Since then, the temptation to stray has grown stronger and stronger. Sometimes I . . . I just feel . . . powerless."

John Sweeney was astonished. If Bill was sterilized, why did Maggie ask his blessing to go on the Pill? Weren't they talking to one another? Might this tragedy have been averted if they were communicating? Why were the lines of communication jammed?

"Bill, why did you do that?"

"Father, Maggie's ovulation cycle is so irregular that it's impossible to determine in any given month when it's safe to have sex. With her migraine headaches and the problems with Moia, I just didn't think she could handle any more children. And I was just not prepared to abstain for three weeks every month. It's unnatural, Father."

"Bill, did you tell Maggie?" He knew he had to be careful here. The Seal of Confession was inviolable. It was Church law. It was the one thing all priests agreed on, even if they agreed on virtually nothing else. He knew priests who no longer believed that their words at the consecration of the Mass initiated the transubstantiation of ordinary bread and wine into the Body and Blood of Christ. But even those men, he knew, wouldn't break the seal. Nor would he.

"No, Father. I knew she wouldn't approve. You know how she is about those kinds of things."

"Bill . . ." John Sweeney was struggling. Canon law forbade him from coercing, even suggesting, that Bill talk to his wife, or anyone else for that matter, about the content of a sealed confession. But there was clearly a serious communication problem in this family. "Would you consider just talking to Maggie about your sacramental relationship? Not about your affair. Just your relationship and how it might be strengthened?"

John felt a hesitation on the other side of the screen. He wondered where he went from here if Bill Kealey was simply unwilling to address the state of his marriage with his wife.

"Father, I'd rather not do that."

"Why?"

"If we start talking and if I tell her I've been sterilized, she'll tell me what I did was a serious sin. She'll tell me I can't receive Holy Communion with the family on Sunday."

Right on both counts, John thought, but wrong about Maggie's response. John knew she wouldn't be giving her husband any such lectures.

"Bill, have you broken this relationship with your secretary yet?"

"No."

"Do you intend to?"

Hesitation. Then, haltingly, "I'm going to try, Father."

"Bill, for you to receive our Lord's forgiveness in this sacrament, you must be prepared to end this affair, and all contact with this woman. I can't give you absolution until you tell me you will."

"Father, I may not be able to. We're together all day, every day. Just seeing her in the morning, uh . . . stimulates me."

John understood all too well.

"And I can't very well reassign her. It would stir gossip. The gossip wouldn't be fair to her, and besides, it would cost me my managing directorship. I've worked too long and too hard to just give that up for reasons that have nothing to do with my performance."

John Sweeney exhaled audibly. Right or wrong, he didn't see himself as a particularly good arbiter of such matters between man and wife. He was a uniter, a conciliator. In his youth he had courted confrontation. No more. He didn't like it and wasn't good at it. It robbed him of his peace. And without his peace, he couldn't carry out his priestly duties in service of the other parishioners.

"Bill, this is not part of your penance, and it's not in any way mandatory, but I want you to know I'm available if you and Maggie want to . . . just talk."

Silence.

"Bill, are you hearing me?"

"Father, I could never agree to that if you're going to bring this affair with my secretary up."

"Bill, I can't do that," John responded, stifling his notorious impatience. "I can't talk about anything that is said in this confessional. That would be a mortal sin for me. And as much as I love you and Maggie, and your family, I will not commit a mortal sin, even to save your marriage."

"What's the topic of conversation then, Father?"

"Communication. The absolute necessity, the indispensability, of married couples communicating openly and honestly with each other about matters of the heart and soul."

"Father, can I get absolution?"

"Bill, work with me here. I can't give you absolution until I am certain you have true contrition—a sense of sorrow for your sins. I'm not getting that."

"Father, I'm sorry for my sins."

"And you'll end this relationship with your secretary?"

"I'll try."

John Sweeney was weary from the struggle. His conscience troubled him, but he didn't know what else to say or do. "All right, Bill, for your penance say three Our Fathers. Now make a good act of contrition and I will absolve you from your sins through the ministry of the Church."

36

As John Sweeney vested for the nine o'clock Mass the following morning, he felt the familiar sensation of a peace that, as the Apostle once claimed, surpassed all understanding. He never felt happier, more at ease, more a priest, than in those moments prior to his celebrating the Holy Sacrifice of the Mass.

He loved everything about this ancient and sacred ritual. He loved the perfectly balanced and integrated structure of its praise, petition, and thanksgiving. He loved the blending of Old and New Testament readings, carefully selected and themed to platform a particular Gospel imperative. He loved the seamless participatory roles of priest and parishioner—the joyous sound of a uniting of spirits and wills for nothing less than the glory of God, even if but for a brief moment in time.

He loved the Consecration itself most of all. He loved the great mystical reality that the Son of God was, against all possibilities, sacramentally present. God the Father's thought and Word had entered time, and now would, in this moment, submit to a sacramental re-presentation of His definitive act of unbounded love. And He would do so, actually re-enter time and space, at the initiation of a sinful *alter Christus*, on behalf of an equally sinful humanity. It was too sublime for words, John thought. It caused him to reflect on what he believed were the most perfect words of the most perfect Preface in the whole of the Liturgy, "Our desire to praise you, Lord, is itself your gift." For him, that about summed it all up.

As he kissed and donned his stole, he moved toward the large oak credenza in the sacristy behind the sanctuary. He glanced down at the large red Lectionary from which he would read for the Liturgy of the Word. It was opened to the readings for that Sunday. He took a moment to read them quickly. When he was younger he prepared his sermons assiduously, but he discovered he was not a particularly gifted homilist and came, gradually, to the conclusion that what Christ said in the Gospel was far more important than what he said about what Christ said.

Perhaps that was a bit of a rationalization, he conceded. But he had preached on all the Gospels for ten years now, and he reasoned that his parishioners knew what to expect from him on any given Sunday, and that he was not a man for surprises. Besides, nothing should overshadow the Consecration itself, he believed. The Holy Eucharist is the source and summit, as the Church held for two millennia, of her very existence. It perfectly symbolized the unbreakable bond of unconditional love between Creator and creature.

John was surprised to see that the Gospel passage for this Sunday was John 6. In it Christ tells His disciples that unless they eat of His flesh and drink of His blood, they would not have eternal life. Many of His disciples simply found this "hard saying" too difficult to embrace and therefore departed, perhaps forever. But Peter did not depart. And when Christ asked him if he was also going to leave Him, he answered with one of John's favorite Gospel responses. "Master, to whom shall we go? You have the words of eternal life."

John re-read the words several times and found his mind drifting back to Bill Kealey's confession last evening. He began to feel a slight tugging sensation, the light warmth of the Holy Spirit shadowing his heart. In an instant, he determined that in his sermon he would challenge his parishioners to reflect on the "hard sayings" that perhaps they too had walked away from—decisions that they now knew were obstructing a more intimate union with their God. And he would do more. He would identify the hardest of those "hard sayings," those involving the Church's teachings on human sexuality, and he would afflict the comfortable right here in the pews of St. Martha's Church in Narbrook.

He entered the sanctuary behind two altar girls and a middle-aged female lector singing the entrance hymn in full voice. He was greeted by the customary smiles and small waves, and he felt the warmth of the lay faithful who had gathered before him. He knew they liked him and they knew he liked them. He was again at peace. Before beginning with the Sign of the Cross, he looked over the assembly, paused, and said, "Thank you all for coming. I really didn't want to have to report you to Monsignor Grogan." This drew light to moderate laughter, and he waited until it settled. He then began with a slow, deliberate, carefully enunciated Sign of the Cross.

At the Gospel he mounted the small, marble pulpit to the left of the altar and read the passage with power and conviction. At its conclusion, the assembly noisily seated itself to await his words of explication. As they did so, he scanned the crowd for familiar faces. He saw the Kealey clan in their usual spot, half way up on his left-hand side. They were all there, save Moia. John thought Maggie looked exhausted and overwhelmed, her complexion unusually sallow. Grace looked like she had lost an astonishing amount of weight. John wondered if she was bulimic. He couldn't read the look on Bill Kealey's face. It was masked in inscrutability, as it often was when he did not want his thoughts known or his emotions betrayed.

John took a quick deep breath and plunged in. "Today, my brothers and sisters in Christ, our Blessed Lord challenges each and every one of us. What are the 'hard sayings' that we have permitted to become barriers to a deeper, more intimate relationship with Him?"

He paused. He saw the large cluster of John Paulistas, as he referred to them, in the middle of the left side of the church, opposite the Kealeys. They were young, and they were on fire with the Faith. Seven couples—the Harmons, Gambones, Avins, Owens, McFillins, Fallons, and Costellos—and already there were thirty-two children among them. The adults were still in their late twenties and early thirties. They were the future of the parish, he and Monsignor Grogan agreed. Their love for the pope was so complete and so contagious that it even attracted the attention and grudging admiration of the lukewarm.

They lobbied with a firm persistence for daily Eucharistic Adoration, which he and Monsignor Grogan reluctantly denied, citing insufficient interest on the part of the parish as a whole. They asked his help in forming study groups to read and discern the providential wisdom of John Paul II's encyclicals, but he told them he simply did not have the time. To John's relief, they seemed to accept his explanation and jumped into other parish activities, undertaking them without appearing to compromise their rather considerable family responsibilities. In fact, their families seemed to be extremely close and remarkably happy.

They were all here, present and accounted for, even the infants. Some forty-six of them clustered over six pews, so thoroughly integrated that you couldn't be sure which sets of children belonged to which sets of parents. What he found particularly instructive was that not only did the parents pay close attention to the homily, but the older children did as well. They sat looking at him with expressions that mirrored those of their parents. He actually found it somewhat unnerving, though he'd never disclosed that to another soul.

He began, "One of hardest of those 'hard sayings' for me

when I was young was our Lord's admonition that we had to forgive our neighbor, not seven times, but seventy times seven times. I can remember getting into trouble with my brothers, and my father would tell us to lay face down across our beds—our little bare bottoms exposed. We'd cry out for mercy. And Dad would say, 'This is the 491st time. Even the Lord Himself is out of mercy for you.'" Gentle laughter followed, and some squeals from the children in the cluster, which he instantly understood were occasioned by his reference to the bare-bottomed Sweeneys. He hoped that one wouldn't come back to bite him on—stop, don't go there, he told himself.

"Another 'hard saying' for some is Christ's comment concerning the rich young man in the Gospel passage of two weeks ago, who went away sad because he was unwilling to sell his possessions and follow Christ. As He watched the man leave, Christ said to His Apostles, 'How hard it is for a rich man to enter paradise. I assure you,' He told them, 'it is easier for a camel to pass through the eye of a needle than it is for a rich man to gain eternal life.'

"His Apostles were so astonished at this statement, Matthew tells us, that they asked Him, 'Master, then who can enter paradise?' Christ saw how hard it was for them to understand this, so He reassured them by saying, 'For man it is impossible; but nothing is impossible for God.'

"The Church teaches that it is not our possessions themselves that can compromise our relationship with Christ, but our attitudes toward what we possess. The danger is in acquiring material goods for their own sake, and putting the acquisition and possession of those goods before our relationships with each other and God.

"God's abundance is to be shared with those who have less. Holy Mother Church refers to our obligation to the poor as a Gospel imperative. It's called the Gospel's preferential option for the poor. It means we all have an obligation to look at the structures of injustice in our society and correct them.

"We all know what it's like to drive through certain parts of Philadelphia and see the atrocious living conditions of our poor brothers and sisters of color. Many are living hand-to-mouth, ravaged by disease, crime, and unemployment. Their families and spirits are broken. They live lives of misery and hopelessness. Yet blocks away, there are high-rise office buildings and apartment houses filled with people who have no such worries. They have good jobs and nice places to live, and their children go to good schools.

"Beyond the perimeter of the city lie the suburbs where we live. We who have so much. As Christians, we are called not just to share what we have but to attack the root causes of social injustice themselves. We are called to be the love of God in the modern world. These people are our brothers and sisters in Christ. They must feel God's love, and it is our responsibility to love them as God has loved us.

"Now some may find this a 'hard saying,' but in today's readings Christ calls us to embrace the 'hard sayings' of the Gospel. Love is sometimes hard. But we are called to love God with all our mind and heart and soul—to love our neighbor as ourselves for the love of God. This is the great challenge of the Gospel. But don't lose heart if sometimes you find yourself unable to love as you ought, because Christ reminds us today that for man many things are impossible—but for God, nothing is impossible.

"So let us ask our Blessed Lord for the grace to love Him with all our hearts, and to love our neighbors, particularly the poor, as we love ourselves. Let us renew our resolve to correct the injustices of society, particularly the unequal distribution of goods, which is the root cause of so much sin in our world. And let us remember that it is through us that God wishes His love to flow into the world, touching and transforming hearts and minds.

"If we can embrace this 'hard saying,' then we will not walk away from Christ sad because our possessions are many. We will instead walk toward Him, drawing ever closer to the great Source and Object of our love. And even more importantly, we will bring many, many others with us.

"And that, my brothers and sisters in the Lord, is what it means to be a disciple of Christ."

He turned and stepped down from the pulpit, and walked to the chair at the top of the altar in front of the tabernacle. He sat down facing the congregation and closed his eyes, signaling this was a time of momentary reflection on the Gospel and the homily.

John Sweeney tended to be hard on himself. His first thought was to castigate himself for not saying what he had intended to say. You folded like a cheap suit, he told himself. Why? Why, he demanded.

But as he reflected further on what he said, he thought perhaps it was the better message for his flock to hear. After all, he reasoned, hadn't he challenged them with the Gospel's preferential option for the poor? Hadn't he afflicted the comfortable in order that they might comfort the afflicted?

And besides, he told himself, it would have been inappropriate to say what he had intended to say about the Church's teachings on marriage and family in front of children. And what would the Kealeys have thought? Bill would have assumed John was lecturing him; perhaps even trying to embarrass him. And what of Maggie? Would she have thought he was admonishing her? He found the thought of adding to her burden so abhorrent that his head started shaking involuntarily from side to side.

But most of all, he was now glad that he would not have to face the stares and glares of the faithful on the steps outside church. And he would not be called to give an explanation for what he had said to Jim Grogan, who would look at him with incredulity and tell him that he had said the most inappropriate of things in the most inappropriate of settings.

No, he concluded, he had been saved from a self-destructive urge by none other than the Holy Spirit Himself. It was He who guided him away from danger and onto the path of wisdom and grace.

He stood for the petitions, feeling greatly relieved. Several minutes later he was sharing with his parishioners what he believed to be the Body and Blood, Soul and Divinity of the Word Incarnate. Maggie Kealey approached with a smile on her face. He smiled and placed the Host on her outstretched hands. "This is the Body of Christ."

Bill Kealey followed, but he was not smiling. "The Body of Christ," John said as he placed the Host on his tongue. "Amen," Bill said, nodding slightly.

37

The call never came. At least, the call John Sweeney was hoping for never came. Three weeks after granting Bill Kealey absolution, he did receive a call from the Kealey home, but it was Grace, and she was asking him in urgent tones to come to the home as quickly as possible.

He left the rectory in haste and drove to the Kealey home on Walnut Lane in South Narbrook. He entered the home through the front door, which was open despite the sub-freezing temperature. He saw Grace cowering behind a sofa in the living room and heard loud guttural noises coming from one of the upstairs bedrooms. He saw a decapitated statue of the Blessed Virgin lying in the dining room, and a framed picture of the Sacred Heart of Jesus lying next to it, smashed to pieces. He entered the kitchen through the dining room to see if any of the other children were in the home, and discovered none were.

In the kitchen he saw plates and glasses, a portion of which were broken, strewn on the floor. All about them lay the contents of various packages of food—cereals and pastas, grains and snacks.

He turned and walked back into the living room, looking for Grace, who had come out from behind the sofa and was now sitting on it with her head in her hands. "Grace, what's happened? Where's your mother?"

Grace Kealey was now twenty and a sophomore at St. Joseph's University on the western edge of Philadelphia. Though she did not possess a full portion of her older sister's beauty and intellect, she was among the most selfless of young ladies John knew, aptly befitting her baptismal name. She excelled in basketball and lacrosse in high school, winning partial scholarships to a number of Division II schools in New England and north central Pennsylvania, but she elected to stay home to help her mother with Moia and the other children. She chose instead to commute to St. Joe's—only five minutes from home. But the problems in the Kealey home were simply too difficult for even two extraordinary women, and Grace was forced to drop out of school . . . twice. The second time was due to bulimia.

John looked at Grace, who was still quivering. "Moia went on a rampage, Father John. She came out of her room screaming and cursing. She had Grandmom's crucifix in her hand and started hitting Mother with it. Mother ran out of the house. I think I heard her leave in the car, but I'm not sure."

John Sweeney looked at the unnaturally thin child before him and tried to imagine the living hell her young life had become. It was in moments like these that his faith was fully tested. He understood, of course, that suffering was part of living. That it had redemptive value, if offered as sacrifice, both for the victim and countless others. But why God would permit such extraordinary suffering to befall a single person, or a family, or even a whole people—as in the case of European Jews—he simply did not understand.

In that instant, they heard a loud scream and a crashing sound from upstairs . . . and then silence. John Sweeney turned and started for the stairs, but before he could get there Grace rushed ahead of him and ascended the steps like a deer bounding a series of small hedges. "Moia! Moia!" she shrieked, heading to her mother's bedroom.

When John came to the doorway of the master bedroom he stopped, constrained by propriety. He saw a physical impossibility he could not comprehend. Moia had somehow pulled her mother's eight-foot, three hundred pound dresser down upon herself and now lay underneath it, semiconscious. Grace was struggling vainly to lift a portion of it off her stricken sister, crying in her futility.

John rushed to the aid of the two girls. Without a word he inadvertently nudged Grace to the side, but having temporarily forgotten the slightness of her frame, he was now surprised to see her airborne and flying, fortunately, in the direction of the bed, where she landed with the softest of sounds. He grappled with the corner of the dresser but could not budge it. Moia's face was turning blue. He said a quick prayer to the Virgin and moved to the front of the dresser, crouched low, and with a Herculean lift and shout, he hoisted the dead weight up and rocked it toward the adjoining wall, where it teetered and settled.

He knelt by the side of Moia Kealey and checked her pulse. Her heart was beating. He leaned over the lithe body, which was curled in a fetal position, and proceeded to give her mouth to mouth resuscitation. Beside him now knelt Grace, hands folded, lips moving in silent prayer. He prayed to the Virgin that Moia Kealey might live.

For several long moments it appeared as if his prayer wasn't being heard, and he immediately chastised himself for his own wretchedness. If I were the priest I was called to be, this child would have lived, he remonstrated. Look not upon my sinfulness, he pleaded with his God, but upon this tortured child who has died without ever experiencing your love. Surely that could not have been your will in this place and time.

Apparently it wasn't. Moia began to stir, suddenly conscious. Her eyes opened, without recognition. She moaned softly and reached for her right leg, which was bent in an unnatural position behind and underneath her body. John gently reached for the leg and eased it back into a more natural position. Moia jerked and yelled out in pain, but then closed her eyes and began mumbling something that John could not make out. He noticed tears now for the first time, running down her cheeks and onto the carpet.

John turned to Grace and said, "Grace, call 911 and ask them to send an ambulance. Tell them there was an accident and say that your sister might have a broken leg." Grace nodded and lit out like a tiny cheetah. John turned again to Moia and bent down to pick her up with the idea of laying her on her mother's bed. As he placed his arms under her back and thighs, though, the child became suddenly alert and began writhing in horror, shouting, "No, no, no, don't touch me, priest! No, please . . . no more . . . don't touch me!"

John recoiled in fear and panic. His hands started to shake. He felt a wave of nausea rising in his stomach. The room began to move about in concentric circles. He sat down on the bed to calm the spinning. But it did not stop, so he lay down, resting his head on one of the pillows.

That is where the paramedics found him, asleep on Maggie Kealey's bed with Moia Kealey lying beside him on the floor, curled once again in a fetal position.

38

Joe Delgado got up slowly from his desk and walked to the large window in his office. He looked out at the lush green rolling hills, all earmarked for development within the next decade. There would be office buildings, specialty shops, sporting clubs, restaurants, and of course parking lots.

As a boy he had played baseball and football in the tracts carved out of those hills by the township. He and his friends fished the streams and camped in the nearby woods. It was an idyllic childhood in an iconic American moment. He certainly was not one for deep societal introspection, but somewhere along the line something had happened, and whatever it was, it was becoming clearer it was not altogether good.

He turned from the window and looked at the folder on his desk again. There was no question it was a time bomb. The question was how to determine if it was ticking. And the answer to that, he realized, could only be determined by identifying the person who'd buried it, face down, in the middle of his inbox.

The file was sealed and stamped "confidential." Its contents included selected copies of the archival material on the origination of Pittman Labs' oral contraceptive business. They were not new to him. What was new, however, was a copy of a letter from Paul Scaramoucci, who was the president of the National College of Gynecology. It was addressed to Al Heyworth, Chief Executive Officer of Pittman Labs. It was dated December 12, 1965.

Joe read it three times, surprised to discover that it both raised and answered additional questions with each reading. Joe thought the letter was an odd mixture of consent and rebuke, and he wondered at the forces that would animate even the relentless Al Heyworth to launch such a bold strike into the very heart of medical science—and to do so in writing.

The matter had been all but closed in Joe's mind. His second conversation with his confessor, Father John Sweeney, had finally convinced him that there was considerable more downside risk than upside virtue in blowing a whistle fashioned after the insider tobacco industry expose, an Insider II, if you will. He did not see himself as a missionary, or a kamikaze pilot for that matter. He was a husband and father first, as Father Sweeney reminded him. And, as a man of faith he had accepted Father Sweeney's counsel on the primacy of family as an intonation of the Holy Spirit. His instructions were clear, and he had followed them.

He would not deny that the matter continued to gnaw at him from time to time. But he had less and less difficulty dismissing it from his mind when it surfaced, and it now surfaced only on rare occasions—generally when he was in conference with Carney, Halifax, and Dalkowitz. Sitting among them, Joe would occasionally wonder if another group of men would be sitting in this very conference room in the not too distant future, accompanied by outside counsel and strategizing on how to defend against a class-action suit brought by women who found themselves the victims of breast and cervical cancer from their use of hormonal contraceptives.

So it was with no small measure of discomfort that he unsealed, read, and re-read the contents of the folder lying on his desk. Who hid it in the middle of his stack of mail? What did that person expect him to do with it? And why is this matter surfacing again?

He picked up Scaramoucci's letter to Heyworth and read it a fourth time:

Dear Mr. Heyworth,

I acknowledge receipt of your letter dated November 1, 1965 and will reply forthrightly to the questions you addressed to me in your correspondence.

First, let me say on behalf of the National College of Gynecology, we are most grateful for your generous pledge, which will allow us to embark on a rigorous program to upgrade the knowledge base, the professionalism, and the overall effectiveness of our membership with respect to the care and treatment of American women.

We believe our physicians are the world's finest practitioners in their field of competence and that the work they do is among the most important work being done in the field of medicine. The timely assistance of Pittman Labs will enable NCG to further extend its commitment to providing our members with all the newest advances in scientific and technological discovery.

As an association, we are always interested in collaborating with healthcare professionals in every sphere of activity within our industry. Our executive board has carefully reviewed the studies that Pittman Labs commissioned through the medical research department at Harvard University in 1962, and we have no major difficulties with either the study's methodology or its fundamental conclusions.

That having been said, Mr. Heyworth, I must advise you that NCG cannot, and therefore will not, involve itself in ethical matters beyond our field of competence. Simply stated, the matter of when human life begins is a religious question and not a matter for medical scientists, physicians, or associations.

However, our board is open to the possibility of making an official pronouncement on when pregnancy itself begins, and we believe this may serve your overall purpose in a more authentic and credible manner. We believe, to be more specific, that it is entirely supportable to posit that pregnancy begins with implantation of the embryo in the uterine wall. That is scientific fact. If your compounds perform as the Harvard University Medical Research Unit observed, your assertion that they are de facto contraceptives and not abortifacients would be entirely defensible, because there cannot be an abortion without a pregnancy.

We quite agree that America's major cultural institutions—those you cited as well as others—will resist mightily the introduction of an abortifacient into the public debate, although they have been surprisingly receptive to the discovery and mass distribution of contraceptives.

Perhaps you might consider a joint statement with a high-profile association of ethicists who might be willing to push the envelope on the question of when life actually begins. In that case, NCG would be willing to help soften the ground by issuing our pronouncement perhaps one year in advance. This would permit a public debate prior to the issuance of the subsequent statement on the religious dimension of the question. It is our experience that these matters are always best viewed from the perspective of a continuum of discovery because this view is intrinsic to the nature of scientific exploration itself.

I hope this clarifies our position on the issues raised in your November correspondence. We are very grateful for your generous support and ongoing encouragement, and we want you to regard us as willing and able collaborators in your mission to provide American women with the most comprehensive package of family and healthcare products and services available anywhere in the world.

Sincerely,

Paul Scaramoucci
President
National College of Gynecology

Joe gently laid the letter on top of the file and closed it. As he did so, he noted a small silver paper clip jutting from the back of the folder that he hadn't noticed before. He removed it with his thumb and forefinger, intending to put it with dozens of others inside his top desk drawer. However, a small index card that was attached fell from the clip, hit the top of the desk at a right angle, and floated to the floor. He stooped to pick it up and saw a name and phone number scotch taped to the front of the card. Both the name and number were printed out from what appeared to be an IBM personal computer of a kind commonly used throughout Pittman Labs.

The name read Dr. Stanley Koblinski, and the phone number had a 215 area code, which indicated that Dr. Koblinski was local. Joe sat down and said a small prayer to the Virgin Mother, asking for what he referred to as "discernment."

He proceeded to take inventory. Clearly, someone knew of his conversations with Carney, perhaps even Halifax and Dalkowitz. Just as clearly, whoever it was went to some lengths to elude detection, or the name and phone number would have been hand written, perhaps even on Pittman Labs stationery.

Joe immediately ruled out the possibility that any of his three senior associates would have discussed their private conversations with another employee. Too much risk. He'd learned long ago that there were no secrets in corporations. If one person knew something of importance about the company or one of its employees, it would not be long before others knew as well. So, someone must have known of the discussions without, perhaps, knowing much about their content.

His initial thought was that it may have been one of the executive assistants on the floor who had observed him behind closed doors in one or more of the three separate instances when the "OC file" was being discussed. Perhaps one of them heard a stray comment or observed his body language during or after the conversations and made a connection. Quite a leap, he concluded. He decided to place a phone call, merely out of curiosity, and as he began to punch up Dr. Koblinski's number he made a mental note to check the PCs in the executive pool after hours to check for remnants of bits and bytes that might shed some light on the identity of his unknown correspondent.

The woman who answered the phone did so in an especially engaging manner and Joe guessed she was in her late twenties or early thirties. She spoke somewhat rapidly, in a manner not uncommon for bright young ladies who have mastered the content of their jobs fairly early in their tenure. He hadn't been entirely sure what she had said, so he asked her to repeat it. This time he heard her say with greater clarity, "Catholic Medical Association. Dr. Koblinski's office. This is Jennifer. How may I help you?"

"Jennifer, my name is Joe Delgado and I'm calling for Dr. Koblinski," he said with all the certainty he could muster.

"OK, Mr. Delgado. Please hold."

She was back in a heartbeat, "Mr. Delgado, does Dr. Koblinski know you?"

Joe tensed. "Jennifer, tell Doctor Koblinski I was given his name by someone who thought the two of us should meet."

"OK, Mr. Delgado . . ."

Long pause. Joe started fidgeting and weighing his options. The voice was back, "Mr. Delgado, Dr. Koblinski can't meet with you for three weeks. He's giving papers in Boston, Chicago, and San Francisco. He hopes you understand."

"Jennifer, I understand next to nothing. I'm very sorry to have troubled you."

"No, no, Mr. Delgado . . . Mr. Delgado . . . are you still on?"

"Yes."

"Doctor asked me to set up a meeting with you. He wanted to know if you'd be free on the last Saturday morning of the month and if you'd be willing to meet him in the cafeteria at Memorial Hospital around 8:00 a.m.?"

Joe paused. Why not? Good location. Decent time. Who would see him, and if by some remote chance someone did, he of all people should be able to explain what he was doing talking to a doctor in a hospital, given his battle with diabetes and hyperten-sion. "Sure. That'll work for me. Tell the doctor I'll see him on the twenty-eighth."

"OK, Mr. Delgado. If anything changes, you let us know. And the doctor now has your number too."

"Right. Thank you, Jennifer." Joe hung up feeling oddly titillated. He couldn't wait to find out why he had called this meeting.

39

Fran Delgado wanted to know where her husband was going so early on a Saturday morning and was not one to be put off by shrugs and grunts. Joe, for his part, was not particularly good at prevarication, having had the non-negotiability of truth drilled into him, often quite painfully, by his father and mother early in life. This occasionally made for awkward, even confrontational moments in their marriage, though they did their best to shield them from the children, not always successfully.

"I don't know why you won't tell me, Joe. Just tell me. Where are you going so early?"

"I did tell you. I'm going out. I have things to do. Let it lie, OK?"

"Well, when will you be back?"

"I'll be back when I'm back."

"Are you going to work? Are you having problems at work? Is the company doing OK?"

"Goodbye, Fran." Then to soften things a bit, "I'll be back

before lunch. Maybe we can have lunch at the club if you're still here."

"I'll meet you there. What time?"

"No, we'll go together." He wasn't going to be pinched into an artificial deadline.

He entered the garage through a door off the kitchen, hit the remote to raise the door, turned the engine over in his BMW 750, and backed out into the circular driveway, which formed an attractive and well-landscaped crescent at the front of their three-story colonial home. In minutes he was headed east on Montgomery Avenue toward City Line Avenue. From there he would angle into the heart of Dixon County, and ultimately into the parking garage of Memorial Hospital.

When he arrived at the hospital he was relieved to see that the sheltered parking garage was nearly empty. He parked on the ground floor and entered the hospital complex through a small door that led to both steps and an elevator. He opted to climb and found himself on the second floor when he stopped to push open the door to the corridor. No sign of life, a bad thing in a hospital, he noted. He turned and retreated to the first floor, found a sign for the cafeteria, and headed in that direction in search of coffee.

The double doors to the cafeteria were shut and it appeared closed, but when Joe peaked through one of the windows he saw a lone cashier idling behind a cash register. He entered to find two nurses in green smocks chatting together with paper cups of coffee in their hands. He saw a tall black man in a white uniform and large hat, and assumed correctly that there was warm food somewhere in the vicinity. He grabbed a tray, a plate, some utensils, and then proceeded to the serving area—loading up with virtually everything his doctor told him was off limits.

As he approached the cash register, the youngish black woman behind it was already calculating the damage. "That a double order of bacon?"

"Uh huh."

"Double order sausage too?"

"Uh huh."

"We got scrambled eggs . . . home fries too . . . that Danish I see?"

"Yep."

"You a hungry man this mornin.'"

"Uh huh."

"Whatcha drinkin'?"

"That urn of coffee over there."

This seemed to greatly delight the cashier. "Jess leave yo wallet with me."

Joe parked himself facing the door, hoping to finish before Dr. Koblinski arrived. He knew it was bad form to talk with his mouth full. He'd made it halfway through his plate when a somewhat balding, barrel-chested man of late middle age entered wearing a white lab coat and black horn-rimmed glasses. He had a distinctive bearing if not distinctive features, and he was scanning the room for a man he hoped would look like a senior corporate executive. Joe watched as he looked at, then past him twice before realizing that the man he was looking for had to be this rumply, middle-aged guy dressed like one of the help.

Their eyes locked momentarily, and the good doctor nodded and began walking to Joe's table. "Mr. Delgado, I presume?"

"Indeed," Joe replied smiling. He gestured to the open chair opposite him for his guest, or was it host, to join him. "Thank you for making time for me."

Koblinski dropped a weighty stack of materials on the table, gestured with his right forefinger that he had one thing to attend to first, and headed to the coffee area, where he selected a darkly blended, highly caffeinated option that appeared from Joe's table to be equal parts liquid and steam. The doctor returned to the table with a big grin on his face. "Now, Mr. Delgado, you will have my undivided attention."

Joe studied the face of the physician sitting opposite him and quickly concluded that it invited trust. "Doctor, I'm not entirely sure why I'm here."

The deep blue eyes behind the coal-black, horn-rimmed glasses twinkled and Stanley Koblinski, smiling slightly, replied, "How long have you had this problem?"

"Since I got married," Joe laughed. "My wife gave me a note, but I seem to have misplaced it."

Koblinski chuckled and offered help, "I must presume you're interested in the Catholic Medical Association; at least that's what Jennifer seemed to think."

"Yes, yes. Please tell me about your association."

"May I inquire as to why we have engaged your interest, Mr. Delgado?"

Joe paused. He wasn't quite sure how to proceed. "Doctor, I work in the pharmaceutical industry. My guess is you have some issues with a few of our products." Clumsy, he thought, but at least the subject's on the table.

"Actually, our issues are less with the pharmaceutical industry and more with some of the medical associations which seem to work for them."

Joe brightened, finding that disclosure of sufficient interest to warrant more inquiry. "For instance . . . ?"

Koblinski stared at Joe and said, "Who do you work for, Mr. Delgado?"

Joe plunged, "Pittman Labs. I'm their chief financial officer."

Koblinski nodded. He made the connection. This was the fellow Sharon Williamson had told him about. His wife, Marjorie, and Sharon had been college roommates at Immaculata, a small Catholic university on the outskirts of Philadelphia. They had been in each other's weddings and remained friends. Marjorie was on call when Sharon suffered through a messy divorce in which she'd lost custody of her only child—a daughter who Koblinski thought was probably a teenager today. Williamson's husband was a divorce attorney, and it was Koblinski's conviction that he'd manipulated scant evidence of occasional alcohol abuse and his knowledge of the court system to gain custody—an advantage as unfair to Sharon as it was unfortunate for the child.

Sharon Williamson, he knew from long experience, was a good woman. She had suffered a great setback and struggled mightily to get back up on her feet. She had re-entered the job market and rose, through years of hard work and personal sacrifice, to become executive assistant to Pittman Labs CEO Bill Carney.

Koblinski could see that his companion hadn't yet made the connection, and saw no reason to make it for him. Perhaps Sharon preferred anonymity in this matter. He couldn't recollect their discussion, so he opted for discretion. That was always the wiser course in matters like this, he assured himself.

"Ah yes, Pittman Labs. The company that gave the world Al Heyworth. Or was it the other way around?"

"That would be us," Joe replied, smiling tightly.

"Well, yes. We certainly know all about Pittman Labs. But as I say, our focus at the Association has been more on, and here's your for instance, a group like NCG."

"NCG?"

"The National College of Gynecology. They have been surprisingly aggressive on the matter of abortifacient contraceptives, and I think I might know why."

Joe nodded, wondering just what the doctor knew about Heyworth and NCG. "What's their position been on the indications for oral contraceptives?" he asked innocently.

Koblinski's eyes narrowed. "Very interesting choice of words, Mr. Delgado. Uncanny, actually."

"Doctor, please call me Joe."

"Yes, of course. NCG's position, though they would have us believe it is rooted in science, remains totally oblivious to scientific discovery. They've held for almost twenty years now that the question of when life begins is unsettled, a religious question, but that science has settled the question as to when a pregnancy begins. It begins with the implantation of the embryo in the uterine wall. This of course is quite devious, and science itself has now proven just how devious."

"I'm not sure I follow," Joe said with feigned confusion.

"NCG initially distributed their statement purely to neutralize what they anticipated would be fierce opposition from the Catholic Church on abortifacients. Your Al Heyworth was determined to focus the national debate on birth control, a debate he was confident he could win even with the Catholic Church lined up against him. He was extremely shrewd. He knew that the Church was largely divided on the issue of how best to regulate births, but he was acutely aware that both shepherd and flocks would never countenance a birth control pill that acted as an abortifacient. At least not in the 1960s."

"So Heyworth induced, pardon the expression, NCG to carry water for him. What was in it for NCG?"

"Money, what else? They needed it. He supplied it. Various research programs, professional development, that sort of thing. And once they abandoned principles and staked a position, they couldn't very well turn around years later and say, 'Hey, we got that one wrong. Sorry. It's now clear life begins at 'first contact' fertilization.'"

"I take it that science is now clear?"

"Absolutely. We now have blood test technology that can pick up products from the embryo, the beta sub unit, even before implantation. These tiny sub units, as they are commonly called, go into the fluid around the baby, then find their way into the fallopian tube and, ultimately, into the mother's blood stream. Now, in fairness, we didn't have tests in the late 1960s that were sensitive enough to read this activity. But we do now."

"It's a pretty slippery slope, isn't it?"

"Come again?"

"NCG must have known that science itself would inevitably make them look . . . uh . . . unscientific?"

Koblinski shrugged his shoulders. "Who knows what they were thinking at the time? They were probably blinded by a great light reflecting off Al Heyworth's gold."

"Bottom line, they got away with it, didn't they?"

"Well, we called them on it. Our membership unanimously passed a resolution condemning the Pill as an abortifacient."

And probably the only people in the country who paid any attention, Joe mused, were the people who voted to pass the resolution. "What about the Church itself? Did the bishops comment on your statement or issue a pastoral letter or a statement of their own?"

"No."

"Why not?"

"You'd have to ask them," Koblinski replied, fixing Joe with a firm but otherwise inexpressive stare.

"Let me try this on you," Joe offered. "It's the late 1960s. All hell is breaking loose. The debate on birth control is over. The Catholic Church has lost. She's not looking for another fight. Her flock is becoming more educated, more emancipated, and therefore more unruly. The 'center' isn't holding, as one very sober Irishman once famously put it. The Church doesn't want to further alienate the upwardly mobile Catholics she sees as her emerging voice in the national debate on civil rights, domestic economic policy, and war and peace. She goes along to get along."

"I wouldn't be that cynical," Koblinski shot back. "Maybe the bishops were waiting for the Vatican to say something they could rally behind."

"So they were split on the Pill like they were on the issue of birth control itself. Any indication they sought help from Rome?"

"No, but the Catholic Medical Association wouldn't be part of those privileged communications."

"Where were the so-called Catholic theologians on this thing?"

"All over the place. No different than today. You had the so-called 'progressive' wing; 'dissidents' is another word for them. Frankly, I prefer 'heretics.' They staked their raison d'être on green-lighting contraception for the masses, throwing a big tent around anyone who could help them . . ."

"Even the enemy?"

"If by enemy, you mean people and organizations that are generally hostile to the Catholic Church, the answer is yes."

"So our progressive theologians were embarrassed to be part of a Church that's so hostile to scientific discovery. They're signaling to the modern world that the post-Vatican II Catholic Church is open for business."

Koblinski squinted and shifted uneasily in his seat. He was not given to conjecture. He was a medical man, a scientist. He lived in an empirical world. Truth was knowable because it was measurable. The data spoke. It was the physician's task to understand what it was saying. "Again, I'm not into imputation. I'll leave that to people who are smarter than I am."

Joe felt stung and struck back quickly, too quickly, "Doctor, you had no such reluctance when characterizing NCG's greed."

Koblinski recoiled and Joe immediately felt a strong sense of self-recrimination. He sought to calm the waters. "Of course you are no doubt right about NCG, and I am perhaps entirely wrong about the U.S. bishops and theologians."

The good doctor accepted the peace offering. "I don't say you're wrong. I simply said I don't know if you're right. There is a difference, I'm sure you'll agree."

"I do, I do. Let me ask you this, Doctor. De facto, your friends at NCG redefined life's inception, yes?"

"Well they attempted to, de facto as you say. They certainly haven't succeeded. They sought to establish a scientific basis for determining the beginning of life. In doing so they based their argument not on what is happening to the child but on what is happening to its mother. This, of course, is the beginning of the depersonalization of the child. Medical science didn't wait for the child to develop into a discardable fetus. It declared it a nonperson by virtue of its pending implantation. This of course is sheer nonsense, as medical imaging technology has now made clear to everyone."

Joe watched as Dr. Koblinski looked around the now rapidly filling cafeteria. Clearly he was uneasy. Two physicians were now sitting one small table away. "Doctor, why don't we take a walk?" Delgado suggested.

Koblinski's facial muscles appeared to relax. He looked at Joe and said, "Good idea."

Joe got up first, but waited for Koblinski to lead the way out. They walked through the double doors, turned down a long, serpentine corridor antiseptically clean of everything, including people, and came to the back of the building. They emerged into sunlight breaking through a high, hazy cloud cover. Koblinski, folders under his arm, headed toward two park benches amidst a half dozen large oak trees maybe forty yards away. As he arrived at the first bench he used his left arm to brush the accumulated leaves to the ground and motioned for Joe to do the same to the opposite bench.

When they were both seated, Dr. Koblinski sat back and exhaled. "I always have to be careful. The hospital administration and a good many of the physicians know of my advocacy work. They don't have a problem with it as such. But there is an understanding that I won't proselytize on the premises. I'm careful to avoid even the appearance of doing so."

"Does this hospital do abortions?" Joe asked.

Koblinski shook his head emphatically. "I assure you I wouldn't be here if they did."

Joe paused to reflect on how best to pursue his line of inquiry. He had two interests. He wanted to understand where the money trail led in the dirty business of oral contraceptives, and he wanted to know what Dr. Koblinski knew about the potential link between the Pill and breast cancer.

"Doctor, is the U.S. government involved . . . or should I ask . . . *how* is the U.S. government involved?"

Koblinski's head bobbed. "*How* would be the better question, and I will tell you. First let me explain the government's interest in this, dare I call it, 'growth' industry. Unlike corporations, who are often chastised for thinking in terms of quarterly forecasts made or missed, official government bodies are often charged with planning twenty to forty years out."

"What are the strategic coordinates for that planning effort?" Joe interrupted. He owned the strategic planning portfolio for Pittman Labs, but hadn't done much with it. Al Heyworth was proven correct. The oral contraceptive business was gushing cash, and it funded development in a lot of other areas. There was not much pressure from the Board, and therefore Carney, for detailed strategic business plans, built around as yet undiscovered categories of pharmaceutical compounds.

"Demography and technology," Koblinski replied summarily, and Joe was reminded that doctors don't like to be interrupted. "Basic needs, wants, enablers. Not exactly rocket science. And they get it wrong as often as right."

"OK, sorry for the interruption doctor," Joe said, having learned nothing of value and sensing that this was his companion's intent.

"Anyway, the U.S. government understood many years ago where medical science was going. They saw the next big thing, the so called 'new frontier' of scientific discovery, would be Life Sciences and Bio-technology. Whole sectors of global economies would be built around products and services that were barely imaginable, yet entirely feasible, if that makes any sense."

Joe nodded. He didn't follow, but he didn't think it important that he did, yet.

"The U.S. government understands, as do the governments of all the developed nations, that discovery is fundamentally a foot race. You throw money at your best and brightest research houses, and you hope they deliver before, say, the Chinese or, God forbid, the French. The stakes are huge. We're talking here about a nation's GDP growth, the ultimate enabler of its dreams, and therefore a civil society."

As a senior corporate executive, Joe certainly understood the growth imperative. He knew enough about market economies to understand that scientific discovery required business systems to deliver new generations of benefits to a consuming public. And he knew capital markets existed to sort out winners and losers among both the products and the systems. The U.S. economy was over heated and had been for the past six years, so the government didn't have to worry about funding the risk alone. There were plenty of private venture capital firms that would be only too happy to lay down large bets on promising "market makers," as breakthrough products were commonly called. In fact, Joe knew from corporate experience that there were more dollars chasing deals than there were deals. It was, in short, a seller's market. Or in this case, a bioscientist's market. All you needed was the glimmer of an idea . . . and an ability to fog a mirror. *Well, one out of two ain't bad* he told himself.

"The U.S. government will not hand over America's future, and therefore its sovereignty, to foreign interests, so it has decided to become a major player in the field of human embryology," Koblinski continued. "They believe the pot of gold at the end of the rainbow ultimately lies somewhere within the mystery of embryonic stem cells."

Joe blinked. His mind began to race, connecting dots, tying fragments of thoughts together in search of a unifying thread. He needn't have bothered. Dr. Koblinski was on a roll.

"Obviously the good folks in and around Washington now have a serious interest in the debate within the scientific community on the beginning of life. If conception does not in fact occur at 'first contact' fertilization, then our children become fair game at their initial stage of development, the first moment of their existence. They're now in play, so to speak."

"So they . . . their cells and tissues . . . can be harvested?" Joe asked. He was now half on, half off the bench.

"Precisely," Koblinski replied. "All in pursuit of admirable ends, we will be told. These embryonic stem cells will produce miracle cures for all sorts of common maladies."

"You don't believe that for a minute, do you?"

"Of course not. How can you believe in a God of love and truth and also believe that He would imbed the secrets of wondrous cures for human suffering in the DNA of unborn children? That would be a bit too devilishly clever, don't you think?"

Well, that was one way of looking at it, Joe reckoned. "Doctor, please forgive my ignorance. But can you break down the science in this debate for me?"

Koblinski looked pleased to take the question. Not so very long ago the best and brightest kids went to medical school, Joe mused. The business dynamics of affordable healthcare, driven in part by demographic trends in the West in general, and the U.S. in particular, had slowly culled out those who wanted to heal from those who wanted to earn. Joe could see Koblinski was a healer. He saw his world changing around him, but he remained transfixed. There were growing numbers of aging people who needed his unique gifts as a medical internist; his primary focus would forever be on them, not on his investment portfolio—which he could, and did manage himself, so modest was its scope and trajectory.

"I can and I will," Koblinski replied, straightening himself into a more erect posture, the preferred position for more authoritative discourse. "Medical science has long specified that forty-six chromosomes are required to be present in any given cell of an embryo before it can be declared to be living. This is both observable and empirical through a microscopic analysis. When the twenty-three chromosomes of the sperm and the twenty-three chromosomes of the ovum are combined, a new, unique, unrepeatable living individual with forty-six chromosomes has been formed. This happens . . ."

". . . at fertilization," Joe interrupted. He couldn't help himself.

Koblinski ignored him and continued, " . . . at fertilization. Now—the genetic identity, the DNA if you will, of this now human embryo, is qualitatively different from that of its mother and father. We're not talking here about a 'blob,' as our opponents like to claim, of the mother's own tissues. This human embryo is already a boy or girl. He or she already has distinctive human enzymes and proteins forming immediately. Momentarily, distinctive human tissues and organs will be formed. The entire DNA loop is closed at this point. There will be no further genetic information added to or subtracted from this tiny boy or girl for the rest of their life."

Koblinski paused ever so briefly. "I could go on and explain how this original genetic information 'cascades' throughout the development of this new life, determining specific molecular information, totipotency, embryogenesis, trophoblast layers and so forth, but I think you grasp the fundamental point. Human development proceeds along a continuum. It is a continuous process, and one phase merges into another without any real point of demarcation."

Joe thought briefly of sliding off the bench and onto his knees, pleading for detailed information about trophoblast layers, but decided that Dr. Koblinski had given every indication that he did not suffer fools lightly. "What's the other side's argument?" he asked with a full measure of seriousness.

"They attack the 'continuum.'"

"On what basis?"

"They point to certain animal species and contend that development is actually initiated without a 'paternal contribution,' as they refer to it. They further suggest that when the male chromosomes are present in these various species they have been shown to have no effect until well after fertilization."

"What's this have to do with humans?"

"Nothing of course. But that is the point, isn't it?"

"Which animal species are they citing?"

Koblinski waved his hand to dismiss the specifics as unworthy of discussion. "They needed a fig leaf to create a new category of nonpersons. Their chief architect, Clark Sifford, came up with this about ten years ago, and they all jumped on board."

"Why? Why a new category of nonpersons, as you call it?"

"At the time, they needed moral cover for in vitro fertilization experiments being conducted in the U.S. and England. Now, of course, it's about greasing the skids for abortifacients. Tomorrow it will be fetal stem cell research. The day after tomorrow it will be human cloning. The day after that it will be bio-engineering whole categories of 'desirable' human beings. And somewhere down the murky line, I'm sure we'll be cross-breeding humans and animals to create the alpha species of existence. You know, Genesis II stuff."

"Genesis II?"

"Yes. Genesis I, God creates man in his own image and likeness; Genesis II, man creates man in his own image and likeness."

Joe shuddered and fell silent. He thought of his three daughters and the men they would marry, the families they would hope to raise in a brave new world that was already being built by godless men working below the surface of the earth, free from the attention of the rest of mankind. Suddenly, without apparent warning, these "breakthrough scientific achievements," as they would be labeled, would surface and humanity would hold its collective breath, enthralled, before exhaling slowly as the old order of moral certitudes began to slip their collective grasp.

But it would not really be sudden, Joe knew. When their beachhead was finally and fully established, it would be clear that the very men who'd attacked the continuum of life had worked equally hard, for many years, to establish a continuum of death. And they would not permit it to be breached by scientific or moral argument, as indeed they themselves were successful in doing to the continuum established by their Creator.

Joe looked at Koblinski and decided to run that by him. "They've decided to establish their own continuum, haven't they?"

Dr. Koblinski grasped the irony at once. "Yes! The definitive nullification. It's exquisitely demonic."

"How do they package it, this 'big lie,' for mass consumption?" Joe asked. "How do they advance their argument in their trade journals and industry seminars and so forth?"

"Well, it always starts with language," Koblinski replied. "They create new terms and supply meanings for them. In this case, they've established a new definition for the embryo during fertilization. They call it a 'pre-embryo.'"

"A thing."

"Precisely. The pre-embryo has a reduced moral status. About five years ago, the Babcock Commission in England embraced the term and declared that pre-embryos are not to be accorded the same status as a living child. In fact, they went further. They said society itself should have no interest in according a pre-embryo the same protected status as a fetus."

"When do they suggest a 'pre-embryo' becomes a fetus?"

"They're divided," Koblinski smiled disdainfully. "Some of course hold that it is implantation which confers personhood."

"When's that happen?"

"Generally between three to six days."

"What do the others claim?"

"Well, depending on their agenda, anywhere from one week all the way up to nine weeks."

"Nine weeks! Isn't that patently absurd merely on the basis of empirical fact?"

"Of course. But you must remember that the abortifacient industry only needs a window of several days. At the other end of the continuum, if I may use that term, bio-medical researchers need eight to nine weeks to harvest fetal brain tissue. So it all depends on whose child is being gored, if I may mix a metaphor."

Joe winced. He was having a very hard time believing his Church was silent while all this was going on. Particularly because the American bishops had been so vocal of late on nuclear arms and the rights of the poor to higher wages and support from the state. Wasn't this debate worthy of their attention? Didn't the question of when life begins and how it is to be protected prior to birth have an existential significance that the other issues, though certainly worthy of debate, simply lacked?

"Doctor Koblinski, help me understand something. Where the hell have our bishops and theologians been while this battle has been taking form?"

"Institutionally, they have been missing in action. Of course, many have been neutralized by the Catholic physicians who advise them—virtually all of whom prescribe oral contraceptives. Some of our self-described theologians, however, have been active, though not always in constructive ways."

Joe thought perhaps he misunderstood. "Did you say some have been working the other side?"

"Yes," Koblinski replied.

"No!" Joe blurted, incredulously.

"You asked earlier how our government got involved. Let me tell you how. About ten years ago, President Carter's Secretary for Health, Education, and Welfare, a Catholic from Brooklyn named Jim DeMarco, formed an Ethics Advisory Board, many of whose members also served on something called the Ethics Committee for the American Fertility Society. DeMarco knew just enough to figure out how to co-opt the Catholic Church on what he understood would be a contentious debate to say the least."

"Rent a theologian." Joe interjected.

This time Koblinski didn't ignore the interruption. "Correct," he affirmed. "DeMarco went right to the list of dissenters from *Humanae Vitae*. At the top of the list he found a Jesuit by the name of Johan Schneider. He offered Schneider what he coveted most, entrée into the inner circle of secular influence. In return, DeMarco got the Church's imprimatur, ex officio of course, on some highly dubious science and some abhorrent ethical principles."

Joe nodded. He intuited that somehow the first step on the continuum of death must have involved an attempt to separate the twin inextricable dimensions of the marital embrace—what were commonly called its unitive and procreative purposes. Bonding and babies, in perhaps clearer terms. "So what did this guy Schneider do to earn his thirty pieces of silver?"

"About what you might expect. He argued that the child does not become a child until fourteen days after fertilization. This was his contribution to what he termed the centuries-old debate within the Church on 'ensoulment'—the moment when God infuses a soul into a human being created in His own image and likeness. Within the institutional Church, there has been no such debate of course. Nevertheless, with this established in his own mind as fact, Schneider went on to define the human embryo as a 'pre-embryo' or 'pre-person,' or perhaps even more absurdly, a 'non-personal human' possessing something less than full moral status as a human person."

"DeMarco's committee probably couldn't believe their ears."

"Yes, here was a gift from . . . well . . . certainly not heaven."

"But surely Schneider must have been taken to a woodshed by somebody?"

"On the contrary, he sought shelter within his order—the Jesuits. And the Jesuits have always been protective of their renegades. At least since Teilhard de Chardin."

Joe understood the reference to the widely acclaimed French Jesuit anthropologist who once claimed to have discovered the "missing link" in support of Darwin's theory of evolution. The so-called 'Piltdown Man' was eventually exposed as a hoax, but that didn't seem to tarnish Teilhard's credentials within the order and their orbit of influence as serious anthropologists.

"So nobody stood up to him?"

"Well, we did. I personally wrote a series of articles rebutting Schneider that the Catholic Medical Association tried to have published in the Kennedy Institute of Ethics Journal . . . "

Joe grinned. "Excuse me, but isn't that what's known as an oxymoron?"

Koblinski indulged him with a small smile. ". . . the Journal of National Medicine, and the Mid-Atlantic Journal of Medicine."

"Tried? You mean they wouldn't publish a counter-argument from an authentic Catholic source?"

Koblinski simply shook his head, and Joe could see he hit a nerve. "Well, so much for the compatibility of faith and reason," he offered, with more than a hint of irony. "I'm afraid our Church has let you down, Doctor."

"I wouldn't say that. Our Church, Mr. Delgado, is the Mystical Body of Christ. She has been the lone indispensable guide to man for going on two thousand years. From time to time she may have some weak men at the helm, but that has never stopped a serious Catholic in ancient or modern times from having access to the truth about what is good for man and what is not."

"Meaning someone, somewhere in the hierarchy knows right from wrong and will tell you, assuming you know where to look?"

Koblinski rejected the cynicism. "Meaning, Mr. Delgado, wherever you find bishops who are united with the bishop of Rome on a doctrinal or moral precept, you can be certain the Holy Spirit is speaking. Christ promised us that. I tend to take Him at His word."

Joe grimaced. This man was obviously a true believer. "And on the matter of the beginning of life . . ."

"The Church has never wavered. Life begins at conception. And conception occurs at fertilization, not implantation."

Joe marveled at Koblinski's fortitude. Somewhere along the line he had made a decision to fight the good fight, in season and out. Nothing would derail him. Not scandal, not cowardice, not ineptness. All of those faults were understood as a mere manifestation of concupiscence present in all men since the Fall. The Church, in his mind and in the minds of men like him, was ever good, ever noble, ever holy. Because at its core it was divine.

"Dr. Koblinski, you have been a blessing to me," Joe said somewhat awkwardly. "I mean that. I don't know what I'll do, if anything, with all the information you've shared with me. I still don't even understand how we ended up together this morning. But I'm going to do some thinking, probably some praying too, and try to figure out what the good Lord wants from me."

Koblinski nodded but did not comment. He began to gather his files, which lay next to him on the bench. "Well, I best be getting to work," he said, getting up stiffly.

"Doctor, just one more question. If I wanted to talk to someone about the link between abortifacients and breast cancer, could . . . would . . . you direct me to someone knowledgeable?"

Koblinski didn't hesitate. "Sure. You have my number. There are several people I could hook you up with." He turned to go, took a step, then swung around again, "You know, there is a substantial and growing body of medical evidence that the link is strong and documentable."

"I don't doubt it for a minute, Doctor," Joe called out as he departed. Koblinski, walking briskly, was now already halfway to the back entrance of the hospital and didn't acknowledge his rejoinder.

Slowly, Joe began to make his way to the parking garage. His wife was waiting for him, no doubt impatiently. She would have many questions. But for once, he would have even more.

40

Michael and Carol Burns sat in lawn chairs under two huge oak trees on the sprawling front lawn of their three-acre property. Their large farmhouse was behind them, a one-acre pond stocked with bass and perch and blue gill lay at some distance in front of them. Around their perimeter romped five children, including two infant boys crawling in opposite directions on an oversized beach blanket. It was a warm mid-summer Sunday afternoon. The sun was bright. The children were happy. And Michael Burns was grateful for his many blessings.

"I wish you didn't have to go out of town tomorrow," Carol said, breaking a blissful silence. Michael sympathized. His wife's family, unlike his own, were all back in Philadelphia. She was inherently reserved and not given to cultivating relationships outside of family. She didn't have to. She was the fifth of ten children. There were more than enough relationships for her to manage in her own bloodline.

She also hated to be alone, particularly in a large home with small children. Their farmhouse was about three miles outside of town. There were neighbors within sight, if not earshot, and the surrounding area was known to be largely crime-free and well-policed. Michael didn't worry about his family's safety. Indeed he had carefully researched the town, including its police records, before settling his family there. He did not regret his decision. Nor did Carol, he knew.

"I wish I didn't have to go too," he replied. This, he knew, wouldn't completely end his wife's lament, but it would direct it away from him and toward his work. Carol did not like the advertising business, but she loved her husband unconditionally and she knew he would never be satisfied unless his competitive fires were tested against the very best in his field. That meant uprooting immediate family, leaving her childhood family, and ultimately disengaging from a way of life that was purposefully integrated and reasonably serene.

They had made the decision to go to New York together, and although she voiced reservations initially, she was encouraged when their parish priest, Father John Sweeney, had blessed the plan, even suggesting there might be a hint of divine intention at work. He reasoned that Michael was a forceful, persuasive, believing Christian who would arrive in New York at a critical juncture in the development of the American entertainment media. As he saw it, the men and women creating the new media would either seize the opportunity to produce material that inspired virtue and hope among America's families . . . or they would veer in the opposite direction, creating instead more nihilism and despair, suctioning the other parts of the media world into a death spiral with them. Carol took some comfort in the hope that their personal sacrifice would bring a measure of relief to good families all over the country who, like the Burnses, were growing increasingly concerned about the content of America's entertainment product.

"Why do you have to go again?"

Michael groaned inwardly. They had been through this several times during the past week, without resolution. In fairness, this would be the sort of extended trip that Michael had been fairly successful at avoiding since his arrival at the Hal Ross agency. He would be gone the better part of two weeks, monitoring focus groups in ten cities, which were carefully selected for their demography and cable television purchase patterns. At the end of the first week he was due to arrive in Southern California, which would permit him, after his work was concluded, to catch up with one of his brothers who was a successful commercial real estate agent in Newport Beach. They would play some golf, catch a ballgame, and hit the beach with his brother's wife and four children. Michael did not share that part of his itinerary with his wife, knowing that she would ask him to come home for the weekend. To him this made no sense, because he had to fly back across the country the following Monday for more focus groups in San Francisco. He really hoped the conversation didn't go there.

"I have to find out why so many families who could buy Cable Movie Network don't, and why those who do disconnect in such large numbers."

"Because the programming is toxic. There, I just saved you two weeks and CMN hundreds of thousands of dollars."

"Stupid me," Michael retorted, smiling. "Why didn't I think of that? How about I schedule a meeting of their senior executives tomorrow morning. I'll introduce you as my wife, the mother of my five children, and CMN's prototypical customer and say you've unlocked the mystery of the vanishing customer base. Then you just get up and say, 'Your network sucks' and sit down."

"OK!" Carol said a bit too enthusiastically. Michael had to concede that, for all her obvious attributes, and there were many, his wife was not a particularly long-term thinker.

"You'll explain it to the kids, then . . . the part about not having a home?" he said.

"Why can't you just tell them?"

"The kids?"

"No, CMN."

"They wouldn't believe me."

"Why not?"

"They would claim I was making excuses to distract attention from what they like to refer to as our horse manure—by which they mean our advertising."

"Well, your advertising isn't as bad as their product."

"Thank you for that magnanimous concession."

"What will you do on the weekend? Why can't you at least come home then?"

Michael on occasion had chosen to selectively withhold information, almost always to serve the interests of marital accord, but he made it a practice never to dissemble. "I'll be out on the West Coast for about five days. It wouldn't make sense for me to fly back and then out again just for a day, would it?"

"No, I suppose not," Carol said, somewhat forlornly. Then she brightened, "Hey, we'll just meet you out there!"

Michael flipped the rest of the *New York Times* on the blanket and scurried after one of the boys, he didn't know which one, who'd managed to roll himself to safety on the freshly cut lawn. He came up for air with grass clippings matted to all sides of his little bald head. This drew laughter from his older sisters, who rushed to his aid, vexing him to tears. "Three women servants to attend your every whim and you're still not satisfied," Michael said to the sobbing toddler. Then to his wife, "OK, hon. You get 'em all out there, I'll get a place for all of us to stay."

That seemed to end the discussion.

41

Michael slept in the following morning and caught a limo to the departure gate at Newark International around 11:00 for an 11:30 a.m. commuter flight to Boston. The first group wasn't scheduled until 5:00 p.m., but he wanted to arrive early to scout the setup and prep the moderator. And, truth be told, the Sox had a 1:30 day game at Fenway against the Yankees. Hey, he assured himself, it was going to be a long road trip.

When he arrived at the terminal, he immediately ran into Ron Ashley, CMN's marketing director. "Hey . . . Burnsie!" he called out from maybe thirty yards away. Michael felt heads turning and wondered which of the Ashley personalities would accompany him through this first leg of the road trip. It seemed the trip was about to get longer.

"Hey, Ron," Michael said, extending his hand as Ashley approached. "Good to see you. I didn't think you guys were coming in until mid-afternoon."

"Most are. But I'm gonna catch Guidry at Fenway. Want to join me? I can get you a ticket. Our cable distributors up there can score anything."

"Can't think of anything I'd rather do," Michael replied, trapped. "Just as long as we can get to the site by 4:00."

"No problem. We'll just leave the stadium at 3:15. We'll catch six, maybe seven innings."

Michael got in line at the counter for his boarding pass. Ashley followed, blathering on about this and that. Michael had little difficulty tuning him out. Men like Ashley, he'd discovered, really didn't require much attention. They just basically wanted to lease your ears for a fairly exhaustive mind dump while they perpetually scanned the vicinity to sight a fresh pair approaching.

They boarded the plane, assigned to random seating. Ashley found an aisle seat next to Michael's. Michael opened the *Times* and gave Ashley the sports section, hoping it would quiet him for maybe fifteen minutes. It didn't. He waxed authoritative on the American League pennant race, the upcoming NFL season, and several pending boxing matches in weight classes Michael didn't know existed. Michael continued reading, nodding his head ever so slightly from time to time.

Soon they were airborne. Michael could hear the hum of the engines and soon realized that Ashley had fallen silent. He looked over and saw his companion napping, mouth open. Michael immediately pulled the research proposal from his black shoulder bag. It included an executive summary from the field survey, an itinerary, and the final discussion guide for each of the two groups they would interview in the ten cities.

The field survey produced something of an interesting revelation. Both the "nonbuyer" cell and the "trier/rejector" cell sited the same dual reasons for not purchasing CMN, or purchasing and disconnecting. Michael summarized the objections as "cost and content," and the research firm, which Camfy had selected from among National Publishing's approved vendor list, termed that labeling as "workable." Michael understood that "workable," roughly translated, meant "we can't at the moment think of a good reason why that doesn't adequately summarize the six to eight problems we've uncovered in the two cells, but give us a little time." They'd had their time and his labeling held, even withstanding the constant niggling that was part of the National Publishing culture, a not altogether inessential factor in their storied success, Michael conceded.

It was an important consideration in Michael's mind. If the decision not to purchase CMN and the decision to disconnect among those who'd purchased could be framed as a "value" issue, not a "content" or "moral value" issue, Michael believed he would have a better chance of making some headway with the people who controlled the network's programming model. Ultimately, this would mean Richard Kloss.

The executive summary of the field survey made it clear that the concept of paying for television was a turn-off, so to speak, for roughly two-thirds of the nation. They responded to their telephone interviewers in the clearest terms that they felt no sense of deprivation from whatever it was they were supposed to be missing out on. Of the third of the country that did elect to buy a cable television service, some two-thirds of them chose only the basic cable package, which was devoid of any so-called "premium" or "pay" channels like CMN. In rural areas, this purchase was driven largely by "reception"—meaning that the only way families in what are called "C" and "D" county areas could get clear reception for network television and their local news was to subscribe to a cable television service.

Cable television's penetration of large metropolitan areas, the country's "A" and "B" counties, generally lagged rural areas for two reasons. Clear reception itself was a nonissue in these areas; and big city municipalities were governed by soul-deadening bureaucracies that demanded the equivalent of every cable operator's first, middle, and last child in return for a license to wire homes. The so-called "wiring" of America was proceeding in a "two steps forward, one step backward" pace that greatly frustrated the men who owned and operated multiple cable systems. They risked huge amounts of borrowed capital to bulk their companies up to wire America's large cities, and they needed to show their bankers and venture capitalist backers that there was a return on their investment out there somewhere.

Yet something was driving the inexorable growth of the cable television industry in the United States. Michael believed the answer lay in "the third" of the third. The third of cable television buyers who bought CMN in addition to their basic cable package. This "third of a third" was the engine driving not only the business in rural American communities; it was also the gun to the head that cable operators used to pressure municipal bureaucracies. "The people are demanding it, your city's coffers require it, what the hell are you waiting for?" was more or less the operators' appeal.

Ultimately, big city fathers believed the entertainment portion of the "wired package" was simply the cherry on the sundae. They understood that real economic growth would be driven by a whole array of information and communications services that were at the moment nothing but a gleam in the eye of Silicon Valley entrepreneurs. So they herded their bureaucratic cats in the direction of constituent demand and opened city hall for business. And thus, slowly but inexorably, the wiring of America proceeded.

But Michael was intrigued by something in the data. The "third of a third" was roughly ten percent. And half of that ten percent made the decision each year to disconnect CMN. The reason they disconnected seemed to have something to do with the actual content of the programming. Perhaps there may indeed be a culture war quietly playing itself out in living rooms across the country. Main Street drawing a line in its resistance to Hollywood values at its own front door. Would that rate of resistance, he wondered, hold through the wiring of major American cities? If it did, what changes would it force in the cable television, and CMN, business and programming models? And how might those changes impact the wiring of America itself?

More importantly, he now mused at roughly ten thousand feet over the Atlantic Ocean, what impact would the wiring of America have on the culture of America? Could the five percent of families living in wired areas that appeared satisfied with CMN's programming content really establish a beachhead for . . . God knows what? What indeed would follow salacious movies into American homes, Michael wondered? He was hopeful that these focus groups would help answer at least the most preliminary of these questions.

Michael requested that the focus group moderator utilize what he liked to call "the rolling why" with the various panels in the ten cities. That meant following up each answer to a question asked by the moderator with a "why." In practical terms, "Why did you buy, not buy, or buy and disconnect, CMN?" "Why was *that* important to you?" "And why was *that* important to you and your family?" This technique, Michael theorized, would help place the purchase decision at the intersection of family values. It would help determine how far up the value chain the advertising could go without hitting a discordant note. It was an "outside in" approach. The technique permitted the ultimate consumer of the product to define its "end benefit" in his or her own terms. This ultimately served to narrow the risk element in creating advertising and buying time and space to place it—which was an enormously expensive and therefore risky proposition.

Michael looked again at the itinerary. He was involved in its configuration and was generally satisfied with the final result. They were starting in Boston, and from there they would head south to Atlanta. They would move west along the southern tier of the country, stopping in Birmingham and Phoenix before arriving in San Diego on Friday. Michael was very much looking forward to that stop and his reunion up the Pacific coast with his brother. The following Monday they would be in San Francisco. Then they would move north to Eugene, Oregon on Tuesday and begin heading back east with stops in Denver, St. Louis, and Columbus, Ohio.

In each of these cities, the actual focus groups would be held outside the city limits in areas that most closely mirrored the demographic and purchasing patterns of cable television customers and those who had tried and ultimately rejected CMN. With ten groups in each cell—cable nonbuyers and CMN trier/rejecters—they would ultimately end up talking with somewhere between one hundred and one hundred twenty consumers. Not quite projectable at a ninety-five percent "confidence interval"—the standard for quantitative field surveys—but the findings would certainly be more than "directional" and would not only "put a face" on the field survey but, at these numbers, define the features and add a "voice." To Michael, it was important that whatever they came back with have a fundamental legitimacy. It could not be dismissible as the unenlightened opinions of a handful of rubes in "red state" America.

"Loosianna Lightnin'!" It was Ashley, awake and hungering for diversion. Mercifully, the plane was in its descent and would be on the ground in less than five minutes. Michael steeled himself. "You're right, Ashman. Ron Guidry is a marvel." This innocuous rejoinder set his companion off on a soliloquy about the improbability of a 165-pound man throwing a baseball past major league hitters at 95 miles per hour for over 2 hours every 5th day of the spring, summer, and early fall . . . and doing it for 10 years. Yes, Michael nodded in silent assent, Yankee ace Ron Guidry was indeed a marvel.

42

Michael was fuming as he entered the cab outside Fenway with Ron Ashley in tow. It was 4:20 p.m. and they were late. He had been unable to extricate his companion from his running conversations with at least three different groups of rabid Sox fans. They'd taken to "playing" Ashley, who was of course oblivious to it. They induced him to bet substantial sums on particular "pitcher–hitter" matchups, the majority of which Guidry, and thus Ashley, won. When it came time to collect, however, the Sox fans pleaded for "double or nothing" stakes in subsequent matchups. Ashley, ever New York confident, was only too eager to roll the bets over. When Michael insisted on leaving at 3:15, Ashley determined that he had too much riding to leave. One hour later, when it became obvious even to Ashley that he would collect no money that day, they finally left—Ashley in full rant, Michael in sullen silence.

The groups were being held in Lynn, a town on the North Shore about an hour from Fenway under normal conditions. With the late start, however, they would catch rush hour traffic out of

Boston and would arrive at the Lynn Shopping Center at least twenty minutes late, a prospect that was totally unacceptable to Michael, who had booked an early flight to avoid just this possibility. He had made an error in judgment. It was a mistake to have accompanied Ashley to the ballpark. Once there, he couldn't very well leave his host in a state of self-induced distress. This was not a good way to begin his business trip, and he berated himself for his poor decision as the cab sat on the Mass Pike going nowhere.

It was 5:40 when Michael tossed a twenty-dollar bill through the window that separated passengers and driver and bolted the cab before it came to a full stop. He reached the door in full stride, looking for the sign directing the respondents to the research center in the rear of the east wing of the mall. He broke into a run that left Ashley, who was not equally gifted moving his legs as he was his lips, struggling to keep up. When Michael finally arrived he was perspiring heavily, despite the mall's perfectly adequate cooling systems. He entered to find a young site co-coordinator representing the mall sitting alone in the reception area. She jumped to her feet, handed him a small towel, and said, "We got started late. It's only been going on for about ten minutes. Let me fix you a plate." She pointed to the beverage table next to the buffet spread and said, "Hey, let me get you something cold first. What do you want?"

Michael signaled for a soft drink and started toweling his forehead and neck. He was embarrassed but relieved. The first ten minutes was only about introductions and ground rules anyway. Moments later, Ashley arrived out of sorts and out of breath. "If you didn't get a head start out of the cab, I would have beaten you here," he said in breathless rasps. Michael heard the young woman break into laughter and watched Ashley fix her with a glare and say, "I was all-conference in the 440 in high school." The girl turned red and busied herself at the serving table. Michael felt badly for her and said, "Ask him how many years ago that was." Ashley laughed, and the tension was relieved.

Michael accepted his cold drink and a small plate filled with various deli cuts and salads, motioning for Ashley to follow him when he was ready into the darkened, bay-windowed, sound-proof room behind the large conference room in which the focus group was presently being moderated. He entered to jeers, as anticipated. "Hey Burnsie, good of you to drop in. Can you stay for both sessions?" And, from one of the CMN programming women, "Burnsie, how'd you ditch Ashley, find him a woman?" Michael grinned good-naturedly and seethed inside.

The first group included seven women and four men who'd elected not to buy the basic cable package offered by their local distributor. Cable operators generally expected CMN executives to build demand for the basic cable package through the aggressive marketing of their own network—which was only offered as a "tier," or an extension, of their basic package. The barriers to purchase, therefore, needed to be understood. The field survey suggested that somewhere between 10 to 15 percent of the nonbuyer segment could be converted, at least to basic cable, if they were convinced there were things being offered that they really wanted to see. An important part of the assignment was to ferret out what those things were and how strongly nonbuyers felt about them.

The groups were being moderated by a woman named Yashima Brown, a partner in the firm of Gaffney and Froehlich Research Associates in New York. Ms. Brown was a Princeton graduate about seven years removed. She was extremely bright and effortlessly gregarious. She was also reputed to be tough, which Michael believed was critical in controlling focus groups that tended to be dominated by one or more outspoken panelists. She was the eldest of five daughters of a Baptist minister and a high school English teacher from Birmingham, Alabama. She was the first in her family to go to college and the first to reach back and help the others. She'd taken in one of her sisters who was trying to break into the New York fashion industry, and was helping to pay the college tuition for another who was studying computer technology at Emory University in Atlanta. Like Michael, she too had planned family reunions around scheduled stops on the itinerary.

The eleven panelists skewed slightly blue-collar, but there was a smattering of people who looked like urban professionals, no doubt helping to re-gentrify a section of the old mill town on the North Shore. Yashima quickly dispensed with the formalities and began probing current viewing patterns and preferences. It yielded little by way of surprises.

She then probed reservations about cable television in general and any biases or preconceived opinions about "pay television" or CMN, in particular. One woman whose tent card placed in front of her identified her as "Yolanda" got heads nodding when she said, "There's a lotta things on cable I don't want my family seein'." Yashima's first instinct was not to explore what, in fact, those things were but the very idea of wives and mothers as gate-keepers—deciding which types of programming made it into the family living room. Michael was impressed.

Another woman, Theresa, responded to Yashima's gatekeeper question by saying, "Somebody's got to be the mommy. You can't have kids decide what the family watches on TV."

"What about husbands and fathers?" Yashima asked.

Several of the women grunted and Yashima reminded them that the sessions were being taped, and that inaudible sounds didn't transcribe themselves in a particularly coherent fashion. This drew a comment from a panelist named Carole, "You certainly can't let the men decide. They'd tell the kids to go to bed and sit there watching porn if you let them."

Yashima asked if this was a "cause of tension" in the home, "No cable. No tension," said Yolanda. A number of the women nodded.

Yashima probed the men, "Who made the cable TV decision in your house, Jack?"

Jack looked to be in his early thirties and, not having heard the introductions, Michael guessed he was a middle manager at one of Boston's large insurance firms. "My wife. I told her we ought to look into it, but she just said we ought to wait until there's more quality and more choice available."

Yashima followed up quickly, "What kind of quality and what kind of choice?"

Jack looked like he had been caught without his homework, and the CMN crowd behind the glass skewered him, "Better check with the boss, Jack, before you answer." And "Quick Jack, top or bottom?"

Jack didn't help himself with the CMN swarm when he answered, "She likes concerts and foreign films . . . and . . ."

"Porn," yelled one of the CMN representatives in the darkness, to raucous laughter. Despite the commercial-grade quality of the soundproofing, Michael noticed the heads of several participants swivel in the direction of the one-way mirror. He immediately tried to shush the group. Another error in judgment. First responder, "Who woke Burns up?" Next voice, "Burns, go tell that whore to untie Ashley." More laughter. Michael winced. He was half tempted to retrieve Ashley, who was no doubt enjoying his dinner and the opportunity to make a pass at the comely project coordinator, but he knew Ashley would enter the back room and immediately look for a seat near him. This grief was preferable to that, he assured himself.

The first group ended about forty minutes later, and the lights went up in the observation room. After the respondents filed out, Yashima left the conference room and joined the group. "What did y'all think?" she asked of no one in particular.

With the lights up, Michael counted about sixteen or so CMN representatives in the small room. Three worked for Kloss. Two of them were young African-American gentlemen who looked to be in their late twenties. Michael had met them before and was favorably disposed to each. The third member of Kloss' group was a single woman, Rhonda Silver; she was in her early forties and did not enjoy the goodwill of her colleagues, who commonly referred to her, less than affectionately, as "the bitch." Nonetheless, she was there to protect Kloss' interests, an agenda she made no attempt to hide, and would therefore be a force to be reckoned with. It was she who spoke first, "I think that group was a total waste of time. Why even bother talking to people who don't have either the discretionary income or the discretion itself to plug themselves into the twenty-first century?"

As elitist statements went, Michael thought it was an interesting first salvo. The "swarm," predictably, fell silent. Where was Ashley when you needed him, Michael wondered? He wanted to avoid staking out a position on anything in these groups, much less the obvious categorical value of talking face to face, through a moderator and a one-way mirror, with the customer. But nobody was rising to meet her challenge. So against his better judgment, Michael heard himself say, "Actually, I think there were a couple of interesting insights that surfaced in that group, and by the way, terrific job Yashima." This drew the chorus of support that Michael thought Yashima deserved, but also served to rid the room, temporarily, of negative energy.

"Such as?" Ms. Silver demanded.

"Such as women emerging as gatekeepers," Michael responded casually.

"That's not new," Ms. Silver challenged.

"Well, if it came out in the field survey, I'm not aware of it. Maybe I just missed it," Michael added diplomatically.

"Of course women are going to have a say. The country's only twenty-five percent Irish, Burns."

Michael heard at least one gasp but didn't look in that direction. He was conscious of a roomful of eyes redirecting themselves toward him. He struggled not merely to bite his tongue but to mask his attempt to do so. "Well, we're working hard on that Rhonda. Some of us harder than others."

The room erupted, breaking the tension. Yashima seized the opportunity and probed, again, "How about others?"

Of the nearly twenty members of CMN's marketing department who made the trip from New York, including Ashley,

Michael thought that no more than four needed to be there, and even one of those was marginal. But the unwritten provision in the contract between the Hal Ross agency and CMN called for the agency to help train the cohort of aspiring marketers at the network. Most of them didn't know what they didn't know, and this always made the task more difficult. Michael promised Zimmer and Camfy he would do the best he could, and indeed he tried. But there were times when his patience simply ran out. As he waited for one of them to say something, anything, constructive, Ashley walked in with a small splotch of mustard on one of his cheeks and announced, "Great group. Super job, Yashima."

"What did you get out of it, Ron?" Yashima asked, gently.

Ashley straightened his carriage. "Great misconceptions about what's in the basic cable package. Total confusion about what we're all about . . . CMN. A general misunderstanding on our part of the role of the woman in the purchase decision." He paused briefly. "Shall I go on?"

"Yes," Michael muttered to himself. "For once, please, go on."

"In other words, a classic marketing challenge," Bob Herbert, Ashley's assistant, offered.

"Not even. Just basic education," Ashley pounced. "It's just telling people the basics about what will come to be regarded as the greatest contribution to American culture since the invention of the kinescope."

Michael sensed eyes rolling in the back, and he wanted to build on the good in what Ashley said, "It'll be interesting to see how the second group handles the same issues. I'm particularly interested to see how the woman in the home factors into the CMN decision—both to purchase the service and to retain it." This, a baldly naked signal to Ms. Silver that he was incapable of being intimidated.

"Anybody else?" Yashima probed one last time.

Silence.

"OK. Second group begins in forty-five minutes," Yashima said. "Anybody with last-minute suggestions on the discussion guide, see me in the conference room, please."

. . .

As the second group of panelists filed into the conference room and around the large elliptical table shortly after 7:00 p.m., the CMN "swarm" behind the glass began to settle themselves into comfortable chairs behind ascending rows of tables. Michael found a seat in the last row. Ashley found one next to him.

On the other side of the glass Yashima initiated a brief discussion of ground rules. "I thank you all for coming. Each of you made a decision to subscribe to CMN; and each of you made a decision to cancel your subscription. We have some folks on the other side of this mirror who are very interested in what you have to say about your experience with CMN. We are recording this session, so please try to speak audibly. It is important that we hear from everyone, so don't be timid. If I sense some of you are holding back, I will come after you like a heat-seeking missile." Big smile. Nervous laughs. "Does anyone have any questions? OK, let's go around the table and introduce ourselves. Names and occupations, please."

The CMN "swarm" edged up in their seats. This was theater, an opportunity to one-up their colleagues as dukes of derision. Michael thought the small room suddenly had the look, sound, and smell of a frat house with the six women determined to prove themselves worthy of the rush. There were twelve panelists, eight of whom were women. They appeared to represent a mix of blue and white-collar families within the target age band of twenty-five thru fifty-four. There were two African-American women and one man, but no Hispanics or Asians, Michael noted.

"Mah name is Tamiqua and my question is, where y'all hidin' Ron Ashley at?" It was Curt Welsh, national field marketing manager and resident mimic. The first of the two African-American women had just introduced herself, and Welsh was the first to get off. Michael waited for the others to advise him he'd just crossed the line. No one did. Instead, John Quinnock, a regional field marketing manager, piled on, "My name is Bruce, and I am a homosexual. I cancelled my subscription because CMN only shows heterosexuals fornicating." From there, things descended rapidly. Michael thought about leaving and monitoring the panel from the reception area, which was miked, but decided against it, knowing that it would only redirect attention to him. Instead, he stood up and made his way down the steps toward the one-way mirror, inclining his head as he did so toward the large speaker up on the wall. A sufficient number of the "swarm" understood the signal and fell into an uneasy silence.

Yashima dove into her work. "First, let me ask this question, and let's go around the table. Why did you subscribe to CMN?"

Woman number one, Peggy, "I thought it was all part of the package. I didn't know until the bill came that it was extra. I canceled right away."

Woman number two, Susan, "We liked the idea of uncut Hollywood movies in the home. But in any given month there are only a couple of good movies, and they repeat them over and over. It just didn't seem worth the extra money."

The first male respondent, Glenn, "I bought it for the specials, the concerts, and the boxing matches. There just weren't enough of them to justify the expense."

Another woman, Alexandra, "My husband wanted it, I didn't. After a while, he lost interest, and I just cancelled our subscription. He never complained."

This got Michael's attention and said aloud, "Follow, follow."

Yashima's instincts were true. "Tell me about that. Why did your husband want to subscribe, and why did you resist initially?"

Alexandra paused. She was reluctant to share private discussions in public. Yashima, sensing this, offered gentle encouragement, "I say this to all of you. Whatever it is you have experienced with a particular product or service, I guarantee you others have experienced the very same thing. So don't be afraid to share. We've all been there."

This helped. Alexandra appeared to relax a bit and said, "My husband wanted the so-called 'great movies.' I didn't think they'd be so great for the family. We watched a few as a family, and they were bad. My husband didn't even like them, but he'd watch anyway, and I had to put the kids to bed. It created a tension between us. Why pay for that?"

"So it was his decision to subscribe, but it was your decision to cancel?" ask Yashima.

"Yes. But if he hadn't lost interest, I'm not sure I would have been able to do it."

"I understand," said Yashima. "Let me ask the group a question. Show of hands. In how many families was the decision to subscribe either made or strongly encouraged by the male head of household?"

Michael counted ten of twelve hands raised.

"Good. Now, in how many cases was the decision to cancel either made or strongly encouraged by the woman of the house?"

Again, ten of twelve hands were raised. Michael looked at the two men who had not raised their hands and wondered if they would have responded in the same way if their wives were present.

Yashima was on the hunt. "OK. Talk to me. Obviously there was an expectations gap, at least with respect to husbands. They expected one thing and experienced another. And I want to probe that. But first tell me why you women resisted initially, and cancelled ultimately."

Brief pause. Gerry, who'd been quiet, spoke first. "I knew it was wrong. I told my husband it would be bad for the kids. He said it wouldn't be that bad. But it was."

Mary Alise: "This was my fault. I don't blame my husband. We were all watching the movie *Lipstick*. It was a Sunday night. All of a sudden there was a rape scene. A rape of a child. It was very graphic. My husband and I were both frozen. We couldn't believe what we were seeing. He turned it off, and I rushed the kids to bed. We cancelled the next morning."

In the dark, Michael shuddered.

Frank: "When we subscribed, I wouldn't let the kids in the room when I had it on, for exactly that reason. So my reason for canceling is a bit different. The movies just aren't any good. The so-called big box office films are driven by what the kids like. They're the ones who actually go to movies. Who in here goes to more than one or two movies a year?"

Yashima permitted the question, but no hands were raised. Again, Michael suspected there were some panelists who did go to more than two movies a year, but he knew from experience that no one in such a setting wants to appear out of the mainstream.

Yashima regained control. "Let me direct this to the women. Why do you think your husband offered little or no resistance when you decided to cancel?"

Alexandra: "In my case, he could see I felt strongly about it."

Gerry: "My husband's out in the world all day and when he comes home he wants a refuge. He counts on me to provide it. If there's tension, for any reason, he'll detect it. So he'll give me wide berth on deciding what's best in the home."

Somewhere in the dark Michael knew that Rhonda Silver had to be writhing in pain. The thought of her distress greatly consoled him.

Yashima: "Let me ask the men—what did you think you were going to get when you subscribed to CMN, and were there any surprises?"

Len: "I thought I'd come home to a good movie every night. That was unrealistic, looking back. But one good movie a month isn't asking a lot. And lots of months there isn't anything on there worth watching."

Glenn: "I think Frank hit on it. The kids make or break Hollywood movies. They're not made for us old timers. We're probably a little slow to get that. To the people behind the glass from CMN, I'd say, 'Make your own movies. And make good ones. You'll end up with more people subscribing and less people canceling.'"

This brought forth the expected full measure of fury behind the glass.

"Thanks a lot jerk! Now get a freaking job."

And, "Hey moron. Go collect your lousy fifty bucks and find yourself another whore."

And this from Ashley, trying to ingratiate himself with the others, "Hey Burnsie, I thought you said you didn't have any relatives up here."

Michael felt the warm flush of anger in the pit of his stomach. He fought its rise and emergence with everything in him, knowing full well that the report of whatever he said or did would be on the desks of both Camfy and Zimmer by morning. He didn't want any wakeup calls to his hotel room asking him to return to New York because he hurled a client through a plate glass window. He put a folded forefinger in his mouth and bit down hard.

Yashima finished the session, probing everything put in play in careful detail. Michael was beyond delighted with her performance, and he realized that she would pull everything there was to pull out of every group put in front of her. A lot of questions were going to get answered over the next two weeks. Despite the grief, it was all good.

The lights went up, and there was some uneasy shuffling. Ashley was the first to speak, "Good group. Very good, actually. Not what we wanted to hear, but it's what we're here to hear."

Melissa McCarthy, an associate field marketing manager, followed, "It was interesting to see the difference between men and women. The acquisition strategy has to be built around the man; the retention strategy has to be directed to the woman. It's an interesting marketing challenge."

This triggered a response from Rhonda Silver, "What did we learn that we didn't already know from our own research?"

Awkward pause. Then Ron Ashley, rising to the challenge, "All of it. The need to balance, or meet, the expectations of men. The need for a technology solution for women to block children from being able to access programming. Most importantly, the need to diffuse the tension the current programming model creates in at least some homes. I would say to all of you that our biggest challenge is how to make CMN an inextricable part of the in-home family experience. I assure you that we will not solve this problem with better marketing alone." Then, looking at Rhonda, "Both sides of the house are going to have to do their part."

"Hot damn," Michael muttered to himself. How he loved that Ron Ashley.

43

It was close to 2:00 p.m. the following day when Michael checked into the Ritz Carlton in Buckhead, an exclusive enclave within the heart of steamy downtown Atlanta. When he entered his room, which was cool and dark with its drapes and shades drawn, he saw the red light on the telephone flashing. He dropped his bags on the oversized bed and picked up the receiver to check for messages. There was one. It was from Ron Ashley, who'd flown in on an earlier flight. He debated whether to return the call now or let it wait until he saw Ashley at tonight's sessions in Decatur, about a half hour east of the city. He decided to dial Ashley's room, hoping that perhaps he'd be out.

"Ashley," boomed the voice on the other end.

"Ron, Michael."

Pause. "Oh, yeah, Burnsie. Hey . . . we've got a problem."

"What is it?"

"The bitch wants Yashima sent home."

"What! . . . who . . . why?"

"She claims she's biased."

"Biased! How?" Michael was fuming and, he was aware, sputtering.

"Toward the agency."

Michael was so outraged he simply couldn't collect himself. The notion that this consummate young professional, who was at this moment enjoying a mini-reunion with her younger sister somewhere in town, was in the bag for anybody, much less the Hal Ross agency, was on the face of it patently absurd. She'd been hired by CMN from among National Publishing's stable of approved marketing research firms. Michael hadn't met her until last night at the sessions in Lynn, Massachusetts. There had been no phone conversations prior to the groups. And it was plainly obvious that National Publishing could provide her with more work over time than Michael or even the whole Hal Ross agency. Who could possibly believe such a meritless charge?

Then it struck him. No one *did* believe it. It wasn't necessary that anyone believe it. By simply making the charge, Kloss, through his minion, put the agency on the defensive. The agency was biased. The moderator was biased. Ergo, the research itself was biased. In other words, Michael realized, why even continue?

"You've got to get Camfy involved, Ron. This is a shot across his bow by a desperate adversary who just got the early returns and doesn't like where this thing is going."

"Well, when I told Burt" . . . Ashley paused for effect, "he just laughed and said, 'I'll bet Burnsie's a walking pant load.'"

Michael felt a surge of anger. He didn't like being played, particularly with so much at stake. "What does he think we should do about it?"

"Nothing. At least not now. He wants me to monitor her performance tonight and call him in the morning."

"Ron, you know this charge is nonsense."

"Of course. We all do. Particularly Kloss. But Burt's not going to sacrifice the whole project for the sake of a focus group moderator. They're interchangeable, as far as we're concerned. He's prepared to fire them one by one if he has to. He knows the next one on the job will uncover the same problems with the network. Then Kloss will be the one on the defensive."

It was outrageously unjust. So egregious that Michael wasn't sure how to even defend the young moderator. "Just promise me this, Ron. Her family's waiting for her in Birmingham. Don't let them fire her before we get there. She doesn't need insult heaped on injury."

"No promises. But I'll see what I can do."

44

The groups in Decatur did not provide any special insights into the issues uncovered in Boston. They did, however, reinforce them, with one mother of a young family saying she canceled her subscription to CMN because, "I wasn't going to sit still while a sewer ran through my living room."

That night after the second session, Ron Ashley pulled Yashima Brown aside and let her know her services were no longer needed. Michael watched from behind the glass as the young woman struggled to compose herself. She'd performed flawlessly, even better, Michael thought, than the first night outside Boston. He was nearly overwhelmed with sadness, thinking of his own daughters who, one day all too soon, would be striking out in careers of their own. What would keep them from being victimized by the politicization of issues and events totally beyond their control? He found this thought so upsetting that it forced him out of the observation room, out of the research facility, out of the mid-rise office building, and into a rainy night in Georgia.

The sessions in Adamsville, just north of Birmingham, were significant, Michael believed. The new moderator was a woman named Amelia Harkins, who appeared to be in her fifties. She had flown in from Chicago. She proved competent, even adept, in moderating what was an unusually opinionated group of former CMN subscribers. In fact, so vociferous were both the men and women in their attacks on Hollywood filmmakers that Rhonda Silver had dismissed them as nothing more than "red-assed, red-necked, anti-Semites."

Michael thought differently. He sensed that they had wandered into the midst of ground zero in a raging culture war between Main Street and Hollywood. He could see that the group's loud and pointed criticism of CMN programming—what they described as "soft porn, at best"—had penetrated the impenetrable. The "swarm" was uncharacteristically quiet after the second group. They reassembled in a pub near the hotel, Michael among them, and sat in clusters of two and three, chugging imported brews from Mexico and South America. When talk touched on the groups that night, most fell silent. It was Bob Herbert who appeared to say what many were thinking, "I don't know if we've got a product for these folks down here."

This prompted Curt Welsh to say, "Man, I was waiting for the sheets to come out. Did any of them follow us back to the hotel?"

Nervous laughter. Michael wondered how the report on tonight's sessions would be received by Richard Kloss in the morning. In fact, when he noted Rhonda's absence, he suspected that Kloss had already been briefed. No doubt all the respondents will be accused of being on the Hal Ross agency payroll, he thought acidly.

"Well," said Ron Ashley as he stood up from the table and dropped what looked like a twenty dollar bill on its surface, "I never thought I'd be looking forward to going to Phoenix in late July, but . . . "

Michael headed to his room, wondering if Yashima Brown was in the air and heading toward her family.

45

The groups in Phoenix were actually held closer to Scottsdale, about an hour north. Michael knew the respondents wouldn't fit the target demographic profile; they would tend to be more upscale, with more discretionary income and therefore more inured, Michael presumed, to the price value issues of a monthly subscription service. But he wasn't going to fall on his sword over it. Ashley told him it was a sop to Kloss, which, in Burt Camfy's ever-agile mind, would cost him nothing.

As expected, the first group, nonbuyers of cable, skewed somewhat older and were largely opposed to the notion of paying for television. There wasn't any kind of programming, they maintained, that would lure them into the web, and certainly not that "garbage," as several of them referred to CMN. They used pet phrases like "rip off" and "grand larceny" to describe the network's offering. Michael wondered if Kloss would be happy with his selection of Scottsdale when he got this report.

The second group, however, had a decidedly different outlook and tone. Most of the respondents were less concerned with

264 / BRIAN J. GAIL

explicit content issues than they were with the issue of value itself. One respondent summarized what appeared to be a consensus among his fellow panelists, "I'm not all that offended by the raw nature of some of the programming. That's today's culture. But at the end of the day, it just doesn't satisfy. You're left with the question, is it worth it? And for me, the answer was no."

Michael would have loved to know what kind of product would have sated this fellow and group, but Amelia chose not to go there. A lost opportunity, he believed, particularly because CMN's own network research—culled from its panel of subscribers—provided at the very least a clue.

Michael went back to the hotel that evening and placed his nightly call home. Carol eagerly awaited his calls, even with the time zone difference in Birmingham and Phoenix. "How are you?" he asked as soon as he heard her voice. "And how are the kids?"

"We're all good. How are *you?*"

He summarized the work result and told her he was looking forward to seeing his brother and family over the weekend. "That'll be good for you," she assured him. "I'm glad you'll see him. Find out when they're coming east again. Tell them they can stay with us."

Michael hung up and called his brother to confirm details of their hookup in Newport Beach on Saturday. He was really looking forward to tapping into a little sanity.

The following morning at the airport in Phoenix, Ron Ashley approached him. He advised Michael that Rhonda Silver had flown back to New York and taken the two young African-American programming executives with her. "Any particular reason?" Michael asked with feigned surprise.

"Yeah," Ashley responded in his odd manner. "She said the whole project was a piece of crap . . . only she wasn't that delicate."

"I'm sure," Michael replied. He noted that Ashley was staring at him as though it were somehow his responsibility to ensure Rhonda Silver's comfort level from group to group. "Am I missing something?" he asked.

Ashley fixed him with a stare and said, "Camfy's not happy. He said he didn't want the 'bitch' coming back to headquarters, splaying her stench all over him and the sales and marketing departments before he even had a chance to arrange a debriefing for Reynolds."

"Ron, how is that my problem?"

"It's a problem for all of us, Burns" he said pointedly.

"Is there something I could have done? Is there something *you* could have done? Is there something *anyone* could have done?"

"Dunno. Just telling you this isn't good." Ashley turned abruptly and headed to a small news shop to buy a couple of papers for the flight to San Diego. It was at moments like these that Michael wished he'd never entered the field of advertising. He should have taught and coached, he told himself. Maybe opened a small bar. Sold real estate. Anything. Who could live, who could build a career, in such a world—a world bereft of reason?

46

Michael removed a John le Carré spy novel from his carry-on, shoved the bag into the overhead bin, and half fell into his seat, exhausted. Two weeks, he mused, is a long time on the road. Ten cities in two weeks had made this trip seem even longer. He missed his wife and children terribly, and took comfort in the realization that he would behold their angelic countenances within the next three hours.

The final groups were held in Worthington, Ohio, about an hour north of Columbus. Each merely reinforced the main themes that had emerged in earlier groups, without enlarging the findings in any material way. Families in general were protective of their sanctuary, wives and mothers especially so. The CMN programming the ex-buyers had sampled just didn't align itself with their concept of home and family. They wouldn't allow it back into their homes "even for free," as one gentleman phrased it last evening.

The CMN "swarm" behind the glass had become increasingly sober, literally and figuratively, as the same themes emerged again and again in town after town. As Peggy Samaric, one of the regional field marketing reps said in a tavern in Columbus after the last group, "I wish the programming people had stuck it out. To grow this network we're going to have to fix it. And to fix it, we're going to need programming and marketing working together."

Michael hoped her "net takeaway" would be clearly and convincingly represented by those in attendance upon their return to CMN's New York headquarters. If it were, and if the senior executives listened and acted on what they heard, he believed the network's growth would be stratospheric. If not, he was certain CMN would hit a wall and flush the business of its costs, including many of its marketing staff, and eventually be forced to settle for a small niche, leeching onto the back of America's mainstream entertainment media.

There was a commotion at the door, a brief heated exchange between a passenger and some of the crew. Moments later, Michael saw Ron Ashley coming down the aisle with an oversized bag that clearly should have been checked. He was smiling, and when he saw Michael he leaned down and said in a stage whisper, "It's charm. Works every time." Michael craned his neck to follow Ashley to the back of the plane, where he sought to stow the bag underneath the seat in front of him. He was in a middle seat and ended up with his feet on the bag, which ostensibly protruded to the base of the seat. The sight was comical, and Michael made a mental note to go back and rag him about it when the plane was airborne.

He never got the chance. The moment the plane finished climbing and the seat belt sign was turned off, Ashley seemed to appear like an apparition beside Michael's seat. Ron had noticed there was a middle seat open across the aisle and asked the man sitting on the aisle if he would switch with Michael so the two "colleagues" could talk. The man appeared even less happy at the prospect of switching aisle seats than Michael was to sit next to Ashley, but agreed to the move.

When they were settled, Ashley asked Michael to summarize his core "takeaways" from the ten-city tour. He thought the question odd, even as a conversation starter, so clearly had the key findings been summarized night after night. So he said the sort of irresponsible thing that he often said in such circumstances, "Just keep doing what we're doing. Sooner or later we'll just grind 'em down."

Ashley grunted. Michael leapt, "What's your bottom line? What you think and report is a helluva lot more important than what I think."

Ashley quickly demonstrated why stroking his ego was so productive and predictable. "There's a hardcore nonbuyer that the cable industry itself will never get. It's a matter of principle. They just don't think they need to pay for television. There's another segment of that universe that's also beyond our reach. They have significant issues with the content of the programming. No matter what we do, it'll never be good enough, pure enough."

Michael did not agree with this last statement but chose not to interrupt.

"The ex-CMN subscribers, they're recapturable, I think. We've just got to do a better job of educating them. We've got to adjust expectations."

Michael was dumbfounded. This was Ashley. Totally brilliant one minute, completely off the wall the next. Michael suspected Ashley might be goading him. He decided to play along, "I think you're right. We can't be telling consumers to buy the product because it's great when we know they'll discover it isn't and just cancel. We've got to find a way to say to them—and this isn't the copy—'We're not going to tell you the product is great; it isn't, but buy it anyway. You're bound to find something you like. In any given year, half our subscribers do.'"

Ashley appeared deeply insulted. "That's not at all what I meant, smart ass."

"Hey, I said I wasn't writing copy." Michael replied lamely.

Ashley fell silent. Michael thought *so that's the way to shut him up, insult him.* But he felt guilty. He didn't like offending people. Actually, he did like it when he was doing it, usually for justifiable reasons he always told himself, but he always felt guilty after the fact. And he drew more pain from the guilt than he did joy from the put-down, so he began a long, tortuous struggle to curb his tongue. It was slow going.

"Ron, I don't think adjusting consumer expectations is a marketing assignment, and I know it's not an advertisable proposition," he began cautiously. "Tell me, though, what you heard our ex-buyers saying."

Ashley looked up from his reading, paused as if deciding whether he wanted to re-engage, then looked at Michael and said, "The man of the house subscribes because of the perceived value of our content; the woman resists initially but relents. When the man recalculates the price value proposition after about three to six months of viewing, the woman seizes the opportunity to cancel." He shrugged his shoulders.

Michael decided to call him on it. "Ron, how do you get from that to the marketing of adjusted expectations?"

Ashley stared at him. "Burns, you know Kloss isn't going to buy any of this."

But of course, Michael nodded. The assignment was never about finding out why the customer cancelled his or her subscription. It was only and always about finding out what Kloss wanted the customer to say about the decision to cancel. And that certainly wouldn't have anything to do with the quality of the actual programming itself. "So who will have the responsibility of doctoring the final report?"

Ashley bristled. "We're National Publishing, Burns. We don't doctor research findings."

No, we just ignore or misrepresent them, Michael thought to himself. "I'm confused. What happens when the report comes in and says pretty much what you just said?"

Ashley looked away, then back, "I don't know what Camfy will decide to do with it. That'll be his decision," he said matter-of-factly.

So the whole thing will just slip quietly into the night, Michael realized. Kind of like the Titanic, without the iceberg. It will be as though the work was never commissioned, never undertaken, never reported. The last two weeks of his life didn't happen. Richard Kloss had assumed the identity of Rod Serling and escorted them all on a brief tour of the Twilight Zone.

"Ron, work with me here," he said, a bit too impatiently he feared. "Play it out for me. The report is deep-sixed. The churn rate continues unabated, roughly fifty percent annually. The wiring of America slows, then stops, its mission completed. Ex-buyers fill the nonbuyer universe. Cost to recapture ex-buyers is a multiple of the cost to hook up initial buyers. At least twice, maybe three times as expensive. So marketing costs escalate as revenues flatten, then plummet. National Publishing tells Rick, or whoever is CEO then, maybe Camfy, to pare the operation back to meet corporate budget projections."

Pause. "And that course of action, or non-action, is preferable to dealing with the 'content' issue head on, now, because . . . ?"

Ashley stared at Michael for a good long while. Michael returned his stare, not sure what he was seeing in his companion's eyes and demeanor at this point. "Michael," Ashley began with a sense of resignation. "I don't argue with your scenario. It all could go down like that. Probably will. But I'm not going to put my career on the line if my boss isn't willing to put his on the line."

Michael nodded and fell silent. He could never exist long-term in a corporate environment, he now understood more clearly than ever before. Advertising firms, even large international ones like the Hal Ross agency, were essentially small independent units that either succeeded or failed on their own. Grow your account and the CEO would throw money and promotions at you. Michael had experienced his share of that and found it exhilarating. Lose your account and the CEO would throw you and your team out the window. Michael hadn't experienced that yet, but he did have a sense that, other than the fall itself, it would somehow be a bit less exhilarating.

He was now forced to confront his options. Going along to merely get along was not among them. He had a family, and sooner or later, he knew, Kloss would succeed in convincing the CMN brain trust that the agency was responsible for the network's "poor marketing performance." There would be a formal review. Other major agencies would be asked to submit "ideas" that, given the size and visibility of the account, would be presented in the form of finished commercials. They would be dazzlingly fresh and vibrant, and they would offer promise of a whole new growth trajectory for the network. The CMN executives would be smitten, and they would notify him and Zimmer that they just had to make a change, difficult as it was. They were truly sorry, they would claim, and they would thank them "for all the good work." They would wish them well, and mean it.

Of course, nothing would change. The new agency would be wise enough to steer clear of the volatile "content" issue, and instead provide cosmetic changes in the advertising approach that would have a negligible impact on the business. In fact, they would probably be the same people who had wooed Kloss, telling him how he was changing the very fabric of American culture single-handedly. Camfy would bite his tongue and accept Kloss' strong recommendation of the replacement agency that he knew would both please Rick Reynolds and seal his own fate.

Meanwhile, the core business issue would go unaddressed and customers would continue canceling subscriptions in massive numbers. Those who did not cancel would be boiled slowly like the proverbial frog in the cooking pot. Slowly, gradually, the heat would be turned up, and before they realized it, they would be inured to the raw violence, profanity, and sex ("VPS" in industry code) that entered their living room each evening. Slowly, inexorably, the cultural forces of this imperceptible boiling would increase the size of this audience. The major networks would take notice and begin to counter the programming strategy, and advantage, of CMN. And the foot race to a cultural netherworld would begin in earnest. Just in time for a new millennium, only fifteen years away.

Michael was just Catholic enough to see that as a true danger for the American family. And just Irish enough to want to thrust a lance into that windmill to at least slow it down.

None of this would happen overnight, of course. He knew it would take a year, maybe two, for Kloss to achieve hegemony over CMN's sales and marketing operation. Camfy would not capitulate without a fight, but that fight would consist largely of a series of tactical maneuvers that Michael knew would be seen as one long retreat when viewed retrospectively.

This presented Michael with a dilemma. If he was correct in his assessment, this was no place for a believing Christian. But his departure would only hasten the agency's exit, throwing a number of good men and women out of work. And if he stayed, if he continued on the account to provide those men and women with additional time to find their next assignments, what would be required of him as a Catholic layman now directly involved in what he knew to be the marketing of . . . was evil too strong a word?

Michael needed pastoral guidance. He made a mental note to call Father Sweeney when he and Carol returned to Philadelphia in a couple of weeks. In fact, he noted, he would see the Father at the parish's 175th anniversary celebration. He would make it a point of asking for some private time either before or after the event itself.

Just then the pilot came on the intercom and indicated preparations were underway for the landing at Newark International Airport. Michael's thoughts returned to his family. He never longed to see Carol and his beautiful girls and those miracle sons more than he did at this moment. He vowed he would never go on another two-week road trip while his family was young. Faith, family, and career—in that order—were drilled into him as a child. He knew he was sometimes guilty of inverting priorities. It was now time to reprioritize. It was now time for family.

47

Maggie Kealey mingled with the mini-multitudes on the platform at 30th Street Station on a humid, drizzly mid-summer morning. In a few minutes she would board Metroliner 1667 for New York. She tried to look inconspicuous, but she was conscious of the attention she was receiving from the early morning commuters. These were businesspeople, and it was estimated that around thirty-five hundred of them made the journey to Mecca every morning and returned home each evening in search of sanctuary. Mothers had a way of looking like mothers, no matter how they attempted to disguise it. The way they dressed or carried themselves gave them away. She imagined herself an object of some curiosity and, moments later, when the train arrived, her suspicions were confirmed. The crowd that huddled at various boarding points actually parted to allow her to board first. She nodded her appreciation and somewhat self-consciously boarded and ducked quickly into the first unoccupied seat, not even stopping to remove her coat or store her carry-on bag. She wished she was extended, if only occasionally, this kind of courtesy at home.

She sat back in the large, comfortable seat and closed her eyes. She said a prayer called the *Memorare*, asking the Blessed Virgin for guidance on this trip. She was scheduled to meet a priest named Father LeClere at the chancery behind St. Patrick's Cathedral at 50th and Madison. The meeting was arranged by Father Sweeney, who, despite his misgivings, contacted the chancery to ask if Father LeClere and one of his parishioners could use one of the unoccupied parlors in the stately home for "official" Church business. An unusual request that was nonetheless granted. Maggie regarded this as a sign, and it alone provided her the necessary trust to board this train.

Father LeClere was an exorcist. Well, not actually an exorcist, as Father Sweeney reminded her. He worked in tandem with another priest who was an actual exorcist, whose name was known only to the archbishop and one or two of his closest advisors. The identity of this priest was always withheld from the laity and, in most cases, even priests themselves. The Catholic Church had always regarded her confrontations with the demonic as life-or-death serious, and there were protocols and procedures in place to guide the actual engagement itself so as not to either sensationalize or trivialize it. One of these, Maggie learned, was an actual on-site visit by Father LeClere, at the official request of the Cardinal Archbishop of Philadelphia, to determine if there was sufficient evidence to suggest demonic possession.

The Church understood actual "possession" to be exceedingly rare, and it required some level of on-site discernment to judge if the ritual was necessary. Far more complex was the discernment of demonic "oppression" and "infestation," which typically comingled with psychiatric illness and eluded simple detection. Before Father LeClere would undertake an on-site investigation he needed hard information about the victim and the family. He needed, in short, to screen the real from the delusional.

Despite Father Sweeney's strange intervention with Moia the previous month, John had maintained his belief that he saw no indication of demonic possession. He held that Moia suffered from an undiagnosed mental illness, he thought perhaps it was a "Borderline Personality Disorder," and that ultimately she would either be healed through the science of modern psychiatry or, God willing, would simply "grow out of it."

Maggie didn't believe that for one minute, so she prevailed upon Father Sweeney to use his connections to permit her to investigate what she in her mother's heart knew to be a problem with a paranormal dimension. He acceded to her wishes with great reluctance, appearing embarrassed even to make the phone calls to set the process in motion. This disappointed Maggie, though she did her best to hide it.

As the train made its way through North Philadelphia heading toward its stops in Trenton, Princeton, and Newark, Maggie reached into her bag for a notebook. She wanted to use this time to prepare for her discussion with Father LeClere. She had categorized all the manifestations of Moia's troubled behavior beginning in her early adolescence; she listed the questions she wanted to ask the priest, including the particulars of the process itself and its approximate timeline. But mostly she would probe to understand what she could expect. Could this priest be the instrument of her daughter's healing by a merciful God? Had he done so successfully in similar instances? Were there people like herself she could speak to, perhaps another mother of a child in early adulthood? A number of unwelcome thoughts suddenly flooded her head that were too painful to contemplate, and she found herself closing her eyes and repeating the prayer to the Blessed Virgin.

. . .

When the train pulled into Penn Station, Maggie was jolted awake by the rustling of commuters gathering their things in preparation for departure. As she watched them collecting and straightening and subtly moving their feet to position themselves for a quicker exit, she wondered how they endured this marathon every day. Just getting to 30th Street Station involved a degree of difficulty. Getting to Penn Station significantly more so. Now these men and women had to make their way uptown or across town or downtown to their offices. And it was in those offices where the true challenge awaited. The day-to-day competition with the most fleet of foot, the most agile of mind, and the most predatory of hearts. Making your way up that most treacherous of ladders or finding an unoccupied rung from which to plot a carefully timed leap into what would appear to be a safe sanctuary but, quite often, proved not to be so. Then, every night, reversing the journey. The struggle to get from the office to Penn Station. The long, tedious journey home. The battle from 30th Street home on the back-end of rush hour. Then what? A quick dinner, perhaps alone. Maybe one or two television shows to unwind, perhaps a CMN movie. Then bed. And tomorrow, repeat steps one through twelve.

Maggie had once asked one of these men why so many people from Philadelphia subjected themselves to this torturous odyssey to New York every day. He looked at her as if she were an alien and said with no small measure of exasperation, "Because that's where they keep the money!"

Maggie exited the train and moved pell-mell with the masses to, then up, the escalator. She stopped briefly once inside the main terminal to get her bearings. She quickly realized she was on the wrong side, and sought signs for Seventh Avenue and Madison Square Garden as Bill told her to do. She didn't see any, so she asked the nearest stranger for help. He was black and blind, and he reached for her hand and said, "Child, God is with you," and pointed in the general direction of the two-story escalators on the other side of the terminal.

Maggie thanked the man for his kindness and turned toward the escalators. As she began to move she heard the same gentleman repeat, this time louder, "Remember, child . . . God is with you."

She thought this odd, yet oddly comforting, briefly pondering its significance.

Once outside she saw an exceptionally long line awaiting their morning taxis to the office. It was warm, but not yet hot. She was running slightly late for her 9:30 meeting at the chancery, so she decided to walk. She crossed Seventh Avenue at 34th and headed toward The Avenue of the Americas. She found herself walking faster than she intended merely to keep up with the pedestrian traffic, and by the time she reached Sixth Avenue she was beginning to perspire. The image of her arriving drenched at the front door of the chancery gave her pause, and she decided to hail a cab, which she was able to do with little difficulty.

She exited the cab on the corner of 50th and Madison, wanting to make a quick visit in the Cathedral. She entered St. Patrick's from a side door and welcomed the cool air and abiding tranquility. She knelt with her head in her hands and begged her Lord and Savior to have mercy on her poor sick child. "You healed so many mother's sons and daughters when you were among us, Lord. Please one more. I will do anything you tell me to do. Anything. Just please heal my little one."

She exited through a side door closer to the altar and descended the steps quickly. She was now seven minutes late, and she didn't like to be late. By the time she pushed the buzzer at the front door of the chancery she was beginning to perspire again. She reached in her bag for a handkerchief to mop her forehead. The door opened and a handsome young priest appeared. "Father LeClere?" Maggie asked.

"No," he laughed. "Father Connors. I'm not nearly so important." His smile was magnetic, and immediately Maggie felt at home.

"I'm sorry I'm late Father. The train . . ."

"Late? You're early. Father LeClere hasn't even arrived. And him coming from right here in town. Why, the unmitigated arrogance!" Father Connors was enjoying himself. He led Maggie into a small but comfortable parlor just off the main hall. In moments, a red-headed woman whose face and voice summoned the image of a rural farm in County Derry appeared at the door. "May I bring you a cup of coffee, Mrs. Kealey?" she asked with a familiar lilt.

"No, thank you."

"How about a nice cold glass of orange juice?"

"Now that I could go for," Maggie obliged.

Father Connors reappeared. "Father LeClere just called to ask if you were here. I told him you were about to leave, and were none too happy about his failure to show."

"Oh Father, you're a troublemaker, I can see."

"How perceptive. And here you just met me." The handsome young priest's eyes danced and sparkled, and Maggie couldn't help wonder how many hearts he'd broken when news of his decision to enter the priesthood circulated. Then abruptly, his demeanor changed, and he took a seat in a chair opposite Maggie. "Mrs. Kealey, I know why you're here. Let's invoke the Lord's Presence."

He closed his eyes, and Maggie closed hers. His voice carried a healing quality, and in seconds she was transported in serenity to a faraway place where she and Moia were safe from all harm. She opened her eyes momentarily and observed the young priest praying with a startling intensity that furrowed his forehead and flared his nostrils. He is praying as though Moia was his child, she thought to herself. She marveled at the mystery and majesty of a Church that attracted such men and women in every age. "Oh Lord, I am not worthy to be even the weakest part of your Mystical Body," she prayed in silent declaration.

When Connors finished his prayer he smiled and squeezed Maggie's hand. "Now," he said as he stood up, "when Father LeClere gets here, you tell him he can dispense with an opening prayer. Been there, done that. And tell him to be on time next time." With that he was gone. An angel who'd flown into her life and out with ostensibly no other purpose than to provide her with a small flash of light in a moment of great darkness.

About ten minutes later she heard the buzzer ring. The Irish housekeeper who'd brought her not merely one large glass of orange juice but a refill as well flew past the entrance to the parlor and opened the front door with a cheerful greeting for her visitor, Father James LeClere. In moments, Father LeClere was in the parlor, hand outstretched and striding toward Maggie. "Forgive me, Mrs. Kealey. One of our communicants turned emergency penitent this morning after Mass. Of course we ordinarily like to see that order reversed, but Holy Mother Church doesn't always get her way in such matters these days. But enough of my problems. We're here to discuss your . . . challenges. Should we begin with a prayer?"

Maggie smiled and said, "Yes Father, and thank you for making time to meet with me."

The priest was darkly complexioned, early-middle-aged, and bore a slight paunch. He took the seat that Father Connors had occupied and closed his eyes. For several moments he said nothing. Maggie's first thought was that perhaps they were each supposed to be praying. But then the silence was broken by the priest's prayer of deep reverence and introspection, and she realized the encounter with the demonic must require a whole different magnitude of fortification.

When Father LeClere finished, he looked at Maggie for a long moment and said in a soft and gentle voice, "Mrs. Kealey, I'm sorry you and your family are suffering so. I don't know if we can help you, but if we can and God wills it, we will do everything in our power to bring Our Blessed Lord into the middle of your suffering, and beg Him to provide the relief you seek."

Maggie began to cry. It was the last thing she wanted to do. His words, however, touched and released a hurt so deep within her that she simply couldn't help herself. Her narrow shoulders shook, her body began to vibrate, and she started to sob uncontrollably.

Father LeClere got up to close the door to the parlor and made his way back to his seat. He sat quietly with his hands folded in his lap, maintaining both his composure and distance, waiting for the tears to wash away years of hurt and replace it with hope. The hope of Christians, he thought, which alone among all of men's thoughts, words, and deeds surprises God.

Slowly, the sobs ebbed. Maggie struggled to compose herself. "I'm so sorry, Father. I'd given up hope." She started to cry again.

"No you didn't, Maggie," Father LeClere replied gently. "You wouldn't be here if you did."

Maggie nodded. "Yes, Father. Thank you, Father."

"Maggie, tell me about your daughter."

Maggie Kealey sat upright in her chair. She ran her tongue over her lips and did a quick sort of all the Moia files she carried in her mind. She searched for the least painful way into her tragic tale. "Father, she was just the best child. Everything a father and mother could want. She was my right hand until she was fifteen. I've suffered from chronic migraines for almost twenty years. Moia ran the house for me, getting her five younger brothers and sisters up and out to school—breakfast made, lunches wrapped. She'd draw the curtains and blinds and bring me my medicine and a continuous supply of cold compresses. If it was a particularly bad day, she'd call Rose O'Rourke, our neighbor, who would come and help when the kids came home from school. She was a gifted student—straight A's—and captained her lacrosse and soccer teams. She went to church every Sunday and every day in Lent. The nuns, the Sister Servants of the Immaculate Heart of Mary, had their eye on her. Sister Pat, the principal at her high school, told me at the end of her freshman year, "Maggie, this one's ours.""

Father LeClere was listening so intently that it might have unnerved Maggie under normal circumstances. "When exactly, to the best of your recollection, did it all begin to change, Maggie?"

A cloud came over Maggie Kealey's face. She paused, pulling back perceptibly. Father LeClere thought she might begin to cry again. "It happened gradually, Father. First, she started losing interest in sports—missing practices, then games. We didn't even know. Her coaches called and asked if she was all right. They thought maybe she was sick."

"How did you address that situation?"

"Well, Bill and I—that's my husband—her dad, took her for a sit-down with the lacrosse coaches. But she wouldn't talk."

"What's your husband do, if I may ask?"

"He's a lawyer, Father. The managing partner of a mid-sized Philadelphia firm, about sixty lawyers."

"How does your daughter interact with her father?"

"Father, Moia doesn't interact with anyone. That's why we're here. None of the medical or psychiatric professionals have been able to help."

"Before she started missing lacrosse practices, how did she get on with her father?"

"Well, I'd say overall, pretty well, Father. My husband is quite a forceful presence. He's used to getting his own way, and I think all the children are a bit afraid of him. But I don't want to give you the wrong impression. He's a very good husband and father. He just has to spend a lot of time at work."

Father LeClere nodded slightly. He made a mental note to circle back on the father-daughter relationship, often no less determinative in adolescent mental illness, he'd come to learn, than the father-son dynamic. "Then what happened, Maggie?"

"Well, she started missing classes. Again, we were the last to know. Sister Pat called to tell us."

"Where would she go when classes were in session?"

"Apparently, she'd walk up to a small shopping center about a mile away. She would just buy something to eat at one of the supermarkets and . . . walk around." The thought of her daughter walking aimlessly amid strangers struck another nerve, and Maggie started to well up.

Father LeClere paused for the moment to pass and continued with tender deference to his guest's emotional fragility. "Maggie, how did you and your husband broach that situation with your daughter?"

"We had a sit-down with the principal. But she wouldn't talk to any of us. Sister Pat suggested counseling, but she wouldn't talk to Ms. Hathaway either."

"So what did you do?"

"We went to our parish priest, Father John Sweeney. He's the assistant pastor and a dear friend. He suggested professional counseling and arranged for Moia to meet with a psychiatrist who sees a lot of priests with emotional problems . . ."

"Can you give me his number? I need help!" Father LeClere was smiling, which Maggie thought made him look at least ten years younger. "So how did that work out? Was this man at all helpful?"

"No, Father. He tried. She wouldn't talk to him. So he had Moia see his partner, a woman with a reputation for being very good with young girls. But after several visits, we all came to the conclusion that this arrangement wasn't going to work any better."

"What did you do then?"

"We started seeing other psychiatrists and psychologists— about sixteen over a three-year period."

"And none of them helped?"

"No, Father."

Jim LeClere shook his head slowly. Quietly, he thanked Almighty God for his vocation. He'd just been reminded yet again that he could never, ever, have been a parent. "God bless you, Maggie," he said soothingly. "You have borne a heavy cross."

"Father, my pain is nothing compared to what my baby suffers every hour of every waking day."

"I know . . . I know," the priest reassured. "While all this is going on, how would you characterize the interaction between Moia and her sisters and brothers?"

"How would I characterize it? I would say Moia brutalizes her younger sisters, particularly Grace, our second child. She is merciless."

"And how would her anger manifest itself in her interaction with Grace?"

"She steals her clothes, rips up her homework, calls her names—tells her she's fat and a loser—neither of which are even remotely true, Father."

"How does Grace respond to this provocation?"

"With extraordinary grace, if I may say so Father," Maggie answered with quiet pride. "She is a most remarkable young woman. She continues to love her sister and brings her books, meals, and gifts that she buys with her own money."

"And how does Moia respond to Grace?"

"All the love makes her hate even more."

Father LeClere nodded. "How does all of that going on affect the others in the home?"

"It polarizes the family, Father. Bill and two of Moia's younger sisters favor a tough love approach. Grace and I don't want any more pain inflicted on her."

"What kind of 'tough love' are they proposing?"

"Basically, shape up or ship out."

"Ship out! To where?"

"That's just it, Father. There is nowhere for her to go."

"So what's happened?"

"Well, one of her sisters in a fit of pique, told her she was going to be thrown out on her ear, only she didn't say 'ear,' Father."

"How did Moia respond to that?"

"She ran away." Maggie Kealey began to sob again and Father LeClere considered ending the session. If he continued to go where he intended to go with his inquiry, the pain would only get worse. He did not think this fragile mother would be able to handle it. "Should we take a break here, Maggie?"

"No Father!" Maggie replied, reacting as though she had just been sprayed with cold water. "I'm fine. That's just a painful memory. Going to her room and discovering her gone, most of her things not there."

"I'm not sure I could ever fully appreciate the depth of a mother's heart."

Maggie smiled resolutely. "I take great consolation in the Blessed Mother, Father. My pain doesn't compare to what she went through."

Father James LeClere marveled at this bred-in-the-bone faith before him. Where did it come from? What sustained it?

He looked at the mother on the couch in front of him and was surprised to hear himself blurt, "Maggie Kealey, you are remarkable."

Maggie blushed, shook her head vigorously, and looked down at the floor.

He recovered and said, "Now tell me, what happened when Moia ran away?"

"Father, she went to Las Vegas."

"Viva Las Vegas! Why Las Vegas?"

Maggie shrugged. "We don't know, Father. But she didn't stay long. We think she sensed she was being followed, which she was. Bill arranged through friends to have her tracked. We were getting daily, sometimes hourly, updates."

"Where'd she go?"

"Hollywood!"

Father LeClere just waved his arms in a dismissive "you can't make this stuff up" manner. "Sure, why wouldn't she leave Las Vegas and go straight to Hollywood?"

Despite herself, Maggie laughed. "I guess she had big dreams. Who knew?"

"So how'd you get her home?"

"Well, she ran out of money. She stole over eight hundred dollars from us and her sister Grace. She spent it all and wired for more. She said if we didn't send it she'd walk in front of a bus on Sunset Boulevard."

"I'll bet your husband the lawyer responded well to that."

"Yes he did, Father," Maggie replied, missing entirely Father LeClere's irony. "He wired back, saying a plane ticket home with her name on it would be waiting at the LAX American Airlines counter the following morning. He didn't say anything else."

"She came home?"

"Yes, Father."

"How did the family react to having her in the home again?"

"Not well. We were all walking on egg shells, Father. But we needn't have worried. She came home, went in her room, and never came out."

"Never? What's never? How long did she stay in her room?"

"She's still in there, Father. She's been in there over sixteen months."

Father James LeClere looked at his guest in absolute wonderment. "Sixteen months? Mother of God."

"Can you get her to come out, Father?"

"I don't know, Maggie. How does she respond to religious figures and symbols?"

Maggie fell silent. No memory was more painful for her than the one that suddenly resurfaced. "Not too well."

"Can you give me an example?"

Long pause. Father LeClere actually began to brace himself. "Father, I read that the devil hates the cross. So I hid one under Moia's mattress, actually between her mattress and box spring. I don't know what I was hoping. Maybe just that it would drive the devil away. I never thought she'd find it. She never lets us change her sheets."

"So she found the crucifix?"

"Yes, Father."

"And?"

"And . . . she attacked me with it."

"Attacked you! Oh my! Oh my. . ."

"Then she went into my room and pulled my dresser down on top of her."

"Maggie, did she hurt you when she struck you?"

"Oh yes, Father. I had welts and bruises on my face, neck, and arms."

"Was she saying anything when she was striking you, Maggie?"

"Yes, Father. She was cursing me and . . ."

"And what else Maggie?"

"She was cursing Jesus. She was saying the vilest things about Our Blessed Lord. I could never repeat them, Father."

"Maggie, what did her voice sound like when she was cursing?"

"Like somebody else. Somebody I didn't know. It was almost like a man's voice."

"Did she seem . . . stronger . . . did her physical strength surprise you?"

"Yes, Father. I couldn't get her off me. Even Grace and I together couldn't budge her."

"Maggie, how much does your dresser weigh, best guess?"

"I wouldn't know."

"Is it very heavy or just heavy?"

"I would say very heavy. It's taller than I am, and filled with clothes. We couldn't figure out how she crashed it down on top of her. Or why she did it. It made no sense."

"How did you and Grace move the dresser . . . I assume she was trapped beneath it?"

"Yes Father, she was. Grace called Father Sweeney. He came and lifted it off her."

"Alone?"

"Yes, Father." Maggie smiled at the memory. "Father Sweeney was a football player in college. He's very strong."

Father LeClere paused to absorb what he was hearing. He'd heard of a priest being ordained in the Philadelphia Archdiocese some years ago who, it was said, passed up a potential career in the NFL. Jim LeClere tended to discount those stories. They always made for good publicity for the Church but, in his experience, men who possessed those unique athletic gifts always wanted to test them first, and were generally encouraged to do so by the episcopacy so that there would be no "coulda, shoulda, woulda" down the road. "But this Father Sweeney . . . he didn't think any of this was unusual?"

"Well, I think he knows, in fact I know he knows Moia is very sick. He thinks she has a Borderline Personality Disorder. But if you mean, does he think the devil is involved in some way in all this, I'd have to say no, no he doesn't."

The priest was puzzled. "Then how'd you get here? These

conferences require some clerical conviction, somewhere along the line."

"Well, I just begged him. I told him I believed with all my heart that the devil is involved with my child. I don't know how. I can't prove it. I just believe it. Sometimes mothers just know things, Father."

Father LeClere smiled. "Mothers know a lot of things that the rest of us don't, Maggie. A mother's heart is God's masterpiece, His final creative act in Genesis. Most of us spend our entire lifetimes trying to understand things that a mother simply intuits within the deep recesses of her heart."

Maggie liked this priest. His humility, wisdom, and gentle pastoral manner put her at ease and drew from her the darkest of painful secrets. She didn't think there was anything she wouldn't tell him if he asked her.

"Maggie, how 'bout we take a little break. Mrs. Kane has no doubt fixed us some lunch. We can continue after we eat."

Maggie blinked. "Father, did you say Mrs. Kane?"

"Ah, I did now. Would you be a knowin' that fine miss?"

Maggie laughed at the priest's attempt at native dialect. It wasn't terrible, but it was obvious he didn't grow up in an Irish home. "I don't say as I do, Father. But I know there are O'Cahaigns from the North on my mother's side."

Father James LeClere laughed. "Oh, this oughta be good. Now I'm surrounded by the IRA. I'll be hearin' confessions all afternoon."

48

The brief luncheon provided a much-needed respite and an opportunity for Maggie to rekindle her ties to the land of her forebears. Although a precise connection could not be drawn, it was clear that both families laid claim to an ancestral home in County Derry, which made it likely the two women were in some way blood relatives. Not that it mattered. Close enough was always good enough for the Irish. That and a pint or two of Guinness could end or start pretty much any war, Jim LeClere believed.

Maggie got on so famously with Patty Kane that the cook actually sat herself down at table and sampled some of her own broth and roasted chicken. She also regaled her guests with stories of her mother and grandmother, women of apparently indomitable faith, who had been born just outside Dungiven in the southwestern corner of County Derry.

When it was time to resume, Patty Kane rose as one with Father LeClere and for a moment the priest feared she was going to join them. But after a brief pause she came around the table and gave Maggie a long and tearful hug and promised to get both her mother and grandmother "working on this thing with Moia." Maggie accepted the promise of prayers as graciously as it was offered. "Thank you, Patty. I will stay in touch. Promise."

Father LeClere led Maggie back into the parlor and closed the door behind him. "What time is your train back to Philadelphia?"

"Three o'clock, Father."

Father LeClere looked at his watch. It was 1:10. "We should be fine. Let me tell you what I want to get done in the next hour or so." He took his wristwatch off and laid it on the coffee table between them. "I want to try to get a handle on whether we're dealing with demonic possession, which is rare, or demonic oppression, which is actually much more common than most people think."

Maggie shifted uncomfortably. She felt a great sorrow stirring in her breast that even the presence of this good priest couldn't still. The thought of an actual demon of some sort living in her home, actively sharing, or crushing, the life of one of her little ones was possibly more than she could bear. Could she, would she, make it through this?

"Maggie, I'm going to give you a brief overview of both possession and oppression, and I want you to stop me if I say anything you don't understand. Then I will ask you some questions. I also want you to ask me questions. It's very important that we leave here today on the same page, regardless of our degree of discernment. That we leave to God, OK?"

"Yes, Father."

"First of all, I want you to understand that the devil is a created being. Like you. Like me. That means his power is limited. Limited by a God who is all-merciful. Are you with me?"

"Yes, Father."

"The devil wants most to be worshipped as God is worshipped. But God will not permit him to show himself openly, until the end of time. So the most he can do is what he does do. He possesses, or oppresses, human beings. God permits this, always for some greater good, reasons that frequently transcend the limits of our human intellects.

"The most telling thing you said this morning, Maggie, was the story of your daughter's discovery of and reaction to that crucifix. Of all religious symbols, this one has a singular power to trip the devil's wires. It reminds him and reminds all his demons of their Waterloo—their great and everlasting defeat at Calvary. Those of us who are involved in the Church's rite of exorcism pay particular attention to that 'manifestation.'

"Now, there are six other 'manifestations' or characteristics of possession. I want to go through each of them, and I want you to tell me if you've observed Moia exhibiting or experiencing any them."

Jim LeClere paused. "OK . . . are you with me, Maggie?"

"Yes, Father."

"You're doing fine so far. We're just going to take it one step at a time. OK?"

"Yes, Father."

"So, we have observed a great fury unleashed at the discovery and presence of a crucifix. The second manifestation is a vile blasphemy directed toward the object itself. And I believe you said Moia's rant was so profane as to at least border on the sacrilegious."

"It did more than border on it, Father. She was yelling and cursing and saying the vilest things about Our Blessed Lord. I . . . we . . . Grace was with me—we were horrified."

The priest simply nodded. "Now, a third 'manifestation' is the emergence of an altered state, a different personality. Is it fair to say that Moia took on a distinctive change in her person? That she almost seemed to be a different person during her attack on you?"

"Oh yes, Father. She became like a . . . a demon. She was so strong and determined. It was frightening."

The priest nodded again. "Maggie, another common 'manifestation' is that this altered state takes on the character of evil. There is a great twitching of facial muscles. The body becomes extremely rigid. The eyes sometimes roll back in the head. Did you observe that happening to Moia?"

"Father . . . I couldn't honestly say. I was so terrified that all I remember is her cursing and her strength, and the pain, the terrible pain. . ." Then Maggie Kealey began to tear up, but caught herself and stiffened.

The priest paused to permit his guest to cleanse the memory. "Maggie, we're going to give that moment, that memory, to the Lord right now. Take my hand."

The priest took the extended hand and marveled at its gentleness and suppleness. He closed his eyes and after several moments began, "Lord, we come before you now pleading for your healing touch. You are the Divine Physician. If we cannot turn to you O Lord, to whom can we turn? The soul of this good woman is beleaguered. She has been as much a victim of evil as her precious little one. You alone can heal her, Lord. In you alone we place our trust. Please heal this bitter memory and replace the evil with the good. Bring a joy greater than the sorrow. For you alone are Lord. You alone are our hope. In you alone we invest our complete trust. Forsake us not, sweet Savior. We ask this as we do all things through the intercession of your Holy Mother. Amen."

Maggie felt a sweet wave of lightness pass over her from head to foot. There was a gentle tingling in her fingers and toes. An enveloping serenity settled gently in her heart and lifted her spirit, sending it soaring in search of sound . . . the sound, she imagined, of cherubim and seraphim. She felt she was slowly being buried in bliss. Immediately, her mother's heart wanted to share the sentience with her suffering child. Oh how she wished her daughter could feel what she was now feeling. Then she would know there was a God. That He was a God of love, just as they were taught. That everything was going to be all right. There would be an end to this awful nightmare, this unrelieved hair shirt of pain and torment.

"Maggie, are you alright?"

"Yes Father," she replied with an undisguised airiness. "I feel like the weight of the ages has been lifted from me. I feel like a child again. I just wish, I just pray, that God would let my child feel what I'm feeling. Just once." She began welling up again.

292 / BRIAN J. GAIL

The priest felt his heart stir. "He will, Maggie. He will. In His time."

Maggie Kealey nodded and shifted her body in the chair to better face the priest. She was ready to continue.

"Maggie, shall I go on?"

She nodded.

"OK. Another 'manifestation' of a person who is possessed is the return to normalcy. It happens slowly. In time, there is no remnant of the altered state, except the memory of it in those who have witnessed it. The possessed person has no recollection of it at all. Did you see that happen, Maggie?"

"I don't know, Father. I don't know what normal is for Moia."

"Did she go back to what she looked and sounded like before she unleashed her fury?"

"Father . . . honestly, I couldn't say. I ran from the house. When I returned, she was back in her room with her door locked."

"No sounds coming out of the room?"

"No, Father."

"No unpleasant odors?"

"No. I called my husband, he came home, and we took her to the hospital. Turned out her leg wasn't broken."

"How was she at the hospital?"

Maggie shrugged, "Almost normal. It was as if nothing had happened."

"OK. Let's move on. There's often another 'manifestation.' It's when the possessed person returns to a completely normal life. The possession itself does not have any effect on social relationships. People who do not know what these people went through would never suspect anything out of the ordinary happened to them. That clearly wouldn't apply here, right? Am I correct in assuming that Moia's current . . . ah . . . dysfunctionality wouldn't allow us to determine that?"

The mother nodded. "Yes, Father. I'd have no way of determining that."

The priest straightened up in his chair and cleared his throat.

"Well . . . finally Maggie, a person who is possessed may hear voices from time to time, or even have hallucinations. Have you or anyone in your family observed any of that?"

"No, we haven't. But how would we know? The poor child has been in her room for the past sixteen months."

"I understand."

"Father, I must ask you this. Why does God permit a young child to go through something so horrific?"

"First Maggie, we don't know if Moia is possessed, or even oppressed. But if God has permitted it, we can be certain it is to obtain some greater good for her—or your family—or other souls of His choosing. Perhaps a priest."

Maggie paused to absorb this last. The thought of Moia possibly suffering for the priestly ministry of Father Sweeney was something she hadn't considered. But now that she did, she rejected it out of hand. She just couldn't believe her God would permit the one to benefit the other. It was—at least to her—unthinkable.

The priest took stock of his guest's emotional inventory and decided to continue. "Maggie, let me give you a brief overview of demonic oppression. And again, don't be afraid to ask questions if something is not clear. OK?"

Maggie flinched visibly and nodded.

"Demonic oppression is materially different than demonic possession. In possession, a person's body, never the soul, is actually occupied by a demon. The actions during possession are the actions of the demon, not the person. There is never any sin involved on the part of the possessed person. The Church requires a formal religious rite, approved by the local bishop, and follows a very regimented protocol once it has been reliably determined that there is in fact a demonic possession."

Maggie shuddered involuntarily, and Jim LeClere thought perhaps he was pushing the boundaries too far, too fast, or both. But no sooner had he concluded he should stop when suddenly this most resilient of women signaled him to continue with a vigorous nod of her head.

He did. "Demonic oppression is said to occur when there is a clear demonic influence in the things a person thinks, says, and does. It is more a matter of what we call a 'shadowing' or 'clinging of spirits.' The devil's intent is to block healing. In this instance the devil attaches himself—carefully hidden—like some kind of insidious leech, to an individual. He lives within the individual's orbit, what we might call sphere of activity. Generally this happens in cases where there is an emotional disturbance of some sort. The tactical advantage for the devil here is great. Overt possession can be ruled out fairly quickly, but because the individual is suffering emotionally one can never be sure where the emotional illness ends and the demonic oppression begins. He can ride these cases for a very long time, causing great havoc in families—good families in particular."

"Why good families, Father?"

"Well . . . there's some pretty heavy theology involved, but let me just say this. We are most like God—we who have been created in His image and likeness—when we are living in a community of relational love. That's what God lives in with His Son and the 'offspring', if you will, of their boundless love—the Holy Spirit. Together, they live a totality of unconditional love. We who live in loving families experience a foretaste of this great love here on earth. We are living as God created us to live in this life. We bear the sign, love unto victimhood, of being created in His image and likeness. This of course is completely unacceptable to the devil. His mission is alienation. A negation of the good, of love itself. It is precisely this image and likeness of God that he seeks to destroy in the loving family. So we see him running the perimeter of these families looking for a seam, an opening, a weakness in one or more of the family's members. When he finds one, he slips inside and enters the very life of the family, causing unceasing torment." The priest paused and fixed his gaze on the beautiful and troubled woman opposite him. "Frequently, Maggie, it seems it is an emotional disorder within one of the family members that presents him with his opportunity."

Maggie sat stunned. "Father," she blurted, "That's our life. You just described our living hell."

Father James LeClere nodded, and forced a pained smile. He said with great gentleness, "We see too much of it, Maggie. That's why we, I'm including the exorcist, got into this ministry. The devil has emptied hell and loosed his charges for what seems like one last desperate push. And his point of attack is the family, particularly the good families. After all, he doesn't have to waste time with the others."

Maggie was very nearly overwhelmed by what she was hearing. Why did she have to come to New York to hear this? Why wasn't there a priest in her own diocese who could have explained all this to her? Her agitation slowly gave way to an emotion she hadn't experienced in some time. She was beginning to feel—how else to say it? Hope. She was beginning to believe there might be relief for her little one, and for her family. But she needed to know at least one more thing.

"Father what are the typical causes of these emotional disorders the devil exploits?"

"Wounds."

"What do you mean, wounds?"

"Sin. Something cruel we do to others or something cruel someone does to us. The demons 'cling' to our wounds, as I say, to prevent healing. It's fairly straightforward. No healing, no peace. No peace, no joy. No joy, no fullness of life. Precisely what Christ came to give us."

"And what types of sin bring this awful abuse into the middle of a family's life? Maggie asked tentatively, not certain she wanted to hear the answer.

"Abusive relationships. Emotional, physical, or sexual. Usually within the family structure."

"Sexual!"

The priest shook his head sadly. "Yes, as astonishing as that must sound."

Without warning, Maggie began to sob quietly. The priest was taken aback. He had already ruled out the possibility of sexual abuse. He thought it much more likely there was emotional abuse from a domineering father with perhaps some physical abuse on occasion.

Maggie didn't know what to do. She felt trapped. Should she just leave? Surely she couldn't repeat what Grace told her. How could she say what she knew to a priest?

"Do you know something you're not telling me Maggie?" the priest asked gently.

Maggie simply wanted to run. She just didn't know how to get up out of the chair and start for the door.

"Maggie?"

"Yes, Father?"

"Is there something I can help you with here?"

"Father . . . I don't know . . . I don't know."

"Just say it, Maggie. The devil loves the darkness. Christ wants us to bring the truth out into the light."

An impulse stirred Maggie to speak, "Father, my daughter was in the hallway and she told me she saw the whole thing. When Father Sweeney lifted the dresser off Moia and tried to put her on my bed, she was screaming. Grace described the screams as . . . like something out of a horror movie. She said . . ." Maggie couldn't go on.

"Grace said Moia was screaming . . . about being sexually abused. Is that it, Maggie?"

Maggie sat stone-faced. She simply could not bring herself to repeat what she'd been told.

She wouldn't have to. "Did someone abuse Moia . . . Maggie?"

Nothing.

"Did Moia's father abuse her . . . sexually abuse her, Maggie?"

"No, no, no, no, no!" Maggie Kealey cried aloud burying her head in her hands. The commotion brought Patty Kane in from the kitchen. She opened the door and peaked in. The priest signaled that everything was under control. The Irish cook blessed herself quickly and shut the door.

"Maggie, who abused your child . . . who was it?"

"A former pastor, Father. Not our current pastor. The one before him. A man named . . . Munger."

A chill ran up the priest's spine. He was seeing more and more of this. He thought it bordered on the pandemic. If it ever came to light—and he knew for a fact that bishops around the country were doing their best to keep this scandal buried in chancery archives—he believed the damage to the Church would be total. Whole dioceses would be bankrupted. An entire generation of children, or at least the better part of it, would be lost, not to mention their parents. The Church's voice as a force for good would be all but stilled at a critical moment in human history. The prince of this world, he believed, would achieve an extraordinary victory of great strategic significance.

"Maggie . . . I'm so sorry," he fumbled. "I apologize to you on behalf of the Church."

"Father, do you think it's true?"

"Well . . ." the priest hesitated, allowing for the possibility of it not having happened, "it's certainly possible. We've seen this kind of thing before."

"Father, I don't believe it. I don't believe a priest, an ordained priest who says Mass every day, could do such a thing. Do you?"

"Yes Maggie, unfortunately, I do. That is not to judge a former pastor. He may be entirely innocent. Moia could have suffered this terrible cruelty at the hands of another and projected it . . . onto a trusted figure in the community. We've seen instances."

"But who else could it have been, Father? I know, I just know, it wasn't my husband."

"I don't know, Maggie. I don't know. Perhaps we'll never know."

"But Father, that priest is dead. Grace told me she recognized the name. She said Moia was yelling this man's name over and over again when Father Sweeney was trying to help her. If it was our former pastor, wouldn't there have been other children in the parish who were also abused?"

"Yes, it would be quite likely that other children were involved, yes."

"But no one has come forward. Wouldn't someone have come forward, Father?"

How to answer? The priest paused and proceeded with careful deliberation. "Maggie, it is entirely possible that your former pastor is completely innocent. That he's guilty of nothing more than a few bad sermons." He smiled ruefully. "On the other hand, it's possible that he did abuse young children in his trust and that it won't come out until these children begin suffering the kind of emotional disorders your Moia is suffering. In the end, these things do come into the light."

Maggie Kealey looked desperate. "But . . . there can be healing, right Father? You said there can be healing."

The priest listened to the plaintive cry from the heart of this mother and marveled at God's handiwork. Nowhere, he knew from years of experience, does faith in God run deeper than in the heart of a mother.

"Yes, Maggie. There can be healing. If God wills it, it will happen."

"But why wouldn't He will it?"

"I can't think of a reason why He wouldn't. I just don't profess to know His mind."

"Well, what can we do to convince Him to do something, anything? How do we get started, Father?"

"I want to come to your home. I want to get a better sense of what we're dealing with here. If we've got a case of demonic oppression, it can be handled by what we call a 'prayer of deliverance.' Your parish priest, Father Sweeney, would be more than capable of leading that prayer. I say 'leading' because generally there are a few lay people—men and women of strong faith—who

accompany the priest, laying hands on the victim's soul and join-
ing in the prayer."

"And that works, Father?"

"It can work, Maggie. In all these matters we leave the actual
healing to the Divine Physician."

At this the mother fell silent. The priest thought she was on
the verge of tears again. Then her face changed and she radiated
a sunshine that softened his own heart—a heart long hardened by
too many encounters with the darkness.

"Well, if it can work, it will work. We'll just besiege heaven.
I'll be like that widow in Scripture, Father. God will answer my
prayer just to shut me up." Then Maggie Kealey threw back her
head and laughed, laughter of pure innocence and delight.

Father LeClere thought in that instant that he'd never beheld
a lovelier woman.

49

It had been a fitful week for Joe Delgado. He had experienced difficulty sleeping and even working since his meeting with Doctor Koblinski. He was on edge, and when he was on edge his wife was always the first to notice. That meant questions, many questions, none that Joe had the interest or patience to answer. This of course only served to make things worse at home, and therefore at work.

As far as he could tell, no one at work seemed to notice his struggle to focus. All his major projects—two overseas acquisitions, a restructuring of the corporation's long-term debt, and the hiring of a new head of human resources—had a momentum of their own and didn't require his undivided attention. This was a blessing, he knew, because at the moment his attention was indeed quite divided.

Over the course of the last week he'd slowly come to the realization that his conscience was speaking to him. He felt obligated to follow the "blood trail," as he called it. He couldn't just let it go. Not now. He had questions, and he wanted answers. Into what other nooks and crannies of medical science had Al Heyworth's cash flowed? What new eddies and streams had been created a generation ago, unleashing more rivers and seas of corporate profit and societal dysfunction today?

It was not an easy decision to reach. His parish priest was clear; he had one responsibility before God, and that was his family. His wife was equally clear; she would take the kids and return to her father's home if he was fired for "meddling," as she put it, in Pittman Labs' link to the creation and perpetuation of the oral contraceptive industry in America. He didn't want to lose his job, and he certainly didn't want to lose his family. Yet he didn't seek this inquiry; it sought him. He felt a certain responsibility, and yes, curiosity he had to admit, about it all. He was also just Italian enough not to like being told what he could and couldn't do, particularly when there was a moral principle involved. That he couldn't, wouldn't abide. It was a blessed burden of his upbringing. No, he decided, he would not go quietly into the night; he would take the next step. He would call Doctor Koblinski and ask him for his contact. He would explore the so-called link between oral contraceptives and breast cancer. And if there was indeed a link . . . well, he didn't know what he'd do. One step at a time, he told himself.

Joe assured himself that he was not being paranoid, but rather than make the call to Koblinski from his home or office he used a pay phone in a shopping center less than a mile from the Pittman Labs building. Koblinski was not in, he was told, but had been "expecting his call." The young secretary was most helpful. "Doctor Koblinski said that if you called you would want the name and number of one of his friends. I have that information, Mr. Delgado. Do you have a pen?"

"Sure do, and tell the good doctor I said thanks and that I will keep him advised of my progress."

"OK, I will Mr. Delgado. Are you ready?"

"Yes."

"The name is Doctor Timothy Kallen, and the phone number is . . . 673–501–8639. Shall I repeat that, Mr. Delgado?"

"No, I've got it. Thanks very much."

"Oh you're welcome, Mr. Delgado."

Joe hung up and thought about placing a call immediately from the pay phone, but decided against it. He just wasn't ready, he told himself. He didn't know why. He just wanted to sleep on it, assuming he could sleep with it.

. . .

It was still dark when Joe quietly slipped out of bed on a midsummer Saturday morning. He wanted to get out of the house and on the road early, without waking his wife. Johnstown was the better part of a four-hour drive from suburban Philadelphia, and Joe wanted to get there and back before dinner. It would be difficult but doable.

True to form, he chose not to fabricate a story for his wife. He simply said he had "business" in Johnstown, and that he didn't want to try to wedge it into his current schedule, which was just "too cluttered." That wasn't good enough, of course, but short of making a spectacle of herself by calling work and fishing around, there wasn't much she could do about it.

So he dressed quickly and quietly, having left his clothes in the bathroom to avoid yet another interrogation. He descended the steps quickly, deciding against making himself some coffee; he'd get a little something on the road. He went out the front door rather than through the kitchen because he'd left his BMW in the driveway rather than in the garage. He also wanted to pick up the early morning paper so he'd have something to read on the interminable drive to Johnstown. Reading while driving was a bad habit he developed in graduate school. He had gone back to school some ten years after earning his undergraduate degree. He had been working as a public accountant, had a family, and he was often quite pressed for time. He discovered the best time to study, the time when there were the fewest distractions, was when he was driving on highways that seemed to have no beginning and no end. He would simply wedge the textbook into the open surface of the steering wheel, just below eye level, and glance down intermittently. Initially it was slow going, as with the development of all new habits, but eventually he became quite proficient at it, even deploying a highlighter with great dexterity in his final year. Of course, he promised himself, if he ever caught one of his children doing such a thing . . .

Once on the road he ducked into a neighborhood Wawa, a popular convenience chain in the Delaware Valley, and bought himself a twenty-ounce cup of rich Columbian brewed coffee, black and hot the way he liked it. He also picked up a copy of the *New York Times* to see if any news about the acquisition he was orchestrating (of the British pharmaceutical house) had been leaked. He had been warned by Pittman colleagues in Europe that the CEO of the target company was notorious for finding all sorts of novel ways to keep his name before his countrymen. Joe told him directly that if any leaks surfaced, Pittman would cease negotiations immediately. They both knew it was pure fabrication, but Joe hoped it would at least slow the man down.

With his *Times* drawn and quartered within the fold of his steering wheel and with his cup of coffee in his right hand, Joe was ready for his four-hour drive to meet one Doctor Timothy Kallen. The prospect of the meeting excited him. Kallen was a true believer, the kind other men often dismiss out of hand because the rationality of their argument was tinged with an element of emotion. Most rationalists believed—and businessmen were nothing if not rationalists—that emotion was laden with risk and therefore expensive. Joe believed it was possible to distinguish between emotion and passion, and generally chose to look beneath the hood to understand what was driving a man's passion, so to speak.

That was why he wanted to conduct this meeting face to face. He wanted to take in the full measure of the man and his alleged scientific discovery.

As he drove through Lancaster, he looked at the dashboard clock and checked it against his wristwatch. If he was correct, he'd only been on the road forty-five minutes. He was ahead of schedule. He decided to stop at a convenience store just off the highway for a coffee refill and a *Business Week* magazine. Back on the road, he made Harrisburg in less than two hours, and Altoona in less than three. He began to think he would make Johnstown before nine o'clock, which would certainly give him more than enough time to see and hear what he needed to see and hear and be home before dinner. Time sufficient perhaps even to take his wife to dinner, because she tended to be far more discreet about her lines of inquiry in public.

Joe prided himself on "making good time" on the road. It was something of a family joke. "Dad got lost on the drive to the Outer Banks, but we made good time." He was making good time on this fine summer morning. He just didn't know who he'd tell about it.

Sometime before nine o'clock, Joe pulled off the road inside the city limits of Johnstown, Pennsylvania. He studied the written directions on his lap. He was not at all certain he'd taken them down with adequate attention. That was another of his many failings. He had a touch of this new diagnosis which was attaching itself to a surprising number of children in school. It was called Attention Deficit Disorder, or ADD, and when he heard of the symptoms, he told his wife he believed he suffered from it. She said at the time, "Anyone who knows you could have told you that." He replied as he often did, "Honey, thank God I have you to remind me of my weaknesses."

Joe thought he loved his wife despite their difficulties, which he knew were only exacerbated by her drinking. He admired her single-minded focus and clear-eyed assessment of what was good and what was bad for her family, and her resolute determination in pursuing the good and following the course once set. He would chide her gently for being a cynic, but she would always reply that she was a realist, a necessary compensating balance for his misty-eyed idealism. Indeed, he thought that she more than he had the right stuff to be the chief financial officer of a Fortune 500 company.

He asked her twice to seek counseling for her addiction. She reacted badly each time, and he chose not to go there again. Then, out of nowhere, she surprised him one Saturday night by saying she had confessed her "problem." She claimed Father Sweeney said to her, "Congratulations. It just means somewhere in your bloodline there's some Irish." He reportedly added, "When I visit on the Block Collection, just make sure there's some Jameson's in the house." He asked Father Sweeney about that sometime later and the priest expressed some surprise at how his comments were construed. "First, Joe, I told her I was the last person to be judgmental about alcoholism given my own youthful indiscretions. But I told her, if the problem was serious, she should get counseling. As far as the Jameson's was concerned, I was only kidding. But hey . . . you guys do carry the stuff, don't you?"

They both laughed at that and Joe departed as he always did from his conversations with Father Sweeney, feeling better. He wasn't always certain he got his questions answered, or fully answered, but he did always feel better when he was around the man. He thought of his parish priest as something of an anti-depressant. A little toke on a spiritual joint.

Joe decided he would just start in the general direction of the final leg of his trip. He reasoned he was no more than ten to fifteen minutes away. He would get close, then call. Some twenty-five minutes later, exasperated, Joe called Dr. Kallen. He tried to suppress his anger at having just discovered that he'd circled the city twice and essentially found himself close to where he started. "Joe, stay where you are," the voice on the other line instructed. "I'll come to meet you. Be there in ten minutes."

Joe sat fuming at the indignity of not being able to complete the trip himself and—of greater consequence in his mind—adding a good twenty-five minutes to what might have been record time from King of Prussia to Johnstown, even on a Saturday morning. The metaphor of his losing his way on this journey to God knows where escaped his notice, such was his degree of dudgeon. But he didn't have long to deride himself, because within minutes Dr. Kallen pulled up next to him in a light blue Volvo station wagon. Surprised at first, Joe was slow to lower his window. When the Doctor lowered his, Joe responded with an airy, "Doctor Kallen, I presume." This drew a chuckle and a hand signal that seemed to say, "follow me, doofus."

Several minutes later they pulled onto a quiet residential street in a development that was straight out of the 1950s. There was row upon row of white frame split-level homes on small tracts with miniaturized driveways adorning one-car garages like bibs. There were not many mature trees, so what passed for grass was more brown than green. From the road, Joe could see quite a number of above-ground pools in the backyards, all apparently installed by the same mass-market retailer. The only external feature helpful in differentiating one home from the next was the shutters, he noted. There were blue shutters, red shutters, green shutters, and gold shutters. And that was pretty much it. That and bicycles. There were plenty of bikes strewn across driveways and lawns, suggesting that this was a teeming kid zone. Joe smiled at the pure nostalgia of it. This, he surmised, is "the way we were." He was looking forward to making the Kallens' acquaintance.

They pulled up to a three-bike driveway, and Dr. Kallen parked in front of the house and waved Joe to a spot behind him. Joe noticed several neighbors observing him, and he felt self-conscious about navigating his BMW into the spot. At least he hadn't brought his wife's Mercedes station wagon. When he popped out of the car he was surprised to see the whole Kallen family at the curb. They were smiling. All six of them.

Tim Kallen, tall and handsome in the classic Nordic tradition, extended his hand, turned to his family, and with his back entirely to Joe immediately launched into the introductions. Joe hoped there wouldn't be a test. By the time he started up the driveway to the front door, he had even forgotten the wife's name. Less than twenty steps and he was already perspiring. He just hoped the house was air conditioned.

It wasn't.

Dr. Kallen directed him to a small family room in the back of the house, just off the kitchen. They sat, Joe somewhat stiffly, on matching love seats. Mrs. Kallen, what else to call her, appeared with a large pitcher of iced tea. Joe considered, but rejected, the impulse to commandeer the entire contents, aware that it might possibly give the wrong impression. Dr. Kallen's wife, Joe couldn't help but note from up close, was also fair of skin with piercing blue eyes and the timeless beauty of a European actress.

When the room was cleared and the house was quiet, Doctor Timothy Kallen looked at him directly and said, "OK Joe, what can I tell you about the Pill and breast cancer?"

Joe liked men who got right to the point. And no group of men and women got there quicker than physicians, he found. "Well, first, Dr. Kallen . . ."

"Call me Tim, Joe—or should I call you Mr. Delgado?" This was said with a smile, but the point was nonetheless made. This would be an informal discussion, devoid of protocol. Joe sensed that at some point he might be asked to fire up the grill and flip a few burgers.

"You can call me pretty much anything you want Tim. Let me start by thanking you for making time for me and for giving me the opportunity to meet your family. How old are the children, may I ask?"

"Michael is eleven, Kevin is nine, Mary Beth is five, and John Paul is fourteen months."

"Hmmm . . . John Paul. Would he be named after the famous French existentialist?"

"No. The pope. Pope John Paul II!"

OK, Joe told himself, no jokes. "Well, it's quite a family you have here, Tim. I've got to ask, how the hell did you find the time to undertake this project with a big family, and everything else?"

Tim answered with a self-deprecating shrug of his shoulders. "I just made the time. We all have mothers. Most of us have sisters. Some of us are fortunate enough to have wives and daughters. About one in eight of them will develop breast cancer in her lifetime. Epidemiologists tell us that, in the last fifteen years alone, there has been about a thirty-five percent increase in breast cancer incidence. What medical science hasn't told us is all of the risk factors. I believe women, and the men who love them, ought to know. They certainly have a right to know."

Joe nodded. Tim was indeed a true missionary. When would he be shot, Joe wondered? Then it struck him that it might be the other party in this discussion who catches the arrow—if for no other reason than he was certainly the more ample target. This unsettled him, but only briefly. "Isn't a lot of this research government funded, at least partially? Why wouldn't the U.S. government insist the scientific inquiry investigate all risk factors, real and alleged, and report the results in an objective, purely scientific manner?"

Tim smiled. "Because the elite medical science community tends to be a closed loop. The people with the most prestige seem to move easily among the top medical schools, the leading professional associations, the big research houses, the most influential medical journals, and the most coveted government positions and commissions. It's always surprising to those of us not included among their number just how little diversity of opinion exists on very large, complex issues within these concentric circles."

"Who are these people, Tim? And what do they want?" Joe asked.

The doctor paused for a moment and said, "If you were at a cocktail party, you wouldn't readily discern a worldview much different from your own. In most cases, they want the same things for their families that you and I want for ours. They want a strong and noble America. They want robust, civic-minded communities. They want good schools, loving families . . ."

"Just not large families," Joe interrupted.

Kallen smiled. "Well, that's undoubtedly true. It's the eco-variant of the Malthusian view. Too much of anything is bad. Particularly people. Particularly people who consume disproportionately to other citizens of the world."

"So how did they end up so . . . 'out there'?"

Kallen laughed. "They're convinced *we're* the ones who are 'out there.' But you have to remember, these good folks were children of exceedingly high expectations. Their high academic achievement opened doors to the kind of places which breed a sense of—well, let's just say—hubris. You see this most clearly in some of our politicians from the Northeastern part of our country. They know more, so they know better. And because they know better, they have an obligation to set things right for the rest of us. So whatever the prevailing orthodoxy of the day is in their circles of influence, it's their task in life to see that it guides the lives of us ordinary folk. All in the interest of a more civil society, of course."

"So they're not really shapers of their own orthodoxy?"

"Shapers, yes. Originators, no. Remember, these are people whose trajectory in life was determined by their ability to surprise and please their academic patrons. They imbibed more deeply, absorbed more fully than their counterparts the 'first principles' of the academy. Their success, ultimately, will be measured by the standards set by their mentors. Were they able to shape public policy, to bring it into alignment with the reigning heterodoxy of the elite centers of learning in this country?"

"So how are they doing?"

"In America as in Europe, they're doing very well, thank you."

"So who are the 'originators'?"

"Look Joe, we're getting pretty far afield from our subject here."

"OK, but suffice it to say it's not amoral capitalists?"

"Oh, God no! Amoral capitalists do not trouble themselves with existential issues. We're talking about the natural selection, if you will, of some three hundred years of philosophical error. As John Paul II once famously said, 'Descartes got it precisely backwards. It's not 'I think therefore I am; It's rather I am, therefore I think.'" What I think he's saying here is that philosophical error draws man away from a fundamental harmony with Original Design, if you will, and the consequences are usually catastrophic. Witness the 'bloody century.'"

Tim Kallen had just given Joe an unexpected gift. He'd shown him the dead end off in the distance. He saw his "blood trail" originated in philosophical error—the very who, what, and why of man's existence—but it was perpetuated by scientific error. An error induced by a metaphysical blindness that, ironically, was not perceived as error because it was so broadly and richly credentialed. The Al Heyworth's of the developed world were just men in the marketplace sensing a convergence of fortuitous events—ideas, wants, technology, capital, and such—all merely requiring only the commercialization of what was and what could be, by men of vision.

Joe thought it best to veer back on course. "Where does money figure in all of this?"

"For the true scientist, it's more an issue of access to grants. They crave recognition. They still want to be regarded as the brightest kids in the academy. So if they can field a rebuttal study that breaks new ground, scientifically sound or not, they will do so, knowing it will provide access to more grants and more recognition."

"How about the others?" Joe wanted to know. "The ones who aren't about the research itself?"

Tim nodded. "Yes, well, remember the oral contraceptive industry in America is a ten-billion-dollar-a-year business. You have deeply entrenched parties around the table whose interests need protection. That protection comes most credibly from the elites within the medical community itself. They are sought out for their well-published views on certain issues, and they are offered high-profile sinecures that are often regarded as career capstones."

"These . . . sinecures?"

"Research grants, as I've mentioned. Commission chairs. Even cabinet posts. Think Everett Koop."

"Koop!" A wave of recognition flooded Joe. Koop was the Reagan appointee as Surgeon General—so warmly received by the president's socially conservative constituency. A pro-life doctor in the country's most important, and visible, position. But it turned out, once confirmed and installed, the good doctor was not actually pro-life. Surprise, surprise. In an announcement that shocked many across the nation, Dr. Koop began opposing congressional bans, then restrictions, on abortion. Later during his tenure he initiated efforts to distribute contraceptives to "at-risk" children to reduce the incidence, he said at the time, of sexually transmitted diseases, known in the trade as "STDs." At the time, pro-life organizations warned that distributing condoms would encourage a separation of the unitive and procreative dimensions of the conjugal act, which would then cause a pandemic of STDs—some were predicting as many as fifty million individual cases by the year 2000. Near as Joe could tell the warning and the predictions had fallen on deaf ears.

"Did President Reagan know?" Joe wondered aloud.

"Of course not. He was as shocked as the rest of us. The question isn't even did the people who advised him know—because it appears they too were in the dark. No, the question is did the people who advised the people who advised Reagan know?"

"And the answer?"

"There is some evidence that yes, they did in fact know Koop's true leanings on the great moral issue of our time, and that is why the Senate hearings and final vote were so swift and lacking in contention. Of course, there are others who claim Koop simply changed his mind. A case of Potomac influenza. Kind of what happened to the little cowgirl from Arizona when she started playing tennis with Katie Graham, the publisher of the Washington Post."

"That would be . . . Justice O'Connor?"

"Right."

"Listen Tim, without getting too deeply into the science, lay this thing out for me. Is the Pill in fact a significant risk factor for breast cancer in women? And if it is, how do you account for so many studies that come to the opposite conclusion?"

"Good questions, both. Let me take them one at a time. First, the numbers speak for themselves—at least to anyone coming at this thing with a blank slate. Meaning no preconceived biases one way or another."

Kallen continued, "The World Health Organization, not exactly a right-wing think tank, conducted a series of experiments around the world from which they concluded, and reported, that women who'd been injected with a progestin, like Depo-Provera, for at least three years before the age of twenty-five had a *190 percent* increased risk of developing breast cancer."

"Wouldn't that be end of story?"

Tim Kallen laughed and said, "No. It's the beginning of the story. Findings like that, it turns out, must be spun."

"But how do you spin that?"

"Simple. You field another study, and that study produces a different conclusion."

"So we have what, dueling banjos?"

"Precisely. The battle of the studies. What we've seen through the years is for every study the purists, as I call them, field that shows the link to be undeniable, the other side publishes two, sometimes three that conclude otherwise."

"They have access to more money?"

"A lot more money."

"Ah . . . I think I'm gonna need an example."

"Sure. The result of the largest meta-analysis done to date— meaning an exhaustive sweep of all major studies in a particular field to develop a composite risk factor—was published about two years ago in several of the most influential medical journals. It attacked the link between oral contraceptives and breast cancer.

There was only one problem with it. It completely omitted data from women who used contraceptives prior to their first full-term pregnancy."

Joe didn't want any of this getting past him. He interrupted, "Tim, why is that omission significant?"

Dr. Kallen permitted himself a small smile. "Well, in the scientific community it was generally known that these young, single women were presenting higher risk factors, but because the meta-analysis chose to be silent about the data, an Italian researcher fielded a study to address the omission. Her name is Dr. Isabella Romieu. Her study found that women who used oral contraceptives for four years prior to their first full-term pregnancy had a 52 percent increased risk of developing breast cancer."

"What's the link between the Pill and first pregnancy?" Joe thought he might know from his prior discussions with Dr. Koblinski, but he wouldn't have wanted to submit to an oral exam.

"A woman's breast is especially sensitive to cancer-producing influences before she has her first child. That's because the breast itself undergoes a maturation process throughout the woman's first pregnancy. Now, if a woman has used oral contraceptives prior to this maturation, this carrying of her first child to full-term, studies confirm there is a significantly higher rate of breast cell division. And there is no disagreement, none, among medical researchers that cells that divide more rapidly are far more vulnerable to carcinogens. That's just a simple, uncontested fact."

"So how did the other side contest it?"

Tim Kallen laughed. "Well, in the Oxford study, they just omitted women from the study who were less than fifty years old."

"But that's so transparent!"

"Of course it is. But they can and will get away with it, at least for awhile."

"How?"

"Because the latent period—the period between the entrance of the risk factor and the cancer it induces—is around twenty years.

Oral contraceptives were introduced in the early 1960s. Now in the 80s, most women who are over fifty would not have had access to them prior to giving birth. Younger women today, of course, not only have access to the Pill, but it is used almost universally by women both single and married. As we know, many use it for years before their first full-term pregnancy. If these women are excluded from the studies, how could you possibly get an accurate read of the link between the risk factor—in this case the Pill—and the maturation of breast cancer some twenty years later?"

"In other words, if I'm understanding you, the other side, if I may call them that . . ."

"You may."

"They've taken, what, a snapshot in time?"

"That's correct."

"And maybe a snapshot at the wrong time . . . at least for our younger women?"

"Right again."

Joe paused to consider the implications for a generation of daughters. "Tim, wouldn't this thing track much better as some kind of documentary? You know, follow these women around through various stages of life and record the data, you know, chart, what, . . . their demise? God, that's awful, positively ghastly."

Tim Kallen leaned forward and said with controlled vehemence, "How's 175,000 women being diagnosed with breast cancer every year in the U.S. sound? How's almost 50,000 women a year dying from breast cancer sound?" His eyes remained fixed on Joe's, and Joe felt the room temperature momentarily soar, something he didn't think possible on this unusually hot summer day. "Anyway, you and I don't have to worry about any docudramas, Joe. That'll never happen."

Joe made a mental note to float the idea of a documentary to his buddy Michael Burns, who was running the CMN business for a big New York advertising firm. The buzz was that Burns was skyrocketing up the corporate ladder and was now a big honcho. Joe figured that if anyone could persuade the powers that be to create a documentary on the link between the Pill and breast cancer, it would be his friend Michael. And it just so happened he'd be seeing him in several weeks at the parish's 175th anniversary celebration in Narbrook. In fact, they would be at a table together, along with the Kealeys and a few others.

"Tim, I think what I'm hearing is that as these younger women mature we're going to see more and more of them developing breast cancer. I mean we're talking about not an epidemic, but a pandemic!"

Kallen made no attempt to hide his distress. "Sad, but true. The 'x factor' now is the high number of girls in high school on the Pill. Soon it'll be junior high. An astonishingly large number of them will develop breast cancer before they're forty, and increasingly, they will die from it."

Joe wanted to get back to the "blood trail." "Are all these studies government funded?"

"Good question. The answer is no. We've got what amounts to the lineal descendant of Margaret Sanger in England, and she provides the lion's share of the funding for many of the major rebuttal studies abroad, and more and more here in the United States, I might add."

"What's her name?"

"Elizabeth Roscommon. 'Libelous Lizzy.' Her family's fortune was made in diamonds, in South Africa. It's a bottomless pit, so to speak." Small smile. "She'll throw a hundred dollars of bad research against every one dollar of good."

Joe found this astonishing. "What's she got against women?"

"She's a true believer, which today of course means nonbeliever. It's actually an Enlightenment mindset. You know, the Catholic Church is the enemy of all that is good and true, particularly as it relates to scientific discovery. Mankind needs to be liberated from the constrictions of organized religion, which is a corrupting and oppressive influence on man's development. Usual stuff."

"Man, how'd you like to take that one to bed?"

Tim Kallen blinked.

Joe coughed and shifted uneasily.

Kallen ignored the comment, or pretended to. "She's not a true Sanger disciple, though. Sanger got her hands dirty. She advised Hitler on eugenics. She created the Birth Control Federation in the U.S. She opened clinics offering contraceptives in cities all across the country. When the Catholic Church objected, she stared them down. Lizzy wants to stay above the fray. Actually, she just wants to fund the war."

"That woman, Sanger," Joe replied, "I've heard of her before. Isn't she the one who put a smackdown on our bishops?"

"Well, let me answer that this way, "Who do you think has more influence on the nation's social policy today, the U.S. bishops or Planned Parenthood—which, by the way, is what her Birth Control Federation morphed into? Who has more influence in the school? In the home?"

This thing with the Catholic bishops bothered Joe greatly. The more he got involved in this seminal moral and social issue, the more he wondered why these men always appeared to be missing in action. Maybe, he told himself, he just didn't understand the role of a bishop. Maybe they do a lot of good things behind closed doors—out of range of their critics and adversaries. Things people like him never heard of and wouldn't understand if they did. Perhaps if they didn't do the things they did, whatever they were, things would be a lot worse.

But how much worse? What was it Alexander Solzhenitsyn said recently? Something about "the West committing moral suicide." And hadn't Mother Teresa of Calcutta said earlier this year, "The most dangerous place in the world today is a mother's womb?" Joe was beginning to understand that what happened in the womb was not only dangerous to the child, but to the child's mother as well. And, he concluded, whatever was dangerous to America's mothers was absolutely lethal to America's families.

To Joe's way of thinking, primitive though he considered it to be, if something was bad for the family, it was bad for society.

What were men like Al Heyworth thinking when they shorted America's prized equity stock, its next generation, for short-term personal gain? How could that possibly benefit even Heyworth's own children and grandchildren in the long run?

He thought about Al Heyworth's moment of reckoning. He hoped it didn't take place in a contemplative, bucolic setting. He thought perhaps a glass-walled docket like those used for the Nuremberg trials would be more appropriate. He must be more charitable, he reminded himself. And why, by the way, was that so difficult for him?

"Tim, what's the bottom line on all this? Best guess. What's a reasonable number for the percentage increase in risk of breast cancer if a woman's using oral contraceptives?"

"Joe, I just explained it's all in how you cut the data. Not spin the data. Cut it. Meaning segment it, analyze it, cell by cell, so to speak."

"OK, OK. Let's work with the most at-risk segment."

"Well, again that would be our young women who are single or who are married but who have not yet given birth to their first child. These are the women who seem most at risk to use oral contraceptives, and therefore, the most at risk to develop breast cancer."

"How much more at risk?"

"For women who use oral contraceptives for four years or more before first delivery . . . well, they're over 50 percent more at risk. That means if the national average of at-risk women is 12 percent, that some 18 percent of the women in that particular category are at risk of developing breast cancer. Almost 1 in 5. That's the predictive power of the 'latent period,' if you let it play itself out."

Joe nodded. He was locked and loaded. "Tim, this has been enormously helpful. I've heard what I needed to hear."

"Joe, may I ask you a question?"

"Certainly."

"What are you going to do with this?"

Joe flinched. "I . . . I don't know."

"You said on the phone you were the CFO at Pittman Labs. They're a monster player in the oral contraceptive business. Are they starting to experience pangs of guilt down there?"

"Oh, no. Nothing like that." Joe was aware he was coming off a bit coy, and he didn't think that fair to his host, who'd been entirely candid with him. "Look Tim, the people at Pittman Labs told me a few months back to let this thing go. But it won't let me go, if you know what I mean."

"I do indeed. Welcome to my world."

"At this point, I don't even know what my options are."

"Well, what's your angle on this thing?"

Joe pondered that for a moment. "That people are making money on the pain and suffering of our women. And, down deep . . . they know. They know."

"You could go to a publisher and try to sell them on the idea of an exposé."

"No, I'm not much of a writer."

"How about a newspaper publisher?"

"Aren't they all pretty much part of the problem?"

"Yes. But you can appeal to their self-interest."

"What self-interest?"

"Pulitzers."

"Pulitzer Prizes? Those things they give journalists for . . . for what exactly?"

"For all sorts of things, including hard-hitting investigative series on some betrayal of the public trust."

"Do you think one of them might really be interested in something like this?"

"I do. I just don't know which one. And therein lies the problem."

"Exactly. It's not like I can go shopping this thing. If word gets back to Pittman Labs, they'd fire me. They've already put me on notice."

Tim Kallen winced. "Joe, I'm not going to encourage you to put your family at risk. Decisions like that are for man and wife . . . and a good spiritual director. Do you have a good spiritual director?"

"I think so."

"You think so? Why don't you know so?"

"I guess I've never really put it to a test before. At least not in this kind of way."

"Well, where is he in all of this?"

Joe paused. He didn't want to sell Father Sweeney out, even in anonymity. "He's told me not to do anything to jeopardize my family. And the reason he said that, I believe, is because I told him that my wife was having major problems with my continuing to pursue this thing."

Tim Kallen nodded. An uneasy silence descended. Mrs. Kallen interpreted it as a natural break and entered the room to ask if she could bring more iced tea. Her offer went unacknowledged. She left discreetly.

"Look Joe, I have no right to say this to you, but I'm going to. And I say it to myself as well as to you. In *Veritatis Splendor*, John Paul II said that all of us have accountability to objective truth 'even to the shedding of blood.'"

Joe's head swung up as though hooked. He looked at his host with an intensity that was palpable. It caught Tim Kallen momentarily off guard. "What does that mean, exactly?" Joe asked.

"It means we are called to imitate Christ, who spoke truth to power and was put to death because He did. That seems to suggest that truth itself, in God's eyes, is important."

"So what you are saying is if I don't fall on my sword on this thing . . . I'll go to hell?" Joe was irritated, if not offended.

"Of course not! And by the way, who talks like that anymore?"

"Tim, I'm not trying to be a wise guy, I'm really not. But I need to understand. Are you saying I have an obligation to see this thing through no matter where it leads—family or no family, job or no job?"

"I'm saying you might. It is possible the Holy Spirit has put this on your heart for a reason. Maybe it's a gift, an opportunity for you . . . a work you sort of muddle through as best you can, in the process of working out your salvation. I don't know that. I'm simply saying it's possible."

Joe Delgado was suddenly as serious as a heart attack. He looked ashen. "Does that mean if I go back and do nothing, I jeopardize my salvation?"

Tim Kallen exhaled slowly and audibly. "Joe, you're asking me fair questions. I just don't have the answers. You really need a good, competent, spiritual advisor. If your guy isn't, find someone who is."

Joe got up to leave. He gathered his notes and picked up his glass to return it to the kitchen. "I see your wife has trained you well," Tim needled him gently. "I was hoping you'd stay for lunch. I was going to put you to work."

"Somehow I got that sense. That's when I knew it was time to leave."

"I want you to call me if you need anything. I'm going to be praying for you."

"I appreciate that," Joe replied, suddenly feeling very alone.

Tim Kallen walked his guest to his car. The street was now alive with the sounds of summer. There were girls riding bikes and skipping rope, and a group of boys in the midst of a wiffleball game in the street. It appeared that the rear of his car was being used for first base. Joe noted the metaphor. He looked at his watch. It was a little after noon. He calculated that he could stop for something quick on the road and still make it home before five o'clock. That would leave plenty of time to frustrate his wife's interrogation . . . and for him to redeem himself by taking her to dinner.

50

Some evenings, Father John Sweeney observed, seemed to emerge as tableaus—ethereal and timeless. Night doesn't so much fall as it gently descends in ever-darkening half measures until all is well and still under a lightly sugared sky.

It was into one such evening, a Saturday evening, that he was headed after showering, shaving, and dressing in his Sunday best. He stared into a full-length mirror on the back of his closet door. It's true, he affirmed, good guys really do wear black. He descended the stairs nimbly and tapped the screen door open with his throwing hand, entering the bliss of a perfect summer night with its evocative summons of youth. His mind filled swiftly with memories of ball games under lights and—thoughts be banished—girlfriends under stars. On the way to the parish hall he ducked into the church, which was dark and vacant, and asked his Redeemer's blessing on the evening and its celebrants. He also asked divine Providence for assistance in meeting Monsignor Grogan's expectations for the evening's take.

He locked the church door behind him and turned in the direction of the lights and the music on the other side of the street near the top of the hill. As he walked up Narbrook Avenue he recalled his own happy childhood in this Brigadoon of dreams. He calculated he was one of maybe five hundred children of his generation to have experienced a sweet, untroubled childhood in this time and place. Five generations had preceded his and one, now two, followed. Each huddled momentarily in sequential periods of the same time warp, which conformed ever so slightly to the conventions and cataclysms of the day. It was his view that each child in each generation left this virginal womb with the same love of God and country, family and community. Most uprooted themselves, replanting in thousands of other communities small and large around the world, forever enriching their citizenry.

A fortunate few in each generation would find their way back, John Sweeney noted with a full measure of gratitude. How blessed he was to be born into the family of Jack and Mary Kate Sweeney in this tiny hamlet and this expansive country. How blessed to be born into a time that the country's finest generation hailed as "Morning in America." And how blessed, too, to have been called back to this place by God Himself, though in this instance, He was going by the name Jim Grogan.

As he made his way up the hill to the parish hall, he took a passing inventory of his life. At thirty-five, he thought he was perhaps in the prime of his life and ministry. He was friend and advisor—and assistant pastor—to some twelve hundred families and almost thirty-five hundred immortal souls. How blessed, how unfairly blessed, to have been given a priestly ministry. How blessed to have been given the privilege of facilitating this flock's encounter with the risen Christ. How blessed to be occasionally asked to thrust one of his broad shoulders under one of their crosses. How blessed to be assigned sentinel duty for people and ideas that might inflict spiritual harm on these, his families. Yes, he was indeed blessed. And because he had been so richly blessed, he was so very grateful. Grateful for his vocation. Grateful for the opportunity to celebrate the tenth anniversary of his ordination with his classmates in Rome next month. Grateful to be an assistant pastor in the parish he believed was nearest heaven's door.

When he reached the top of the hill, he made his way to the steps that led to the entrance to the parish school. He paused and peaked through the doors and the decorations that adorned them, surveying the gymnasium carefully. Each of the fifty tables, twelve souls to a table, appeared to be filled. He smiled. His boss would relax and enjoy himself, which meant his assistant would be able to relax and enjoy himself as well. The band was playing, and a number of young people were dancing. Waiters in white tuxedos were carting trays of hot and cold hors d'oeuvres to clusters of parishioners dressed in colorful summer dresses and suits. There were two open bars at either end of the floor—each of which attracted a mini-throng of thirsty revelers. On the stage a 1950s dance band was playing, and the musicians were wearing patches on their lapels proclaiming the parish's septaquintaquinque centennial.

This would be a good night, John Sweeney concluded. A very good night. The kind of night that would strengthen the bonds of community; the kind of night that would validate the work of a parish priest through the happy witness of his people's joy and gratitude. Standing there, John was half tempted to remain indefinitely or at least until observed. He reasoned that he could absorb more from his present vantage point than he could from inside, where he would be forced to be a participant. Inside he would engage and be engaged until ultimately rendered disengaged. Here, he could listen without hearing and see without seeing, observing more fully the fruit of his priestly labors to bless and heal and unite.

He opened the door and was greeted by a rush of cool air and the sound of a familiar page from the great American songbook. He suddenly missed his father very much. He longed to see him again, to hear him sing from this stage, alternately exciting the crowd and frustrating the band. He pictured him whirling his mother about the dance floor, singing just loudly enough to be heard above the twelve-piece orchestra. Too soon, Papa, John chided. You left us far too soon, and none of us has ever been able to take your place. The joy of your being has never been reclaimed within our family. And every time we're all together we feel it so intensely that none of us can or will give voice to it.

The thought of his mother sitting home with his sister Mary Eileen, just beginning what would become a painful protracted battle with Alzheimer's, filled him with more sadness. Mary Kate Sweeney occasionally would forget the name of her dead husband. Every day he would slip in and out of his former home mere blocks from the rectory, sometimes just holding his mother's hand while she napped. She remained the central intention of his daily Mass, during which he also gave thanks to God for the gift of his sister, who was now mother to the child that was, that forever would be, their mother. One life sacrificed for the other. History reciprocating.

"Father! Father John. Over here."

The voice was familiar and came from a table of older parishioners seated with party hats slightly askew on heads, themselves slightly askew. He immediately flushed the sadness from his head and heart and moved to those who'd beckoned him out of himself, thanking God for their summons.

"Father John, where have you been? We've all been waiting for you." It was Harriet Munger Greer, youngest sister of former pastor, now deceased, Monsignor Timothy Munger. She was smiling, her eyes dancing with merriment. Beside her sat her husband Fred, who appeared to be trying to determine which end of a party favor to blow. "Father, sit. Sit. Fred, get up and give Father John a seat."

John was embarrassed. He needn't have been. Fred Greer either hadn't heard or had chosen to ignore his wife. For her part, his wife now appeared to have forgotten what it was she asked her husband to do and why in fact she had summoned her parish priest to the table. She looked at him as if he was there to take a drink order, but she couldn't seem to remember what she was drinking. "Fred," she asked morosely, "what is it you're drinking?"

Fred grunted something unintelligible, and John thought this an excellent time to circulate. He turned to the bar at the far end of the gym and saw one among another group of parishioners waving him over. As he headed in the gentleman's direction, he was stopped twice by middle-aged women asking him to pray for one or more of their children who were suffering from drug or alcohol addictions. He promised he would, and was reminded anew of how a mother's life is essentially one of quiet and interminable suffering. Just as it was, he reminded himself, for the mother of the Redeemer.

As he approached the bar, the man who'd waved him over thrust a bottle of imported beer in his hands, saying, "Go ahead, Father. Grogan isn't looking."

John accepted it graciously, having no intention of drinking from it. "Thank you, Tom." Then to ease his awkwardness, "When will Tom Jr. be leaving to return to Yale?"

Tom Centrella was an influential attorney with a Center City firm with a large and varied client roster that, it was said, included a number of highly placed members of a local crime family. Somehow, it hadn't come up in confession. "Next Saturday, Father, and I'll tell him you were asking for him. He likes you, you know."

"Well Tom, I like him very much too." Pause. "And his father and mother."

"Thank you, Father." Strong clap on the shoulder. "Now drink that beer. We need you up there singing like your old man."

John laughed and noticed out of the corner of his eye a group of men and women from the parish choir huddled around two tables. He approached and was welcomed warmly. "Father, we miss your dad." It was Susan Littenauer. "We were just saying how much he and your mother would have loved this night. How is your mom doing, Father?"

"She's pretty much the same, Susan. You know how that disease is. It's unsparing."

"Father, how are *you* doing? You look good," remarked John Cunningham, spirited baritone and father of seven daughters.

"I'm good, John. Happy to be on this side of the grass . . . and in Narbrook."

"We're glad you're here too, Father," added Anne Mathers, mother of five.

John nodded and made his way to a table of women from the Sodality sitting quietly with their husbands. "Is this table behaving itself, or am I going to have to send Sister Patricia over here?"

Respectful laughter, "It's too late, Father." It was Jim Gentile, husband of Mary Ellen and coach of the school's football and baseball teams. This man John liked. He had a mischievous idea of what was fun, and John tended to gravitate to that quality in others. John motioned with the two fingers of his right hand, alternately pointing between his own eyes and the eyes of the other gentleman to indicate he'd be paying strict attention to the goings-on at this table.

John heard a familiar voice. "Hey, Fadder Sweeney! You buy a ticket? Who let you in?" It was Patrick O'Rourke, one of Rose's sons. He was a full-time attorney and part-time heckler extraordinaire, or maybe the reverse, John thought. He couldn't get enough of O'Rourke, which worked out fairly well because most people soon had enough of him.

"Where's your leash, big dog?" John asked, looking at his long-suffering wife, Mary Theresa. It was one of the delicious ironies of life he thought, that two women of such probity would have each been given the same thorn. He did note, though, that mother Rose appeared ten years younger, now that she was at least technically off the clock.

"Hey, I want to see your ticket! Did you scam your way in here? I better not see you drinking our beer if you didn't pay— and I know you didn't." O'Rourke was angling toward him now, with a large magnetic grin and a turned shoulder for a big hug. John embraced him and said, "Just remember, you do have to go to confession at least once a year."

O'Rourke laughed and said, "You don't have the authority to hear my confession." He then thrust his beer, pre-sampled, into John's hand. "But in case you ever get it, I want you drunk . . .'cause you know I'll be!"

John laughed and moved on, placing the beer on a semi-vacant table at the first opportunity. He picked up an unopened soft drink that was still cold to the touch, and headed toward a table of early middle-aged, blue-collar men sitting quietly with their wives in clothes they must have worn only to weddings and funerals, judging from their discomfort. He liked these men and women very much, and pulled a chair from an adjoining table and wedged it into the group. "Hey, how's everybody doin' here?"

"Good, F'er, how's youse and yours doin'?" It was Guido Carrozoli, a foreman on a local construction crew and one of the toughest men John knew. As always, he was smiling, a smile John particularly loved because it revealed the goodness in his heart— and the absence of his teeth. The teeth had been knocked out one by one in sandlot football games and industrial league basketball games. There was never enough money for both kids and teeth, so Guido simply never bothered replacing them, the teeth that is. It didn't seem to bother him or his wife. Indeed, his wife was also missing her upper plate, though it was not known under what conditions it had taken its leave, and John never actually inquired.

"Good, Guido. Everybody's good. How about youse?"

"Good F'er. You know we wuz just saying, me and the guys here, you still look like you could help the Iggles. Ever think about it?"

"You mean as a chaplain?" John deadpanned.

"Naw, naw." Big toothless grin. "We meant as QB. Member how y'cud tho' dat thing?"

"Yes, well Guido, there was a little nuance of the game called 'reading defenses.' It always kinda looked like a Chinese fire drill out there to me. That used to steam my coaches up pretty good."

"Yeah, I know whatcha mean. Use to confuse me sum, too. Hey, F'er any truth to that rumor sometime goin' 'round you hadda become a priest because, you know, you wuz a wild kid, knockin' up girls 'n all, and your mom and Grogan made a deal?"

"No truth to that at all, Guido. But hey, thanks for asking."

John got up and waved to the rest of the table, who waved back so enthusiastically he thought perhaps he had just spent an hour with all of them rather than several minutes with one of them. Must be glad to see me move on, he mused. No doubt concerned I might start hitting on their women.

He scanned the room for Bill and Maggie Kealey. He saw a table of their friends in one of the corners. The Kealeys weren't there. He looked on the dance floor. He didn't see them. He checked the lines at the two bars. Nothing. He felt a quick stabbing pain in his heart that surprised him. He really wanted to see the Kealeys. He hadn't caught up with Maggie since she returned from New York several weeks ago. This in itself was a bit unusual, but he reasoned that it was summer and perhaps she and Bill had taken the younger children to the shore.

He started to move toward the table of their friends when he felt a large hand on his back. He turned to see Monsignor Jim Grogan with a grimace on his face. "John, did you hear about Maggie?"

"No . . . no Jim . . . I didn't. What happened?" John's heart began to race.

"She was rushed to the emergency room at Lower Merwood a couple of hours ago."

"What! Jim, what the hell happened to her?"

Grogan shook his head. "Don't have the full story. Some kind of stroke. Bill took her. He's with her now."

John froze. He hoped the look on his face did not reveal the true level of his concern. "Jim, who'd you hear it from?"

Grogan nodded in the direction of the table and said, "Fran Delgado told me about twenty minutes ago. Where you been? I've been looking for you."

"Just mingling, Jim. This is terrible. Who's watching Moia?"

Jim Grogan shrugged his very round shoulders. "Dunno. If you hear anything, let me know, OK?"

"Right." John stood in place, dazed. Then, slowly, he began to move about aimlessly. He decided he needed that beer. He headed for the bar nearest the band and found himself beset with questions. What was the origin of this poor woman's latest problem? What induced a stroke? Should he leave and go to the ER at once?

"Hey, Father, how 'bout a cold one?" It was young Rick Ferguson, a big, redheaded former basketball star at the U.S. Naval Academy. John Sweeney very much liked and admired the charismatic young man, and he did want to catch up with him and his group of friends. Just not now. "Sure. Thanks, Rick. How are you and Joan doing?"

"Great, Father. C'mon over and join us. Everyone would love to see you."

"I will, Rick. Where you sitting?"

The young man pointed to a table near the door. "We're over there by the exit, Father. In case the place gets raided." Big toothy grin.

"OK, give me a few minutes. I got something I gotta do first. I do want to find out what you've all been up to. Haven't seen you in a while."

Ferguson nodded, but John noted that the smile was gone.

He turned and headed for Fran Delgado, who was sitting with Carol Burns, talking animatedly. He thought perhaps he knew the subject of their conversation. He approached the table and said, "Monsignor Grogan just told me something's happened to Maggie Kealey. Do we know how she's doing?"

The women stopped talking and looked up at their parish priest. "A complication, Father," Carol Burns said guardedly.

"What sort of complication? Do we know?"

The two women looked at each other. Fran Delgado spoke, "A woman's thing, Father. She's where she needs to be."

Just then, their husbands returned from the bar, drinks in hand. "Hey Padre, you here to pick up women?" It was a grinning Michael Burns who spoke first, but Joe Delgado who reached him first, hand outstretched. "Good to see you, Father. I was hoping you'd be here tonight."

John gave them each a big pump. He was immensely fond of both men, and drew genuine satisfaction from their having sought him out for spiritual counsel, each independent of the other. In fact, he wondered if each knew he was advising the other. "Hey, what's up with Bill and Maggie?" he asked with evident concern.

Michael looked at Joe, much as their wives had looked at each other. "Some kind of problem with . . . ah . . . medication, Father. A complication of sorts. Think it kinda . . . caught them off guard."

John didn't like the sound of that. Nor did he like the sound of what he *wasn't* hearing. Clearly, Maggie or Bill had confided in someone at this table who had shared it with the others, but just as clearly, no one was prepared to share that confidence with him. This pained him.

"Sit down, Father. Relax a little bit." It was Joe, motioning to an empty chair. He sat a bit uneasily, realizing for the first time he did not enjoy the full confidence of some of his own families. But he forced his apprehensions to the back of his mind, telling himself to live in the present moment, which, as he was taught in the seminary, was a necessary precondition for peace of mind.

Just then the band stopped playing, which delighted John. He had a genuine aversion to loud noise, particularly when he was trying to have a conversation. "So what have the Burnses and Delgados been up to?" he asked, placing the bottle of beer squarely in front of him and picking slightly at the label.

Michael Burns debated two alternate answers to that question. On the one hand he wanted to keep it light, this after all was a social setting; on the other hand, he and Carol were heading back home tomorrow immediately after Mass, and he did have nagging doubts about his moral dilemma at CMN and the spiritual counsel his priest was giving him. What to do? He hesitated for a moment, then leapt. "Well, Father . . . I got myself a Class A dilemma."

John winced slightly. This was a problem all but unique to the Irish, he believed. They go looking for fights, and finding none, start one. "OK, give me the headlines." He wanted to keep this one short and sweet, this being neither the time nor place for this kind of discussion.

Burns jumped right in, either oblivious to the sensibilities of the others or confident of their interest in the operatic quality of his drama. "Father, I'm now getting pretty clear indications that CMN has committed itself to an irreversible course of counter programming network television down. 'Down,' as in broadcasting increasingly excessive doses of violence, profanity, and sex—the likes of which would put broadcast licenses at risk. The programming side of the house is driving this, and is in near total control. The marketing side knows that selling this programming will be a long, slow grind with plenty of risk to their revenue base, but appears powerless to challenge it and resigned to its inevitability.

"In short, it's no place for a Christian, Father. I know we both thought it was, but now I see it isn't. It just isn't. If I continue to speak out, I'll be summarily fired, and my family will be at risk. If I don't speak out and stay, I'll be a party to bad things happening to American families."

He paused and shrugged his shoulders at the sheer improbability of it all. "What would God have me do, Father?"

John Sweeney groaned. He noted the other couples at the table were talking among themselves and were paying no attention to this conversation. He also noted that Carol Burns and Fran Delgado were stirring uncomfortably and indeed were now in the process of excusing themselves. They stood, smiled a bit painfully at his predicament, and headed to the bar.

It was just him and Michael Burns . . . and Joe Delgado, who was now pulling his seat closer to the two men. John looked at each of them and felt a sense of unease—as though he were about to be ambushed. His head began to ache. Why on this night must he be subjected to this? He now understood the Old Testament references to kings wanting to rend their garments when they felt trapped in moral or ethical conundrums.

"Michael," he began slowly, choosing his words with great care, and hoping to quickly dispose of the topic, "I think we've been over this. God has given you a rare gift, the gift of a very special family." He nodded in Carol's direction. "What He wants most from you is your love and protection of that family. He is not asking—He would not ask—you to do anything that would put them at risk."

Silence at the table. Then abruptly, "I think you may be wrong about that Father." It was Joe Delgado. His face was slightly flushed, the light from above casting it in a rosy hue.

John was stunned. He swallowed hard and said, "Joe, what makes you say that?"

"I don't know," he said, sounding anything but irresolute. "Just doesn't seem right, is all."

John felt his own cheeks flush. He looked at Joe, then Michael, then back to Joe. "Men, work with me here. What did I say that doesn't seem right to you?" He'd landed a bit too hard, he feared, on the "you."

It looked like Michael Burns was prepared to speak, but it was Joe's voice John Sweeney heard again. "Well, I've been reading up on what the pope said in his letter to the laity. All of us have a duty to evangelize the culture, particularly in our places of work. We're supposed to speak truth to power, regardless of consequence. In other words, even if bad things happen to us and our families."

Suddenly and without warning, a grenade had been thrown into the middle of the conversation. Its pin was pulled. Michael was nodding in agreement and looking at John for an explanation, or at least a response. For his part, John felt as though his primary focus needed to be on picking shards of shrapnel from his exposed body parts. Thank God he was sitting, he told himself.

"Well fellows . . . I'm sure the pope wasn't calling fathers of large Catholic families to make kamikaze runs into their employers' buildings."

"Then what exactly did he mean, Father?" It was Michael Burns, and the glint in his eye signaled he was digging in for an argument.

John stumbled. "I don't know, precisely. I didn't . . ." He let his words hang in the air, their meaning clear.

"Father, I thought you guys had to read that stuff so you could explain it to the rest of us," Joe Delgado again.

"Well yes . . . certainly." He hesitated. "I just haven't caught up to that one yet. This pope has been . . . unusually prolific."

An uneasy silence.

"Father, if I may . . ." It was Michael Burns, and, despite his better instincts, he was tracking what he no doubt suspected was wounded prey. Burns, John knew, tended to be uncompromising, which he thought odd for an advertising executive, and he was certainly no great respecter of position or titles. "Maybe you could . . . ah . . . speculate." Brief pause. "Just what *could* he have meant?"

"Michael, not having read the statement, I don't know how to answer you."

Michael, John realized to his astonishment, was prepared to thrust his sword. "Well Father, I read the pope's letter," he said rather pointedly. "I was looking for . . . confirmation that what you've been telling me . . . is right. Father . . . I don't think it is."

John turned from Michael to Joe, who was nodding ever so slightly and rocking gently in his chair. He said nothing.

Michael looked into John Sweeney's soul and asked in the voice of a child, "Now, what does a duty to evangelize the culture in your place of work mean in my situation, Father? Am I to simply ignore all of that and just . . . just go with the flow as you've been telling me to do? Is that what God wants from me?"

John felt weak, and looked around for relief. Anyone. Surely there was someone who would wave and call him over—even just to run an errand. Nothing. Even Harriet Munger Greer appeared to be content for the moment. He needed time to think, but there was no time, and no place, to think. He turned to Michael and said, "I suppose it means you may have to resign your position, Michael; but as head of family, I wouldn't do that before I had another job."

John fell silent. More words would only bring more problems. He was now in a bad place both literally and figuratively. He waited for the conversation to change, or die, or something . . . anything. It didn't.

"What about me, Father? What should I do?" It was Joe Delgado, leaning in, breathing heavily.

"I don't know, Joe," John answered simply.

"Does God want me to just go with the flow too? Should I ignore what I've found, even if it means certain death to hundreds of thousands of women and millions of babies?"

Complete silence.

Michael Burns broke the silence. "These ministries come with a license, Father?" He said this with a smile, and John understood he was trying to change the tenor of the conversation, but it was too late. Much too late.

John felt the question penetrate his chest cavity and lance his heart. He hunched over in his seat, physically pained and utterly humiliated.

Then, without so much as a word, he got up and left.

Head down, heart crushed, he made his way to the table of "John Paulistas," as he called them, on the other side of the gym. He desperately needed a lift. Slowly, he raised his head to scan the table for young, happy, innocent faces. He saw them—the Fergusons, the Gambones, the Avins, the Fallons, and the Costellos. A welcome sight. He dropped his head, determined not to be intercepted along the way and, to his relief, he wasn't.

As he approached the table, Andrew Avin saw him first and stood out of respect for his collar. John liked this big bear of a man. At 6'3" and some 290 pounds, he had played football with some distinction at the University of Michigan. He had been a center, and he and John, who had been a quarterback, occasionally compared notes on how the whole game was ultimately dependent on the action between a center and the quarterback, because nothing commenced until those two players decided it would. "Hey, Father, good to see you. Sit with us. Ferguson here was just leaving."

"Nobody's going anywhere," John said, grabbing Rick Ferguson's arm with one hand and an unoccupied chair from an adjoining table with the other. He placed the chair between Joan Ferguson and Cheryl Avin. He sat, knees creaking, on the chair back to front, resting his arms on the bowed ribbon of wood adorned with festive crepe. "OK, I want a full accounting of all—twenty-six, is it?—children. Who's going to start?"

Bill and Janet Costello laughed and said, "We'll start." But Tim and Sara Fallon had other ideas. "OK, Father, are you strapped in?" Sara wanted to know. She unleashed a torrent of words that were rendered as a spot-on send-up of a popular Fed Ex television commercial that spoofed the hyper-paced absurdity of business communications. She ran through every school and every activity of each of their six children, top to bottom, finishing in what seemed to be less than two minutes.

John was impressed. "Sara, how many times did you rehearse that?"

"All just top of my mind, Father," she demurred with a laugh.

"Just like your sermons, Father," bellowed Tim Fallon. The laughter around the table was swift, sudden, and far too robust for John Sweeney's comfort. He decided not to go there; he'd had enough pain for one night. He redirected, "So where have you folks been? Monsignor Grogan and I haven't seen you since what, Easter?"

An uneasy silence greeted this simplest of questions. The conversation ground to a halt. John looked from couple to couple. He sensed his question might go unanswered. He waited patiently, awkwardly, until it slowly began to dawn on him that these young families had found spiritual nourishment . . . elsewhere.

He stared at Rick Ferguson in disbelief. "You haven't all registered at another parish, have you?"

A chorus of no's.

The table grew quiet again. "Then where have you been?" he asked, quietly.

Nothing. Suddenly, he found himself very much engaged. "Are you all still going to church on Sunday?"

A chorus of yes's.

John looked directly at Joan Ferguson. He knew he would get a straight answer from this small woman of large faith. He need only ask the question directly. "Joan, where'd you go to Mass last Sunday?"

She eyed him evenly and answered, "Mary, Queen of Peace, Father."

"Mary, Queen of Peace? That's in Chester!" John looked at Rick Ferguson, now sitting tight lipped. Chester was a ship-wreck of a town about forty-five minutes south of Philadelphia. It was an old manufacturing port town nestled along a bend in the Delaware River. Jobs, families, and hope had departed long ago, leaving behind a calcifying underclass and monstrous social problems. John couldn't conceive of his families, his best young families, leaving a leafy enclave at the front door to Philadelphia's storied Main Line for an all-but-abandoned Catholic church on the outskirts of downtown Chester.

John was incredulous. He looked again at Joan Ferguson. "Joan, what's going on at Mary, Queen of Peace?"

"Father John McGinty's going on." It was Tim Fallon. "He's the real deal, Father. He packs that church every Sunday with young families."

John felt a stabbing pain of inadequacy that he struggled mightily to mask. He sought to lighten the mood with a little humor. "What's Father McGinty serving down there, free cham-pagne brunch after Mass?"

Another awkward pause. Then, from Carmella Gambone,

"Truth." This was said so matter-of-factly, John almost didn't absorb it.

He blinked, not quite comprehending.

"He trusts us with the truth, Father." It was the diminutive Joan Ferguson.

John immediately made a decision. He was *not* going to get up and leave the table, which his every instinct was urging him to do. He was going to sit and hear what he needed to hear. He wasn't going anywhere until he understood what had driven these families out of his church and into the spiritual arms of another . . . Father.

"I'm not sure I understand, Joan. What do you mean, he trusts you with the truth?" He felt, more than actually saw, knowing glances being exchanged out of the corner of one eye—he didn't know by whom—and would not be told until much later how his unwitting paraphrase of Pilate struck the group in this moment.

Joan Ferguson shrugged her tiny shoulders and said, "He challenges us. He tells us we were created to be holy, and that we can be . . . if we're willing to pay the price."

John was now leaning forward, shoulders hunched, on the edge of his chair, "What does Father McGinty say the price is?"

"Being counter-cultural, Father." It was Drew Avin.

John turned to the large young man and said, "Well, of course. We'd certainly all agree with that, right? That's what it means to be a practicing Catholic." Heads nodding. "Did the Father offer any specifics?"

Yet another awkward pause. John wasn't about to answer his own question. He'd sit, wait, and let them work through it.

The answer finally came after several embarrassing moments of silence. It was Rick Ferguson and he was—how to say it?—on message. "He says contraception is a grave evil, Father. He says it just ruins marriages, families, and whole communities. He calls it a 'spiritual cancer on the Mystical Body of Christ.'"

"He says . . ." Tim Fallon broke in, "that no man who truly loves his wife would treat her like an object, just use her for his own pleasure. Especially now, with all the news reports about the side effects of the Pill—women having strokes and getting these . . . these cancers. Who would do that to someone they loved?"

John started to ask a question, but stopped when he heard Carmella Gambone's voice coming once again from the other end of the table.

"He told us something else, Father—something important." She said this quietly, yet the whole table heard it as clearly as if she were speaking into a microphone. "He showed us the divorce rate for couples who use natural family planning to space children. It's less than one percent, Father."

John correctly sensed that Carmella wasn't done. "He compared that to the national average, Father. It's now up over fifty percent; and for couples who cohabitate and contracept, then marry, it's over seventy percent." She paused, a bit too theatrically for John's sensibilities. "See why he's got our attention?"

John sat back and exhaled. So that was it. Nothing more than an old-time fire and brimstone teaching on the great taboo, without the fire and brimstone. But what was new here? And more to the point, how had this vanquished dogma from yesteryear been resurrected right under his nose without his knowing it?

John pondered all this for several moments, saying nothing, aware they were watching him. Had this priest in Chester lured his best young families away simply by channeling John Paul II? He began to feel adrift. He needed to find a way to bring them home. He needed them. But at this moment, he had absolutely no idea how to even begin.

"Let me say this to each of you," he began haltingly. "I want you to return to St. Martha's parish. This is your home. You belong here. I would ask you—each of you—to come back to your church. We, Monsignor Grogan and I . . ." He felt his voice tremble slightly and let it trail off. He was surprised at how emotional he was getting. Why? What was it about this defection—this "Mass" defection—that he found so unsettling?

His plea, he was surprised to discover, fell on hearts unmoved. He saw the band beginning to reassemble on the stage. He noticed an army of waiters and waitresses appear in formal attire, carrying trays of plates laden with exquisite foods to tables that were now filled. He saw at least one older couple rising from their seats in anticipation of the band beginning to play again.

And still no one responded.

Finally, Rick Ferguson said in what for him was a measured tone, "Father, we can't. We're addicted."

John blinked. "Addicted?"

"It's a truth fix, Father," the big redhead with the incandescent smile added. "What we get down there feeds us for the whole week. And during the week, we all just look forward to going back and being fed again."

Janet Costello said gently, "Father, we love you. We really do. But . . . you don't feed us. We're hungry. We've had a taste of the whole truth, and we want more."

Drew Avin, not wanting to pile on but wanting his friend to understand, said quietly, "Look, Father. Please don't take it personally. Like Janet said, everyone here loves you. But this priest is working hard at this. He's offering classes in NaProTechnology to help us space our children. He's leading study groups on the Holy Father's encyclicals—like that new one, *Veritatis Splendor* which, by the way, is just outstanding. He's got experts who come and speak to us about Marian devotions, apparitions, and the lives of the saints—like this Polish nun, Sister Faustina. And, best of all, he's got Eucharistic Adoration 24/7. A bunch of us get up in the middle of the night and drive down there. We're talking about driving to Chester, Father . . . in the middle of the night!"

John sat quietly, hands folded in his lap.

"Hey, Father, why don't you come with us some night?" It was Rick Ferguson, totally oblivious to the annihilation he was inflicting. John just wanted to scream—but what? That he, too, was an ordained priest? That he woke every morning with *their* spiritual needs and wants, not his own, uppermost in mind? That he had been 100 percent faithful to his vows since the day of his ordination? That he had a prayer life, too, that brought him before the Blessed Sacrament all hours of the day and night?

What did they think drew him to this most difficult and lonely life? He followed the scriptural exhortation of Christ. He left father, mother, brother, and sister—everything and everyone—to follow Him whom he loved with his whole mind, heart, and soul. He'd been promised in return that his reward would be great in the afterlife, and that he would have "many more children" of his own in this life. He was fully invested in that promise. Yet his very own children, the ones who'd been entrusted to him, were leaving him. Leaving him virtually childless in his own parish family. He'd never, ever, experienced such devastation.

The band resumed playing. The first song in this, their second set was an old Sinatra standard, "All of Me." The lyrics opened with the verse, "All of me. Why not take all of me? Can't you see . . . I'm no good without you?" Waiters and waitresses appeared with plates creatively adorned with delicacies from the sea and choice cuts of beef from the heartland. People, his people, "the people of God," were eating and drinking, singing and dancing. They were happy. In fact, Father John Sweeney sadly conceded, he'd never seen them happier.

For the second time that evening, this most promising and now most painful of evenings, John Sweeney was forced out of his chair. Evicted from his own seat in his own parish hall by the sheer inadequacy of his life's work. He stood without looking at anyone and slid his chair under the table, inadvertently bumping the arm of a waitress who was positively apoplectic at having jostled a priest. "Oh, forgive me, Father. I'm so sorry. Are you OK?" This was said with authentic concern. He smiled at the middle-aged woman who, he guessed, was working late on a Saturday night to help put a son or daughter through college. "I'm OK. Are you OK?"

She smiled with a pain John felt searing. He looked at her with tender affection and whispered. "Truth be known . . . I'm not

OK. And I know you're not OK. But it's OK." And with that bit of inverted transaction analysis completed, he headed for the exit.

Outside, he paused for a moment to consider his next move. Should he go back to the rectory and—what? Should he go bathe in what he referred to as the "supraviolet" light of the Blessed Sacrament and beg his God to heal his wounded heart? Or should he simply go home? Just walk down Narbrook Avenue, cross Haverhill, climb the hill, cross the bridge, take a right on Winthrop, and search in the darkness for his mother? A mother he knew would not recognize him. Who may not even remember him.

"Father . . . Father John." It was Drew Avin, huffing his way alongside him. "Father, you never answered Rick. Would you like to come with us some night? It would be good to have you and . . . it might even be good for you."

John felt the piercing flash of pain anew. He did not want to say anything that would in any way offend this fine young man. He didn't trust himself to speak, so deep was the pain rooted in his heart. "I don't know, Drew. I don't know what I'm going to do . . ."

"Father, we had to go. Please understand."

John nodded, too numb for words.

"For people who really want to live holy lives, as dumb as that may sound, we've got to go where we get fed. It's too hard for us otherwise. We just can't do it. It's like we've been orphaned out there in the world. Father, we're spiritually . . . fatherless."

John winced visibly. He felt that thrust penetrate into the very depths of his soul. There was nothing more to say. Mercifully, there were no more words.

He descended the steps rapidly, wanting to create as much distance from the source of this pain as he could, and do so as quickly as he could. He angled across the parking lot, heading toward the other side of the street, which was darker and therefore further removed somehow from the harsh glare of reality. As he started to cross the street, he heard his name called. He turned and squinted to detect the identity of the figure emerging from the shadows. It was Fran Delgado. In the darkness, she appeared even larger and more formidable—a princess of privilege poised to pounce. As she approached, John saw she was inebriated.

"Father . . . Father John. I must talk to you." She approached him with arms outstretched, her breath smelling of alcohol. "Father, give me a hug. I'm so worried about Maggie."

The sound of Maggie Kealey's name momentarily jolted him out of his semi-catatonic state. He allowed the woman to come closer and to put her arms around his shoulders. His own arms remained at his side. "Oh Father, it's so terrible what happened."

"What's terrible? What happened to Maggie, Fran?"

"Oh Father," she started to sob. "She clotted. The blood stopped flowing to her brain. She had a stroke. Father, will she be permanently damaged? Please, please tell me no."

John felt a wave of panic spread quickly from his head to his toes. He turned to run, but felt the woman's hand on his arm. He removed her hand so forcibly she lost her balance and fell to the ground. John was momentarily stunned. He was suddenly aware of other parishioners who'd left the party to fill their lungs with a bit of fresh air—only to replace it with ingested carcinogens from their cigarettes. He felt their eyes upon him—and Joe Delgado's wife—and he was filled with horror that what just happened might be misconstrued. He stooped to lift her to her feet, and was astonished at how heavy she was.

Fran Delgado was talking even as he was lifting her. "Father, Maggie told me she was on the Pill. She said you knew. That it was OK. Do you think that's what caused this? Do you, Father?"

John Sweeney stood in the shadows of the light that flooded the parking lot from the uppermost corners of the three-story school building. He began to mumble. Anything but this, O Lord. Anything. He then did something he had never, ever, done before. He asked God to take his life this very night. He begged his father, whom he prayed was in heaven, to ask God to allow him to die on this spot. Suddenly, to his utter amazement, he had lost completely—and in this instant he believed irrevocably—the will to live.

He settled Fran Delgado more or less on her feet and motioned one of the parishioners who was observing them over to assist. It was Jim Gentile. "Jim, please see that Mrs. Delgado gets home safely."

"Will do, Father."

John Sweeney then turned and did what he wanted to do from the moment he spoke to Jim Grogan. He walked out of the light and into the darkness.

51

_____

Father John Sweeney was not about to rush. Not on this morning after. He would be late, in fact he already was late for the 9:00 a.m. Mass, which he knew would surprise the congregation and anger its pastor.

His head was still buzzing from too many mixed drinks of uncertain origin and a night of pain spent on the unlit back streets of Narbrook. At its blurry conclusion, he'd found himself on an end stool in the Turks, a small, popular tavern in the middle of town with an outrageously irreverent Irish bartender named Barry McDyer.

It was shortly after midnight when he arrived, and he stayed until well past closing. McDyer saw him enter. He took one look at his boyhood friend and knew he was hurting. He came out from behind the bar and whisked him to a booth in the back, gently guiding his seating so his back would be to the door and the crowd.

McDyer sat with him for awhile. He listened, interrupted with an assortment of profanities, and left every now and again to go behind the bar and return with a margarita, an assortment of stingers, and finally some "really good" tequila. At some point, the bartender removed John's collar, lest it give scandal to those stumbling out of the men's room and past his booth on the way back to their stools. Unfortunately, it was McDyer who then gave scandal by donning the collar and dispensing penance with each shot and beer. At closing he offered to hear confessions but reconsidered, telling the stragglers that any patron of his was not worthy of absolution. He admonished them to either "go home or go to hell." One of them, no doubt thinking of the reception he would get at home, asked if McDyer would mind telling him the difference.

McDyer dropped John off at his home and walked him inside, where he helped him find a spot on the floor next to his mother's bed. Mary Kate Sweeney awakened and called for her dead husband, then fell back to sleep, snoring lightly. John was asleep almost as soon as his head hit the floor. He awoke with a start several hours later from a nightmare that frightened and distressed him. He and his classmates had decided at the eleventh hour to travel to Rome by ocean liner rather than airplane. Somewhere in the middle of the Atlantic the ship struck something, and hundreds of passengers were thrown overboard, including John and his fellow priests. Within moments, one by one, the passengers in the water began to disappear below its surface. John began to panic, and started swimming toward a group of young couples, maybe twelve to fourteen of them, who he believed were on their honeymoons. The men were trying to help their wives, who were flailing wildly and crying hysterically, but the women resisted, endangering the men. John was swimming frantically toward the undulating knot of people, but he couldn't seem to close the distance. He swam harder and faster, and still he was no closer. He stopped and begged God to allow him to reach the couples in time. He resumed swimming harder and faster, entirely exhausting himself. After what seemed like several minutes he looked up only to discover to his astonishment that not only had the distance not been shortened

. . . it had actually been lengthened. In that moment, he lost hope and started to sink. He awoke unable to breathe.

He stood now next to the bed of his mother and gently called her name. Her eyes remained shut. He told her he was her son and that he loved her. Then he bent to kiss her, thanking her for all she'd done for him and the others. His sister Mary Eileen came into the room in her bathrobe, her head covered in a large bath towel. She appeared more surprised than delighted to see her older brother standing by the bed looking tired, rumpled, and somewhat disoriented. "John, did you sleep here last night?"

"Yeah, I did. Right here by my favorite gal."

"On the floor?"

"Yep."

"I didn't even hear you come in."

"Well . . . it was late."

"John, are you all right?"

He looked at his sister and saw the beauty that attracted so many men over the years. She was tall and dark, but fair of complexion and disposition. Her eyes were a deep blue and her features possessed a delicate porcelain quality that made her appear even younger than her thirty years.

"I'm late, 'Weenie,'" he said, using the name he'd given her in childhood.

"John, what Mass do you have this morning?"

"The nine o'clock."

"My God, John! It's already a minute past."

John shrugged his shoulders and looked back at their mother.

"John, get in the car! I'll be ready in one minute."

"What about mother?"

"Mother would approve, believe me. Get in the car, John!"

John Sweeney was vested and on the altar by 9:16. The church was nearly filled and the congregation was coughing and fidgeting—much as it often was during one of his homilies, he couldn't help but note. As he processed out of the sacristy, his thick, black, curly hair still disheveled, he walked behind two altar servers and the lector and immediately reconsidered his decision to offer no explanation for his delay. It just didn't feel right. He got to the top of the steps and turned to face the "people of God." He was uncharacteristically nervous. He bowed his head as in preparation for the Sign of the Cross and the opening prayer and . . . suddenly looked up, exhaled dramatically, and said, "Hey . . . that was some party, huh?"

The laughter rolled through the church in waves deluging the sanctuary, receding, then returning to lap the foot of the altar again and again for what only seemed like several minutes. John let it wash over him, asking God to allow it to heal, cleanse, and renew his broken spirit.

Still somewhat disoriented, he stumbled through the Gospel, raising more than a few eyebrows. He then gave the shortest sermon of his ordained ministry. He didn't know what he said, indeed didn't know even as he was saying it, and suspected that no one else did either. He kept his head down during the distribution of Holy Communion, not wanting to make eye contact with any of his parishioners for fear that his eyes would reveal a truth he didn't want revealed. He got through the closing prayer and final hymn, made it to the sacristy, perfunctorily thanked the altar servers, disrobed, and was back in his room in the rectory in less than two minutes.

He stripped to his boxers, sat in the easy chair in the sitting area of his suite, and shut his eyes. The pain would not go away. It was now clear that he was going to wear this one for awhile. Its roots went deep, finding their way into a location of his being he did not know existed.

Who was he, now that his emperor's clothing had been summarily removed?

What was he, now that his inadequacies were laid bare for all to see—or soon would be?

Why was he? Why was he here in this room, in this rectory, masquerading as a priest?

Why did he think he'd been summoned to a life of priestly service? Why didn't the bishop and the authorities see his fatal flaws and weed him out before ordination?

He was a disgrace . . . a fraud, an embezzler, a squanderer of spiritual patrimony. If his line of work required civil licensing, as Michael Burns suggested, he knew his would have been revoked. "Nolo contendere." He could hear Patrick O'Rourke entering the plea to a nodding judge, Jim Grogan, and a jury of his own parishioners—the John Paulista table.

He got up out of his chair and shut his window—which provided a view of the Virgin Mother's grotto below—and turned on the air conditioner in the bedroom. It was warm on the way to hot, and John wanted cool. Cool, quiet, and dark he thought, as he pulled the shades and made his way to the bed to lie down. He lay still on the bed, staring at the ceiling and listening to the droning sound of the wall unit. It was only then that he remembered Maggie Kealey lying in a hospital bed, five minutes from his room. What happened? Did she suffer a stroke? Was the stroke, if it was a stroke, in any way related to her use of an oral contraceptive . . . the "Bitter Pill"? Had she suffered brain damage? Would she live?

Was he in some way responsible?

His mind attempted to replay the soundtrack from her confession a year or so ago. He couldn't retrieve it. He remembered only that what she did, she did for Bill. He wondered if Bill now knew what he knew. Would it matter? Had Bill ended his relationship with his secretary or were they now so . . . so deep into one another that he simply couldn't end it? If he didn't . . . couldn't end it, would he be able to generate the single-minded, selfless, unconditional love that Maggie Kealey now needed to will herself back to a normal life?

John felt himself welling up. He loved that woman, though not, he quickly told himself, in a carnal way. He'd never lost that idealized view of her, and Bill too for that matter, as his generation's best and brightest. She was achingly beautiful and terrifyingly smart. She was also naturally and effortlessly engaging. She could and did make people feel better simply by smiling at them.

That she suffered, and suffered more terribly than anyone he'd ever known, only enhanced her mythical appeal in John's eyes. For better or worse, he'd made this woman and her hopes and dreams for her besieged and broken family the centerpiece of his pastoral ministry. In his mind, he'd done everything he could possibly do to help lighten her cross, to lift her sagging spirit, to bring her closer to her Lord in those moments when she was too weak to pray. He knew he'd been good and faithful . . . and ruinously negligent.

He felt tears running down his cheeks and onto his pillow, and their warmth surprised him. His eyes grew so watery he couldn't tell at what speed the overhead fan was circling. He thought about getting up to adjust it, to accelerate it, but couldn't find the will to move his body.

Another thought pushed its way to the front of his mind. Had he spent too much time tending the outsized needs of the Kealeys, and not enough time cultivating the spiritual growth of the younger families in the parish? Would they have stayed if he had simply asked them what was going on in their lives, and listened? Couldn't he have brought in outside preachers, speakers, and teachers, whoever and whatever they were, and kept those families fed and content? How many others would they lure to greener pastures, and what would Jim Grogan say to him, and about him, if there was a Mass exodus from his parish?

John rolled over and tried to sleep, but his mind was racing and he found it impossible. Why did Michael Burns and Joe Delgado jump him last night? Hadn't he made himself accessible to each of them? What about all the late-night calls and unannounced drive-by visitations he'd been only too happy to accommodate? What had he said to them but what anyone in his position would have said? What was wrong with advising them not to jeopardize their families? What, in God's holy name, was wrong with reminding them that their family was their God-given, sacramentally covenanted responsibility—first, last, and always?

He didn't understand. He really didn't. Why did he work so hard, so faithfully, only to end up feeling so worthless? He couldn't give voice to the abject futility he was experiencing. Never had he felt so far from God—his God—the God he had vowed, at great personal cost, to serve. He was, canonically at least, an *alter Christus*. Why, then, could he not feel Christ? Where was He? He was groping in the dark, reaching for Him, feeling for Him, crying out to Him, and yet, his Lord was hiding. Hiding from him who sought Him. From him who loved Him. From him who'd made Him first in his life. From him who left father, mother, brothers, and sisters for Him.

John cried out in his anguish and pain. He cried out for his Lord and Savior. He cried out to the Blessed Virgin. "Surely you will help me, Mother. My own mother doesn't even recognize me anymore. Have you forgotten me too? Will you abandon me the way your Son has?" He thought about getting up and going back into the church, but realized the 10:30 Mass would be starting soon. He would wait until the church was empty again.

He rolled over and said the *Memorare*, beseeching the Blessed Virgin's intercession. He asked that his consciousness, with all its present accusations and torments, be stilled and silenced. He asked that he might find rest. He asked that he might find the yoke that was said to be easy. He needed sleep. He desperately needed sleep. He rolled over again, this time onto his stomach, and mercifully, within minutes he was sleeping.

52

Late summers in and around the Philadelphia suburbs, like those in other large Eastern cities, were generally slow and serene. Most families were off to the beaches or mountains for their annuals, and the relatively few who remained had their run of the air-conditioned malls, restaurants, and movie houses. For parish priests with schools, it was a good time to make sure all the teaching posts were properly filled, the budget was settled, the textbooks were ordered and inventoried, and the athletic schedules and social calendars were finalized. It was also a good time to get away for a retreat, or at the very least, a brief "period of reflection" over a weekend.

John Sweeney wasn't going anywhere. He had decided not to join his classmates on their tenth anniversary trip to Rome, though he hadn't notified his brother priests. He had spent the last week doing his best to avoid people—foregoing even visits to Maggie Kealey in Lower Merwood Hospital and his own mother, five blocks from the rectory.

He said early Mass and spent quiet, uneventful days at his desk in the rectory, only occasionally venturing over to the school to review planning and operational issues with the principal. At night after dusk he took long walks alone, around the perimeter of the little town, generally stopping at the park to sit on the bench in deep-center field, where he listened to the cicadas and watched the fireflies dart about.

It was on one such night that he rounded the corner on Wynncoate Road, angling toward the park and looking for a familiar figure on the bench under the trees. The light from the street silhouetted the outline of an older man, bent as though reading, and rocking back and forth slowly. John's heart skipped. As he approached, the figure rose to greet him. He moved toward him slowly, not stopping until they fully embraced.

"Good to see you, John."

"Good to see you, coach. Thanks for coming."

The old man shrugged and sat down, patting his knee softly as a signal to John to do the same. John half fell onto the bench beside him. The older man silently appraised him and said, "You're hurting."

"I'm hurting, yes."

"Want to tell me about it?"

John opened his mouth and out spilled a torrent of words and emotions so raw and so relentlessly self-critical that Hal Schwartz thought for a moment that somebody else must have slipped onto the bench next to him. He could never recall John Sweeney giving voice to such introspection. Initially, he didn't think he was hearing anything that unduly alarmed him in his young friend's soliloquy, which all but leapt from the pages of Lamentations— a book with which he was all too familiar. But his body seized involuntarily when he heard the young priest say he was thinking of taking a leave of absence from his ministry.

"Would you repeat what you just said, John? I'm not sure I heard you clearly."

"I said . . . I'm going to tell Monsignor Grogan that I'm going to petition the cardinal for a leave of absence."

The older man nodded. "That's what I thought you said."

They sat for maybe four or five minutes with neither man saying a word. It was humid, and in the distance peals of thunder grew more audible, signaling a wetter, cooler end to the evening. Hal studied John, now silhouetted in the muted glare cast by the streetlight. He could almost feel the intensity in the young priest's clenched jaw and sinewy back and shoulders, which were bulging under the black short-sleeved shirt. He has thought this through, Hal mused, or at least convinced himself he has.

"John, I want you to listen to me. Will you do that?"

John turned to the older man and reproved him mildly. "Hal, when have I ever *not* listened to you? Why would I come to you for help and not want to hear what you have to say?"

Hal nodded and said nothing. He was now certain he had his young friend's attention—which was always the first order of business when you were about to hit someone between the eyes with a two by four.

"I'd like to ask you a few questions, if I may, and I'd like you to think before you answer."

John did not reply.

Another pause, then, "John, what do you suppose is the origin of this sense of entitlement?" Brief pause. "I never detected any trace of it in your father or mother."

John wanted to get up and leave, but something restrained him. He found himself formulating a response that began, "You haven't listened to a word I've said." The words never made their way out of his mouth. Instead, he sat in sullen silence.

Hal Schwartz shifted uncomfortably. "Maybe this isn't a good time for this discussion." Then, half turning to face John, "Maybe another night would be better."

John did not move and did not speak. Hal Schwartz sat back on the bench; he would simply wait for human sound. After several moments, the young priest's body seemed to go limp. He shook his head and said, "I really don't know, Hal . . . I really just don't know."

The older man exhaled slowly and smiled, patting John on the thigh, "Good, John. We can work through this."

John leaned forward on the bench, elbows resting on his thighs. He stared into the darkness and said, "Hal, what's going on here? Why is this happening to me? I know this sounds terrible, but I don't think I deserve this. It feels like God is holding me by the scruff of my neck and plunging my head into a bucket of sludge. Every time I raise my head, He slams it back down into the muck. Why? To what end . . . to what purpose? I don't deserve it, Hal! I really don't deserve it!"

Hal Schwartz nodded and said quietly, "You're right. You don't deserve it, Sweeney. Yet God, in His infinite mercy, has seen fit to grant you this extraordinary gift anyway."

John turned fully to the older man, "What!"

Hal Schwartz bent and reached down next to the bench for something in a small, dark pouch. He straightened and placed what appeared to be a relatively thin paperback on his lap. "When our son was killed in Vietnam, my wife and I had very different reactions. She brooded, I searched. One day a friend of mine from Tennessee who heard about our loss—a fellow I served with in Europe . . . we hit the beach together in Normandy—came to see me.

"He lost a son in Vietnam too, and then lost his wife to breast cancer. He had a rough time of it, but you'd never know it to listen to him. He was the kindest, gentlest soul, which surprised me greatly because he was the fiercest warrior in our whole company. Before he left, I asked him if he thought his suffering had transformed him and he said—and I'll never forget this—he said, 'No. God transformed me through the suffering.'

"Before he left he asked if he could spend some time with my wife . . . and he did, though she was not particularly responsive. To this day we still don't talk about our son's death. And truth be told, it's created a distance between us that wasn't there before.

But as he was leaving, he gave me this little book, all dog-eared and highlighted. I found peace in this book. Maybe you will too."

He handed the book to John with both hands as though it were Waterford Crystal. John took it and tilted it into the light. On the cover were the words "The Dark Night of the Soul."

John looked up at the older man, whose face was an inscrutable mask. He didn't know what to say. He'd been assigned John of the Cross as required reading in the seminary, and like the others he'd read the works of the great sixteenth-century mystic and reformer. However, none of them had really understood much of what they read, including this small tract—*The Dark Night of the Soul*. It was all just too mystical, and so unrelievedly austere.

What to say to his friend?

"Hal, how did this . . . this book . . . help you?" He did not want to insult this man whom he knew to be both wise, and like all men, not without his measure of pride, but . . .

Hal Schwartz smiled and reflected on the wonders of aging, which he viewed as a choreographed ballet of maturation and decomposition. Even as our cells begin to blink, die, and ultimately disconnect one from another, our minds begin to cast overboard the ballast we've accumulated over a lifetime. All the pretense of who we are, and all the affectation rooted in what we've accomplished, tends to slip its moorings, along with the mental acuity that gave it life and dimension, until finally, we simply say what we think.

Hal Schwartz looked at John Sweeney with affection and said, "Are you asking how I dealt with 'the Jesus factor'?"

"Uh . . . yeah."

"Transposition."

"Transposition?"

Hal Schwartz nodded emphatically, "Every time I read the name Jesus, I just substituted God. It wasn't Jesus who was purging my senses and breaking my attachment to the material, it was God.

"It wasn't Jesus who was purging my spirit and burning off the dross of self-attachment, it was God.

"It wasn't Jesus who was illuminating my intellect, letting me see how worthless I am and how unfathomable, nonetheless, was and is His love for me. It was God.

"And, though I don't believe I've ever gotten there, it wouldn't have been Jesus who drew me into the unitive state, that bliss of divine intimacy known only to the privileged few. It would have been God. The God of Abraham. The God of Moses. The God of David."

John was incredulous. "Hal, you read this, you absorbed this, you found peace from this, yet . . . yet you never . . ."

Hal smiled. "Never! I was born a Jew; I will die a Jew. My friend, we both await the Messiah. For you, it is His return."

John was incredulous. "Hal what triggered this; what made you bring this book tonight?"

"Something you said on the phone. You said it seemed like God had abandoned you. I've felt that. My guess is that most people do at some point in their lives. I've come to believe it's just God moving even closer to us. He kind of tiptoes in on us without our sensing it. The problem is, the closer He comes, the more pain we feel. But that's not His problem; it's ours. It just reflects the state of our souls."

John winced. He found all of this surreal.

Hal wasn't finished, "Anyway, my army buddy changed my life a second time. Through the gift of this book, he opened the door to a deeper understanding of the way God deals with us in this life."

"Was your friend . . . ?"

"Catholic? No, no! He was a good Southern Baptist. An evangelical. Finest Christian I ever knew, present company included of course."

John laughed, and as he did so a good bit of the tension pent up within him gently released itself, "And how does the God of Abraham deal with us, Hal?"

"He draws us as close as we let Him. And the closer we come, the more we suffer. And the more we suffer, the more we experience the joy of Him."

John nodded. "We erect barriers."

"And He is perfectly content to blast through them, as he is demonstrating to you."

"But why me? And why now?"

The older man shrugged his shoulders. "So ask Him. He'll tell you, in His time."

"This sense of abandonment—this sense of detachment from things and people . . . this pain of humiliation and futility—it's not going anywhere anytime soon, is it?"

Hal shook his head. "No. If it was gone in days, it would all be for naught. The whole point is transformation of the soul. That's the work of God . . . and He works on a different calendar."

"Years?"

The older man smiled and said, "Think marathon."

John fell silent. He recalled from his seminary reading that the purgation of the senses alone could be a particularly long and painful process, and that was the good news; the purgation of the spirit could be an even more exhaustively dark and difficult leg of the journey. For saints it was often measured in years . . . dog years. And John Sweeney knew he was no saint.

"Hal . . ."

"John?"

"What happens now?"

"You will surrender to it . . . ultimately. You'll be led to see that sanctification—holiness—is not in doing. It's in letting 'it'—this purification—be accomplished within you. In His time and in His way, your God will reintegrate Himself within the deepest recesses of your soul. You will be remolded in the true sense of that term, and the new and improved John Sweeney will have gained wisdom from the great darkness and dryness of his suffering; and this wisdom will be given to others as a gift to strengthen them, as they too are drawn more deeply into the mystery of their own relationship with 'I Am.'"

"In short, my friend . . . God is at work in you; apparently, He intends to make you a better priest."

Just then, a clap of thunder startled them. Seconds later, a shaft of lightning seemed to strike at very close range. John and Hal exchanged tight-lipped smiles, concern etched deeply in their eyes and the corners of their mouths.

As they stood and moved out from under the cover and danger of the trees, the heavens opened. Together, they ran for shelter.

53

Michael Burns was convinced that he could persuade virtually anyone of . . . well not anything exactly, but anything he was sufficiently convinced was in their best interests. That he wasn't always successful generally came as a shock. He was at his best on his feet. He could be charismatic, at times magnetic, able to move a crowd this way and that before drawing them to his view of things, his conclusions, and his course of action.

On the downside, it was said of him that he was often wrong, but never in doubt. He didn't see it quite that way of course. And this presented problems when he went one on one with colleagues and clients. Without a large group to summon his humor, and charm, he could be, and often was, overbearing and off-putting. Were he aware of this and truly understood it, he never would have done what he did, which even he came to regard as an "error in judgment." Of course, Michael Burns was not then aware of his blind spots—because he had yet to pay a price for them.

The way he saw it, he had three "sell jobs" to do in succession, each progressively more difficult. They were difficult, but not "unmakeable" shots. He would have to persuade Ron Zimmer . . . to persuade Burt Camfy . . . to let *him* persuade Richard Kloss . . . to change the CMN programming model.

The way he saw it, he had one important thing going for him. He had his wife's full support. Carol Burns was every bit as convinced as her husband that the demise of the American family could only be hastened by the threat that Cable Movie Network posed to the control the major networks exercised over prime-time viewing. If the pay cable network's current course was not disrupted, she believed, the broadcast networks would fill their schedules with increasing levels of violence, profanity, and sex, believing it essential to "hold" their audiences. CMN would of course "up the ante" through the creation of their own productions, igniting a spiraling effect of soft and increasingly hardening porn flooding into living rooms across the country.

No, Carol Burns had no problem with her husband standing up to that. In her mind, someone had to. As she told her parents, "If not them, who; and if not now, when?" And if they failed, as it was likely they would, then at least they'd met their accountability to the "Splendor of Truth." They would leave the rest—including the fate of their family—in the hands of divine Providence.

Michael Burns was waiting in Ron Zimmer's office when the Hal Ross agency's president arrived at work the Monday before Labor Day.

Zimmer did a double take and pantomimed a swatting of flies. "Never a day without a shamrock; where's the cow dung when you need it?" he grunted.

"Ron, I've got an idea," Michael replied undeterred.

"Ah yes . . . speaking of meadow muffins."

Michael smiled, despite his best efforts not to. He thought back to the evening Zimmer and his wife, Cheryl, had hosted him and Carol for dinner at their Gatsbyesque mansion in Greenwich, on the North Shore of Long Island Sound.

Michael and Carol were nothing less than awestruck at the massive structure and the spectacular setting, which on this evening came complete with a breathtaking sunset. The mansion sat on five acres and included a swimming pool with a pool house, a tennis court, a basketball court, several garages with an indeterminate number of vintage automobiles, a formal garden with a huge fountain, and a two-hundred-foot pier with four Jet Skis and three boats—the longest of which was a sixty-foot yacht.

When they got to the front door, they saw a sign, professionally designed and printed, which read, No Irish Need Apply. Carol, for some reason, didn't find this funny and opened the front door and marched in only to find Ron Zimmer holding a case of Guinness with its double lid covered with uncooked spuds.

Zimmer quickly read the look on Carol's face and said, "Hey, you're wearing shoes and you're not pregnant . . . you're not Carol Burns."

Carol, disarmed, burst out laughing.

Michael wished he had that gift.

Now Ron Zimmer was looking at Michael in his corner office and motioning him to sit, pantomiming putting plugs in his ears. "OK Shamrock, let's hear it."

Michael dove right in. "Ron, I think we've got to do something dramatic . . ."

Zimmer interrupted with the loud buzzing sounds of those dead to the world.

Michael ignored him and continued. "The American family has spoken. They don't want that crap Kloss is dumping into their living rooms. In three years, maybe less, that network's gonna hit a wall and all the king's men won't be able to put Humpty Dumpty Kloss and his network back together again. We gotta convince them of that and suggest their only option is to alter the programming model now, before it's too late."

Zimmer snored louder.

"Ron, I want a sit-down with Kloss."

Zimmer shot bolt upright. "You're drunk!"

"What's the downside?"

"Oh, about twenty jobs, including yours. On second thought . . ."

"That'll happen anyway . . . eventually."

"Sure. Why wait till tomorrow if you can throw people under a bus today?"

"Ron, none of that has to happen. These guys pay us to tell them what we think. We think—we know—that their business is going down the crapper. We owe it to them to show them how to fix it."

Zimmer stood and shot Michael a "spare me" look, then went to the floor-length window, which offered a breathtaking view of the Hudson River. With his back to Michael, he proclaimed to all below, "You and Camfy had your shot with that research—half a million dollars worth. Sunk without a ripple. Kloss even boycotted the presentations. Just blew it off. Stuck it right up Camfy's Ivy League ass." Then turning to Michael, "He's history. You're history. We're history."

"Then what are we doing here?" Michael asked politely.

"We're harvesting. We're going to make as much money as we can for as long as we can." Then with feigned solicitousness, "You Catholics don't have anything against money, do you?"

Michael shook his head vigorously. "I'm not going down without a fight. Nor would any self-respecting ad agency, Ron."

"Oh . . . and because you have a death wish, it's my job to embalm the whole agency?"

"People talk. You more than anyone know that."

Zimmer didn't appreciate the low blow. "Let them talk. Some of them might even live to fight another day."

"Standing up to this bully will win you respect, Ron. Stuff like that gets around."

"That's Grade A Irish manure."

Michael didn't argue. He reasoned that Zimmer was the more seasoned judge of such extractions. He paused and said, "Why not give Camfy the option? We're billing him for it."

He was not surprised that his "closing" argument seemed to find a room in Ron Zimmer's home. The integrity of the transaction and the concept of fair value—the right of a man to what he paid for—that was a governing tenet of the marketplace and its best practitioners. They believed the marketplace, when properly respected, provided its just rewards, and that those rewards helped define a man.

Zimmer leveled his gaze and said, "I have no objection to that. But if he's smart, and I think he is, he'll want no part of it. And if he asks my opinion, which he might, I'll tell him he'd be crazy to let you in the same time zone as Kloss."

"Deal."

Michael didn't think Camfy would ask Zimmer's opinion for a very basic reason; he would know what Zimmer would say simply by the way he would present it. And Michael knew that Camfy would like the idea of his laying out the business case for the programming model's overhaul. He knew of course that Kloss would listen, perhaps even politely, given his end game, and disregard everything Michael said. But his CEO Rick Reynolds would also get a full report of the meeting, and that would help Camfy. It would also elevate Reynolds' respect for the Hal Ross agency . . . which would also help Camfy. He didn't want Kloss choosing his advertising agency, and he might need to enlist Reynolds' support to keep that from happening.

Zimmer looked at Michael and shook his head as if to say, "You just don't get it." He slowly made his way to his desk to begin his day.

Michael smiled and quickly got up and left, shutting the door behind him. He had work to do.

54

The call came at night, when Michael and Carol were in the den reading. The twin boys were in bed, and the girls were either studying or on the phone talking to boyfriends, safely out of earshot. The sound startled them, and Carol reached for the phone to lower the ringer. Still ringing, she handed it to Michael, saying, "It's for you."

It was. It was Ron Zimmer. He said simply, "Just heard from Camfy. You're on, Shamrock. He'll give Kloss a heads-up and you can schedule it yourself."

Michael felt his heart begin to race. Two down, he thought, and one to go. "Thanks, Ron. I'll be ready."

"How do you Irish prepare for an execution?"

Michael laughed and hung up.

He gave Camfy a day to give Kloss the heads-up. The following day he called Kloss' office and scheduled a one-hour meeting, two weeks to the day. Apparently, Kloss would be traveling in the meantime to Cannes or Toronto or Sundance—one of those film festivals, his secretary wasn't sure which.

Michael called Camfy to confirm the meeting and to see if he wanted to schedule a briefing, either before or after his meeting with Kloss. "Burt, Michael. I've got Kloss in two weeks. Want to schedule a preview?"

Camfy snorted. "Nah. I'll just ship Zimmer a case of Preparation H."

"Want to schedule a debriefing?"

"Yes. That I do want to do. Got your calendar?"

"What looks good?"

"When do you have Kloss?"

"Four o'clock."

"How about Gallagher's Steak House at six o'clock? I'll buy you a steak . . . if you still have a stomach."

Michael laughed, delighted at his good fortune. He had absolutely no fear of Kloss. When he crossed the threshold of his office he'd be locked and loaded. In the meantime, he'd follow the formula his mother taught him and his brothers when they reached school age, "Work as though everything depended on you; pray as though everything depended on God." He was a believer that God could extend a man's reach, particularly when he was reaching for something good.

"I've got plenty of stomach for Kloss, Burt. I'll see you at Gallagher's."

"Ok. Tell Zimmer to start looking for work."

"Why? That's the last thing he wants to do."

Camfy laughed and hung up. Michael immediately called Zimmer, who was out on "new business," and gave his assistant the dates. "Any questions, have him call me."

"Michael, he'd rather have a colorectal exam," she replied, on cue.

Organizations, Michael mused, really were the length and shadow of their leaders.

55

Michael did not like afternoon meetings, and he particularly disliked late-afternoon meetings; in his experience they were often subject to re-scheduling due to delays and any number of other distractions to which busy executives were particularly vulnerable.

Once in San Antonio, he'd been asked to give a somewhat routine forty-five-minute presentation immediately after lunch. Lunch, unfortunately, was a five-course meal served at a Mexican restaurant in the heart of the downtown business district. The presentation was scheduled for a back room just off the main dining room. The lights went down. The power-point went up. Michael went on. When he finished and the lights went back up, the heads of every one of the forty mid-level executives in the room, save two, were lying on the small tables in front of them. And those two were rubbing their eyes.

Michael didn't worry that Kloss would be less than fully awake—he took far too many uppers before, during, and after his business day for that to be a concern. He worried that he'd get "slid"—that the meeting would be postponed to another late afternoon in another two weeks, and that this would repeat itself until the topic of discussion was no longer a topic for discussion.

That didn't happen. Sometime after lunch, Michael received a call from Kloss' assistant that he was running "about twenty minutes late." She was a most proper early middle-aged English-woman whom Michael found particularly interesting, given Kloss' randy reputation; she inquired ever so deferentially as to whether it would be "an imposition" if they were to push the meeting back "slightly" to 4:30. "No imposition whatsoever," Michael replied, relieved. "Tell Richard I'll see him at 4:30."

At 4:00, Michael left the Hal Ross offices on the West Side and headed for St. Patrick's Cathedral. It wasn't on the way, but it wasn't that much out of the way, and Michael wanted a blessing on this meeting. Once inside the great cathedral he prayed for the grace "to be led by the Holy Spirit." To "listen and be listened to." To be "clear and persuasive" in representing the legitimate interests of his family, and millions of others. And finally, he prayed for the grace to keep his ego "the hell out" of the way.

He arrived at National Publishing's headquarters and imme-diately signed in, allowing himself to be directed past security to the proper elevator bank. He arrived at the eighteenth floor lobby and presented himself at 4:27. He was asked to sit and advised that "Mr. Kloss" was running a few minutes late.

As he sat waiting, gazing at the Monets and Manets pin lit discreetly from above, the import of what he was about to do struck him full force, surprising him. This man he was about to confront currently had a billion dollars worth of original "proj-ects" in various stages of production; industry analysts noted it was an amount that exceeded the total of the seven major American film studios combined. His company, CMN, was gushing money; the country's leading actors and actresses were competing for his favor; the nation's elite media were profiling him every week or two, as often as not on their covers.

And here sat Michael Burns from Narbrook, waiting for the opportunity to tell him what he was doing wrong. Somewhere in his stomach, an elevator was in a free fall.

"Mr. Burns, Mr. Kloss will see you now."

Michael rose quickly and attempted to thrust aside his doubts with a sudden, violent shoulder roll, the way he often did before tipoff of an important conference game. He promptly put on his game face and followed the receptionist back to Richard Kloss' corner suite.

He entered to find his host on the phone. He waved to Michael, and motioned for him to take a seat in the reception area of his suite. To Michael, it sounded as if Kloss was on the phone with a film studio executive. His tone was civil and detached, almost aloof, as though he were the court of last appeal and this executive would find no relief on this issue at this time.

Michael surveyed the immaculate suite, with its sunrise view of the East River and its sweeping vistas of midtown clear down to the Village. The walls were an off-white and sparsely adorned with several original paintings of postmodern masters and a few lithographs of recent cover stories in national magazines that featured the office's occupant. The furniture—desks, tables, chairs, and artifacts—was redolent of musky dark leather from the interior of Africa. The small tables that abutted the sofas and thickly cushioned easy chairs featured a series of discreetly sized and framed photographs of Kloss with celebrities from the worlds of cinema, sports, and politics.

Michael noted that there was also a well-appointed conference room that adjoined the office, and that it was equipped with several Sony television sets of various sizes and a surprising number of telephone lines. This was no doubt where Kloss screened his many investments and ordered the "re-makes" for which he was famous, or infamous, depending upon your point of view.

Michael studied Kloss from the side as he attempted to wrap up his telephone conversation. He was in his late thirties, and by all accounts a confirmed bachelor. He lived alone in a large, custom refurbished apartment in a luxury high rise overlooking Central Park that was said to have no fewer than six television sets scattered throughout.

He was a handsome man, Michael conceded. His sharp features and porcelain-white teeth were close to perfect. Somewhat short with an athletic build, dark hair, and piercing brown eyes, he projected an effortless self-assurance that Michael quickly noted exceeded his own rather healthy self-confidence. When not among his staff or industry insiders, he was nearly always self-contained, possessing the requisite "gears" that almost all the *über* executives seemed to have on call. He could deploy charm and aloofness, wit and satire, graciousness and ruthlessness, all in the same conversation.

Today it would be charm, wit, and graciousness, and it caught Michael completely off guard. In fact, it unnerved him and threw him off stride for several key moments at the outset of their conversation. Kloss hung up the phone, turned to Michael, and said, "I know you don't drink, Michael, but don't make me a bad host. Can I get you a soft drink or some bottled water?"

Michael smiled, shrugged his shoulders, and said, "Sure. Either will be fine."

Kloss directed his assistant to the small refrigerator in his conference room to secure two bottles of imported water and ushered Michael to the sitting area with its unobstructed view of the reflection of the setting sun on Lower Manhattan. Kloss sat on a sofa, and Michael sat in a wing chair across from him.

Kloss took a bottle of water from his assistant without saying anything, removed the cap, looked at Michael, and narrowed his gaze slightly. "So Michael, tell me." Three-swallow gulp. "What's on your mind?" This was said matter-of-factly, as though it could well have been his children or marital difficulties or a downturn in his investment portfolio that brought him to his godfather's feet.

Michael felt a knot in his stomach. Ready or not, he was on. He always found moments like this a bit surreal. You prep for them, you pray for them, you attempt to choreograph them, and somehow they are never as you imagine them. He learned the hard way that you cannot let the moment direct you. You must direct the moment.

He looked at Kloss and the natural intensity in his eyes . . . and he stumbled. "I . . . I'm worried . . . I think . . ." He paused, unsettled.

"Michael, relax. You're among friends." Kloss said this with apparent sincerity that had its intended effect. Michael began to relax, though it would take him many months to forgive himself for launching an "air ball" to open the discussion.

"Richard, the churn rate is just too high. It's killing the business." He paused briefly to gauge the impact of his words. Kloss was revealing nothing. Michael plunged on, slightly off stride. "And refilling the base from hardcore non-buyers and burned-out ex-subscribers is going to be too expensive. We need a War Council to fix it. We've got two, maybe three years before this becomes a major-league problem for the network and National Publishing. We've got to put all our best minds on it and tell them to leave their portfolios behind. The fix is the thing. Nothing else matters."

Richard Kloss removed the cap from his bottle of water and took another long drag, then another, before responding. Too much salt, Michael thought, probably corned beef.

"And this War Council would conclude . . . what, Michael? That the programming model needed some work?"

"Maybe. Or maybe that your advertising is some previously unknown form of human excrement and you need a new agency."

Kloss' eyes narrowed further, furrowing the thin brows above each. He took another long slog of water, finishing the bottle. He called for another one. "The churn rate is high because we are marketing a new concept—asking people to pay to watch television. Eventually it'll all settle, and we'll establish a natural floor for the business. Then we'll leverage our rather considerable investment in original productions, properly advertised, to expand the base incrementally over time."

A shiver ran up and down Michael's spine at the reference to the advertising. He harbored no illusions. Kloss would ultimately find an agency, his agency, which would, in his mind, "properly" advertise his original productions, stabilizing the customer base and stimulating new demand among non-buyers.

"Isn't that a marginalized view of the business?" Michael said, wanting to keep the focus on alternative perspectives of the industry's potential.

"I don't think so," Kloss replied. "Once we've basketed the low-hanging fruit from the initial wiring of American cities, it'll be a grind-it-out business. It won't be quite as glamorous from a financial perspective as it is today, but the cash flows will be strong and that will finance a lot of new projects at National Publishing, and [small smile] even a few here at CMN. That will keep those guys on the upper floors of this building out of our hair, which I know is something your boy Camfy wants at least as much as I do."

He was a master at sending signals, Michael conceded. If you were smart enough to decode them, and cool enough not to react to them, so much the better. But Kloss really didn't care one way or the other. He was going to do what he was going to do and no one was sufficiently well-positioned to stop him, even the executives who ran National Publishing, which owned his division.

"Why settle?" Michael asked, searching for a seam in Kloss' ziplocked scenario.

"Who's settling?" Kloss responded, inadvertently secreting a morsel of steam.

Michael noted the slight change in room temperature and decided to adjust the thermometer. "I dunno. It just doesn't seem like you. You're famous in your industry for never settling. Nothing is ever good enough. Why be content with a marginal, grind-it-out business?"

This Richard Kloss did not wish to hear. He was the master manipulator, and here was this pup of a vendor attempting to pull his strings. He affected a slightly contrived, dismissive air of detachment and said, "There's nothing marginal about a multi-billion dollar business operating at forty percent gross margins,

Michael. I'm sure Zimmer wouldn't object if you could run those on our account, would he?"

Michael didn't react to the dig. "Those numbers aren't a problem if they were to continue indefinitely. But they won't. You and I both know there are other numbers that portend great danger. But that aside, the larger issue is one of opportunity. The major networks are pumping pure crap into American living rooms every night, and American families don't much care for it. In fact, from all indications, they deeply resent it. The networks are ripe for a fall. They're fat, dumb, and hopelessly vulnerable. Why not counter program them, create a run on the bank? Why not take your business from a niche play to a mainstream alternative to lowest common denominator programming?"

Kloss smiled coolly. "So it is about the programming?"

Michael flinched. The bridge had been too abrupt. That was clumsy. He chose, however, not to retreat, knowing Kloss was the type to pursue and butcher enemy combatants in disorderly retreat. "Richard," he paused for emphasis, "the product is programming."

"Are you sure?" Small smile.

"Well, I'm sure it seems we forget that from time to time, and you're right to call us on it; but don't we all share the same . . . the same accountability to point out opportunities in the market?"

"Opportunities?"

"Opportunities to give your customers more of what they tell us they like."

"And in your opinion . . . what is that, Michael?"

Michael leaned in, now on the edge of his chair, "Uh . . . movies with happy endings. Films and shows that families can watch together. Stuff that uplifts spirits, that at the very least attempts to balance the higher angels of our human nature with the lower."

Kloss sat impassively.

Michael continued, "Your research, the Total Satisfaction Scores from your customer panels, all point to this kind of programming as the veritable pot of gold. Your customer couldn't be clearer. She—and it is a she in the final analysis—she is saying,

'Make us feel a little better about the world after the program ends.' That's all. Just a little bit of hope."

Kloss fell momentarily silent, pondering what he'd heard. Michael had to concede that the man was listening, and apparently struggling to internalize the message. "You know . . ." Kloss began thoughtfully, " . . . the things you object to about our programming, I actually find cathartic. I enjoy the grit of today's reality. The violence doesn't make me want to go out and shoot someone. The sex doesn't make me want to go out and screw someone. If anything, it provides a release."

Michael didn't know what to do with that. He shook his head involuntarily, which he instantly regretted. "Richard, with all due respect. You are a mature adult; you are not the average teenager whose mother fears a different kind of release if her child is exposed to this kind of programming."

Kloss leaned forward on his sofa and peered intently at Michael. "You know what your problem is?" Then, not waiting for a reply, "You're too Catholic."

Michael jumped on that belt-high fastball. "Richard, 'catholic' means universal. My job is to universalize the appeal of your product. That's precisely what brings me here today. You've hired me to be too 'catholic.'"

Kloss appeared to take deep offense at this. It was only later Michael was able to recall Billy Conn's famous line. He was asked by sportswriters after being knocked out by Joe Louis in the eleventh round of a twelve-round World Championship fight why he chose to mix it up with the champ so late in the fight; he was, after all, far ahead on all the score cards. "What's the sense of being Irish," he reportedly said, "if you can't be a little stupid?"

Kloss glared at him and said, "Your job is to tell America that 'home isn't home without Cable Movie Network.' If you can't or won't do that, Michael, you really ought to tell me so I can find someone who will."

"Richard, I've spent the better part of the last four years listening to your customer. I dare say no one in your company has listened as carefully and understood what she is saying as clearly. And what she is saying is this, 'My home *isn't* home with Cable Movie Network in it.'"

Kloss all but leapt off the sofa and walked briskly to the work area on the far side of his office. He walked around to the large, black, ergonomically designed chair behind the desk and sat down. He looked at Michael, who was now standing, moving uncertainly out from the reception area to the middle of the room.

"The business comes down to gut, my friend. Either you have an intuitive feel for what people want, or you don't. I've got it. I've got the golden gut. That's why they pay me the big bucks. Somebody's got to make the call on these properties, and these projects. National Publishing's shareholders have decided it should be me—not you—me."

To his lasting regret, Michael loaded up for one last shot. "Even if that gut of yours ends up gutting the business?"

Richard Kloss instantly swiveled in his chair, back now turned completely to his guest and buzzed his assistant. She answered swiftly and he said, "Please show Mr. Burns out of the building . . . and get me our LA office on the phone."

Michael Burns picked up his binder, the one with all the notes and charts and survey highlights, and followed the petite, ever-charming Englishwoman out of the office and to the elevator bank.

He entered the elevator and looked at his watch. It was ten minutes past five o'clock. He had some time to kill before his dinner with Burt Camfy.

He didn't feel particularly hungry.

56

As the numbness began to set in, toes first, then legs and arms, Maggie Kealey's first thought was of Moia. Is this the beginning of death? What will happen to my child? Who will care for her?

There was a further complication. Father LeClere had called earlier in the day to schedule a visit and "an investigation" for the following week. And, yes, he said, he would stay for dinner to meet and observe "the family dynamic."

Now what? If she was in the process of having some kind of seizure or stroke—and why was she suddenly feeling so dizzy— would Bill cover for her? Would he leave work early next week and meet Father LeClere and introduce him to Moia?

She called out to Bill, but he didn't hear her over the hissing torrent coming from the shower, and it was Grace who rushed to her assistance. She tried to explain what was happening, but she sensed Grace didn't understand her. She wondered if perhaps she wasn't being clear, possibly her speech was garbled.

Then . . . nothing. No pain, no noise, no visions of a warm enveloping light through an extended tunnel. Just gray, then black.

When she regained consciousness, she knew something was different. Her physician, Dr. Philip Tabor, told her she had suffered a thrombotic stroke, which was technically some sort of ischemic stroke. She didn't know what that meant, and it frightened her. He explained that a blood clot had formed in one of her arteries, which severely constricted the flow of blood to her brain.

The good news, he said, was that Bill had delivered her to the ER within a half hour of first symptoms. This allowed the doctors to inject what they referred to as clot-busting drugs through an intravenous tube within the first hour; this apparently not only saved her life but also limited the damage from cells that either died or very nearly died. The right side of her face would bear the attack's lasting scar, in this case a slight paralysis around the cheek, jaw, and corner of her mouth. With medication and therapy, Dr. Tabor believed, the effect on speech could be, should be, slight.

Initially, there was some mystery as to the cause of the stroke in the minds of her doctors. They asked if there was any history of strokes, or "brain attacks," as they referred to them, in her family, and she said no. They also inquired about high blood pressure, high cholesterol, diabetes, and cardiovascular diseases—afflictions that Dr. Tabor affirmed she had never presented the slightest traces of during his twenty-year treatment of her.

She was certainly not old at forty-two, and not overweight at 132 pounds. Nor was she a smoker . . . or drinker, although that didn't seem to matter much to the doctors questioning her. She assumed it was because doctors drink heavily, or so she thought, and because they didn't, or hadn't, suffered strokes, they didn't regard alcohol as a risk factor.

It was a woman physician, Dr. Laura Lippmann, who seemed to discover the missing piece of the puzzle. She came in the afternoon of the third day just after Maggie awakened from a fitful nap, and she asked a very direct question, "Mrs. Kealey, are you on the Pill?"

Her first instinct was to dissemble and, in fact, she started to shake her head but there was apparently no discernible movement or sound, and Dr. Lippmann repeated the question. This time Maggie nodded, nothing more. Dr. Lippman, too, nodded and left without saying anything.

Within the hour Dr. Tabor arrived, demanding to know who was prescribing oral contraceptives for her and why he wasn't advised. Maggie grew so flustered at his line of inquiry and its tone that she babbled incoherently, and the good doctor made a hasty exit. He never inquired again, at least not of her, though she suspected he might have asked Bill the same question. She didn't have to guess how Bill would have answered that revelation, but she did wonder and worry why Bill never asked her who supplied the pills, and how she paid for them.

She was released after a week in the hospital and immediately began the medication—anti-platelets, the doctors called them. They were supposed to reduce the stickiness of the platelets in her blood stream and make them less likely to clot. Within days she began in-home speech therapy, which surprised her with its tedious, painful demands.

Bill did not react well to the news that there would be lingering effects from the stroke. Maggie sensed it made him angry, though he never addressed the subject with her directly. He was visibly more on edge and markedly less intimate. She found him looking at her less, and she worried that the partial paralysis on the lower right side of her face made her less attractive in his eyes.

But all of that was of secondary significance to a mother of a disabled child—for how else to describe Moia? Yes, she was emotionally disturbed. Yes, she may even be a veritable shelter for a demonic presence that had ridden her into the midst of the Kealey family like a Trojan horse. But in the final analysis, she was a child with a disability, and that was the way Maggie wanted the others to see her—particularly her husband, who tended to grow increasingly angry at his daughter's intransigence on the most mundane matters.

Having to reschedule Father LeClere, however, caused her more anguish than all the other difficulties combined. The priest was very understanding, of course, when Bill explained their most recent problems and he indicated his willingness to come another time; it was just that now, he advised, he couldn't book anything before Thanksgiving, so great was the demand for him and the exorcist. He proposed she "stay at the ready," in case he had a postponement of some other investigation, or even an actual "rite," which would free him on short notice to come to Philadelphia. Bill assured her that he had promised the priest they would.

The postponement broke her heart. It meant another three months of torment for her daughter, and the rest of her family. Maggie would endure, but she wondered if Bill would endure. Her husband was spending more and more time at work, and less and less time at home. He was growing increasingly distant, and increasingly disinterested in the affairs of the family. Maggie was finding it harder to engage him. She was slowly coming to the conclusion that somewhere along the line she had lost a piece of her husband. She no longer believed he loved her, and indeed, he stopped telling her that he did.

She also wondered if Moia would continue as she had for the past eighteen months, or whether she would soon descend to yet another plateau, complicating things even further. The thought of her daughter possibly harboring a demonic spirit in some form—possession or oppression, to her it didn't really matter—filled her with absolute dread. It made even the simplest household tasks exceedingly difficult.

If there was a silver lining in all of this, Maggie mused, it was that her migraine headaches were somewhat less acute since the stroke . . . owing to what, she really didn't know. She hadn't had a real corker in over two weeks.

At this point in her life, she was thankful for any favors, even small ones.

57

On the morning of the first day of the second week of her return home, Father John Sweeney paid her a visit. Maggie found him—she couldn't find the right word for it—less himself. She wanted to ask him about it, ask him if something was bothering him, but decided not to do so, unless he brought the subject up. There would be other opportunities, she told herself, perhaps when she was doing a bit better herself.

John Sweeney thought Maggie Kealey's physical beauty was forever compromised. Her jaw sagged slightly, and the facial muscles on her right side appeared slack. Her mouth, the loveliest accent of Maggie Kealey's arresting beauty, was moderately distorted. The corner on the right side hung limp, giving her a somewhat churlish look at first glance. It was almost, John thought, as though the devil himself was permitted one slash of the Mona Lisa and was told he couldn't touch any of the features. The cut was deft, strategic.

He was viscerally saddened at the sight of her—faithful wife and mother stoically maintaining her cheerful disposition, wishing to put him at ease and redirect the conversation away from herself. She chatted about the septaquintaquinquecentennial celebration and how she heard "everyone had a wonderful time" and that "people were still talking about it."

John Sweeney redirected that part of the conversation, continuing to find it painful in the extreme. He asked about Bill, Moia, Grace, and the other children. She was, he was surprised to discover, every bit as reluctant to talk about Bill as he was the parish social. She did talk about Moia, and it was clear her concerns were at least somewhat assuaged by her trip to New York. This, Father John Sweeney wished to hear more about.

"How did you feel when you left the chancery, Maggie?" he asked softly, hesitant to intrude into a field of pain.

"Hopeful, actually. Father LeClere was wonderful. I'm almost an expert now on the devil!"

"That ought to get you invited to a lot of parties."

Maggie Kealey laughed, and John thought that if he could find more ways to make her laugh it just might reverse at least a few of the five years she had appeared to age in the last two weeks. "So what happens next? Should I rent *The Exorcist*?"

Maggie shuddered involuntarily. "Father LeClere said the only way he could tell if Moia was possessed was to come to the house and conduct an investigation."

"Wow! When?"

"Last week, unfortunately."

"Oh . . . I'm sorry."

"Me too. I'm very worried, Father."

"When can he come back?"

Maggie's eyes momentarily welled. "Not until after Thanksgiving. They're just that busy. Although he did say they might have a cancellation . . . and if they did he would come on very short notice."

"Well, you're not planning any overseas trips are you?"

She laughed again and John felt lighter. "Hey, call me when

he comes. I want to be here, if he doesn't mind. Maybe I can help in some way."

Maggie moved quickly to reassure him. "Of course he'll want you here, Father. And, more importantly, I want you here. You've been an enormous help to our entire family. In fact . . ." she began to falter, welling up noticeably. "I don't know if we'd all be together if it weren't for you."

The combination of what she said and the sound of her voice breaking loosed something within John, and he found himself having to first turn away, then leave the room, and then leave the house entirely. Tears streaming down his cheeks and onto his coal black suit coat, he headed for his car and realized he hadn't said goodbye. He turned to go back into the house, and he heard her voice calling out to him again. It triggered another jet stream of tears, cascading now down his face and into his mouth and onto his collar. He turned again to his car and quickened his step.

He didn't understand this emotion, either its origin or its seemingly bottomless depth. He felt in this instant both frightened and oddly comforted. He got into the car and sat for several long minutes with his elbow resting on the open window on the driver's side. What had just happened? Why did he lose it? What would she think of him? Did Grace or any of the other children see him crying on the way out the door?

Suddenly he felt the soothing warmth of a gentle peace wash over him, releasing a cleansing sensation that was most unfamiliar. He thought perhaps he'd just been jolted by a healing current of divine love—something rare and wonderful that shouldn't be wasted on a pitiable wretch like him.

Why didn't this woman blame him for her condition? She came to him not so much to tell him she was on the Pill but to ask his blessing, hoping and trusting he would take her frightful life circumstances into consideration and give her his tacit approval; and, more importantly, give her the Church's absolution.

And he had.

From what he understood from her doctor, Phil Tabor, who was also a parishioner, Maggie Kealey's stroke could not be explained in terms of conventional risk factors. In the opinion of the medical team attending her at Lower Merwood Hospital, it was clearly triggered by the oral contraceptives she was using.

Yet for her part, there was no anger, no bitterness, and no blame. In fact, there wasn't any discussion of what happened to her, much less how it happened. She simply accepted it. It was as if the conversation in the confessional several years ago never took place. Or perhaps . . . it did take place, was recollected, maybe blame was assigned . . . but now there was forgiveness. Maybe it was her forgiving him . . . or just maybe, it was God forgiving him.

John would not claim to know into which crosswinds the forgiveness front was ultimately blowing, but he was certain that the cleansing and healing sensation he experienced could only have been triggered by the gift of forgiveness. The kind of total, unconditional forgiveness that forces open every pore and ventricle of a person's being and infuses a limitless love that surpasses all understanding—ultimately replacing exquisite pain with even more exquisite joy.

John pulled away from the curb and headed back to the rectory. In moments, he was guiding his black Acura into the rectory driveway and drifting into his space in the back, near the garage. He got out and headed to the back door of the rectory, going so far as to open the screen door before he turned and headed in another direction.

Before he did anything, John Sweeney decided he was going to make a visit to the Blessed Sacrament. He was going to thank his God for lifting him from the muck and touching his heart.

58

Joe Delgado made his decision, and he didn't waste any time acting on it.

He called a woman reporter at the local newspaper, the *Philadelphia Chronicle*, and asked her if she might be willing to meet him and review some material that he thought she might find very interesting. The woman's name was Sondra Lichtman, and "yes, thank you," she was very interested.

Joe had made his decision after very careful deliberation. He was not an impulsive man, he told himself, like his friend Michael Burns. He tended to think things through and work back from the most likely set of outcomes.

The first decision was the hardest, of course. Did he have an "accountability" to speak up about what he knew, now that he understood the dangers oral contraceptives posed to women who use them? He ultimately concluded that he did. He realized the cost of living with what he knew—and having to render an account some day for what he'd done with that information—was unacceptably high. At the end of the day, he knew he simply wouldn't be able to reconcile the "who" he would become if he did nothing with the "who" he felt called to become.

He was not unmindful that his decision might exact a staggeringly high cost. That it might well jeopardize both his family and his career. He was hopeful, of course, that he wouldn't lose either, but both his wife and his boss had put him on notice, so he understood that he couldn't ignore, nor could he fully manage, those risks. He would simply do everything he could to be as discreet as possible.

He arranged to meet Sondra Lichtman after work one day near the waterfront at a small restaurant with a very good northern Italian menu. He selected Ms. Lichtman because he'd read and greatly admired her fearless reporting on a wide variety of municipal corruption and corporate malfeasance stories. She was an award-winning reporter who, Joe thought, was never given a fair shot at a Pulitzer caliber opportunity. Perhaps she was too young and hadn't paid her dues. Maybe she'd stepped on too many toes in her own newsroom. Possibly her senior editors simply wanted better credentialed reporters on the bigger investigative stories.

Joe didn't know or particularly care. He was, however, certain of two things. One, the *Chronicle* regarded the Pulitzer hunt as big-game safari. They threw more resources at it each year as a percentage of their gross revenue than any other newspaper in the country. And two, they were inordinately skeptical of free enterprise, often going out of their way to ignore or sometimes even to impugn local companies that were successfully competing with national or even global companies.

The *Chronicle*, like virtually all metropolitan newspapers, tilted left in the great culture wars, something they appeared loathe to acknowledge for many years. But as the chasm widened between red- and blue-state America, they became more assertive . . . and shrill. Circulation deteriorated, advertising revenues plummeted, and morale in the newsroom sunk to levels previously unthinkable. There were many people who believed the leftist slant of the paper's editorial page had caused, or at least hastened, the paper's demise. The newspaper's publishers would tacitly concede this point but would quickly note that all newspapers were suffering—it was "a generational thing"—and point to the wall ownership erected between "church and state," suggesting they were powerless to affect change.

Joe knew that nothing quite so salved the wounded editorial pride of a once-great newspaper like the public acclaim accorded by a Pulitzer Prize, particularly if it were won by exposing the corruption of businessmen. And nothing quite so incented an above-and-beyond performance from an ambitious but relatively unknown journalist like a potential Pulitzer-worthy story being dropped in her lap.

Joe walked out of an Indian summer evening and into Benedetto's on South Front Street, secure in the understanding that he was carrying a file with him that would address each of those two great hungers. As he approached the hostess station, the maître d' appeared out of nowhere and greeted him warmly. This surprised Joe because to the best of his recollection, he'd only been to the restaurant on one other occasion—when he was entertaining senior executives with the French pharmaceutical house Pittman was thinking of acquiring but decided not to pursue because, as so often happens with the French, they couldn't agree on a fair valuation.

"Mr. Delgado, to what do we owe the pleasure of your return?" asked Giovanni Fittipaldi with a broad smile.

"My wife, John. I get one night a month out, and I usually use it to go to the gym. So please don't tell her I was here."

The maître d' laughed and led him to a small table for two in a darkened corner of a side room just off the main dining room. "Listen, I'll be joined by a Ms. Lichtman," said Joe. "It's strictly professional. I don't want to scandalize you, Giovanni."

The jowly maître d' winked theatrically and shook with mirth. "Mr. Delgado . . . Giovanni Fittipaldi understands perfectly."

He disappeared, and in moments a small, slight woman with bronze skin and dark hair pulled back into a bun appeared to take a drink order. "I'll have a dry martini," Joe said before adding, "I'm expecting company shortly." The woman smiled, nodded, and departed without saying a word. *Now that's discreet,* Joe thought.

After about fifteen minutes, Joe began to fidget. He ordered another drink. Another fifteen minutes and he was getting up to leave when Ms. Lichtman appeared, on the arm of Giovanni Fittipaldi, who was anxious to provide an explanation. "Mr Delgado, this wonderful young lady . . . she have a problem with transportation. Please take no offense. Drinks on the house."

Sondra Lichtman smiled sheepishly at Joe and soundlessly mouthed an "I'm sorry" before turning to her escort and giving him a peck on the cheek. This appeared to greatly please the gentleman who pecked back, twice, slightly flushing Ms. Lichtman's cheeks. Before she could turn back to Joe and provide a fuller explanation, the waitress reappeared for a drink order—a Coors Light—that she took quickly, and departed even more quickly, but not before looking far too deeply into his soul, Joe thought, and smiling.

"Mr. Delgado, I'm sorry. My editor demanded a rewrite, the third today, for a page-one story that is going to run tomorrow," she said contritely. She was somewhat short and blond, and her hair fell ever so gently on her shoulders. She was slightly heavy, rather than grossly overweight and much younger than he expected. He guessed she was in her early thirties, but she looked a good five to seven years younger.

Joe waved his hand dismissively, a "not to worry" signal that didn't accurately represent his feelings at the moment. "So what's the story you're breaking?" he asked, more out of politeness than interest. He was here to talk about his story, not hers.

"Sworn to secrecy," she smiled disarmingly.

Joe liked the answer. He hoped it meant she'd bought into the old-school code of never violating deep background sources. "Good. Now I have something to look forward to tomorrow," he replied, with a disarming smile of his own.

The waitress reappeared with a Coors Light and, turning to Joe, asked if they would like to hear the evening's specials. "Not yet," he said, wanting to set the ground rules with Ms. Lichtman before doing anything else. "Why don't you come back in about ten minutes?" She nodded and left.

"Ah, Ms. Lichtman . . ."

"Sondra . . . Joe." This was said with a large smile, and it struck him that he was probably talking to the smartest and boldest girl in her journalism class at Columbia.

He smiled and nodded. "Sondra, yes . . . let me just set some parameters, if I may."

She nodded and edged forward in her seat. Out came a note pad, pen, and a micro-cassette recorder. Joe grew anxious immediately. "How about we put those away for awhile?" he suggested, stifling his annoyance or at least making an attempt to do so.

She looked surprised but removed them quickly.

"Thank you. There'll be plenty of time for that—Sondra—if we can agree on some ground rules."

Her head bobbed back and forth like a piston, confirming she was as keen to hear and tell his story as he was to tell it.

"Couple things. First, my identity is not to be revealed. That has to be signed in blood. I have a family and a career to protect. I am not into self-sacrifice. Before any documents are shared or exchanged, I must have that covenant acknowledged, in person, by your Managing Editor."

"Certainly, but Mr. Delgado . . . Joe, that's our modus operandi. No serious newspaper could remain in business very long if it revealed its sources—which I know I don't have to add are constitutionally protected."

Joe waved his hand to indicate he'd heard what he needed to hear. "Second thing. You will not contact me. Ever. I will contact you. I don't want my wife or my secretary put in compromising positions, should it hit the fan, which I accept as a possibility. Hopefully, a remote possibility."

Sondra blinked. "But what happens when I have questions? When I want to fact-check or corroborate something new I've uncovered?"

Joe shook his head emphatically. "Let me worry about that when the time comes. I want to control the pace of this story. I don't want us getting ahead of ourselves. That's when mistakes happen. And when you're walking a tightrope as I am, mistakes can be very costly."

Sondra Lichtman clearly did not like this ground rule, and she made no attempt to hide her displeasure. She merely nodded uncertainly, which alerted Joe that he would have to put her commitment to this agreement to the test, early in the process. "And finally, this is not a story of one corrupt pharmaceutical house killing women and babies for obscene profits. It's the story of a whole industry sliding down a very slippery embankment, simply because nobody flashed a red light in protest at any one of dozens of intersections this train roared through over the past twenty-five years. That's the story. What parallels, if any, you or your editors wish to draw with respect to anything else going on in America, I'll leave to you."

Sondra Lichtman did not quite know what to make of this early middle-aged corporate suit opposite her. Clearly, he appeared to possess the courage and principles of a would-be whistle blower and, as was readily apparent, he was as nervous as a hare at the prospect of actually placing the whistle in his mouth. This one was going to be a handful. She doubted her editors would agree to the third ground rule, and hoped it would be "negotiable." Her biggest concern at the moment, however, was not whether Joe Delgado would have the guts to pull the trigger at the moment of truth, but whether he'd let her eat something before she was reduced to gnawing on the edge of the table.

"Joe, I'm clear on everything, and, although I want to discuss the story angle with you some more, I have a more immediate question. Can we eat?"

Joe smiled and nodded in the direction of the waitress, who

just finished taking a drink order at another table. She nodded in acknowledgment and arrived forthwith to announce the specials—none that interested either of them; they instead decided to consult the menu.

Sondra fired first. "I'll have the veal piccatta and a green salad with the house dressing."

Joe was not hungry, which surprised him. He attributed it to nerves. "Surprise me," he said to the waitress. "Tell the chef I said, his call."

The waitress' eyes danced at the openness of his request and a small smile played at the corners of her mouth. She obviously didn't think him capable of such spontaneity, Joe noted. Nor, apparently, did his companion, judging from the arch of her eyebrow. The waitress turned to leave, glanced back at him, and for the first time made an attempt to engage him, "I'm going to tell him to send out for some Chinese."

Joe laughed. "Chinese will work."

Sondra pulled her hair back and said, "Well . . . aren't we full of surprises?"

Joe reached for a file in his black carry bag and placed it on the table in front of him, but did not open it. He had no intention of actually opening it; it was there for effect.

Sondra Lichtman took one look at it and practically pounced, "Whatcha got there?" she asked, with every confidence she would be leaving with its contents.

"Archival files from our law library," Joe replied matter-of-factly. "Let me lay out what's in here, and the conditions under which I will make them available to the *Philadelphia Chronicle*."

Sondra nodded and sat back in her chair. Too many games, she thought. This train may never get out of the gate.

"Sometime in the summer of 1960, Al Heyworth, then chair of Pittman Labs, got wind of some lab research on an oral contraceptive that was underway in Europe—England, to be more specific. He scheduled a trip so he could look in on the work and talk to the research team conducting the study. He returned home with two things of value, a conviction that he'd seen the future of life sciences, and a right of first refusal to manufacture and market here in the U.S. what would come to be called 'the Pill.'"

"Smart man." Sondra interjected. The comment momentarily threw Joe off stride. He wasn't sure how to read it. He had assumed that any woman would be properly cynical about the Pill's origin and utopian claims. He hoped he wouldn't be selling here, because he had no interest in doing so. He was "going retail" with the story because he believed the integrity of the medical industry's relevant associations and journals had been severely compromised. If the *Chronicle* wasn't interested, or questioned the authenticity of the files, well, he would have met his responsibility as a Christian, and his conscience would be at peace. He didn't believe he had an obligation to "shop" the file across America.

"Oh, he was that and more," Joe said as an aside. "Now, according to the files there were two early questions about the Pill's performance. One, was it effective? And two, was it safe? In addition, there was another issue that the files show caused Heyworth more than a few sleepless nights."

"And that was?"

"What he expected to be the Catholic Church's response. Looks like Heyworth was anticipating a massive groundswell of opposition; he seemed to believe the legislation most states had enacted to prohibit the sale of any contraceptive would never be overturned. He was particularly concerned about the reaction in the U.S. where the Church was thought to be . . . more 'doctrinal', I believe was the expression."

"More authoritarian?" she asked, her eyes beaded and intense.

"Yes, precisely. As it turns out, he needn't have worried. Once the Pill was available, Catholics, like virtually all other segments in American society, voted with their feet, and their priests and bishops pretty much followed. But we must remember that at the time, no one really had all the facts because at least some of the facts were . . . let's just say withheld." Small smile.

"By the pharmaceutical industry?"

"Yes . . . and by some of our leading medical associations . . . and by some of our most influential medical journals . . . and by whole departments of the U.S. government. And also by a few Catholic theologians who sold the Church's integrity for thirty pieces of silver . . . metaphorically speaking."

At this last reference, Sondra smiled. "You're one of those true believers, aren't you? Most Catholics I know think the Church has been on the wrong side of all the important issues involving science since Galileo."

Joe merely nodded. He did not want to get sidetracked in a discussion, or debate, about what the Church had gotten right or wrong. He had a certain amount of ground he needed to cover. He plodded on. "Heyworth proposed the two questions of efficacy and safety be answered by an extensive field study in Puerto Rico, and he offered to 'arrange' the funding. The U.K. research team jumped at the offer. I'm just going to cut to the chase here. Pittman's study answered both questions. One, the Pill was not sufficiently effective at the recommended dosages of estrogen and progestins, and two, when they increased the dosages to make it more effective, the drug became unsafe.

"We've got data here that reveals there were a surprising number of Puerto Rican women who died from excessive hemorrhaging and strokes either during or shortly after their participation in the study, and those numbers do not include, by the way, women who lived in the most remote rural areas where no records were kept. Or at least, no records that I've been able to locate. Maybe you'll have better luck."

Sondra Lichtman's eyes darted back and forth between the file and Joe, and he had no doubt that if he excused himself to go to the rest room he would have to take the file with him, or he might come back and find that both his companion and the file had vanished.

"What was done with that information, Joe?" she asked with appropriate gravity.

"Nothing, ultimately. Word leaked out, of course, and the FDA did a cursory investigation, if you can call it that, but nothing ever came of it, not even a written report. The research team was confident it would eventually get the alchemy right and increase the Pill's effectiveness while lowering, if not totally eliminating, the nasty side effects.

"But that was not the most startling discovery. The real story is in what they call the 'action' of the compound itself. And although it's true that the Pill was effective in suppressing ovulation and therefore fertilization, it was also clear that by altering cell adhesion molecules, called integrins, which are chemical receptors crucial for uterine receptivity, it was also capable of preventing the embryo from implanting itself onto the endometrium, which is the lining of the mother's womb."

"Why is that such a big deal?" Sondra asked, with what Joe regarded as the shocking innocence of postmodern youth.

He looked at her and said, "Because some of us believe abortion is wrong." He paused for effect, then softened his tone. "And whether we agree on that or not, we should at least agree that women be told that this abortifacient 'action' is possible, and actually quite likely for many women who stay on the Pill for a number of years, which of course many women do. We do agree on at least that . . . do we not?"

Sondra Lichtman nodded uncertainly. She understood the scientific distinction, but not the social significance of the two "actions" of the Pill. Women took the Pill to avoid getting pregnant. What was the difference whether that happened by suppressing ovulation or preventing implantation? The result was the same, wasn't it? No baby.

Joe thought perhaps he'd lost her, and debated whether to continue. He paused for a moment, and seeing what he perceived to be genuine interest in her eyes, decided to continue, rationalizing that the whole process was going to involve a degree of "education."

"Well, here's where it gets interesting," he continued.

"Heyworth's correspondence indicates he thought the American culture was poised to become more . . . 'progressive,' is the word he used, and sufficiently 'open' to permit him to manufacture and distribute the Pill as a safe, effective contraceptive. He was also counting on Margaret Sanger's Birth Control Federation to help divide and conquer Catholic opposition with the help of . . . let's call them 'friendly Catholic theologians.' But he harbored no such illusions about the Pill's moral acceptability if it was labeled as an abortifacient. That, he knew, would never fly. The Catholic Church, he correctly understood, would have used that labeling as a rallying cry to oppose the Pill's distribution as a grave evil, and would have proscribed its use by Catholics under pain of excommunication. Remember, we're talking about the early 1960s now."

Sondra nodded and smiled, "Doctrinal."

Joe permitted himself a small smile. "So what did our Al Heyworth do?"

"He cooked the books?"

"No, he didn't alter the study's findings. He knew that if he did that he'd lose a portion of the scientific community whose support he knew he needed. And here I'm speaking of American gynecologists and pediatricians. So instead of suppressing the findings he went to the leading medical journal of the day—the *Mid-Atlantic Journal of Medicine*—and the leading medical association—the National College of Gynecologists—and he got them involved 'downstream,' in the study's aftermath."

"How? Did he have them 'spin' the findings?"

"Yes, but not directly. Mr. Heyworth, as you noted, was a very smart man. He simply funded, most discreetly, some published commentary that posited a new definition of when life begins." He paused to see if his guest had absorbed the full measure of Heyworth's ingenuity.

She had. "Wow! How the hell?" she inquired with evident astonishment.

Joe was delighted with her reaction. "He had each group propose, seemingly independent of the other, that the question of when life begins was intrinsically existential and could only be answered by ethicists or, as a last resort in their minds, 'religionists.' This last, of course, would include secular atheists who would, they knew, be only too happy to weigh in on this issue."

Sondra nodded. "But doesn't your Church hold that life begins at conception?"

"Yes, of course," Joe replied patiently. "But Heyworth's money ultimately bought him a way around that little nicety—the creation of a whole new category of human beings called 'pre-existing embryos,' or simply 'pre-embryos.'"

Sondra was incredulous. "What! What is a pre-embryo? Why haven't I heard that term before?"

Joe smiled. "Because Heyworth succeeded. He co-opted the Association and the *Journal* to basically say, 'we can't determine when life begins, but we certainly can determine when pregnancy begins. Pregnancy begins with implantation.' They argued that until an embryo is implanted in the uterine wall, there is no pregnancy. No pregnancy, no child. What exists before implantation can only be called a 'pre-embryo.'"

Sondra's mouth dropped open. She seemed, Joe thought, speechless. "How," she asked, "did they sell that one to American women?"

"The U.S. Government was helpful here. President Carter's Secretary for Health, Education, and Welfare, a fellow by the name of DeMarco, pulled together a blue-ribbon panel of 'experts' from every major current in American life—including a Catholic theologian, as I mentioned earlier. Mindful of course of the hundreds of billions of dollars that would be involved over time—mindful, too, of the influence of secularists among them who were demanding a seat at just such tables—they essentially ratified the whole package. It was ultimately the Catholic theologian, a known dissenter from Notre Dame University by the name of Father Johan Schneider, who provided the 'theological' cover, if you will. He claimed that these proposals dovetailed nicely with the long-held Catholic tradition on life's inception, dating from Augustine and Aquinas.

He reintroduced the term 'ensoulment'—the moment when a soul enters a newly created being—and suggested it covered that period between fertilization and implantation; he even went so far as to suggest this period might well extend for weeks. And he added— and this was actually quite damaging—that pre-embryos were not entitled to the same protections as 'actual' embryos."

Sondra Lichtman was genuinely puzzled. "How did that fly in your Church? Weren't your fathers . . . your bishops, angry? Didn't they . . . what do you call it when you censure?"

"Ah, excommunicate him?"

"Yeah. What happened to that guy?"

"Nothing . . . which is why I told you I don't want this story focused only on the pharmaceutical industry, or one man and one company within the industry. That would be inaccurate and just plain wrong.

"There were a whole lot of active partners in this enterprise over the years, including some misguided leaders in the Catholic Church, who were initially deceived along with everyone else, but ultimately proved no less acquiescent than the other enablers and dissemblers."

"But Heyworth did fund the study and was the first to . . ."

"Actually, I said he 'arranged' funding. Heyworth was careful to get four other pharmaceutical houses involved in the study, and ultimately the manufacturing and distribution of the Pill here in America."

"Why would he do that?"

"He wanted to carve up what he knew would be a monstrously large and lucrative market even before it was created, so any blame or legal judgments would be equitably distributed." Joe permitted himself another small smile.

Sondra nodded ever so slightly, indicating she got it. "This all went down when?"

"We're talking about the early 1960s now. With the American woman buying into the argument that the Pill would help regulate her monthly cycle, the question of its early side effects was downplayed, its most abhorrent 'actions' were concealed, and, of course, with the question of life's inception itself now in play, the alliance, the coalition, whatever you want to call it, was able to get the Pill introduced, distributed, and ultimately mainstreamed into American society."

Sondra startled Joe with what she said next, "Your guys kinda messed up, didn't they?" Joe noted that she said this with a pronounced assertiveness that had an odd effect on him. It made him feel closer to his Church for perhaps the first time in this whole odyssey. He realized how all peoples, not merely those who identify themselves as Catholics, depend on his Church to one degree or another to protect them . . . from themselves.

"Some of them, yes. But at the core, no, never. The popes and the bishops who teach in union with them were never fooled. They understood all of this for what it was—just so much misdirection to encourage people to do what they have always wanted to do . . . but used to be much better at restraining themselves from doing."

"Gittin' it on!"

"Ah . . . yes. What I like to call URO."

"Which means?"

"Universal Right to Orgasm. Anyone, anyplace, anytime. The cultural centerpiece of our time. The main tenet of our new lowest common denominator religion. The new and now universal entitlement . . ."

"Stop, stop! You're scandalizing me!" Sondra Lichtman was laughing.

The food arrived. Sondra greeted it with as much or more enthusiasm, he noted, than anything he'd said. The veal piccatta looked like art, he thought. When the waitress placed his plate in front of him, she was smiling and her eyes danced in anticipation of his reaction. It was, he suspected, the chef's masterpiece—an attractively presented veal saltimbocca that featured tender medallions of veal seasoned, sautéed with sage and lightly covered with prosciutto and fontina cheese, and dipped in a chardonnay wine lemon demi-glaze. Joe was not a gourmet, generally preferring steaks and seafood, so it was not difficult for him to quickly concede his expectations were exceeded.

"My compliments to the chef," he said to the waitress, smiling. "You do know of course that I was expecting a cheese steak."

She laughed and said, "If we could have figured out a way to give you one of those and charge you for this . . . believe me, we would have."

Sondra cackled and said, "I think she's on to you."

Joe nodded magnanimously and replied, "Who isn't?"

For several minutes, food was devoured and nothing was said. Finally, Sondra broke the silence by asking Joe about his family. He responded guardedly, clearly signaling his discomfort. She filed this away for further reflection. She also asked him why he decided to go to the *Chronicle* with the story and not *60 Minutes* or one of the other broadcast newsmagazines.

"Well, I thought about doing that . . . thought about it a good bit, actually," Joe replied. "But in the final analysis I thought you'd do a better, more thorough job."

"Me? You think *I'd* do a better job?"

"Yes, you!" he said smiling. "I've been reading your work for over a year now, and I've been very impressed. I think you're the best reporter at the *Chronicle*, and I think you should get a shot at a Pulitzer-worthy story."

Sondra Lichtman blushed and, for a moment, Joe thought she might tear up, but she appeared to manage that emotion quite adeptly and said only, "I very much appreciate your trust in me."

Joe decided to use this "bonding moment" to lay the crown jewel on the table for her consumption. "Sondra, I mentioned on the phone the link between the Pill and breast cancer. Let me take a minute to top-line it—and once again I have empirical documentation in the file here."

She nodded, mouth full again.

"Does the name Tim Kallen mean anything to you?"

She shook her head.

"He's a physician and a medical researcher who lives and works up in Johnstown, Pennsylvania. Well, he lives up there. His work takes him all over. He's been studying a possible link between the Pill—oral contraceptives in general—and breast cancer."

"Hasn't that been pretty much disproven?" she asked with a dismissive tone.

"Yes," he said, surprising her, and himself. "But every time a study is fielded that contradicts the link, another study emerges from the field that supports it. Facts, as a statesman once said, are stubborn things."

"OK, I'm aware of some controversy there. I could never run with it; I mean it's all got to get sorted out first. Is this Kallen saying anything important?"

"As a matter of fact, yes," Joe answered, nodding. "Kallen does what are called 'meta-analyses.'" That means he's not actually conducting studies; he analyzes the findings of particular clusters of studies and uses mathematical models to factor cause and probability. Now—and this is key—he filters out any studies that do not take generational factors into consideration."

Sondra blinked and asked, "What's that mean?"

"Well, a number of studies omit data from women who have used contraceptives prior to their first full-time pregnancy. One such study, a major one called the Oxford study, that's Oxford as in the university, actually screened out women under the age of fifty. Women over fifty of course tend to have already delivered their babies, and delivered them prior to the Pill's availability about twenty years ago."

"OK, I get that. But why is using the Pill prior to having babies so different?"

"OK, bear with me here. There's some science involved, and I'm not sure I'm the best guy to be explaining it. As I understand it, a woman's breast is especially sensitive to what are referred to as cancer-producing influences prior to the delivery of her first child. Apparently the breast itself undergoes some sort of matura-tion process throughout the first pregnancy. Using the Pill before this maturation causes cells to divide—and divided cells, science has confirmed, are far more susceptible to carcinogens."

Sondra understood. "So you're saying that some of these studies are ignoring the segment most affected."

Joe nodded. "You got it. In the trade it's referred to as the 'latency period.' Ignore the younger women and you end up skewing the data. In time, of course, it will all come out in the wash. Kallen understands this. He's trying to alert the medical community that it's already in the data, if they want to look a little more carefully."

"And they don't."

"No, they don't."

"Too much money involved?"

"Too much money involved."

Sondra Lichtman whistled, which startled Joe and drew the attention of at least two other tables of diners. She immediately ducked her head and glanced up at Joe furtively. "That was completely involuntary, I assure you."

Joe smiled indulgently. He was not at all unhappy that she found what he was telling her surprising.

"Joe," she said after regaining her composure. "What's the bottom line? What does this guy Kallen say is the . . . severity, if that's the word, of the risk factor?"

"That's a perfectly good word. His regression models calculate that women who use the Pill before a first pregnancy have a minimum of 40 percent higher risk of developing breast cancer later in their lives than women who don't. It takes, on average, about 20 years to develop a cancer. Women who use the Pill for at least 5 years prior to first delivery and are between the ages of 15 and 35 are at 50 percent greater risk."

"Fifty percent!"

"Correct."

"What's the incidence of breast cancer in the general population of women?"

"Twelve percent. One in eight."

"So in that segment, those five-year or more users between fifteen and thirty-five, about eighteen percent, roughly one in five, will develop breast cancer?"

"Correct. And that percentage will only increase dramatically in the years ahead, as more and younger women . . ." Joe let his voice trail off.

Sondra Lichtman was speechless. Joe thought she might be calculating her own odds and none too happily. She fell silent and appeared distressed. "Why haven't women been told this?" she asked softly.

Joe looked at her and suddenly felt older. The woman across from him now looked younger, smaller, and somehow more vulnerable. "Now you know why I decided to come forward," he answered. "And why I selected you."

She appeared to shiver perceptibly. She made an effort to regain her natural ease and informality and said, "Joe, I'm on board with all this. Where do we go from here?"

Joe had no doubt that she was indeed on board. It had been a productive first meeting. "Nowhere . . . yet," he said as he signaled for the bill with his MasterCard, which arrived in a small dark binder and, to his amusement, included a card with the waitress's phone number on the back. So he was a player after all, he allowed himself. Well, that was good to know if Fran ever followed through on her threat to leave him.

He signed the chit, adding 50 percent for a gratuity. After all, he reasoned, this woman made my day . . . or night. He stood and smiled at the waitress as she removed the closed binder from the table. He waited, a bit impatiently, for Sondra to rise from her chair. She did so only after gathering her things, too many things he thought, and looking at him uncertainly. "What'll I tell my editors?"

"Tell them you had dinner with a very interesting man . . . who promised to call you."

And with that, he turned and walked out of the restaurant and back into an absolutely exquisite Indian summer evening.

59

John Sweeney was waiting, and he was a man who hated to wait. His own confessor told him repeatedly he would spend his purgatory with bags packed, books read, prayers said . . . waiting interminably for the air tram for heaven. John did not find this funny.

But here he was, bags packed, books knapsacked, Mass celebrated . . . waiting interminably for Father Bob DiGregorio to pick him up as promised and drive him to Philadelphia International Airport, where they would join their five confreres for the overnight flight to Rome, the site of their tenth reunion.

John was surprised to find himself looking forward to this vacation, and realized it was because he thought it would be more of a pilgrimage than a getaway. He knew he needed a regeneration of his priestly ministry, and he believed his best chance of experiencing that would be in the Eternal City, which was once and forever the seedbed for many of the Church's great martyrs. He wanted to feel alive again, to be born anew in the Faith, to "rekindle the fire of divine love," as one of his favorite prayers petitioned.

Since the first anniversary of their ordination in Sea Isle City, New Jersey, the "mediocre seven" had vacationed together in some very un-mediocre places. They'd been to the Pacific Northwest, Jackson Hole in Wyoming, several Caribbean Islands including St. Thomas, St John's, and St. Bart's, Ireland and England, and France—which included side trips to Biarritz, Napoleon's summer headquarters on the Atlantic Ocean, and Lourdes.

The trips bonded the men in ways none could have imagined, and John believed they were closer now than they were as seminarians. They were truly a band of brothers who counseled, supported, and prayed for one another. If one was struggling, the others knew it and stayed in touch, silently offering their Masses and sufferings for him until he was upright and functioning again. Though all but Rick Stuart had at least one parent still alive and quite a number of brothers and sisters—forty-four at one count— in some ways they were very much alone in their rectories, and they regarded each other as family.

John, however, decided not to cut the others in on his purgation, and he felt guilty for having told them when they called to check in that all was fine. He sensed that they knew this was not the case, and he figured the men would probably select a time during this ten-day pilgrimage to sound him out and gently probe his state of mind. He did not look forward to that spiritual colonoscopy, but he'd prepared himself for it, at least to the degree possible.

Sitting there on the rectory porch on a spectacularly beautiful mid-September afternoon, John was forced to concede that he was incapable of describing his mental or spiritual health. He was on a ten-milligram daily dosage of an antidepressant. He was not sleeping well and felt listless for the better part of each day—something that exercise seemed to relieve only slightly, causing him to wonder where his endorphins had gone to die. His interactions with parishioners were forced and labored, almost as if he were figuratively doubled over in pain and communicating with them with his head on his chest.

He knew that people sensed something was wrong, but he

didn't know what the "buzz" in the parish was, or if his boss, Monsignor Jim Grogan, had noticed anything unusual. If he did, he wasn't saying anything. Truth be told, John admired that in his pastor. He was a "man's man" and gave John plenty of leeway to do his work. Their conversations typically reflected parish needs—strengthening the pre-Cana program for engaged couples, reinvigorating the RCIA program for converts, resuscitating the men's choir and the women's sodality—and Jim Grogan made himself very clear on what he wanted and what he expected. John never took issue with his pastor, even on those rare occasions when he did not agree. He believed obedience was the foundational virtue for spiritual growth. Besides, if he disagreed, John would just do what the pastor wanted done, but in his own way. He was certain that Grogan had observed and absorbed his modus operandi, but if he had a problem with it, he never brought it to John's attention, something he had routinely done with John's numerous predecessors.

The sudden honk of a car horn broke John's train of thought, and he looked up to see Bob DiGregorio waving at him from the driver's side of a fairly spent Ford Escort. The car had been an ordination present from an uncle who was a car dealer in Germantown, a historic section in the northwestern corner of Philadelphia that at one time was regarded as one of the city's cultural treasures. Father DiGregorio was an unpretentious man and a good priest who served in an inner-city parish in North Philadelphia. He couldn't bring himself to accept or buy a new or even newer car. "I won't drive a car my parishioners can't afford" was the way he characteristically replied to the good-natured teasing of his classmates.

Now he was getting out of the car to help John with his luggage. John waved him off, but it didn't discourage DiGregorio, who approached the porch with a large smile and his arms extended. "Stop at Dunkin' Donuts?" John said, gently teasing his friend, who was overweight and far too florid of complexion for a thirty-seven-year-old man.

"No, the Turks," he replied with an even wider smile. "And they were all asking for you."

John laughed despite himself and handed his friend a large black suitcase with all his clothing, saying, "Here, you need the exercise."

They were in the car and on their way in moments, heading for the expressway to the airport, which was now backed up with rush-hour traffic. John looked at his watch and wondered if they had miscalculated. The plane to Rome was scheduled to depart at 9:00 p.m. and they were expected to arrive in the overseas hangar at 7:00 for check-in and boarding passes. Father DiGregorio arrived at 6:00, not 5:30 as agreed, and John thought it could take more than an hour to get to the airport in heavy traffic. But his companion was unperturbed. "Not to worry, Father Haste. We will arrive in God's time."

John smiled and turned to look at him, "You should have been a Franciscan. You know that, don't you?"

They were stuck in a crawl, inching forward in the heat, and a number of the motorists were beginning to express their dismay in rather colorful language. Bob DiGregorio wondered aloud if he should get his stole and climb onto the roof of his car to hear confessions. John offered that "about five more minutes of this and I'll be your first penitent."

They made it to the overseas terminal a little before 7:30, and as Bob DiGregorio promised, they had sufficient time to be processed through luggage, passport, and security check points. In fact, they found themselves at 8:15 sitting in the passenger lounge, waiting for their brother priests to arrive, which gave John something new to worry about because the plane was scheduled to board in fifteen minutes.

At 8:45 John grew alarmed and at 9:00 he felt panic, though Bob DiGregorio, who also hadn't boarded, showed no signs of being even a little bit disturbed. He sat quietly working his beads, head slightly bowed. An official from the airline approached and said with a tight smile, "The other Fathers are here. They are being processed through and should be here and able to board with you in a few minutes. The plane will not leave without you. We know the skies will be even friendlier if you're flying them with us."

John was immediately relieved until he saw the small group emerge from the narrow tunnel that separated the boarding area from the terminal. At a glance, John could immediately tell someone was missing, but it wasn't until the priests were within twenty yards of the gate that he realized Rick Stuart was not among them. He elbowed Bob DiGregorio and began striding toward the group. "Hey, where's Rick?" he asked trying to mask the concern evident in his voice.

There was no answer until the group reached John and Bob and then in almost a whisper Paul Krueger said, "There's been . . . a problem, John. Rick won't be coming with us."

"Is he all right?" Bob DiGregorio wanted to know.

There was a strange and awkward pause and then Joe McManus, who looked as though he were about to cry, said, "Rick received a phone call and a letter today from Cardinal Porreica telling him he was under investigation for . . . abuse, and that he had to report to a treatment facility until the cardinal received the final report."

John felt a cold wave of nausea sweep over him, leaving him limp and speechless. Rick Stuart was the last man, the last priest, that John would ever believe was capable of abusing a child, or anyone for that matter. He was a good and faithful priest. He was a dear friend. It just didn't compute. He had many questions, and he knew intuitively there would be too few answers. He looked at Joe McManus and asked, "What did he say to you?"

"He said he was shocked and sickened and . . . innocent," Paul Krueger answered. "He said the charges were baseless, that he wasn't even told who it was he was supposed to have abused. He swore to us that he has never touched a child improperly in his life. He looked awful. We told him we weren't going without him, all of us, but he insisted, saying it would only make him feel worse knowing that his tragedy, he called it that, was now afflicting us. We stayed with him until almost eight o'clock. He finally just begged us to leave. None of us wanted to. On the way here, we all just wanted to turn around and go back."

"Fathers . . . Fathers. We need to board you now." It was the airline official at the gate. "We've been holding the plane for you and the other passengers are beginning to stir."

Slowly, as though in a trance, the men moved toward the gate and the narrow tunnel that led to the entrance of the plane. No one spoke. No one would speak during the entire seven-hour flight to Rome.

60

It was a little after ten o'clock the following morning when United Airlines flight 1667 prepared to land at Fiumicino Airport, about a half-hour outside Rome. John hadn't slept, and felt drained. He squinted into the midmorning sun and looked out the window at the blue sea below, which was dotted by small vessels, its shore ribboned by modest breakers. He looked around and found the other men, only one of whom had his eyes open. It was Joe McManus, and his eyes were red.

They were processed though the passport gates and funneled into the baggage area, where they awaited their luggage. As they were standing by the carousels—each dressed in black slacks and socks, loafers, and white short-sleeved polo shirts—two men walked past, viewing them with apparent contempt. When they were about ten feet past, one of them actually looked back and said something in Italian that made the other laugh.

"What'd he say?" John asked of no one in particular.

"He said, 'Just what Rome needs—more perverts.'" It was Bob DiGregorio, and he wasn't smiling.

John was always surprised at how quickly anger boiled up from deep within him. He prayed constantly for a "gentle spirit," and did not believe his prayers were ever heard, much less answered. Not now, not on this morning, he said to himself, trying to fight off a murderous rage and not succeeding. Suddenly, his feet were moving. Bob DiGregorio grabbed him by the right arm and Bill Bradford now had both his arms around the left. Two others—Jim Cafano and Joe McManus—were now in front of him, slowing his progress. They soon brought him to a standstill. Joe McManus looked at him solemnly and said in a whisper, "We've already lost one good man, John. We can't afford to lose another."

John glared at the men, who seemed to taunt him from a distance, a safe distance. Slowly, he unballed his fists, unclenched his jaw, and allowed his powerful body to go limp. He said a quick, silent prayer to the Blessed Virgin, asking her for a special grace. He struggled to will the past several moments out of his mind and turned to head back to the baggage carousels. As he did so, Bob DiGregorio said to the group, "We're not in the country five minutes and already the Irish have declared war." John laughed with the rest of them, a bit sheepish at his manifestation of weakness. Whatever Rome had in store for him, whatever graces, whatever spiritual treasurers awaited him, he knew he needed them more desperately than anyone he knew.

In that moment, he knew he was either going to return from Rome a better priest, or he would return an ex-priest.

The luggage arrived intact, and they were escorted by several sky caps to a waiting bus that would take them to the North American College on Gianicolum Hill, only a hundred yards or so from St. Peter's Square. The half hour bus ride into the city was unremarkable, but all the men sat up when the first of the famed "seven hills" came into view. It was the first time for each of them in the Eternal City, and they watched spellbound as the bus turned onto Via della Conciliazione, which ran from the Tiber and led to St. Peter's square.

Bob DiGregorio narrated their arrival. "Via della Conciliazione," he began in perfect dialect, "was built by Mussolini as part of the Lateran Pact in 1870. Pius X accepted it and the 109 or so acres that now make up Vatican City as part of a conciliatory gesture from the man who had wrested control of Italy from him. Of course, if Sweeney were the pope then, we'd still be fighting."

They watched silently as the bus glided past the Vatican compound and its office buildings and apartments where the curia, the cardinals, and bishops who ran the various Church dicasteries lived and worked. Then the great square appeared off the right side of the bus and a hush fell over the group as they saw the iconic Cathedral for the first time, and glanced up to the far right corner of the square to what each knew was the papal apartment.

A great yearning swelled within John. He found himself wanting to stop the bus and run out into the square and fall to his knees and pray. He wanted to run into St. Peter's and have his confession heard. He wanted to find the pope, tell him he loved him, and ask him if he would pray for him. He felt a child-like excitement that surprised him, and as it continued to build he felt almost buoyant. "Hey, can we get out here?" he yelled to the driver, who did not speak English and therefore did not understand. He looked in the rearview mirror, and Bob DiGregorio pointed to John, then circled his right ear with his forefinger. The driver smiled.

They pulled up to the North American College, which had a hint of Art Deco in its otherwise stately architecture. They spilled out of the bus and fairly raced up the steps to see the inside of the building where so many American bishops and cardinals had lived and studied as young seminarians and priests. The Carrara marble columns and floors in the foyer nearly overwhelmed them. They were met by a petite Italian nun, and six seminarians from South America who were now reaching for their luggage. The nun spoke Italian, and Bob DiGregorio handled the exchange for them. Once in the elevator he turned to them and said, "She said not to worry about registration. We are to take a nap; then she will prepare a light meal; then she will help us register. She said she was happy we arrived safely, but . . . she thought there were supposed to be seven of us, and she asked about the priest who was missing."

61

Michael Burns was pacing back and forth in his office and dictating a memo to his staff when the intercom buzzed and he was told Ron Zimmer was holding. "I thought I told you not to interrupt me when I'm working?" he said, tongue firmly in cheek.

"Who'd know the difference?" came the reply, swift and sure. Then a bit too ominously for Michael's taste, "Michael, come on up. We need to talk."

Michael immediately laid his black dictation unit on his desk and headed for the elevator. He found nothing in that twenty-second call reassuring. Too businesslike for Zimmer, for one thing. And he never called him Michael. Plus, he didn't mention a topic. The whole thing elevated his blood pressure. The advertising business was a bit like Russian roulette, Michael believed. The more you kept firing ideas, campaigns, and yes, occasionally arrows at the few clients who shamelessly put career interests before their business, the more you increased your chances of getting shot. It was simply a matter of time. A small number were able to dodge the single bullet in the chamber through extraordinary skills—equal parts strategic, creative, and diplomatic—but for most mortals the bullet was an unavoidable destiny.

As he got off the elevator and walked into Zimmer's office, Michael had a growing sense that somehow his destiny would be the topic of conversation. Zimmer was behind his desk—a good sign? He looked serious—a bad sign? As Michael sat, Zimmer stood. He looked at the floor. Michael had an empty feeling in the pit of his stomach. "Michael, I just got a call from Burt." Michael felt a sense of panic. "They're going to put the account up for review."

Michael felt like he'd been hit hard in the solar plexus.

"HKB, R. Thomas Halston, and MMK&J are the other agencies invited to pitch," Ron Zimmer added, looking grave. Michael quickly realized this was a disaster for him, too. He was new in his job as agency president—not yet a full year. When this hit the papers, there would be open speculation about his fate.

"I'm sorry, Ron," Michael said, head bowed. He was crushed. It was Kloss' answer to the last question he put to him in his office before he was summarily dismissed. The Hal Ross agency would pay a high price for his hubris, and none more than his own team of twenty-two skilled executives in research, media planning and buying, creative and production.

"He had something else to say." Zimmer was looking intently into his eyes and awaiting his full attention.

"What was that?" Michael asked weakly.

"He recommended you not be part of the pitch," Zimmer replied, giving no evidence of his deriving any satisfaction from his subordinate's misery.

"What did you say?" Michael asked without even looking up, certain he knew the answer to his own question.

"I said the Hal Ross agency was not in the habit of letting its clients cast its pitches," Zimmer replied, with a firmness that surprised Michael. In that instant, Ron Zimmer won Michael's heart forever. For all the frivolity and vacillation he thought unbecoming a company president, Zimmer had stiffened his spine at crunch time and stood behind his team leader, despite having openly disagreed with his approach. He'd just taught Michael an important lesson in leadership.

"Ron . . . I don't know what to say," Michael mumbled, head still bowed.

"You can get your head off your chest, for starters," Zimmer chastised. "Call everybody together," he ordered. "We're going to unleash the hounds. And we're going to win this thing."

Michael stood and thanked him again, but Zimmer would not accept offers of gratitude. He had a war to fight, and he was already in battle mode.

. . .

The following morning Michael was in Zimmer's office when he arrived, which was shortly after 7:00 a.m. Zimmer looked surprised to see him and said, "Why aren't you at Mass?"

Michael smiled, "They didn't want me either."

Zimmer liked that.

"Ron, I got an idea . . ." Michael began tentatively.

Zimmer shuddered.

Michael ignored the theatrics and began, "Best defense is a good offense, right?"

"I thought it was the other way around?" Zimmer interrupted.

Michael was not going to be diverted. "We chart the trajectory of the growing hurricane. We make the case, airtight and ironclad, for a programming overhaul as the only way National Publishing can avoid a major disaster within the next two years; and we lean on Rick Reynolds to champion the work as worthy of solid study on CMN's part before any agency decision is made."

"Michael, we've been there. That's what got us here, remember?" Zimmer appeared exasperated.

Michael said, "Wait, hear me out."

Zimmer was incredulous, "Just blow off Kloss and Camfy? Are you off your meds?"

"Yes . . . I mean no . . . Ron, please hear me out. Yes, of course we'll be pissing off Kloss. Our existence pisses him off at this point. We can't let what he thinks about us—or anything else—be a distraction. The only issue is, can we neutralize his influence at National Publishing? I think there's at least a possibility we can, if we stick to irrefutably stubborn things called facts."

Zimmer recoiled, thinking he must have misunderstood. "So you wouldn't even present creative . . . ?"

Michael tried to modulate his tone to soothe his CEO's apprehensions, without success. His emotions overpowered his thoughts. Out came a torrent of conviction, white hot, "Yes, of course we present creative, Ron. But I wouldn't go to the expense of finished TV commercials. You know there's no way in hell we win a creative shootout against those other shops. They're too good . . . and we pretty much suck. Our only chance is to engage Camfy—and through him Rick Reynolds—convincing both that what we're proposing is in National Publishing's shareholders' best interests. We are the doomed agency, falling on its sword to awaken them to dangers now clearly visible on the horizon. We'll be doing Camfy's heavy lifting—which he can privately disavow—telling Kloss and Reynolds and the rest of them that he tried to caution us off this approach. But if anybody over there listens to what we say and thinks there may be a modicum of truth in it, we separate ourselves from the pack. How else can we hope to do that, Ron? And if we're able to do that successfully, we'll be making the case at the same time that we're the only agency in the hunt worthy of being their long-term business partners."

Zimmer's silence surprised Michael and suggested he just might have some heart for the strategy. "What do I say to Camfy when he says we're just feeding into our perceived weakness over

there, that our creative is terrible, and our account team—you—
doesn't listen?"

"Tell him you agree. That's why you're going outside for a
new creative team, and why you, not me, are heading up the pitch
and making the presentation."

Zimmer grunted. A good sign, Michael thought. "How do
you propose I—meaning you—structure this thing?" he asked.

It was the only question Michael had dared to hope Zimmer
would ask him. The one question whose answer would engage
his head and heart for the next month—and provide him with a
justification to cash his checks.

"Two parts to the pitch," he replied succinctly. "First part,
what the market wants; second part, how we market what the
market wants."

"Tell me some more about part one," Zimmer asked, eyeing
him warily.

"We start off with an analysis of their business," Michael
replied. "We show them the penetration patterns and trends across
the country and pinpoint, to the quarter if not month, when the
marketing challenge will become principally one of luring ex-
subscribers back to the network, as opposed to signing up first-
time buyers. We then lay out the economic implications for not
just CMN, but National Publishing too, because the network
provides roughly half its profits. With the cost of recapturing ex-
buyers being about three times the cost of signing up first-time
buyers, we'll demonstrate that even massive layoffs at both won't
sufficiently sate shareholders. We'll lay out some likely scenarios,
one of which will be their looking for a merger partner, mostly
likely in the entertainment field to help bail them out. They'll get
the picture—the one of a new group photo of senior corporate
officers in the annual report, with them missing."

Zimmer was incredulous. "If I didn't know you better, I'd
charitably assume you're just nuts. By the way . . . are you?"

Michael ignored him. "We assemble a blue-ribbon panel to
help us make the case. We bring in Stanley Rothman of the Lichter

Rothman Group, whose survey of eleven groups of American 'in-fluencers' will demonstrate that no single group has core values at greater variance from those of Main Street America than the Holly-wood film community. We bring in Neil Postman, the media maven from NYU, who recently published 'the Disappearance of Child-hood,' which posits that Gutenberg created what had heretofore been unknown, a protected phase of life called childhood, through the invention of his printing press, which essentially permitted adults to keep secrets from children. And Sarnoff, as he contends, basically eradicated that phase of life through his invention of the television some four hundred years later, which made keeping adult secrets from children all but impossible . . ."

Zimmer had heard enough. "Michael! Listen to yourself, dammit. What the hell does any of that . . . that crap, have to do with why we're standing in front of them asking for their busi-ness . . . again!" Michael had never seen his boss truly angry. Now he was.

"Everything," Michael replied calmly. "We're demonstrat-ing to Kloss' superiors that he is just flat wrong to make this thing a Hollywood beauty contest. Their business is at a crossroads. They're either going to take the necessary steps right now to create a mainstream business, or they're going to remain a marginal '10 percent play,' which they'll eventually have to explain to direc-tors and shareholders. We're the only agency in this pitch who can define the core business issue for them. That's got to count for something."

Zimmer calmed himself and grunted, "Yeah, they'll be so grateful . . . they'll thank us as they torch the work and give the account to the next agency."

Michael smiled. "Ron, let me just finish laying this thing out. We'll get Postman to go through his content analysis of prime-time television since its inception thirty years ago. He will correlate the rise in violent and sexual programming content in each decade with increases in television viewing among adolescents under the age of eighteen in each decade. Then he will correlate that data with concomitant increases in violent and sexual behavior among adolescents on a case per thousand basis."

"Concluding what!" Zimmer placed his hands around his neck as though he intended strangulation.

"That television, more particularly its increasingly violent and sexually explicit prime-time content, has halved childhood. Cut it from ten years to five years. That kids seem to be growing up quicker today because their exposure to 'adult secrets' has eroded their shame and eviscerated their sense of guilt. No secrets, no shame. No shame, no guilt. No guilt, no childhood. No childhood, no civil society."

Zimmer looked at Michael as if he had just relieved himself on one of the large, well-tended plants in the corner of his office; agency lore held that one angry creative director had actually once done such a thing upon hearing from Zimmer that his work would not be presented to a prospective client. "Michael . . ." he shook his head sadly. "Work with me for just a moment here. These men will see this for what it is—some lame Don Quixote attempt to change the world, to make it something people just don't want it to be. Michael, listen to me. The world is not filled with Irish Catholics who listen to the pope. These men are running a publicly held business. Their business is buying and selling those meadow muffins that Hollywood turns out. If not enough people want to buy it, they'll just raise the price and figure something else out. That's what business people do. And as far as the content is concerned, if that was a problem for any of them, they wouldn't be working there. So why pretend it is? Why rub their noses in it? To what end, Michael?"

Michael fell silent. Put that way, he had no answer.

An awkward silence ensued. Zimmer broke it, "Look, I didn't mean to cut your gonads off. You know I generally defer to you on these things, but I just think—this time—you're way off base." Zimmer looked weary, Michael thought. The last thing he needed at this stage of his presidency, with everything else that was on his desk, was to invest a lot of time structuring a pitch he knew was a lost cause. He was not eager to begin pouring good hours after bad into a bottomless pit. "Listen," he resumed, "we don't have to decide today. Think about it, and we'll talk tomorrow morning. You'll come up with something good. I know you will."

Michael left feeling deflated. He thought about his options. It took him about one floor of a swift elevator descent to realize that he didn't have any. He understood this thing was just going to play itself out; he would be powerless to hold back the tsunami about to strike land; and when its waters had receded, Michael knew, those surveying the wreckage would find certain desolation among many families—of which his was but one.

62

John Sweeney slept through the afternoon tea that Sister Fulginetta prepared, complete with its crusts of Italian bread and prosciutto. When he awoke, he reached for his watch and realized he hadn't reset it to Rome time. He had no idea what time it was, though the angle of the sun streaming into his modest room at the North American College told him it was sometime in the late afternoon.

The room had a bed, a desk, and a sink. The bathroom was down the hallway. For fifty dollars a night with a breakfast thrown in, it was more than sufficient, John reasoned. He smiled at the thought of his father trying to negotiate the little nun down to say . . . ten dollars for the week. His fondest recollections of his father were of him firing lowball "offers" at the unsuspecting, then stepping back to watch the outrage build. It was sport for him. And nothing was sacred to him, not even the possessions of the Catholic Church. At Christmastime he would move trees from the expensive twenty-dollar bins into the cheap five dollar bins, and then ask the parish volunteers to hold them up. He would make a great pretense of inspecting the expensive twenty-dollar tree carefully for flaws, and, finding none, would tell the gentleman from the Knights of Columbus that OK, he would pay five dollars for the tree, if the man put a stand on the bottom of the tree, carried it to his car, and tied it to the roof. This all took place after dinner, on Christmas Eve.

John showered, dressed, and swiftly descended the steps to the foyer, only to see Sister Fulginetta coming out of the kitchen. "Oh, Father Giovanni . . . you hungry . . . yes?"

She was a little doll of a woman who John guessed was in her late forties. She had a lovely olive complexion and dark eyes that radiated genuine warmth. Her precise features were worthy subjects for a high Renaissance painter. "No, Sister. Not hungry yet. But could you tell me what time it is?"

She looked at her watch, fastened loosely around her tiny wrist and said, "It 6:00 p.m. Father. When you are hungry for dinner, maybe 8:00, maybe 9:00?"

John nodded absently. "Sister, where are the others?"

She smiled and said, "They take walk. Say no wake Father Giovanni. He much tired."

John smiled. He was on his own. He liked that. He headed for the front door and out into a beautiful, warm Roman evening just as the sun was beginning to set. The distant hills beyond the Tiber River were golden. He bounded down Gianicolo Hill and toward the Vatican. He entered St. Peter's Square within minutes and found it relatively deserted. He walked its perimeter, drinking in the ambience and fantasizing about running into his old friend from Poland under one of the historic arches.

He entered the basilica and was immediately awestruck by its power and majesty. He noticed markings on the vast marble floor and made his way over to inspect them. They were markers that revealed precisely where the other great cathedrals around the world would end if they were to be inset back to front within St. Peter's. Notre Dame in Paris, the National Cathedral and Basilica of the Immaculate Conception in Washington, even Westminster

Abbey in London—all were represented at various lengths and depths within the marble—and all at considerable distance from the front door of St. Peter's.

John noticed the Pieta out of the corner of his eye and went over to the first alcove near the entrance. He stood and gaped at the exquisite perfection of Michelangelo's artistic vision and his incomparable attention to detail. He thought of the young Virgin Mother, and how little she could have imagined of what awaited her when the angel appeared to her that morning so long ago and asked her if she would be the Mother of God. He was struck by something the great Archbishop Fulton J. Sheen had once written of that very moment, "And all of heaven and earth paused to await the young virgin's reply." The thought of God Himself, Creator of the universe and all that is in it or of it, awaiting permission from one of his creatures to do the miraculous—on behalf of fallen man—elicited a lump in John's throat. Why, he wondered, was he perpetually unable to give adequate voice in his own life's narrative, to the pure humility in that divine pause—the pure love in it?

He walked as close as he could to the majestic altar and saw the Scavi Tour of St. Peter's tomb forming below. He started down the steps, but noticed a middle-aged woman leaving a confessional in a wing of the cathedral jutting out from the main altar. He could think of no more fitting way for him to begin his pilgrimage. He retraced his steps and got in line behind a young man who looked to be in his early twenties and an older man who was stooped and barely able to stand. He turned and tried to get a glimpse of the Scavi, but discovered he was too far removed to have a field of vision. He found himself contemplating those ancient words anew, "Thou art Peter and upon this rock I will build my Church." The Master once said this to a humble, impulsive fisherman who promised he wouldn't leave him over some very "hard sayings" that scattered a good many others. Who could have known then, John wondered, that Peter's Lord and Master meant those words, not figuratively, not metaphorically, but literally? And what must those construction workers have thought in the middle of the twentieth century when they had discovered the very bones of a man believed to be St. Peter below this church and its main altar?

The woman behind John nudged him, and he turned to see the confessional door open. He entered into the darkness and knelt. The screen opened and a priest from what John thought might be India blessed him and invited him to "make a good recitation of his sins." John crossed himself and began, "Bless me Father, it's been one month since my last confession. Father . . . I'm a Catholic priest from America. From Philadelphia, actually."

"Yes, yes," The confessor replied, gently signaling John to get on with it.

"Father, I'm afraid I haven't been a very good priest. I . . . I . . ."

"Just tell me your sins, Father, and I'll give you absolution in Jesus' name."

John felt doused. He immediately realized this man had probably heard scores of confessions on just this day alone. He was tired. He was hungry. He wanted to get out of that box. He wanted John to say something, something absolvable, to just get on with it, puhleeeease!

"Father I've compromised what I know . . . what I've sworn to uphold . . . as Church teaching . . . as a confessor myself." This was hard to explain, he realized. "I have misled . . . not given good guidance to some of my parishioners, and the things I told them seem to have brought great pain into their lives. I think I have . . . I think I've failed the truth I was given to share with them."

"Is that all?"

"No, it isn't all," John suddenly felt a flash of anger, realizing he should have taken the tour. "I lost my temper at the airport this morning and had to be restrained from thrashing two men to within a millimeter of their lives."

"OK, OK, say three Our Fathers and three Hail Marys. Now make a good act of contrition."

And welcome to the Holy City, schmuck, John thought to himself. *Burial site of Saints Peter and Paul and untold thousands of other martyrs, not to mention home to the Vicar of Christ. But hey, neeext!* He recited his contrition and left the confessional with a bit of tail between his legs. He looked for a place to kneel and offer his penance. Not finding one, he moved to the front of the main altar, bowed his head, and said his prayers. As was his habit, he finished by asking the Blessed Virgin to drown him in grace, so even he couldn't screw up what God expected of him.

He left the Basilica after checking the times for the Sunday Masses. He walked to the middle of the square and took in the entirety of the compound. It was, he thought, an impressive fortress, mystically impregnable at its core. There was a bank, a commissary, a post office, a barracks for the Swiss Guard, the famously filmed and photographed Paul VI Audience Hall, which was the site of weekly papal audiences and innumerable concerts, two colleges—one German, one Ethiopian—several office and apartment buildings where the bishops and cardinals who assisted the pope in governing the Church lived and worked, and, of course, one very famous apartment whose current occupant bestrode the age like a mythical colossus.

John wanted to see it all. He wanted to wallow in it, be enveloped by it, be subsumed within it, as though the molecules, particles, myths, and mysteries would somehow penetrate his subconscious, transforming him into a new creation worthy of the name "Christian," worthy of the identity of Catholic priest.

He and his band of brothers had scheduled side trips to Assisi, Florence, and Siena—day trips—but in this moment, John wasn't sure he wanted to take those trips. He felt at peace right here within the shadow of this great Basilica. He wanted to stay as close as he could, for as long as he could, to the "Eternal City's eternal flame."

Who knows, he mused, maybe that flame could even reignite his priestly ministry.

63

Maggie Kealey was as nervous as a schoolchild as she jumped into her SUV and headed over the bridge and down Haverhill Avenue to the train station. She had been surprised to get the phone call from Father LeClere earlier that morning saying there had been a cancellation and he could catch the 3:00 p.m. train from New York. "Was today a good day?" he asked. Maggie fell to her knees in a silent prayer of gratitude and said, "Father, any day you grace our home is a good day."

She felt bad that Father Sweeney was in Rome, because she knew how much he wanted to be present for her and for Moia. She'd taken to worrying about him. Something about his demeanor suggested that a struggle was taking place somewhere deep within him. Others had noticed, too. He just wasn't himself. She hoped and prayed his trip to Rome with his classmates would bring him peace of mind and heart.

She pulled into the circle that adjoined the train station on its northern side and found a metered parking spot. She maneuvered the SUV into it and dug into her bag for a coin but couldn't find one, only loose singles. Bill would not accept that she wasn't able to talk a borough policeman out of a ticket . . . while she was in her own car, waiting for a priest. She said a quick prayer that Father LeClere's train from 30th Street Station would not be too late.

As she waited, she pulled her rosaries from her handbag and began praying silently. Moia was still in her room, impervious to prayer or entreaty. Her sister Grace brought her a tray with food and books every evening. In the morning, Grace would remove the tray and the dishes with the food barely touched. Occasionally there would be books on the tray, which indicated that Moia did not care to read them. Other than that, there was nothing. No more tantrums, no notes of any kind, just a veil of silence descending on that corner of the house, bringing with it an eerie calm that only served to unsettle its occupants.

Maggie couldn't help but wonder what effect Father LeClere's visit would have on her frightened child. Would Moia allow him to question her? Would she refuse to answer his questions, as indeed she had refused to answer the questions of every other professional from whom they'd sought help? Would she throw a fit, scream, and curse as she did occasionally when a priest reappeared in her life? Maggie was horrified at this last possibility, already beginning to feel a sense of embarrassment at the prospect of an explosion in front of this kind and gentle priest. It was an embarrassment undiminished by the realization that this kind and gentle priest was no stranger to such . . . abominations . . . or so she hoped. In any event, she would not have long to wait for the answers to her questions. It was now 4:55, and Father LeClere's train was right on time.

A steady stream of students and administrative types disembarked; the executives and attorneys would not arrive for another hour or two, but Father LeClere was not among them. Maggie felt a surge of panic. Was the train from New York delayed? Did Father simply miss it, she fretted? Then, out of the corner of her eye, he appeared, the last one off the train, carrying a small black suitcase. Maggie honked the horn but did not get out of the car, afraid she might get a ticket and anger her husband. The priest did not appear to see her. He stood in the middle of the platform, craning his neck like an ostrich and appearing confused. Maggie thought perhaps he was wondering if he'd gotten off at the right stop, so she jumped out of the car and ran to greet him. "Father! Father Jim, over here."

The priest turned and squinted through his dark horn-rimmed glasses. A big smile broke suddenly over his broad face. "Maggie Kealey! I have indeed arrived at the right place." He started toward her, hauling his small black bag over his shoulder.

"Father, what do you have in there? Are you planning to stay for awhile?" Maggie needled, gently. The priest looked at her and smiled, but his smile was considerably more tightlipped, "I have whatever I might need, Maggie, for whatever I might need it for."

The priest carefully placed his bag into the back of the SUV, opened the passenger side door, and climbed in next to Maggie. He shut the door, fastened his seat belt, and turned to Maggie, noticing for the first time slackness around the right corner of her mouth. He immediately chose not to mention it directly, instead asking, "Now, tell me. How are *you* doing?"

Maggie turned toward the priest from behind the wheel and smiled, "Oh fine, Father. Much better, actually, now that you're here."

"Maggie, I'm not a miracle worker and I've only come to investigate." He said this gently, wanting to readjust expectations, though he had every intention of leading a prayer of deliverance if he believed the child to be demonically oppressed—as opposed to possessed. He'd said his own Rosary on the train from New York for just that intention, knowing from experience that such a prayer could provide relief, in time. But it took time. It always took time. He'd learned that Heaven operated on an entirely different concept of time, permitting suffering in particular individuals that was often beyond his ability to comprehend; but always, he trusted, for the good of the many.

In less than four minutes Maggie pulled into the Kealey driveway, parking the car just outside the one-car garage. The two boys, now eleven and twelve, were throwing a football on the street with some friends. They came to the back of the house to inspect the alien who was dressed in black like Father John and was now following their mother into their home. They said nothing . . . and they did not come in. Hearing the back door open, Grace rushed in from the living room, where she was helping one of her younger sisters with her homework.

"Hello, Father. May I get you some iced tea?" she asked with a natural ease that Jim LeClere found entirely welcoming. He noted how much this one favored the mother. Her long dark hair, deep blue eyes, and Celtic complexion lent her appearance a striking quality that the priest imagined young men would find irresistible . . . as no doubt they once found her mother.

"A glass of iced tea would be wonderful, dear," he said with a smile. "Your mother has told me an awful lot about you. She's very, very proud of you."

Maggie smiled at Grace, and at that moment the priest thought the two women looked more like sisters than mother and daughter. "Father, Grace . . . is a great . . . grace!"

Grace did not respond, reacting instead as though they were talking about someone else. She busied herself with her task and seemed to share her mother's single-minded focus. "Father, do you think you can help Moia?" she asked with an arresting innocence.

The priest took the glass of iced tea and fiddled with the slice of lemon inset into the mouth of the glass. "Grace, it's really a question of what God intends. Only He has the power to heal. And sometimes He permits a great suffering for a reason known only to Him. But our trust in His goodness brings with it His favor. And that's a very, very good thing for a family to have."

"He sounds like Father John, doesn't he, Mom? Only Father John doesn't really believe in devils. Or at least he doesn't think there's a devil inside Moia."

Father LeClere dropped his eyes to the floor. He had no wish to create a tension between the family and its parish priest. But he couldn't help but note that such views among parish priests today, which were unfortunately quite common, certainly did not make his job any easier. Nor did they help facilitate a disorderly retreat among the devil's minions from good families all over the world. Jim LeClere believed John Paul II got it precisely right when he said, "the devil is more active in this period of human history than in any previous period." The priest wondered how many Catholic priests, let alone Catholics in general, knew that the pope was performing exorcisms himself in Rome.

"Father," Maggie interrupted. "I'm not sure I did such a good job explaining the difference to Grace between demonic oppression and possession." She said this deferentially, clearly asking his assistance. The priest did not want to get into a long discourse so he offered a truncated version of his explanation to Maggie in New York. "Well Grace, possession is very rare, and fairly easy to diagnose. If a victim shows unusual physical strength and a virulent hatred of religious people or symbols, and if she speaks in languages that she couldn't possibly know and about things she couldn't possibly know, and, if after her physical and verbal assaults, she returns to her normal state as though none of it ever happened—in fact may not even remember anything of what just happened—we can safely conclude that the victim is possessed of a demonic spirit that is now acting within her body."

"Sounds like Moia, Mom!" Grace interjected.

"Well, as I say" the priest continued, "possession is nonetheless exceedingly rare; why should the devil risk exposure when he can hide very effectively in emotional illness? Today, it is far more common to find a demonic spirit hiding within a victim's illness, prohibiting the illness itself from being correctly diagnosed or treated. Here the devil's intention is to negate Our Lord's work as healer and reconciler. This is, as I say, now quite common and is almost always incorrectly perceived as intransigence on the part of the victim, when in reality the victim is powerless to rid herself of this demonic influence and regain her functionality."

"Wow, does *that* ever sound like Moia, Mom!"

Maggie laughed. "Grace, listen to you. Grasping at anything."

"Like you, Mom," The daughter replied gently.

"Yes honey, you're right. Lord knows I'm guilty of that."

"That is quite common too," the priest said soothingly. "Families like yours, good families, don't know where to turn. Most clinical professionals, virtually all clinical professionals, are inexperienced in this area; and as you say, many of our priests discount its possibility as an unwelcome remnant of a pre-conciliar Church, and want nothing to do with it or, for that matter, with exorcists," he added with a thin smile. "Unfortunately, that leaves a lot of families . . . a lot of good families like yours . . . out in the cold."

The daughter grimaced and said with alarm, "What do those families do, Father? Where do they go to get help?"

Father Jim LeClere studied the young woman's face and thought he might be looking into the face of an angel. Since their introduction, he noted that she hadn't expressed a single thought that was not entirely focused on the well-being of another. "Well Grace," he shook his head slightly, "there are so many of them . . . and so few of us."

Grace grew animated, "We must fix that, Father! We must get help to those families, so they don't lose hope. They could lose their faith, Father!"

The priest nodded his head and said quietly, "Yes, we must do as our dear Lord asked us to do, Grace. We must 'pray to the Harvest Master because the harvest is great and the workers are few.'"

64

Inner was served promptly at 6:00 p.m., though it was clear to Father Jim LeClere that Maggie very much wanted to wait until her husband arrived. She was, however, equally concerned about the priest's 8:24 train home to New York and wanted to allot as much time as possible to his work with Moia. The priest noted a certain sadness penetrated Maggie's façade at the sight of an empty chair at the head of the table, offering an inadvertent hint of a promise broken.

With the head of household absent, the priest confined his investigatory probe to fairly general questions about life in the Kealey household that revealed nothing he considered remarkable. He thought the family seemed shell-shocked from the everyday trauma of hosting an unwanted intruder whom they could neither see nor imagine. He found the younger children remote, as though they'd simply dismissed the whole notion of a sick sibling holed up alone in her room for a year and a half as a nonevent—something that wasn't really happening to them. Their sister was ill, she was away, and they didn't see her; someday she would be well, she would return, and they would see her again, and that would be that.

This was fairly typical, he noted, of most families' coping mechanisms when faced with a loved one who was demonically oppressed and family life itself was disintegrating. Life under these circumstances often became a tortuous grind.

After dinner, Father Jim LeClere asked if he could go to Moia's room unescorted. Maggie consented, and Grace led the priest to the top of the stairs and pointed to a corner room where her sister spent her days and nights. The priest made his way down the hall, disciplining himself not to look into rooms with open doors. When he arrived at Moia's room he paused and said a prayer, then knocked once. Without waiting for a reply, he opened the door and entered the room. What he saw convinced him immediately that there was at the very least a demonic spirit of oppression at work. The room was devoid of light. The shades were drawn; the curtains were tied together over each of the two windows; clothes, books, and food were strewn about the room. The child, a young woman of about twenty or so, he guessed, was lying face down at a right angle on the bed. There were no sacramentals visible—no pictures of the Virgin or other saints that typically grace the room of a sick Catholic child—no rosaries, no religious objects or books, and certainly no crucifix of any kind.

The priest approached the bed carefully, thinking the child might be asleep. "Moia," he whispered. "Moia . . . my name is Father Jim LeClere. Your father and mother asked me to come talk with you. I've been able to help other young ladies like you get well again. Would you like to get well again?"

No answer.

The priest sensed the child was awake. He decided to dispense with the niceties and try to provoke a response. "Moia, I'm a Catholic priest. I've come to command the devil to leave you under the power of Jesus Christ."

What happened next would, in years to come, become a staple in his talks on deliverance ministry. Moia Kealey bolted from her bed as though electrocuted. She hissed and cursed and spat at him, and tried to push him back through the door he had used to enter the room, which he had carefully closed behind him. Her strength surprised but did not overwhelm him, and he was able to fight her off. She ran to a window to try to open it and presumably jump from it, and after struggling with the curtains and shades and the lock on the window she simply pulled the whole casement down upon her; in a panic, she threw it all to the floor and ran into the room's only closet which had a two-way lock. Once inside she closed and locked the door behind her.

The priest followed her to the closet and tried forcibly to open it, without success. She became hysterical, clearly frightened of being attacked. He heard her frantically ripping clothes from hangers and gathering all manner of shoes and other garments, placing them between the door and her body, which he could now imagine cowering in the rear of the closet, all but invisible were it not for the white surface areas of her eyes surrounding her enlarged pupils.

The priest stepped back. He knew communication was futile. He did not know if this frightened child was possessed or oppressed. Without some direct communication, it was virtually impossible to ascertain. But he knew there was a demonic spirit hovering within the room. He could feel it. It was a feeling cold and menacing and eerie, which to Father LeClere was all too familiar. He determined to do the only thing he could do under the circumstances. He reached into the small black bag he carried into the room and withdrew a book of prayers for deliverance of the faithful from demonic spirits of oppression. He also removed his stole, which he placed around his neck, and some water that he reflexively blessed and began sprinkling over the closet door and throughout the room.

Then he stepped back three paces and opened the book. In a hushed, urgent voice he read the Catholic Church's canonically approved prayer of deliverance from demonic oppression. As he did so, he became aware of Maggie and Grace huddled by the door on their knees, trying to peer through a thin crack; they were crying and praying along with him. The sound of their lamentation only hardened his resolve to invoke his God in the strongest terms possible to rid this family of this menace forever. When he finished the prayer, he walked to the door, opened it, and invited the two women to join him in a final invocation.

When they flanked him he took the hand of each woman and faced the closet. He bowed his head and said, "Lord, we are gathered here in your holy name. As you can see, there are more than two of us, so we know we can safely invoke your everlasting promise of aid to those who seek their recourse in your holy name. In your name we command Satan to depart from this child and this family and return to you, for you to do what you will with him. Jesus, Jesus, how powerful is your holy name. All of heaven and earth are subject to its power and majesty. Jesus, this child has not willed this evil upon herself or this family. We call upon you to command this diabolical spirit of evil to depart her at once, for he has no power over this child of yours, and no power over this good and holy family. Command him, Lord. Exercise your great power. You and you alone heal the sick and give hope to the weary. Lord, please look not upon my great unworthiness as a priest, my many sins and failings, but look instead upon the pain and suffering of your children and love them back to a peace and a joy that is only and always of you. Lord, we ask this through the powerful intercession of your holy Mother—the Mother of God, Mother of the Church, Mother of the people of God—Amen."

The priest squeezed the hands of the two women to signal the prayer's completion. What happened next sent chills running up and down his spine. Grace dropped to her knees, forcing him and her mother to do the same. She opened her mouth and gave voice to a plea that would forever leave an imprint on his priestly ministry. "Oh gentle and loving Savior, your goodness knows no bounds. How we love you and cling to you, never wanting to be separated from you in this life or the next. We thank you for the gift of our sister Moia's life, and we thank you too for the great gift of suffering you have visited upon our unworthy family. May it deepen our love for you and bring the reality of your unfathomable love to many souls who do not know you or whose love has grown cold. Oh how easy it is for us to forget the infinite mercy you extended to each of us from your bed of unimaginable pain on Calvary."

"But my Lord . . . if I may. Would that I might suffer instead of my poor tortured sister? Please, Lord. You are all good and merciful. You alone are our hope. Please lay a cross of your choosing upon my shoulder that this diabolical spirit may be forever banished from my sister and this entire household. You see what it has done to her, Lord. And look at my mother! I beg you. Send me a suffering. Please Lord, send me a cross. I beg you. I don't care what it is, Lord. Please, please just send it."

She was breathing heavily when she finished. Unselfconsciously, she took several deep breaths to fill her lungs and normalize her breathing. Then, calmly and deliberately, she resumed her petition: "Immaculate Mother, would you please intercede for me? Would you please make my prayer your prayer? Please, Mother. Take the imperfection in it—the pride and the vanity, the anger and the rebellion—and replace it with your sublime, immaculate perfection. Our Lord can refuse you nothing. Mother, please, ask Him to do this for you. For you, Mother. Not for me. Not for Moia. Not for our family. But for you, Mother. What son can refuse his mother anything in his power? And our deliverance from Satan is always within Jesus' power, Mother. Please ask Him to deliver Moia from this endless, ruinous existence. Mother, please I beg you."

When Grace opened her eyes, she found her mother and the priest bowed, foreheads resting gently on the carpet, bodies rocking back and forth gently. They were crying.

65

The morning of their first full day in Rome broke gray and drizzly, which did nothing to dampen the spirits of the priest contingent from Philadelphia. They assembled around a large table made of marble and granite in the dining room of the North American College, entirely ready to take on the elements, the gypsies, and the kamikaze taxi drivers who terrorized tourists by blasting through seemingly impassible streets at top speeds.

Sister Fulginetta laid out a breakfast of Polish hams and sausages, and an assortment of French omelets and Irish scones—covering most if not all of the important ancestral bases. John looked around the table at his friends eating and chattering away, much as they had done virtually day and night during their four years together in the "upper college" at the seminary. The plight of their brother in Christ, Rick Stuart, had been temporarily placed in a dark corner of each man's mind; no one, he knew, would mention it during their ten-day pilgrimage. They would think of it from time to time, but no one would dare bring the subject up, and each man would find it easier to push the sheer trauma of it from his mind as they got caught up in the schedule of activities for each succeeding day. They would only find it difficult, enormously so, as they prepared for departure on the last day. Then it would reappear as a nightmare, awakening each man's fear of his own vulnerability to temptation and sin, as well as to calumny and slander.

This day was to be a Roman holiday, meaning it would be spent entirely in Rome. The priests decided they would attack their "must see list" and defer their "want to see list" for another day—one presumably between their unscheduled side trips to Assisi, Florence, and Siena. That they were perhaps being a mite unrealistic in attempting to "do Rome" in a day seemed not to have occurred to any of them.

They donned their slicks, packed their cameras, and made sure their wallets were securely wrapped around their waists—and inside their clothing—and started out on foot, descending Gianicolum Hill like a group of schoolchildren, laughing and teasing each other, particularly about appearance. John thought several of them were entirely capable of frightening away even the gypsies.

First on their list was the visitation of the other six of Rome's seven major basilicas, which they tried to navigate on foot but eventually succumbed to taxis, taking by John's reckoning at least five years off each man's life. They began with the queen of the basilicas, St. Mary Major, which was named in honor of the Mother of God. Once inside, each man appeared to grow deeply introspective. After about twenty minutes of quiet contemplation of the art and architecture, the history and epic grandeur, Bob DiGregorio suggested they kneel and say a Rosary. The group negotiated him down to a decade, which Bill Bradford led in some haste.

Across the street from St. John Lateran, the men beheld the very steps Christ was said to have descended after receiving his death sentence from Pilate, which had been transported to Rome and installed at the cathedral. They joined a small group of German tourists who were ascending step by worn step on their knees, stopping at each for a silent prayer. John's football injuries (two operations on his left knee and one on his right) made kneeling excruciatingly painful, though he did attempt it and made it up seven steps. The rest he navigated on his rump facing the door, which made him feel uncomfortable and, he feared, might have given scandal to some of the Germans.

The men were overwhelmed by St. Paul Outside the Walls—its extraordinary size, its incomparable gardens, its strategic positioning and significance in Church history. Several of them, Joe McManus, Paul Krueger, and Jim Cafano, didn't want to leave and decided to stay and complete the rest of the schedule on their own pace. As John was leaving, he turned and saw his three friends sitting and talking on a marble bench amidst the gardens, wholly unmindful of the misty drizzle descending upon them like so many graces dispensed from the prayer of the property's namesake.

John, Bob DiGregorio, and Bill Bradford visited the other basilicas and were also determined to see the famed Andrea Pozzo ceiling of San Ignazio, which was flat but was designed to appear vaulted, creating an ethereal effect. They arrived to find the front door of the church locked, and the church itself closed for renovation, but Bob DiGregorio found a rear door and ushered them inside. Two men on scaffolds observed their entrance but said nothing, and the three of them walked to the middle of the church and gawked in silence at the ceiling. Their silence was broken by DiGregorio who turned to John and asked, "Father Sweeney, how do you suppose the Irish would have approached the creation of such an effect?"

John nodded, still studying the intricate and ingenious design, "Well I suppose . . ." he began thoughtfully, "we'd have just told the men of the parish to lift the ceiling."

They left the church and ducked down a side street, stopping at what was called a "bar" but was actually a coffee shop, and ordered cappuccino and biscuits. The shop was a veritable United Nations, and they overheard patrons speaking Spanish, German, French, Greek, and Polish—but no English, which permitted them to share some observations on the surprisingly sharp cultural distinctions of peoples even within nominally Christian nations. Bill Bradford offered what John regarded as a noteworthy insight, "How good it must be for God," he said, "to look upon the mosaic of his creation and see purpose where we see historical accident, order where we see disorder, and unity where we see division."

They found the Church of Santa Maria del Popolo and entered in search of the famed Caravaggio painting depicting St. Paul's dramatic conversion on the road to Damascus. They saw it just off the back of the altar on the right-hand side and quickly approached. John found the work mesmerizing and was unable to remove himself from its grip. The conceptualization, the size, the lighting, the realism, and the detail all served to create an effect within him that no artistic work ever had. He studied the juxtaposition of the saint's body after its fall from the great beast and his look of fear and utter helplessness before his all-merciful "Enemy" and thought—*is that not Man? Why must we see our God as enemy? Why must we see His law as manacle?*

John told the others to go ahead, and he turned and walked to the first pew and forced himself onto his creaking knees. Pulling out his rosary, he began to pray for his vocation and for his parishioners. And his eyes never left the fallen figure on the great canvas before him.

· · ·

The following morning, the talk at breakfast was of the weather and of Assisi. A cool front had arrived from the ocean, dropping the temperature a good fifteen degrees and invigorating all the men around Sister Fulginetta's table. The priests wore light sweaters and sneakers in anticipation of a day trip that promised a good walking tour of St. Francis' mountain caves. There was an air of excitement, and it was contagious. John was fighting the tide. He knew he would not, could not, make the trip with his brother priests. He was simply unable to withdraw from the magnetic field that had enveloped him since he arrived in Rome. He knew he had to tell them, and tell them now. "Fellows . . . would anybody be upset if I stayed here today?"

Five heads turned in unison. Ears perked, eyebrows lifted, and jaws dropped, revealing half-eaten morsels sandwiched by jowly cheeks. The silence was broken by Paul Krueger who said, "Was it anything we said, John boy?"

Jim Cafano also chose to make light of what each man thought a peculiar request, suggesting that John was planning to pickpocket the pickpockets. To a man, they were as excited about seeing Assisi as they were about seeing Rome. Scores of brother priests, not to mention countless numbers of lay friends and family, had testified to the otherworldly peace that surrounded the gentle hills and its cathedral, which housed the bones of what many thought was the Church's greatest saint. For a Catholic, much less a priest, to come to Rome and not make the two-hour side trip to Assisi was all but unthinkable.

"John, you OK?" It was Joe McManus, and he asked his question with evident concern.

John didn't respond at first, and when he did, he answered indirectly, "I just feel I should stay here."

An uneasy silence greeted his reply, and he sensed the men felt him growing remote. "I promise I'll make Florence and Siena. I'm just not ready to leave yet."

"Ah, who the hell wants you anyway?" Bill Bradford growled, drawing laughter from Paul Krueger and Bob DiGregorio.

Truth was, John thought, he did not know how he would spend the day, and if he told them that, they would have thought his staying even stranger. He simply wanted to walk, pray, and reflect, all within the shadow of his Church's majestic symbol of unity. He wasn't a believer in apparitions or locutions, though he did know and respect people who were; he just wanted to be close by, in case his God had something to say to him while he was here in the Holy City.

He watched as the men left the college and boarded a small van that they had hired for the day. The driver appeared to be a Pakistani, properly tunicked and turbaned, and John heard Bill Bradford say to the group that he felt like he was in New York. They boarded and the van pulled away with no heads turning to see if he was watching. He felt wistful, and for the first time uncertain as to whether he had made the right decision. He genuinely loved these men and longed for their companionship, and he didn't really know now why he had chosen to stay behind.

He went back up to his room and grabbed his notebook. He started to reach for his camera, but thought better of it. Instead he brought his breviary so he could say his daily hours, and he would do so, he determined, in St. Peter's. He closed but did not lock the door—what possessions did he have that he would not give to any man?—and bounded down the steps and out the door and into a brilliant Roman morning, crisp and clear and limitless in its possibilities.

He walked down the Hill and onto the Via della Conceliazione, walking briskly and nodding "Bon giorno" to passersby, most of whom were only too happy to smile and respond, "Bon giorno, Padre." He turned onto the first side street and saw a bookstore down on the left called Ancora. He entered and noted its distinctly Catholic content—row upon row and shelf upon shelf of texts thick and thin on theology, philosophy, religious art, and spirituality. He moved toward the theology section, wanting to see if there was a book or two that might help him understand some of the things with which he'd been struggling.

He entered the aisle and noticed a small, slight figure clothed in black from head to toe at the far end. His beret was resting at a bit of an odd angle, and he was perusing a section of texts at eye level, peering over a thin pair of black bifocals that rested on the bridge of his nose. John immediately took him for a seminary instructor and thought briefly about asking him for some help in locating a useful text, but noting the man's absorption in his own search, decided against it.

He began looking for a subsection with a moral theology designation and was unable to find one until he saw what appeared to be something fitting that description protruding from a shelf just above the small man's head. John decided to wait until the priest finished what he was doing and moved away before entering the space to conduct his search. But the priest was not moving and John, impatient to the core, decided to see if he might entice the man to at least move his feet a bit, permitting John a cursory look at the shelves he was blocking. As he approached the far end of the narrow aisle, he was surprised that the man took no apparent notice of his arrival. He was deeply immersed in the text in his hands, and John was now certain that he could have gone and stood right beside him and the man would still not have noticed the large figure now casting a shadow on the pages of his text.

Then, suddenly, he stirred, closed the book, and replaced it on the shelf. Turning to move, he saw John. He appeared startled, bowing his head and saying, "Forgive me, Father." Then, motioning to the shelves he said, "Please, please. I am finished." He spoke with what appeared to be a soft German accent, perhaps Bavarian, and in a most gentle and solicitous manner. John was immediately drawn to him. He felt the sense of guilt that he always did when his impatience caused others to rush what they were doing in order to accommodate his perpetual sense of urgency.

"Father, I didn't mean to rush you, I was just wondering what . . . that section was all about."

This seemed to puzzle the older priest. "Ah, what is it you are saying, Father?" The man had a kindly face that John thought oddly familiar.

He felt his cheeks redden. "Those books. Are they moral theology texts, Father?"

The older priest understood. He nodded his head. "Yes, yes. Moral theology, yes."

The older priest moved to permit John to slide in front of him, giving him full access to the shelves.

John nodded his appreciation. "Thank you, Father. I won't be long."

"Is there something in particular you are looking for? Perhaps I might be of some assistance."

John was struck by the man's genuine solicitousness. He smiled and said, "Father, I'm not even sure what I'm looking for, so I'd only be wasting your time . . . which I'm sure is a lot more valuable than mine."

The older priest opened his mouth in a captivating smile, revealing a set of perfectly white teeth that were a striking complement to the silver hair ringing the perimeter of his black beret. "You are the parish priest, yes?"

"Yes, Father."

"From America, yes?"

"Yes, Father."

"Ah . . . then your time is more valuable than mine."

John felt something stir within him. This man was gentle and humble in the extreme, yet he gave evidence of a hint of authority that his words and manner could not entirely belie. "Let me be of some assistance if I may, Father, for there are many things for a young priest to see in Rome, and he should not spend all his time in a bookstore."

"Father, I'm looking to strengthen my understanding . . . of the Church's teachings in areas of moral theology."

The older priest nodded but said nothing, and turning to the shelves, he studied the various texts intently. As he was doing that, John noticed a brightly covered book jutting out from the end of the shelf and reached for it. It was entitled *Christianity and the Crisis of Modern Culture*. He opened it and began reading the dust jacket, and the more he read, the more he was drawn to its contents. The publisher described the book as a probing analysis of the Catholic Church's proposal to modern man. As John continued reading the overview on the back of the dust jacket, his eyes were drawn to its author's photograph at the bottom. Suddenly, his blood ran cold and he felt all the color drain from his face. The author was the

Catholic Church's Prefect of the Congregation for the Doctrine of the Faith, the controversial, the legendary, the almost mythical . . . Joseph Cardinal Ratzinger. The same man standing next to him.

John felt his hands begin to shake, and his knees begin to knock. He quickly closed the book and replaced it on the shelf. He turned to find the cardinal waiting for him with a text in his hands. He was smiling. "I do not blame you, Father, for rejecting that one; he's a bit difficult to understand."

John started to choke. He opened his mouth to speak, but it was dry. He felt his pulse beating. The cardinal observed all of this and smiled gently. He took the younger man's hands into his own and said, "Father, please do not be nervous. The Church wishes to thank you for your vocation, and your great love for your flock. God will bless you richly, and He will guide you in drawing them closer to His Son."

John immediately began to well up. Tears spilled out of the corners of his eyes and ran down his cheeks, which the other man made no attempt to interrupt. Instead he reached into his pocket and produced a handkerchief that he handed to John without further comment. John took the cloth and dabbed at his eyes; he felt a great warmth rise within him; it seemed to nestle into a painful corner of his heart, which beat now at an even quicker pace.

"Father . . . Your Eminence, I . . . I don't know what to say. It's been so hard, and I've been so unworthy."

The cardinal smiled and nodded, "I just left the pope. He was saying the same thing."

John laughed, despite himself. He wondered if this man knew the fear and, in some quarters, loathing with which he was regarded. John was struck by the stark incongruity of image and reality. He opened his mouth to speak, having no idea what he was going to say but wanting to say something to show his appreciation for this man's great kindness. What he heard come out of his mouth embarrassed him. "Cardinal, can I buy you a cup of coffee?"

He immediately sought to retract it, but before he could

formulate a discreet way of doing so, he heard the other man say, "Yes, yes, by all means. You Americans are richer than us, so yes, you will pay." He turned and headed for the door and said over his shoulder, "Follow please, Father. I know a good place just down the street."

Once outside John caught up, surprised to find the sprightly older man moving at such an accelerated pace. He said nothing, moving with silent purpose, nodding politely to waving passersby who seemed to recognize him. Within minutes they arrived at a small, nearly deserted "bar" that served small cups of cappuccino. They entered with John following the older prelate to a small booth in the back. He removed his beret and his coat, revealing a plain black cassock and modest silver chain and pectoral cross around his neck. He hung his coat and beret on a hook behind the booth, and reached for John's light pullover to drape over his coat. John pulled it over his head and handed it to the prefect, revealing his large, muscular forearms, which drew his host's attention but not his commentary. This courtesy extended, the cardinal slid into the booth opposite John and awaited someone to arrive and take their order. He said nothing as he waited, and presently an older man appeared and said something in Italian that John did not understand but which revealed his familiarity with his customer. The cardinal smiled and spoke quietly in Italian, eliciting laughter from the waiter, perhaps owner, and a hasty retreat into his small kitchen.

"Now, Father, we shall be undisturbed," he said, looking intently into John's eyes. Then he smiled, signaling John to begin, his eyes radiating a surpassing kindness that yet again warmed John's heart and melted any resistance to opening his mind and heart. And so he did. He told the older priest everything. Pretty much the contour of his life story—at least its most significant headlines. As he was doing so, a voice within him kept repeating, "Stop! Stop! John, please stop. You're killing this man . . . and embarrassing yourself." But each time, the look in the other priest's eyes said "continue." He was clearly interested. Keenly interested.

Seemingly hanging-on-every-word interested. He never blinked, never yawned, never looked at his wristwatch, never cleared his throat, and never even looked away. His gaze seemed to be directed to a fixed point somewhere within the depth of John's soul, and he would have become completely unhinged were it not for the other's eyes being so gentle and kind, and his manner so humble and solicitous.

So he continued. Right up to and through his moment of crisis and purgation, telling the man everything and hoping he wasn't making such a muddle of things that the other wouldn't be able to guide him. He told him of Michael and Carol Burns, and of Joe and Fran Delgado, and of Bill and Maggie Kealey, and of the John Paulistas who had left him for another priest—one who was better prepared to feed them and challenge them and nurture their desire for holiness. In all of this the older priest never registered surprise, reproach, pity, or disdain. His whole aura was one of consuming interest and gentle empathy, and when John finally brought his . . . what? . . . soliloquy . . . to its rather abrupt conclusion, the other man simply smiled and nodded, paused, and said, "You are a good priest, Father, and your parishioners are fortunate to have such a faithful man of God in their midst."

John blinked. He was incredulous and started to protest, but saw the older priest was about to say more and decided he'd said quite enough, so he zipped it up, "put a sock in it," as his dear mother had often advised, and instead rested his forearms on the table and prepared himself to listen.

What he heard he would never forget, remembering the wisdom and challenge of the words even unto his own final bed of pain many years in the distance. "Father, we must thank the good and merciful Lord for the gift of His truth, which is itself a manifestation of His great love for humanity. And we must thank Him, too, for the faithful people of God who hunger for the truth and who know in their own hearts when we priests speak it and affirm what the Church teaches—and when we offer to them the help and the encouragement they need to live it.

"The French philosopher, Jacques Maritain, once said something about political figures which I believe is true for us priests. He said we must be prepared to incur the displeasure of our people, and yet also be prepared to live in communion with them. He then explains how this can be so. In what he called the 'common psyche' of the people, he says there are several degrees of desire and understanding. At the superficial level, people follow the currents of popular opinion and thus give evidence of all manner of fear and anxiety and momentary passions. At another level, there are the real needs of the people for subsistence, love, and security, which are best evidenced within the family. At the deepest level, there is the desire to live together and a sense of common destiny and vocation—a general inclination to the good that is a good for all men.

"Maritain says most of us are distracted from our larger aspirations by the struggles of our everyday lives, filled as they are with toil and suffering. We priests can be said to 'live in communion' with our people only to the degree to which we awaken them, educate them, and challenge them to live what they themselves have been made aware of and now desire as the true good for their lives. It means we priests must be focused on what is deep and lasting in man and in this life, what is most worthy of his aspirations. In doing this we will occasionally incur his disfavor, but if we continue with our work, if we stay faithful to the task, we can still be said to 'live in communion' with our people, and, with God's providence, even build a deeper level of trust with them."

He paused, then smiled and said simply, "And in this, I believe Maritain is correct."

He was finished. That was it, John realized. There would be nothing more. No lecture, no required readings, no quoting of Sacred Scripture, no reference to Church fathers, no citations of the Church's magisterium. Just the ruminations of a French philosopher and how it might be applied to the obligations of a parish priest. So much for the image of the rottweiler prefect of the CDF, John thought to himself. This man defied categorization.

He was brilliant and deft, wise and humble, kind and encouraging, and . . . he would never be pope, John realized in that instant. He was given what most in the Church would regard as a dirty, thankless job—the job of saying "no" to an age that wished only to hear "yes." And he was doing that job with a fidelity that was timeless and instructive . . . and heroic.

The older priest signaled his friend for the bill, and paid for their cappuccinos before John could even get his wallet out of his pocket. Dad would be pleased, he thought perversely. As they got up to leave, the cardinal prefect put his hand lightly on John's shoulder. "Father, please come to the bronze doors tomorrow morning at 5:00 a.m. Will you do this for me?"

What could he say? That he would head butt his way through those bronze doors if this man asked? "Yes, Father. Yes . . . Your Eminence. I will be there."

The older man smiled and patted his back gently, and having nothing more to say, quietly took his leave.

66

Joe Delgado was nervous. The dinner meeting with Sondra Lichtman was one thing, and indeed it went well from Joe's perspective, but late afternoon drinks with Roseanne Gilbert, managing editor of the *Philadelphia Chronicle*, to nail down their agreement was quite another. This would be the point of no return.

He was glad that Sondra Lichtman was going to join them because she was of a different generation, and he was counting on her intuitive charm to ease the inevitable tensions he knew would be rising from the great cultural divide. Joe had no doubt that Gilbert had been protesting the Vietnam War from some elite Northeastern university—probably Wellesley or Vassar or Smith—at the very moment he had been flying reconnaissance missions over the dense and ever-dangerous jungles of Southeast Asia. He had found it difficult to be in the same room with such people when he returned home, and his discomfort hadn't abated in the years since. Indeed, the very fact that the enemy's sympathizers now occupied the most influential chairs in newsrooms, classrooms, and government bureaucracies across the country was perhaps an even greater outrage. He did not look forward to meeting Ms. Gilbert, but he believed they would find common cause, however awkwardly, in fingering their late 1960s classmates and their mentors, who had put careers and profits ahead of their integrity . . . and the health of the nation's women.

He was particularly anxious to see Sondra again, because in their last telephone conversation, she promised a "surprise," and he expected it might have something to do with some independent research she may have undertaken to keep the project moving. He was happy that Carney was in Europe and Peter Halifax was on the West Coast, which he regarded as fortuitous, given his prevailing need to keep this little neutron bomb away from any and all tracking devices.

Joe said nothing to his administrative assistant; nor did he turn off the lights in his office, which he normally did if he were leaving and not planning to return. He simply removed his jacket from the hook on the back of his office door, slung it over his shoulder, and headed for the elevator. Executive secretaries get to be executive secretaries because nothing, absolutely nothing, escapes their individual or collective attention. So Joe's elevator hadn't even arrived at the main lobby before the full gamut of speculative theories as to his ultimate destination was launched, evaluated, and discarded. He was having an affair. He was going to the club to play nine holes of golf, alone. He was interviewing for another job, probably a CEO position, with a rival pharmaceutical house. He was shopping for an anniversary present for his wife—no doubt at a liquor store. He was meeting with a school principal in a final attempt to keep one of his rebellious daughters in one of those expensive convent schools. It was anybody's guess, but there was a free lunch for any one of them who could ferret it out and document it through one of their labyrinth of networks.

Joe avoided the deadly crush of rush-hour traffic on the expressway by taking a back route that followed the sweeping bends in the river. These "river drives" always relaxed him and helped remind him why he'd returned to his hometown after the Vietnam War and chosen to settle and raise his family here. He liked, if not loved, Philadelphia and, like virtually all Philadelphians, his complaints about the city—largely its dysfunctional municipal government and stultifying provincialism—stopped at the city limits. Once out of town, he boasted shamelessly about its livability, cultural treasures, great ethnic neighborhoods, historic Main Line, and its proximity to important places like New York and Washington, not to mention the popular beaches and quiet mountains. In fact it was not that many years ago, he remembered, that the Chamber of Commerce actually ran an advertising campaign to boost the city's image as a destination site that claimed, "Philadelphia is not as bad as Philadelphians say it is," which was certainly true enough, but he always had a hard time explaining that to out-of-town guests and prospective employees and customers.

Joe entered the city from East River Drive, which funneled traffic around Philadelphia's cultural jewel, the Museum of Art, and onto the Benjamin Franklin Parkway, named in honor of its most distinguished historical figure and indispensable seminal force in the American Revolution. He half-circled city hall, the seat of municipal government, such as it is, with its iconic statue of William Penn—the visionary Quaker who helped peaceably settle the City of Brotherly Love, and for whom the state itself was named. The statue stood some forty-four stories above the street and faced northeast to welcome, presumably, those who had found New York intolerable even then. He guided his BMW down Market Street East to the waterfront, where he was to meet Ms. Gilbert. He was now primarily looking for parking spots, always problematic, and finding none. Not wanting to have to explain a parking ticket to anyone, he headed down Front Street all the way to Head House Square before commandeering an unmetered spot, which left him with a long walk on what he hoped would be a short night.

Toomey's was a popular drinking spot for the city's media, literary, and political class, and Joe generally avoided it for just that reason—save for an occasional business lunch which, he lamented, was quickly becoming a quaint vestige of another time with the introduction of a new Iron Age that consisted of vigorous work-outs and quick health-food lunches. He entered and nodded to the owner—a dour sort who Joe thought would have been bet-ter suited to public accounting—like him. He scanned the back of the main room and, not finding Sondra, assumed neither of the women had arrived. He was not pleased, remembering the good forty-five minutes Sondra had kept him waiting for their first meeting. He would give it fifteen minutes this time, he told himself, then the hell with them, he would go home and forget the whole thing. Out of the corner of his eye he saw a waiter approaching. "Are you Mr. Delgado?" he inquired discreetly.

"I am."

"Ms. Gilbert is awaiting you at a table in the back."

Joe peered through the smoke and saw a large, formidable woman sitting with her back to the wall; she was looking directly at him and gave him a slight nod of her head. He signaled his recognition and started back, wondering where Sondra Lichtman was and hoping she was in the ladies room. He did not want to break the ice with Ms. Gilbert alone. He just didn't trust himself. She and her editorial colleagues at the *Chronicle* had just pub-lished a strident series of editorials denouncing Ronald Reagan for ignoring the demands of anti-Western liberals who opposed his administration's insistence on shipping 300 cruise missiles to Europe—at the request of NATO—to offset 225 Soviet SS–20s now dug in on East European soil and targeting West European capitals. He'd gotten a pretty good look—up close and personal—at the true face of communism in Vietnam, and he did not find it as benign as the American left seemed to think from a safe dis-tance; nor did he think its hegemony in the East and even parts of the West were a historical inevitability. He and his fellow vets thought that Reagan was right to do what he did, and believed it treasonous that the left's doyen, the shameless senior senator from Massachusetts, reportedly made an overture to Soviet leader Yuri Andropov to suggest ways to neutralize the U.S. president's efforts to rebalance power in Europe and help the indigenous peoples of Central America successfully resist Soviet proxies in El Salvador and Nicaragua.

As he approached her table, Joe expected Ms. Gilbert to rise to greet him. She didn't. Instead she extended her hand limply across the table, which Joe was tempted to ignore but thought better of—leading him to reluctantly take it and shake a bit too vigorously, which seemed to arrest her attention and excite her imagination. "My, my, but aren't we primed and ready for battle?" she said sardonically.

Joe ignored the jibe and said, "Where's Sondra?"

"She's pulling together some information; she should be along any minute . . . you're not afraid of being alone with me, are you Mr. Delgado?"

Joe looked at her with barely disguised disdain and reminded himself to play nice—or at least try. "No, I just don't like to repeat myself, if I can avoid it."

"Not to worry, Mr. Delgado. Sondra's a quick study."

"That she is. I've been very impressed with her. You've got a real good one there." Joe tried but could not yet bring himself to call her by name, and he wanted to be extra careful not to call her Roseanne, despite her physical likeness to the comedienne who had recently drawn middle America's ire by grabbing her crotch during a rendition of the Star Spangled Banner before a major league baseball game—in prime time.

"They're all good at the *Chronicle*, Mr. Delgado. We have a whole newsroom of stars, and Sondra Lichtman is only one among many."

This woman is arrogant, and quite possibly nasty, he thought. She obviously resented his having gone directly to a reporter, preferring instead that she wield the power of selection, which she no doubt used to great effect in an effort to keep all the young lions and lionesses currying favor—perhaps on and off the job. "Well, I don't know that, but I'll take your word for it. After all, you've never lied to me."

Roseanne Gilbert seemed taken aback by this comment, but quickly masked her surprise and said, "Lying is not good policy—nor very practical I'm afraid, Mr. Delgado—for the managing editor of America's fifth-largest daily newspaper."

"Lying is not good policy—nor very practical in the long run—for anyone, Ms. Gilbert."

"Well, I shall take your word for that, Mr. Delgado."

Joe wanted to express himself in more colorful terms but fought off the temptation. Instead he waved to a waitress and said as she approached, "I'm afraid I'm going to need a good stiff drink—maybe a Dewar's on the rocks, and while you're at it perhaps you can get some Chablis, I'm sure, for Ms. Gilbert."

The young blonde waitress, perhaps in her late twenties, smiled at Roseanne Gilbert and said, "Hey, how'd he know Ms. G . . . ?"

"Oh, Mr. Delgado is full of surprises, Samantha."

"Are you expecting anyone else?" the waitress asked as she began clearing the first of two table settings away.

"As a matter of fact, we are," Joe said quickly. "Our daughter."

The thin and just a bit too heavily accented eyebrows of the waitress arched quickly, and she looked at the older woman with mild surprise. Ms. Gilbert was not amused. "We will be joined by Sondra Lichtman from the *Chronicle*, Samantha, and I assure you that she is neither Mr. Delgado's daughter, nor is she mine."

Ms. Gilbert waited for the young waitress to leave before turning abruptly to Joe and saying, "Mr. Delgado, as regards the reason I've agreed to meet with you this evening, you ought to know that I'm highly skeptical of your story, your sources, and your motivation."

"But other than that, do we have a deal?" Joe deadpanned.

From the way she reacted to his question, Joe got the impression that most people probably did not joke with the *Chronicle's* managing editor. "There is no deal, Mr. Delgado, and I very much doubt that there will be a deal, unless I hear a lot more from you than Sondra did."

Joe didn't think that likely. He didn't believe he was bound by even the strictest code in all of Catholicism—guilt—to "sell" this story to anyone, and he made it perfectly clear, he thought, to Ms. Lichtman that there would be certain conditions to his participation. "Ms. Gilbert," he began deliberately. "I do not believe we have a basis for discussion, and though I very much enjoy the pleasure of your company, I'm not at all sure we even have a basis for extending this until the arrival of our drinks." He was standing now, and reaching into his pocket for a twenty-dollar bill to cover the drinks and a gratuity for the waitress. Once again, something he said or did seemed to surprise his guest, who looked flustered and started to stammer. "Well, Mr. Delgado . . . I didn't quite expect you to go all . . . all huffy on me."

Joe looked at her coldly and replied, "Now, now, Rosie, I very much doubt any man has ever gone 'all huffy' on you."

At that precise moment Sondra Lichtman arrived, breathless and puzzled, sensing trouble on the playground, "Hey, what's going on here? Joe, are you coming or going?"

"I was just going. Listen, I know you're a Coors Light gal, but I've got a perfectly good Dewar's on the rocks coming; you're going to need it."

"Whoa! Wait just a minute. What's going on here?" she said this looking at her editor, who restrained herself from commenting, not wishing to further acerbate the tension. She then turned her gaze to Joe, silently demanding an explanation. Joe returned the steady gaze from the young reporter and said evenly, "Turns out, Sondra, we really aren't as far along as I needed us to be. Your editor apparently thinks I've concocted this little Shakespearean tragicomedy all by my lonesome and want nothing more than to 'spoof' the *Philadelphia Chronicle* to entertain a few of my Vietnam buddies."

Sondra was nearly apoplectic. "Joe, sit down! Please, sit! I have something very important to show both of you."

Joe did not like being told what to do. Not when Bill Carney tried to micromanage him. Not when his wife tried to mold him into her image of the ideal husband and father. And certainly not by a young reporter from what he considered a left-wing, America-hating propaganda machine. But he sat down. He didn't know why he did. He wasn't happy he did. But he did. He sat down and avoided looking across the table at his nemesis, fearing he had just fatally compromised whatever integrity and self-respect he brought to this conversation.

Sondra Lichtman was indomitable. She had a story, and she now fully believed it was a big one, and she was not going to let two useless boomers who were splaying each other from across some mythical cultural divide separate her from it. "I need both of you to listen to me," she said pointedly, looking at each one of them as though they were recalcitrant children. "We've got another angle on this thing that is thoroughly legit, and I think it can crack the code among secular progressives." She looked to see if she'd provoked curiosity, and seeing that she had, she continued, "Now Joe, I'm not saying, I repeat, I am *not* saying that the trumped up redefinition of the beginning of life, the abortifacient action of hormonal contraceptives, and the studies confirming the Pill's link to breast cancer are not important factors. They are. I'm simply saying that in and of themselves, they may not have the heft, the political rectitude if you will, of what I'm about to share with you."

She peered again into the eyes of her two listeners, and thought she now saw genuine interest. *They're hanging with me*, she told herself. *They've forgotten whatever it was that agitated them about each other, and are now focused on the story*; this is where she wanted their focus and where she needed it to remain. "OK, listen to this." Pause for dramatic effect. "I've come across a study conducted by the Environmental Agency in the U.K.—that's the U.K. as in the

United Kingdom," she paused to let the boomers' worship of all things European settle in. "The study confirms beyond all reasonable doubt that the Pill is a 'major pollutant,' and I'm quoting the report when I use the word 'major.'"

Roseanne Gilbert spoke first. "Sondra, how did you obtain this report?"

"From a former classmate of mine at CSJ who works for the London *Times*."

Joe had to ask, "CSJ?"

"The Columbia School of Journalism. We alums are spread out all over the world, and we help each other get anything and everything one of us needs for a story." She said this looking at her editor, to see if it was having the desired effect. It was. Roseanne Gilbert was now sitting up in her chair, and it was clear she had more questions, but Sondra intended to preempt as many of them as she could, and quickly continued, "Let me quote from their own statement, 'The synthetic steroid ethinyloestradiol—that would be the Pill—is showing up with increasing frequency in sewage effluent, which has seeped into our rivers and streams, increasing pollution at a level equal to or greater than DDT and PCBs and feminizing our fish stocks.'"

Joe suddenly felt lightheaded. Never in his wildest imaginings could he have expected this. He immediately intuited that the study's impact in the States, when released, would cause roughly the same effect as a live grenade thrown into a newsroom, or an Ivy League classroom. What was the term for this? Cognitive dissonance? He immediately fantasized whole armies of editors and academics frantically attempting to reconcile the Pill's contributions to "equality between the sexes," and its contributions to the inequality of the sexes, among America's fish.

He too had many questions, but he didn't want to derail the young woman who'd shown such resourcefulness. He had indeed hit a home run with his choice of investigative reporter, he told himself. He wondered if his skeptical guest was thinking the same thing and at least giving him credit for doing his homework.

"Let me give you some more on this," She continued without looking up. "The U.S. Geological Society is currently in the field with a study that's examining the effects of what they call 'OWC's—organic wastewater contaminants—in 139 streams in 30 states. The sites, they report, are biased toward streams susceptible to contamination from upstream urban areas where there are great concentrations of people. It says they are particularly interested in what they call 'the ultimate fate' of synthetic, hormonally active chemicals that are designed to stimulate a physiological response in humans—in other words, the Pill."

"Sondra, when will that study come out of the field?" It was Ms. Gilbert, and Joe couldn't help but delight in her heightened interest.

"The final report is supposed to be out within six months, but—and here's the startling thing as far as we're concerned—a top line report is already circulating, and it indicates that steroids are off-the-chart leaders as far as the incidence of their being observed among all the other chemicals found in our rivers and streams. They're showing up at about a 90 percent rate, and stuff like disinfectants and pesticides are being observed in only about 65 percent of the same rivers and streams.

"Pretty incredible, huh?" she asked, quite pleased with herself.

"Yes," Joe replied. "And so are you, Sondra, as I was telling your boss before you arrived."

Roseanne Gilbert didn't react, but it was clear that she too was impressed with her enterprising young reporter—she of the global network of CSJ bandits. But she thought she had better tone down the enthusiasm, lest they all get swept away in the euphoria. "Well, I don't think we can use what sounds like a floating top-line report of anything, much less one involving the U.S. Government, but I am sufficiently interested to ask you to continue to dig."

"I've been digging. I've been doing nothing but digging since Joe and I first met last week," Sondra fired back at her boss, endlessly delighting Joe in the process. "And I'm here to tell you it's all checking out. Everything. I've been reviewing the studies—and the meta-analyses of studies—on the abortifacient action of the Pill and its direct link to breast cancer, which is particularly high, in fact outrageously high, in young women who stay on it for more than five years before they deliver their first child; something by the way that's a lot more common today than when your generation was coming of age." Then, to take the edge off, "I mean, it's shocking; these kids are starting on the Pill in high school."

Sondra studied her boss's face. No offense ostensibly taken. She continued, "I've also been poring over back issues of the *Mid-Atlantic Journal of Medicine*, and I can now pinpoint to the year when the terms of the debate changed on the beginning of life. And its locus is right around the time our Mr. Delgado here claims it was. So—and I'm speaking just for myself—I have no problem believing Joe's archival material will reveal what he says it does. I believe we've got something here. Something real that could rock the country. Something that's going to wake American women the hell up to what American men have been doing to them." Slight pause, then in a less frenetic tone, "And Roseanne, I want the *Chronicle* breaking it . . . at least as long as I'm with the *Chronicle*."

The threat hung thick as cigar smoke in the air over the table, curling, rising, and eventually dissipating, but not before changing the room temperature in their corner of the restaurant. Joe immediately glanced at the editor to observe how she had absorbed the thrust, and could see she was somewhat unsettled, even embarrassed, by the unmasking of her aura of command in his presence. His first thought when Sondra Lichtman had concluded was to wonder what would become of such a precocious young woman. Would she stay in journalism? Would she take to writing Pulitzer-worthy exposés? Would she become an acclaimed novelist? Perhaps a government lawyer? Anything was possible, he thought. She just had the right mix of . . . everything. She certainly had defused the tension at the table. She had also accredited everything Joe claimed without his having to so much as even open his file—which he intentionally hadn't brought with him. And now she had stood up to her boss, and done so with genuine poise and presence.

She also, he was forced to admit, had ordered his butt back into his chair with his tail tucked not-so-neatly between his legs.

She was the real deal, and he wanted to hug her right here, right now. But there was business to conduct first. "Well Sondra, you are everything I dared hope you'd be; I only have one question at this point, does the *Philadelphia Chronicle* accept the three conditions that I have placed on the release of the Pittman Labs archival material?"

Sondra looked at her editor, who shifted uneasily in her seat. The woman was clearly uncomfortable and felt trapped, Joe observed. If she said no, she knew she would not only lose Joe and what might be a huge and legitimate story, she might also lose a very fine young reporter and those, she well knew, were difficult to replace. If she said yes, on the other hand, she'd be giving in to the insufferable boor across the table—a man who embodied all the self-righteous moralizing she despised in reactionary men of the right; and she knew she might be signing on for a career-ender if he was the fraud she still suspected, indeed half-hoped, he might be.

"Let's go over the three conditions once again so I'm certain I'm clear on what I'm being asked to warrant," she demanded. Joe thought she was simply stalling for time, and that she'd already made up her mind one way or the other. Nevertheless, he decided to reiterate each of his three conditions slowly and clearly for what he determined would be the final time. "Number one, my identity is never to be revealed. Number two, I am never to be contacted. All communications will be initiated by me. And finally, the story is not to be centered on Pittman Labs to the exclusion of all the other players in this sordid business. I am not asking that Al Heyworth's role in all of this be minimized; I am instead insisting that the role of the research houses, the medical journals, the pharmaceutical companies, the U.S. government and, yes, even the role of our religious leaders—Jewish rabbis and Christian pastors and Catholic theologians and bishops—also be reported fairly."

He paused and leaned back in his chair. "Now, Ms. Gilbert, do we have a deal or don't we?" He was satisfied that he had posed the question with directness, but absent an edge.

Roseanne Gilbert did not blink or flinch. She looked Joe Delgado dead in the eye and said summarily, "We do, Mr. Delgado."

Joe stood up, reached across the table and shook her hand, then turned and moved to his left and hugged Sondra Lichtman, saying, "You're very special." He pulled out two twenties and laid them on the table, then said to both women, "I've gotta run. Sondra, I'll call you in a week."

Sondra Lichtman and Roseanne Gilbert watched Joe Delgado make his way out of Toomey's, head down, avoiding all eye contact, and leaving the way he entered—through the front door—without either of them saying a word.

67

John Sweeney set his alarm for 4:30 a.m., and when it went off he didn't recognize the sound and for several moments flailed about, trying to locate and ultimately silence it. He was irritated at the sheer volume of noise coming from such a small electronic device, because he'd gone to some lengths to avoid awakening his confreres who returned from Assisi quite late and in high spirits. He had heard them come in and inquire as to whether he was awake, and he feigned being asleep because he didn't want to particularly hear about their day, and he certainly didn't want to tell them about his—at least not yet. But most of all, he didn't want to have to explain this morning, and though he didn't know himself what was going to happen after those doors opened in thirty minutes, he somehow sensed it would be momentous.

He showered in the common bathroom last evening so he wouldn't disturb anyone's sleep at such an ungodly hour in the morning, then laid all his clothes out so he could dress quickly and quietly and descend the front steps with his shoes in his hand

and be on his way before anyone was the wiser. At the bottom of the steps, he made a spur-of-the-moment decision to enter the exquisite chapel in the North American College to say a quick prayer and to ask the Virgin's guidance during the next several hours—specifically that she might help him understand anything he experienced in the light of faith.

He stepped out into the early darkness and was surprised at the chill that accosted him. Yesterday the air temperature had been in the mid to high seventies, and John thought it now was in the mid fifties. He realized he needed a sweater under his suit jacket but decided against returning to his room, so loathe was he to risk awakening the attention of his friends. He fully expected he could meet the cardinal and get done whatever the prefect intended—perhaps an exchange of some further reflection on his challenges and, possibly, a few books and other materials John would find useful—and return to the College in time for breakfast with the other men. No, he decided, he'd forego the sweater; he'd just suck it up, get it done, and get back before Sister Fulginetta spread the table in anticipation of her guests' arrival in the dining room.

The walk to the Bronze Doors was a short one, and John took his time; he reveled in the stillness of the Eternal City slumbering under a dark canopy, soon to yield to the orange glow of a rising sun. He arrived at 4:54 according to his watch, and was surprised to see a small crowd under the sloping archway in front of the doors. There were at least a dozen or more lay people and perhaps a half-dozen priests, and as he drew closer, they greeted him with warm smiles and what he now realized were Chinese salutations. He nodded in every direction and took every hand offered and bowed slightly and said "Bonjourno" quietly and repeatedly, musing that the ubiquitous prefect had indeed been very busy yesterday.

At 5:00 a.m. the huge doors opened and out stepped two very tall Swiss Guards in full regalia. They assumed their posts at either side of the doors, looking at no one and saying nothing.

They didn't have to; their large, pointed, embroidered silver lances spoke quite effectively for them. Inside, a small, fidgety Italian cleric beckoned, and they began to enter in twos and threes. John came in with the last group—two older and quite deferential Oriental priests who seemed awestruck at finding themselves suddenly inside the beating heart of one of the world's most powerful and controversial religions.

Once inside they were asked to present credentials, submit to an electronic screening with the aid of a large wand with bright red flashing sensors that was run quickly up and down both sides of their bodies—and bags for those who brought them—and proceed through a metal detector that seemed somehow manifestly out of place in this setting. When the processing of the twenty-five or so of them was complete, they were directed to begin ascending the marble stairs—stairs without end—stairs that were a veritable "stairway to heaven," . . . stairs that John feared might take the entire morning and at least half the afternoon to climb.

John's knees began to bother him at the halfway point, which is to say after about the third staircase. For several painful moments he feared he would have to stop and pause until the pain subsided, but he was determined not to demonstrate such weakness, American weakness, to people he was certain lived a far more spartan existence than he did. When he eventually came to the last step of the seventh and final staircase, John looked back and decided . . . the hell with breakfast with his friends. He was going to stay overnight.

What happened next swept John off his tired feet and would leave him airborne for many, many months after his return home. He followed the Chinese pilgrims down the simple but elegant hallway, towering over them, very much aware that he was presenting the appearance of a Gulliver among Lilliputians. Together they entered a small, breathtakingly beautiful chapel with plain white marble walls and a floor that seemed to be an actual mosaic of intricately cut and spun multi-colored glass. John's first thought was to remove his shoes, but none of the others were doing so, and he reasoned that Asians were the world's authorities when it came to knowing when to remove shoes. He decided to keep his on.

There was an audible gasp from several of the women, and John turned to see what, or who, had drawn it. It was, he could see, a person. It was a man, and he was lying prostrate on the floor in front of a simple altar that was framed by huge paintings on either side. As they moved closer, he observed that the painting depicted the executions of Saints Peter and Paul. Beside the man on the floor was a common kneeler, which was used by priests everywhere for praying, reading, and meditating before the holy altar. On the kneeler rested a small book of prayers and meditations. In the darkness, John could now make out the figure, dressed in white and beginning to stir and moan softly. Chills ran up and down his spine and goose bumps formed on his arms and neck, and he too gasped audibly, drawing the attention of several of the others. The man lying on the floor was not Cardinal Ratzinger. It was Pope John Paul II.

John felt a hand on his arm. It was the officious Italian priest. He was signaling John to join him and the other priests as he led them to a small sacristy just off the right side of the altar and pointed them to the open doors of floor-to-ceiling bright oak cabinets, within which hung priestly vestments of all sizes. John now realized for the first time he wouldn't just be witnessing a papal Mass, but would actually be concelebrating it. He would assist the pope with the liturgical prayers and readings, and with the consecration of the bread and wine, which would become the Body and Blood of Christ even as it continued to remain under the appearance of common bread and wine. This ritual was the central tenet of the Catholic faith, one whose legacy was traceable to the Last Supper and Christ's own divine command to his disciples, "Do this in remembrance of me." This request had followed Christ's own consecration of otherwise common bread and wine and His pronouncement that it was now His very Body and Blood that He was about to share with His Apostles. For a Christian to believe this was to enter into the very existential mystery of the

Incarnation of Christ, and into a full communion with all believers—symbolically represented on this day by a Chinese delegation, one American, and at least one Pole.

John vested quickly, and eagerly awaited the arrival of John Paul himself in the small room to vest for Mass. But as he was trying to figure out what to say to him when their eyes met for the first time, he was distressed to see the small Italian cleric taking vestments off hangers in an adjacent cabinet and carrying them out of the sacristy and into the chapel. Apparently the pope vested on the altar itself. Well, John reasoned, he was the pope—he could vest wherever he wanted.

The hyper little cleric reappeared and signaled the seven priests to proceed to the altar, and John suddenly felt as he often felt before the first pitch or play of an important game. The knot in his stomach felt like an anchor, and his palms began to seep. He started moving and immediately felt lightheaded. Everything surrounding him seemed to be moving in slow motion—a series of stills randomly sequenced—and he entered the chapel behind the other priests to see the pope standing at the foot of the altar waiting for them. He was smiling. Their eyes met ever so briefly, and the pope nodded, but John did not detect any recognition. He reasoned that this most peripatetic of popes had no doubt met literally tens of thousands of priests on his numerous trips to all corners of the globe during the first ten years of his pontificate. He certainly met more priests as pope than John would meet parishioners during his entire priestly ministry. Though this momentarily saddened him, he accepted that this man, now just mere feet in front of him, could not be expected to remember one very confused young man from long ago. A man who had not yet heard a call to religious life. A call this man himself had triggered.

Together, the priests followed the pope up the two white marble steps to the altar, flanking him on both sides. John was surprised to see with the aid of subtle lighting that, unlike altars at home, this altar faced the wall—the way altars did when he was first taught to serve Mass. The pope now stood with his back to the small congregation. He began the Mass with the Sign of the Cross, said in Latin, and at the sound of his strong, baritone voice John again felt chills and a quickening of his pulse. He suddenly found himself marveling at the designs of Providence in bringing a trained actor to the world stage at such a critical juncture in human history. This man was saint and artist, world pastor and evangelist, philosophical genius and global statesman, and here he was putting the entirety of that powerful machinery in play in world events behind a voice that somehow struck chords within the masses in a way no other voice ever had. That voice seemed now to rise and fall effortlessly in concert with the meaning and rhythms of the powerful, interlocking prayers of the Mass, which lead inexorably to its core—the consecration itself. At the confession of sins, early on in the liturgical rite, the pope paused . . . and paused . . . and paused some more. John looked at him from the side and saw his eyes hard-wired shut and his jaw clenching and unclenching, and realized he was examining his conscience and apparently canvassing every interaction from the previous day to identify points where he, even as pope, had somehow failed love. For over one minute and well into a second, the Vicar of Christ stood impassive and resolute before the tabernacle, sending a very explicit signal to all present that sin, personal sin, is a reality in every life, and that it must be confronted and confessed if we are to fulfill the promise of our Baptism and enjoy the full intimacy of our sacramental encounter with Christ. It was a moment that John would never forget, and one that would leave its mark, indelible and eternal, on his priesthood.

At the consecration, the pope raised the Host and held it aloft mere inches from the tabernacle for what John believed to be almost a full minute; when he knelt before what was in that instant the very Body of Christ, he paused again dramatically. His eyes were shut, his body rigid, and he remained like this for what John found to be an interminable period of time; he was a man transfixed and transformed. John had never witnessed, never experienced, anything quite like it. There was suddenly a palpable presence of something mystical emerging from the ether, now enveloping the altar. As the pope raised the chalice, initiating the transubstantiation of mere wine into the very Blood of Christ shed on Calvary for the sins of humankind, John again felt chills. *He's bringing it alive,* he heard himself say within the silent recesses of his mind. John felt the pope actually summoning a dynamic if bloodless reenactment of the Sacrifice of the Lamb on the Friday known in human history as "Good."

John felt himself begin to well up, and very large and very warm tears soon began to roll down his cheeks and onto his vestments. He was immediately self-conscious, and hoped that none of the Chinese priests noticed. He was also grateful that the altar was facing the tabernacle and not the congregation. He had feelings that were literally inexpressible; he couldn't help but wonder if he was experiencing what was there for every priest and every parishioner to experience every time a celebrant invested himself fully in those imponderable words that echo through the millennia, "This is my Body . . . and This is my Blood."

A question formed in John's mind. How could he do this for his people? What did he need to believe that he did not believe, or believe sufficiently? He wanted to experience this again and again, and he wanted his parishioners, his family, and his brother priests to experience just what he was experiencing in this moment. He wished all men and women of goodwill throughout the whole world—Jew and Christian and Muslim and Hindu and Buddhist and agnostic and atheist—could experience it, too. He imagined that if other men could experience what he was experiencing, there would truly be a unity within mankind. Men may well remain of different minds, he reasoned, but their hearts would beat as one.

At the Communion, John realized he would be the first of the concelebrants to take the sacred Host from the hands of the pope, and he again battled a case of the jitters. He decided to take the Host on the tongue, lest his hands betray him and he fumble the Body and Blood of his Redeemer in his own end zone. At the moment when John took the Host, he felt an electric current through his entire body, almost bringing him to his knees. He was suddenly aware of the pope reaching out reflexively with his right hand to steady him. John did not know what happened in that instant—a moment that would remain frozen in time for the rest of his life—but he now felt he was in a place he'd never been before. All was peace and light. All movement was in slow motion. All sound was muted and ethereal. In moments, the pope returned with the chalice that held the Precious Blood. He handed it to John that he might drink from it, and then turned to the congregants who were now assembled in two lines before the altar.

After all the consecrated bread and wine was consumed, the Holy Father went to the kneeler, which the Italian cleric brought to the front of the altar. He knelt and placed his head in his hands. He remained in that position for forty days and forty nights, or so it seemed to John. He had never experienced such a profound and enduring "moment" of thanksgiving, which in the Catholic rite is the time when all who have supped at the holy altar give praise and thanks for having done so; and also petition forgiveness for their venial, or lesser, sins, and divine assistance for their earthly pilgrimage—and that of their loved ones and others whose special intentions they carry within their heart. This period lasted not less than ten full minutes, and John thought perhaps as much as fifteen minutes. When he said Mass, it generally lasted two minutes.

At the conclusion of the Mass, the people were led out of the chapel and into a stunningly bright papal library where they would soon be joined by the concelebrants. The pope returned to his kneeler, where he once again invoked his God for who knew what intentions. He would remain deep in prayer for another twenty minutes, and this astonished John because he did not pray for even one full hour a day. He had read somewhere that the pope prayed for some seven to eight hours every day. Like most everyone else, he wondered how this pope managed to be so productive and prolific with such a heavy prayer schedule, but perhaps, he reasoned, the answer might well be found in that very prayer schedule . . . that and a reported four hours of sleep a night.

John removed his vestments with the other priests, and hung them in the closet. He wished for a way to communicate with them something of what he'd just experienced, knowing that they too must have experienced something deeply mystical from the sound of them; they were chirping happily in hushed tones and were using strange sounds as often as words to give voice to what they no doubt experienced during Mass. Suddenly, a priest none of them knew appeared at the door and he walked over to John and introduced himself in English, "I'm Monsignor Jeevish," he said—which John later discovered was spelled Dziwisz, "and I work for the pope." Big smile. "Follow me into the library, so you can meet the pope and have your picture taken with him."

John's heart leapt. He was going to have the opportunity to meet the pope again after all. He waved to the other priests to follow him as he followed the pope's assistant from the sacristy to the library. When they entered, they saw the others from the delegation already assembled on the far side of the room, and they welcomed their priests with expressions of great joy. They swarmed them and began engaging them in that clipped, staccato, occasionally sing-song language and tone that is so distinctive to Western ears. Several would turn from time to time toward John, smile and bow, and say something to which John only wished he could respond. He looked at his watch and was surprised to see that it was now almost seven o'clock. The Mass, a weekday Mass, had run almost one hour. Somehow, John didn't think Jim Grogan or his parishioners would react too favorably if he ever tried to duplicate such a liturgy some hot summer morning. John figured he had about another forty-five minutes before McManus would be up—he was always the first to rise and welcome the new day as a gift from his Creator. John was usually the last, and the others would not expect him at table until sometime around eight-thirty—so he thought there was still plenty of time to get his picture taken with the pope and be on his way.

Presently, the pope entered the room to the kind of adulation from the Chinese pilgrims usually reserved in the Western world for a rock star. The women gasped and yelped and cried; the men clapped their hands and made sharp high-pitched noises and began closing the distance between the pope and their group. Out of nowhere, a photographer appeared and began snapping pictures with astonishing speed. He repeatedly circled and crisscrossed the room, seeming to click with each step and, when the pope noticed him, he began moving to each person individually, giving them a small gift that looked to John like rosary beads in a small black pouch. He positioned himself to either the right or left of his visitor so that the photographer might perfectly catch the moment of wonderment. When he came to John, he bent his head close to John's chest, and John feared his thumping heart would burst a papal ear drum; it was not the pope's intention to give him a physical, but rather to extend an invitation. "Father," he said in his distinctively Polish dialect, "you come with me. We have breakfast together."

John immediately looked around to see if anyone else heard what the pope said, and determined no one had. He looked at the pope, who was staring at him with the bluest, wisest, kindest pair of eyes he'd ever beheld. He was awaiting an answer. John's heart was racing and he didn't trust his voice, so he simply nodded and immediately reproached himself for projecting weakness, apathy, or anything else that any alert host would read into his underwhelming response. It apparently didn't matter to this host because he smiled and put one very strong arm on his forearm, leading John into a small dining room just off the library.

When John entered the room he immediately noticed that the table was set for the pope to sit on one side of the table, and for two priests who were already seated at another end of the table. There were two chairs and place settings opposite the pope. One was clearly for John, and the other he would soon discover was for the Holy Father's aide, Monsignor "Jeevish." As he approached his designated seating, the men at the far ends of the table got up and approached him to introduce themselves. They, too, were monsignors, and their role, John would learn much later, was to make sure nothing would be reported as said that had not been said—Vatican protocol.

The pope walked around to his place on the other side of the table and waited for Monsignor Jeevish to arrive, and when he did, he closed his eyes and bowed his head . . . and to John's absolute astonishment, he asked John to offer the blessing. He steadied himself and recited the prayer he had learned at his mother's table, "Bless us O' Lord for these thy gifts which we are about to receive from thy bounty, through Christ our Lord . . . Amen." When he finished, he looked up and saw that the pope was already in his chair and motioning the others to take theirs.

Two small Polish nuns with mischievous smiles appeared, carrying large trays of Polish ham and sausage, scrambled eggs, an assortment of fresh fruits, dark toast, and tea. The trays were set on the table, and the plates of hot food were systematically removed and offered to each guest in turn. The pope was served last. A small dish of fruit and a cup of tea were placed in front of him, and he said something in Polish to the nun serving him that made her laugh like a schoolgirl.

John discreetly took what he regarded as small portions of everything, about half what he would have liked to have taken and was happy he had done so when he heard Monsignor "Jeevish" say to the pope, "The Americans eat like there is no tomorrow."

The pope smiled, looked at John, and said, "For America, there will always be a tomorrow."

His remark recalled something President Reagan had once said in his reelection campaign, and John said in reply, "Our president said it is Morning in America."

John Paul II nodded and said, "America has a good president."

He noticed a crease formed in the pope's forehead, and John studied him intently as he edged his fork into the middle of a large strawberry and halved it before taking a first bite. The pope looked up suddenly and said to John, "Your good friend the prefect tells me you have been favored with some very complex challenges for such a young priest."

John felt his heart quicken. He did not know how to respond. He mumbled "Yes, Your Holiness," and added "but nothing compared to priests in your country."

The pope appeared to like this response. He smiled, nodded, and said, "Yes, but prosperity is far more dangerous than poverty."

John immediately grasped that this conversation, wherever it went, would only and always be about souls—the immortal essence of temporal human existence. And he had read that this pope always saw man within the prism of his primordial origin and ultimate destiny.

John felt the pope waiting for him to say something, so he said, "Yes, we have many seductions in America, and it is particularly difficult for our young people."

"Tell me about the problems your parishioners bring to you," he gently interrupted.

The question was like a hammer dropping on John's head. The last thing he wanted to do in his once-in-a-lifetime meeting with the Vicar of Christ was to reveal his painful inadequacies as a confessor. Yet he grasped intuitively that it was just those inadequacies that had opened this extraordinary door in his life. But what to say? How to begin? How much detail?

He began slowly, intent on communicating only the basic outline of what Michael Burns, Joe Delgado, and Bill and Maggie Kealey brought into his confessional, and what he had offered, or not offered, by way of spiritual guidance; he concluded by reporting how it all played out, or at least appeared to be playing out. He was unsparing in his self-portrayal, without being unduly harsh, which he knew would only reveal a deep-seated pride that was most unattractive and most difficult to root out. He had no idea what response, if any, his account would draw from his listeners, particularly the one whose blessing, if not approval, he most sought.

When he finished, the pope looked at him, pointed to his plate, and said, "Eat!" He didn't have to be told twice, and as he began stabbing at the ham and sausage, one of the little round Polish nuns reappeared with a piping hot plate of replenishments that he received gratefully, because his own plate had cooled considerably. As he dug in, he heard the pope place his fork on his half-eaten plate of fruit. He was looking at John and smiling in a way that reminded him of the look on his father's face on those rare occasions when he had brought home a good report card.

"You have been tested early," the pope said with great gentleness. "God must have a special plan for your ministry."

John stopped chewing. For a long moment he couldn't swallow. Then a wave of relief swept over him. His candid account had induced not harsh judgment, but pastoral empathy. He was not sitting before the Bishop of Rome as the worthless, irredeemable wretch he knew himself to be. He was someone of intrinsic value who was at this moment being embraced by a loving and merciful—and holy—Father. He suddenly felt a powerful surge of love for the man on the other side of the table, and he wanted to give voice to it in some way, but did not know how, and so he said nothing.

It did not matter, because it was clear that the pope wanted him to eat. It was also clear the pope had something he now wished to say. John lifted his head and sat forward in his chair.

"The devil is alive and active in the world in a manner unprecedented," he began with some deliberation. "In the East, it is liberty he denies. In the West, it is responsibility. You in America who have much are a particular target. He must greatly diminish your moral energy to suit his ultimate purposes. He does this in our time by distorting the human image on the screen; this he does to excite the impulse for gratification within man. Through the alchemy of the Pill, he deludes man into thinking he is protected from the natural consequence of the act itself." He paused to let John fully absorb what he was saying. John nodded, more in wonderment than in understanding.

"This produces alienation in man—toward himself and his God," he continued. "This alienation has as its ultimate aim the destruction of family, which is the communion of love wherein man, as husband and wife, image Trinitarian love. This is the fundamental negation that the devil must first create."

"Why?" John was dismayed to hear himself interrupt, but before he could retrieve the question, it was being answered.

"So he can create disorder within divinely created order," The pope replied matter-of-factly. "This is what he does, or seeks to do in every age. In some ages he is more successful than in others," he added with a small smile. "With man unable to summon the moral energy to traverse the great divide between what his technology permits him to do and what his heart instructs him to do, he becomes powerless to face the great existential challenges of his age."

John's eyes were immediately opened. The West, America included, was "playing soft." As a former athlete, he understood the metaphor. This man with the piercing blue eyes, whose own granite character was forged in the fire of godless communism, was saying this softness was an inevitable consequence of the West's embrace of the illusion on the screen . . . and the delusion in the Pill. They were inextricable deceptions, and by their very nature demonic. Their near universal acceptance was not without consequence. Western civilization had allowed its moral energy to be systematically drained by sexual license; and it now lacked the intellectual, emotional, and yes, spiritual toughness to face the great crises confronting it.

A question began to form in John's mind. He wanted to ask if the pope was suggesting that the correct use of man's greatest God-given power was of primordial importance to his survival, but he couldn't frame the question in a way he found acceptable. Instead, he asked tentatively, "Your Holiness, what do you see as the great existential challenges of our age?"

The pope looked at him with what John thought was some degree of surprise, and said soberly, "The depletion and exploitation of God's creation, the inequitable distribution of goods, the clash of cultures, the desire of man to recreate himself in his own image, and an all-pervasive global culture of death that extends from the womb and now hangs over all peoples as a sword of Damocles."

John gasped at the darkness of the cloud cover enveloping the globe; he couldn't help but note it was man-made. "Your Holiness," he asked diffidently, "do you have a sense . . . a sense that these challenges will soon come to a head, perhaps in connection with the new millennium?"

"This is a question, as Christ tells us, for the Father only," he replied, without elaboration.

"Then Your Holiness, how is it that you say repeatedly that the Church is on the verge of a new springtime?"

"The two are not mutually exclusive. They are mutually dependent," he replied enigmatically.

"Your Holiness, I don't understand."

"We see the Holy Spirit is more active than ever before in humankind, precisely because the unholy spirit is more active than ever before in humankind."

"Such is the mercy of God," John said quietly.

The pope nodded and said softly, "Yes, yes. We are living in an age of Divine Mercy."

A number of questions formed suddenly and raced each other to the front of John's mind. He knew his time was drawing to a close, and he wanted to maximize every precious second of it and return to his parish better equipped to guide his parishioners. "Your Holiness, I know you have written extensively on marriage and family . . . on marital intimacy. I've tried to read what you've written, but I'm embarrassed to say that I don't really understand a lot of it. What are you trying . . . I mean . . . what are you say-ing to us?"

The pope smiled and Monsignor "Jeevish" said something to him in Polish, and they both laughed. Not wanting John to take offense, the pope said, "My friend here says you are humble and therefore we must reexamine your credentials to see if you really are American."

John laughed and hung his head sheepishly. When he looked up again, the pope was waiting with a reply to his question. "The Church proposes to modern man that he consider woman his equal. It is together that they are the image of God in the world. Therefore, she is the full partner and indispensable companion to man—as he is to her. When man is aggressive toward the woman and asserts his rights to the exclusion of hers, he denies the truth of her equality. He objectifies her, and denies the existential truth—as well as the biological truth—of her being. This is not what the Creator intended when he made a gift of woman to man.

"The marital act is an icon of the Trinity. It is a gift whose truth is inscribed within the very bodies of man and woman. When they give and receive love without condition—without artificial man-made-barriers—they act in accordance with the very nature of love. This love mirrors the love of the Father for His Son, and the Son's love in return for the Father. It is precisely this perfect love that begets the eternal offspring, which is the Holy Spirit. When man and woman love in this way, they too form a union based on a gift of self. This openness to the full humanity of the other opens their love to offspring in accordance with the dictates of the divine plan. In doing this, man and wife fulfill God's plan and give living witness to man's unique privilege as co-creator of humanity."

John thought he understood, more or less. He was tempted to ask several questions but thought better of it, deciding he'd already displayed sufficient ignorance for one breakfast. But his host was observing him carefully and he said, "Am I still not being sufficiently clear?" He said this with a humility that John found stunning.

John cleared his throat and said, "What happens to good people . . . who love God and love their families . . . but decide to take steps to see that they don't have any more children?"

The Holy Father nodded and said, "Love grows cold. When man is aggressive toward woman, it carries over into other areas of his life. He becomes aggressive in pursuit of power. He becomes aggressive in pursuit of profit. In all of this, he begins to see others not as God has created them, but as he wishes to see them. He sees them not as subjects created in the image and likeness of God with an inviolable dignity, but as objects that he believes he can manipulate for personal gain. This is most destructive to the man himself, who by asserting self rather than donating self, denies himself the truth of his own identity. And the absence of authentic identity is most ruinous to a soul, indeed to whole nations."

"Is that what's happening to us in the United States, Your Holiness?"

The Supreme Pontiff paused before replying, "I can safely say it is happening here in Europe, which has lost her memory and, without memory, a nation or a continent of nations cannot maintain its identity. The impact of this we see always in culture, which turns inward and therefore no longer offers hope. And a people without hope cannot survive."

John felt chills run up and down his spine. Did this man believe some sort of "course correction" was off in the distance? "Your Holiness, do you think Europe as we know it . . . will fall?"

The 264th successor to Peter paused and assessed John carefully before replying. "Let us say that Europe cannot be allowed to fall. It alone holds the spiritual patrimony of all the other churches, upon which whole nations depend. And none of those churches wishes to be orphaned."

"Yet you are clearly . . . apprehensive?" John felt emboldened by the concern evident in the lines which re-creased the pope's forehead.

"I am ever hopeful," he replied quickly. "To be Christian is to be ever-hopeful. But we now see on the cusp of a new Christian millennium that the Islamic world is preparing to reinvade Europe in a manner unprecedented . . . and we see that Europe is unprepared for it."

John's eyes widened.

The pope added, "It is difficult, but it is not impossible for a people who have yielded their moral energy to a great deception to summon the will to preserve their sovereignty."

John thought he was referring as much to the United States as to Europe. He now sensed a window closing on the most extraordinary moment of his life. He wanted more. For the first time since he was ordained he truly hungered and thirsted for truth—the simple timeless beauty of it, the raw yet ineffable power of it, the magnetizing allure of it. "Your Holiness," he asked for a final time, "what is it that the Lord asks of his priests at this moment in history?"

The pope liked the question. He looked at John with great love and spoke as a father speaking to a son. "What He asks in every age, Father. That we speak to, and for, the human person, always. That we defend, challenge, and exhort this person created in the image and likeness of God and redeemed in Christ. That we speak truth to power, to protect the divinely granted rights of this person. That we summon this person to holiness and help guide his journey—which is the sole reason Christ created His Church. We are asked to facilitate man's great sacramental encounter with Christ Himself—wherein Christ reveals Himself to this person, and reveals this person to Himself.

"We are called to proclaim a new evangelization with a new ardor, new explanations, and new methods, which will unleash the Holy Spirit to rouse the people of God to reclaim their memory and identity—their vision and purpose—their love and hope. And when this has been accomplished, and by God's favor it will be, man will experience a new springtime of his existence.

"This is the task the Lord has set before you and before me, Father—to make all things new in Christ."

John was enraptured, totally captivated, and found himself welling up. The strength and suddenness of the emotion rendered him momentarily speechless. He could not summon a voice to express the raging desire within him to be that priest for his people, and for God's people.

He suddenly felt strength draining from his body. He felt limp, and was overcome with a physical and emotional fatigue that was unfamiliar. He looked at the pope across the table. He sat head slightly bowed, shoulders hunched, projecting an aura of great strength and equanimity. John felt almost as if he were shrinking before the great man's eyes; he wondered if anyone else at the table noticed.

The pope stood and nodded to the two priests at the end of the table, who immediately departed. He began to walk around to John's side of the table, and John moved to meet him. When they closed the distance, the pope reached out and put his arms around John's neck, pulling his head toward him with a strength that shocked John. He kissed him on the forehead and said to him, "You are a good priest, Father. And I believe you will be an instrument through which the Blessed Virgin will draw many souls to her Son."

The floodgates opened, and John started to weep. His body shook involuntarily. He looked at John Paul II, his vision badly blurred, and felt an overpowering urge to cry out, "What is God asking of me? What do I do with what you are telling me? I am frightened by it. I am overwhelmed by it. Who will help me understand it? Where do I go, to whom do I go with this?"

But he said nothing.

The pope then clapped him twice on the cheek—making John wish he had his football helmet on—turned, and walked out of the dining room.

Monsignor "Jeevish" took him gently by the arm and said, "May I show you the way out, Father?"

68

Michael Burns was happy with the compromise. As Ron Zimmer explained it, Burt Camfy had agreed to two presentations from the Hal Ross agency. The first was to be an analysis of CMN's core business issue—its alarmingly high subscriber disconnect rate, and "appropriate" recommendations; the second, presented in competition with three other agencies, would be the agency's entry in the CMN "beauty contest"—a proposed new advertising campaign by which one agency would secure, or in their case hopefully retain, the fifty-million-dollar account.

As Michael pointed out, the fairness of it lay in the sequencing of the two presentations. If the business case did not precede the advertising campaign, there was no sense in presenting it. Zimmer agreed, accepting Michael's premise that Kloss would simply select his agency and then question aloud why CMN should review anything further from Camfy's lame-duck agency. So Zimmer pressed Camfy on the issue. "Camfy agrees too," he told Michael. "And he's prepared to fall on his sword over it."

Today was the day he and Zimmer were to meet the new creative team that Michael had requested and Zimmer hired. The two were high-profile veterans of whom Michael had read and heard only good things. Together—the woman was a writer and the man an art director—they'd created some of the country's most popular advertising campaigns for its most iconic brands. The woman was said to be a "high concept" genius and extremely tough, as Michael had discovered all successful women in the advertising business were; the man was supposedly a gentle, introspective soul who was brilliantly talented—an acknowledged master in the use of arresting image for commercial purposes. Their talent, and more importantly their "star power," would reenergize Camfy, dazzle Kloss, and ensure that the Hal Ross agency retained the account. Or so it was hoped, and hyped.

Michael took the elevator to the fortieth floor to meet Zimmer. When the door opened Zimmer was waiting. "Ah Shamrock, good of you to join us today."

Michael nodded and held one of the doors, lest his diminutive boss be pancaked. When the doors shut, Michael turned to Zimmer and said, "If these S.O.B.s turn out to be relatives of yours . . ."

Zimmer quickly checked to confirm Michael was speaking in jest, then replied, "I don't have any relatives I'd give this much money to, and that includes my wife and children."

The elevator descended rapidly to the thirty-fifth floor; the door opened and a group of executives who were awaiting its arrival made a large fuss over Zimmer as he exited. Zimmer was all but oblivious, returning the greetings and the kind words with an effortless stream of insult and invective. Michael never ceased to be amazed at how some men could say the most outrageous things to other men, even women, and elicit only affection. He'd discovered if he even so much as intimated one of his harsher judgments to or about another, he stood an even chance of severing a lifelong friendship.

They arrived at the large corner office now occupied by the formidable Rebecca Peterman and found her and her partner,

Nelson Harmon, sitting on a sofa sipping tea. Zimmer walked over to the sitting area and handled the introductions with his usual deft touch. "This is Michael Burns. It is your job to save his job . . . which will help save his marriage . . . which will help save his seventeen children from a life of poverty and misery."

Rebecca Peterman neither laughed nor rose to greet Michael. Taking his cue from his partner, Nelson Harmon remained seated too and continued sipping his tea and eyeing Michael with suspicion. Michael understood. The code on Madison Avenue was to disdain "suits"—those pitiable wretches who cozied up to clients and fought to keep "good work" off the air. The greater the creative talent, the greater the disdain accorded to the philistine account man. Michael did not object. Codes were codes. But he took merciless exception when lesser creative talents projected disdain out of all proportion to their work. Michael's practice was to rip those types new rectal cavities and, ultimately, have them removed from his business. It did not necessarily endear him to the creative community—a surprising number of whom lived in abject fear that whatever talent they possessed might vanish overnight.

Michael merely nodded at his new creative team and sat down on an opposite couch, hoping Zimmer would not sit down next to him and suck all the air out of the room. All he wanted from this initial meeting was a serious debriefing about the untapped equity in the CMN brand. If the "fresh eyes" now staring at him could pick up something in the research that no one else had seen, and if they were able to come up with a creative way to exploit it, then Hal Ross had a chance, albeit a slender one, of holding onto a very large and very visible account that was quite useful in attracting other high-profile clients. A loss of such an account, Michael knew, could sometimes ignite a run on the bank, loosening the tenuous bonds that held many client-agency relationships together. Clients, like everyone else, wanted to be associated with winners.

Zimmer teed up the discussion. "Michael will debrief you, and he will serve as my general on this pitch. He knows this business better than his clients do, and he speaks for me in all matters."

Michael studied the faces of his new creative team, which remained impassive. "We ought to explore anything and everything you think is potentially differentiating. There are no restrictions—no encumbrances—none whatsoever. If you discover you have need of resources we don't have, tell Michael, and he'll see that you get them. We will not ask you to paper the walls with work to justify the manpower we're assigning you. If you wouldn't shoot it, don't put it on the wall. I don't care if we go in with only one campaign, as long as it's the winning campaign. Any questions?"

"We got it, Ron. Thanks," Rebecca Peterman said, speaking for both herself and her partner. As Michael was to discover, the woman would continue to do all the talking for her partner right up until his death from AIDS less than two months later.

Zimmer got up to leave, turned to Michael, and said, "Play nice."

Michael moved to the center of the couch, eyed both of his new business partners, and said, "May I have some tea?" He did not drink tea, but he wanted to understand from what he referred to as the "get-go" just how hard this would be. After a momentary pause, Rebecca slowly gathered herself and went to the credenza behind the sofa and poured Michael a cup of tea. "Lemon or sugar, Michael?" she asked evenly.

"Sugar," he replied, ever so slightly relieved.

She brought him the cup and saucer, a spoon, and a small piece of porcelain china in which he found his sugar. She placed the tea cup on the coffee table between them, returned to her seat, and said to him, "Why is this account up for review?"

Michael immediately understood that the woman understood. She'd done her homework and picked up the buzz on the "Avenue" that he'd had a run-in with Kloss. "Because Richard Kloss wants a new agency," he replied matter-of-factly.

"And why would Richard Kloss want a new agency?"

"Power. He's kinda addicted to it, and from time to time he likes to help himself to more of it."

"Does he always get what he wants?"

"So far."

Michael was not about to demonstrate weakness by spinning the buzz from the street. He did not intend to duck any question, believing this pair well understood that they'd signed on for a long shot and deserved better. He'd read their deal was structured to reward their courage as well as their skill—it was a five-year deal involving millions of dollars—and he was extremely grateful they were here. He was prepared to turn the agency upside down to help them.

"How do you get along with Kloss?" she asked, cutting swiftly to the heart of the matter.

"I don't."

"Why?"

"Because he doesn't understand the business dynamics of his own business; and because I think he's a wannabe riding the crest of a huge wave that is about to crash on the shore of the CMN balance sheet."

"And what exactly is it that he's not getting, Michael?"

The sound of his name coming from the woman's mouth momentarily surprised and slightly disturbed him. "Well, I don't believe he's listening to his own customer," he said evenly.

She processed this with the airy condescension of a clinical psychologist. "And what do you think the customer is saying, Michael?"

He liked neither the question nor its tone. "It's not a matter of what I think the customer is saying . . . Rebecca," he responded in kind. "As you will learn when you get around to reading the research, the customer has been quite clear and extremely consistent."

She quickly took and processed his measure. Clearly this one would not be pushed beyond certain limits—limits he himself would set. He was the sort, she'd been told by her male colleagues, who likened creatives to baseball players who hung, all arms and elbows, over the plate. The business was his plate, and he was the pitcher and he would throw at them—even behind them—to back them off. "OK Michael, just what is the CMN customer saying?" she asked, absent an edge.

Michael softened a bit and sat back on the sofa. He now wanted to relax her and help her ramp up the learning curve, without coloring any of her own judgments and limiting the scope of her creative exploratory. "Their customer is—at least demographically—the parents of the archetypical American family. They are A and B county, 25–54, middle to upper middle, skewing dual income, households, two plus children, some college, white-collar occupational."

He paused and modulated his tone. "The man buys, the woman pays. He buys because he wants to see the 'great' movies. The movies, he discovers, became 'great' because teenagers, needing someplace to go on weekends, made them big box office. When he gets to see them nine months later, he wonders what all the fuss was about. So, gradually, he stops watching; the woman seizes the moment, and disconnects. Turns out she never wanted CMN in her house in the first place."

"We have surveyed those people," he continued. "CMN has surveyed those people. They all say the same thing. They like the movies and other programs that they can watch as a family. They particularly like the stuff that uplifts—the movies with happy endings, the shows that portray people in balanced light, equal parts good and bad. They say there isn't enough of this stuff on the network, so they don't watch it as much as they thought they would. They also say they are greatly offended by what they consider to be excessive amounts of gratuitous violence, profanity, and sex. This makes it hard to justify the monthly cost, which they tend to multiply by twelve and regard as an annual cost. So they disconnect. About half of them every year. Pretty much the entire base every two years."

"When the wiring of all the big cities is completed in the next couple of years, CMN is going to have to recapture a lot of the families who bailed on them if they want to maintain their growth. Their experience demonstrates this is very difficult to do, and very, very expensive." Michael stopped abruptly. Her turn.

The woman gave every indication of having assimilated the essentials by the nature of her follow-up question, "What does Kloss say when he is shown the research?"

"He doesn't deign to review the research. When it's present-ed, he blows it off and makes sure none of his senior programming executives are there."

"So he knows, but he doesn't know."

"He knows, and he knows you know he knows . . . but he doesn't care, because what he thinks is more important than what you think—even more important than what actually is."

"And what does he think?"

"He thinks the great networks are run by people who have a gut instinct for what the American family wants. And he's one of those rare and very special people."

"What does he think of the advertising?"

"He thinks it's pure bull."

"Do you think he's right?"

Michael smiled. "It's far more important what you think. I'm way too invested in it." He waited to see if she would take the bait. She didn't. He was impressed. He had no doubts that this sophisticated woman had already conducted her own review and found the work wanting.

"Michael, what does Kloss think the advertising should do that it's not doing?"

He paused before answering, wanting to make sure that he gave Kloss his due in a way that would benefit her and her partner. "He thinks it should project a Tiffany image of exclusivity; he believes that would inoculate it from churn—who would discard a bauble from Tiffany's? The difficulty is, that strategy is in fun-damental conflict with the way he wants it executed."

This interested her. People of her stature, Michael observed, were absolutely masterful in showing clients how they were get-ting precisely what they wanted in work that had almost nothing to do with what they wanted. "What's he saying about execution?"

"He talks about a platform that would suggest that 'the American home isn't home without Cable Movie Network.'"

Rebecca Peterman nodded and smiled. She liked it. Michael thought this was a problem. "And what problems do we have with that?" she asked, discreetly avoiding a personalization of the creative difference.

"We have two problems with it. One, their former customers have told them it's not true. They have said 'our home is not what we want our home to be with Cable Movie Network in it'; and two, it's a universal positioning that is compatible with neither their programming model nor his exclusivity strategy."

She appeared to find these reasonable suppositions. "So I take it you've pointed this out to Kloss?"

"I have."

"How did he respond?"

"He put the account out for bid."

"Ouch," she winced. "Our Mr. Kloss plays for keeps."

"Do you think we should ask for a meeting with him, Becky?" It was Nelson Harmon, speaking for the first time. He looked frail, and his voice had a hollowed-out quality to it.

His partner did not reject the suggestion out of hand, which both surprised and disappointed Michael, who thought it was a terrible idea. She paused and looked at him in an almost tender manner and said gently, "No . . . I don't think so, Nels. He would see it as weakness. Better we should go in behind our reputations and our work. I'd rather surprise him than give him time to gin up reasons why we're not a good fit for his brand."

She's good, Michael thought to himself. *Pretty much the real deal.* For the first time in a long time, he felt the warm and wonderful sensation of hope stir within him.

She turned to Michael abruptly and said, "Kloss wants someone to package the 'Big Lie' for him."

Michael wasn't sure he understood. He was not familiar with the term. "What do you mean by 'Big Lie'?"

"Haven't you heard that expression?" she asked, with more surprise than disdain.

"No. What does it mean in this context?"

"Big lies are a lot easier to sell than little ones. It's counterintuitive. But history has provided ample demonstration that it can work—for a while. I would guess Kloss is well aware of that. In the advertising world it means flying right into the teeth of the research. Not so much simply ignoring it, but rejecting it outright. If your customer says your brand has the least efficacy of all the personal care products in a particular category, and efficacy is what drives demand, you run advertising that says your product has the most efficacy. Same with soft drinks, tourist destinations, computers, cars, wealth advisory services, and pretty much anything.

"Most advertisers are far too wise to ask their agencies to package up a classic 'Big Lie' and most agencies—self-respecting ones anyway—want no part of it. But every now and again, you run into a client who demands it for one reason or another, and the agency has to decide whether it needs the business badly enough to do it. I take it the Hal Ross agency has decided it does."

Michael immediately felt ashamed. "Rebecca, I'm not asking you to do that. In fact, I'm asking you *not* to do that. We've been straight up with these people from the beginning, and I don't want to go down—if we do—having compromised who we are."

"Good, because Nels and I don't want any part of that either. Life's too short, isn't it Nels?"

"Yes, far too short," Nelson Harmon replied.

"So, Michael, what do you propose?"

Michael looked at both of them and said, "Let's go in with an aggressive campaign that speaks to the business case we're building. We're going to demonstrate how close they are to crashing and burning and the impact it's going to have not only on the network but its parent company—National Publishing. Then we'll show them how they can come out of their death spiral by simply synching their investment in original productions to their own customer research. We'll make the case that the network should be restaged around brand attributes reflected in the new original productions—that the new stuff will create a far more universal appeal among American families than the current product, which is mostly recycled Hollywood movies. This, we will assure them, will not only sufficiently increase their rate of penetration among basic cable subscribers, it will also greatly diminish the rate of customer disconnects."

Rebecca Peterman nodded. "So throw it all on the original programming that's in the pipeline."

'Well," Michael hesitated "We have a slight problem there."

"And what is that?"

"The current CMN pipeline is filled with . . . some very bad stuff."

Rebecca Peterman showed a hint of exasperation for the first time. "You're asking me to execute a strategy the client has rejected and link it to product he won't produce. Do I understand you correctly?"

"You do."

She stood, looked at Michael, and said, "We need to get Zimmer back in here; Nels and I didn't sign on for a 'tour of Oz.'"

Michael well understood her frustration. It was indeed a fool's errand, he conceded. But simply creating different, even better advertising around CMN's existing product would only acerbate the network's problems with current customers. The old saying in the advertising business was that nothing kills a bad product faster than good advertising. CMN's problems, Michael firmly believed, were rooted in the incompatibility of its business model and its programming model. The Hal Ross agency, already facing long odds, could not hope to succeed unless it addressed that reality and created advertising that authentically captured the nature and aspiration of a strategically altered programming model. Ignoring what they knew to be true and competing with the other agencies on the basis of creative execution alone—executions unanchored in a viable business strategy—played to their weakness, did a disservice to their client, and ultimately would end in certain failure.

Michael knew Zimmer had given him power to pull rank, but he decided against doing so. He thought it only fair that this woman and her partner be given an opportunity to air their grievances and be active participants in a debate with figurative life and death significance. "OK, Rebecca. You've made a fair point, and a reasonable request. I'll set something up for later today with Zimmer. In the meantime, I've scheduled a full brand review in the 30th floor conference room at noon. We'll show you all the work that's been done over the past five years—most of it is broadcast, but we'll make sure the print is up too."

"Michael, have you made luncheon provisions?" she asked with a tentativeness he thought out of character.

"Yes, we'll have a deli spread set up," he replied.

"Would you please arrange for some potato leek soup?"

Michael smiled, "Yes, yes, I'll have some potato leek soup brought in for you, Rebecca."

"It's not for me. It's for Nels. He hasn't been feeling too well lately."

Michael looked at Nelson Harmon and agreed that he did not look particularly well . . . but then, he'd just met him. "Not to worry," he said to both of them. "I'll have it taken care of."

He nodded and took his leave. He had two weeks to build a very complex and controversial business case. Rebecca Peterman and Nelson Harmon had two weeks to create a jaw-dropping advertising campaign. There wasn't an hour to spare.

69

The sound itself was so piercing and so disturbing that it seemed to have its origin in some dark corner of the netherworld. Neighbors would say in the years to come that Father John Sweeney, had he been in town, would have heard it from the altar a good six blocks away.

It was the sound of life encountering death. The sound of a mother discovering the lifeless body of her child.

The sound of Maggie Kealey finding Moia Kealey in the garage, in Maggie's car . . . with the engine running.

It was a weekday, a school day. Bill Kealey was up before dawn and at his desk in town as the sun was coming up. Grace sent the younger ones off to school before being picked up by a friend for a morning class at St. Joseph's University. Maggie Kealey awakened with a terrible migraine and remained in bed until it partially subsided. She came downstairs to a quiet house and wandered into the kitchen to make herself some coffee and toast. She sat down to eat, looked at the clock on the kitchen wall, and saw that it was just after nine, and wondered why there was no sound coming from

Moia's room. At this hour her daughter was normally filling the house with the sounds of her bouncing and grunting to an aerobic workout video. As strident and unwelcome as those sounds were, Maggie drew great comfort from them. They signaled that her troubled little one was alive and was still a part of her life, however remotely. They were the sounds of a hope that Maggie invested a part of her heart in everyday. Anything was possible with God, she believed. Anything is possible for one who believes. And she did believe, would continue to believe, for as long as there was a breath of life in her body.

She thought it odd on this morning that Moia was sleeping in, because she knew her eldest daughter slept very little, and then only with great difficulty. Every morning Maggie would come downstairs to find small signs of her child's nocturnal habits. The 2% milk placed in the front of the top refrigerator shelf, rather than the back where Maggie purposely placed it. A few precious crumbs of pantry food under the kitchen table, which must have fallen from her lips. A magazine or a newspaper returned to its place on a coffee table, just slightly removed from where it was carefully set. Some evenings, Maggie would awake in the middle of the night and hear sounds coming from the kitchen, and she would crouch at the top of the stairway just so she could hear the daughter she could never see.

But on this morning, it was the absence of sound that drew Maggie back upstairs and to the door of her daughter's bedroom. She leaned her head against the door, and still not hearing sound, knocked twice. Nothing. She turned the knob and found the door unlocked, itself quite unusual. She opened it, and what she saw jolted her. The room was immaculate. The bed was made, the floor was clean, the curtains and drapes were open, and light was spilling into the room and bathing it in warmth and tranquility. On the bed, Maggie saw a small envelope that was unmarked resting on the pillow. She went over and opened it, and immediately saw that it was written in Moia's hand. There was no salutation, it simply began:

He's screwing his secretary. The same whore granddad made him hire. I heard him on the phone talking to her when you were out praying to your worthless God who never listens to you because he doesn't exist. She wants him to leave you, and he said he would but he wouldn't say when, and the lying bitch started crying, and he told her he loved her and that it wouldn't be long. He's played you for the stupid bitch you are. You both deserve each other. See you both in hell.

Maggie felt death. She could smell it. She knew in moments, somewhere close by, she would find it. She wished in that instant that the death she would encounter would be hers. She wished for an end to pain, an end to fear . . . an end to life. She sat on the bed in shock, unable to move or think or cry. She was shattered. Her life as she knew it had just ended, because somewhere, though she did not know where, life of her life had just ended. In that instant, for the very first time in her life, she questioned whether there was a God. The one thing, the only thing, of which she was now certain, was that if God did exist, He was not a God of love. He was not the God of the New Covenant. He was the punishing, vindictive, occasionally even cruel God of the Old Testament. And now, He had chosen to punish her. He had decided to mock her, pummel her, and strangle the very life within her. It was OK, she told herself. He could take her life. She no longer wanted it. Would that she had never been born. For in living, she was now irrevocably scarred, and no balm from any such mythical eternal life would remove the indelible scar or assuage the memory of the searing pain.

She rose from the bed and began her search for death. She did not find it on the second floor of her home. Nor on the first floor of her home. Nor in the basement. She walked through the kitchen and looked out onto the back porch. She saw that her car was not parked in the driveway where she left it last evening when she returned from Bible study. She walked to the front of the house and saw that it was not on the street. She walked out the front door and into a beautiful late-summer morning, and was immediately surprised by the strong smell of noxious fumes. She turned in the direction of their origin and began walking toward the garage. Twenty feet from the door, she knew. With each step she understood with greater certainty just how she would find her daughter. The last steps required an act of will greater than the bearing of the very pain that accompanied her child's birth. It was this image that filled her mind in that instant. The indescribable pain of life passing through what felt like certain death, and the unfathomable joy of seeing, now holding, a new and immortal creation. What was not possible for a child born of their love, a love without boundary or condition? *How many lives would this child touch?* she remembered thinking at the time. Would Bill and Maggie Kealey live to see the destiny that an all-powerful God would no doubt call her to?

She now heard the low humming sound of her car's engine on the other side of the door, and bent to lift it. She was unable to summon the strength to budge it. It was a heavy wood door to a single-car garage, and she had asked Bill on numerous occasions to replace it with a lighter aluminum door. He always said he would, but never did, and now it stood between her and the lifeless body of her daughter. She would not allow that. She bent her knees and coiled her body, tugging and groaning, and with a great final effort she felt the door begin to move. The fumes immediately knocked her back several feet and made her feel nauseous and light-headed. She turned away and felt her eyes burn and tear. She summoned the will to return to the door, and holding her breath and moving forward quickly, she resumed pulling it up until it was resting horizontally on its track above her head. Again, the power of the fumes drove her back down the driveway. She began to panic, thinking that she might not be able to get to her stricken child. What if she were still alive? Immediately she sensed the absurdity of that denial, realizing that she herself was barely able to breathe outside the garage.

Once again she summoned the indomitable spirit of her Irish ancestors and willed herself into the garage, all the way to the front door on the driver's side. Her child was not there. She looked across to the passenger side, and again saw nothing. She opened the door, slid in, and turned the ignition off. It was then that she saw her child in the rearview mirror. She turned and saw Moia's lifeless body curled in a fetal position on the back seat, facing the trunk. She immediately jumped out of the car and tried to open the back door on the driver's side, but the fumes were still too strong, and she was forced out of the garage and back onto the driveway. For several long moments, she stood there gasping and trying to rub the pain and water from her eyes. But an overwhelming impulse arose within her and sent her back into the garage. She opened the back door this time, determined to remove the body from the darkness of its coffin, and to lug it into the sunlight and fresh air, which she knew her child would never again breathe.

This she did. With a mighty effort, she cradled Moia in her slender arms and struggled to back out of the car on her knees; she struggled onto her feet, groaning mightily, and carried the dead weight of her child out of the garage and down the driveway, almost as far as the house. Finally, her legs gave way, and she fell to the ground. The body of her child fell from her arms and landed heavily on the driveway, gashing her forehead.

It was then that Narbrook first heard the wail of Maggie Kealey. A wail so loud and so incessant that, at first, neighbors thought it might be a wounded animal signaling a mortal and imminent danger. In time, the sheer volume and intensity of the sound began to subside. It was then that the first of her neighbors ventured outside in the direction of the Kealey home, and when they turned up the driveway, they saw the figure of a mother holding the lifeless body of a child on her lap, her head raised to the skies, crying out to an unseen God.

When they reached her, they found her inconsolable. Both mother and daughter were beyond their reach.

70

Joe Delgado smelled his wife before he heard her, and heard her before he saw her. It was a little after 9:00 p.m. and he was returning home from a long and difficult day. It was budget season, and the task of pulling the forecast together for a corporation's next fiscal year fell always to its chief financial officer. Joe found it to be an ungainly mating ritual. The heads of all of Pittman's individual business units in the U.S. and abroad would come in with their tale of woe about the inevitable pressures on their business—the resurgent strength of primary competitors who were bulking up on acquisitions and now possessed a fearsome new portfolio of compounds to market, the difficulties of replacing senior executives who weren't cutting it, the gravitational pull on earnings from currency devaluations that required compensatory levels of revenue and profit.

It was of course a most familiar story; one he heard every year. And every year he would patiently explain that the corporation set its forecast to the demands of the Street, as in Wall Street. The large brokerage houses who represented the nation's top institutional investors required a certain level of "organic" growth in a company's annual top-line revenue and its EBITDA, which captured earnings before interest, taxes, and depreciation. "Organic" growth, sometimes called "same store," meant growing your base business—"managing" growth as opposed to "buying" it through acquisitions or mergers, which the Street understood any CEO could do to inflate earnings. The companies in every industry who outperformed their competitors in these two metrics were rewarded with the highest multiple—represented by the price of its stock relative to earnings.

Joe would patiently explain to the senior executives that Pittman Labs owned "Big Pharma's" highest multiple for two very fundamental reasons. One, it demonstrated over time that it could consistently deliver annual "organic" sales increases in the 8 to 10 percent range, and just as consistently drop 12 to 14 percent of those increases through to the bottom line. This achievement demonstrated to the Street that Bill Carney's executive team had built an efficient operating model to manage growth. And two, none of its major competitors were able to match, let alone sustain, Pittman's performance. This meant that investors who bought pharmaceutical stocks as part of a "growth" or "value" strategy would buy Pittman Labs' stock in disproportionate quantities, which would further drive its multiple beyond the range of its competitors.

All of this would also do one other rather important thing, which Joe never neglected to point out to Pittman's "sandbagging" division heads; it would make each of them and their senior executive teams, all of whom held large blocks of shares in the form of options, worth a great deal of money. To his continuing surprise and irritation, even this was sometimes insufficient to convince some of these men to submit forecasts he could knit together to show Carney how he would "make his numbers" the following year. Carney in turn counted on Joe to make these numbers "work," so he could demonstrate to NHP executives how Pittman Labs would make its numbers, and keep them off his back.

Joe was normally mindful of the need to pay homage after these annual mud-wrestling tournaments to Al Heyworth, the man whose oral contraceptive business insulated Pittman from the vagaries of the business cycle and ensured the buoyancy of its multiple. He would remind himself that no matter what was going on in the world—war, famine, depression, plagues—people would continue to "git it on," in Sondra's idiom. And that meant there would always be a place in their hearts for the reliable products of Pittman Labs.

This year, however, he felt different. It bothered him greatly that he too was getting wealthy, extremely wealthy, from a portfolio of products that included compounds that did severe and lasting damage to women and killed their babies—without them even knowing it. Knowing this made this particular budget cycle ferociously difficult, and several times on this particular day his mind had wandered, and he found himself wondering just how much longer he could perform this task for this company.

He arrived home tired, dispirited, and hopeful there might be a smile and a plate of warm food to greet him. The mere opening of his own front door, however, quickly encouraged him to abandon that hope. The smell that wafted through the house alerted him to what he knew would be a long, painful night, filled with a familiar sound and fury, which he hoped would signify nothing.

"Honey, I'm home!" he said, tongue planted firmly in cheek. He'd never said such a thing, not even on those rare good nights when his wife ran out of Jim Beam or Chivas Regal and was drinking his Michelob. She suddenly appeared in the doorway of the kitchen, and the look in her eyes induced a fear that surprised him and left him slightly disoriented. This was going to be ugly, he immediately realized, and ugly was going to arrive in mere nanoseconds.

"You miserable S.O.B. You . . . loser." she began with a sneer, or was it a leer, on her round, otherwise youthful face? She stomped forward like a character in a stage play, a Eugene O'Neil antagonist, and thrust her palms upon his chest, shoving him backward two or three steps. "Who do you think you're trying to fool? You were nothing when I met you and you're even . . . nothinger . . . now. Don't you know you can't do anything without me knowing? Everything gets back to me. My father was right. He said you were an ass, and you are. My mother told me I was making a huge mistake marrying you, and she was right, too."

Fran Delgado then began to cry. Within moments, she was collapsed on a living room sofa and sobbing hysterically, which brought the children down from the second floor. The three girls took turns trying to comfort their mother and sneaking furtive looks at their father. They were no strangers to what they were about to witness anew. But this somehow promised to be of a different order of magnitude, and it frightened them. They loved their father, but it was their mother who was the hub of their lives and their home. It was she who plotted the course, and she who commandeered the ship. It was their mother, they believed, who had made their lives into lives of privilege—the private schools, the country club social life, the biannual vacations to exotic locales warm and cool. It was their mother who initiated and choreographed these things. Their father signed the checks, but often did so reluctantly, sometimes complaining loudly about their mother's spending habits. She never seemed to pay him much heed when he behaved this way, which in and of itself communicated something important to them.

At this moment, none of them knew which line in which particular mound of sand their father had just crossed. Theresa, the eldest, went to a light switch in the living room and flipped it on. Now all the children could see the mascara running down their mother's cheeks, her stomach protruding above her fitted slacks, and her eyes very wet and very red. Theresa sat next to her on the sofa and put her arm around her mother, who buried her head in her daughter's chest. Theresa instructed the others to go back upstairs and finish their homework. She looked at her father, who was looking at his feet, hands on his hips, and said, "Dad, there's some sliced turkey and some potato salad in the refrigerator; and there's some beer out in the garage."

Joe Delgado looked at his daughter and nodded. He was thinking of going upstairs and packing a suitcase, but he was hungry. He went into the kitchen, opened the refrigerator, and removed the plate of turkey and the container of potato salad. He put them on the kitchen table, removed a fork from the silverware drawer, sat down, and started eating. The beer would have to wait.

He tried to put the ugly scene that had just transpired and was at least partially witnessed by his three daughters out of his mind, but could not do so. Attempts to focus on his challenges at work failed. Thoughts of his ailing mother slipped in and out of his mind. His next meeting with Sondra Lichtman emerged, lingered, and dissipated like a summer squall. He found himself unable to sustain a single diversionary thought.

He finished the plate of turkey and the contents of the container of potato salad, and decided to head into the garage for a couple of cold beers. When he returned to the kitchen, his daughter was sitting at the table waiting for him. "Hi, Kitten," he said with a weak smile. "I'm sorry you had to hear that." He sat down heavily, only to get back up and paddle off to search one of the drawers for a bottle opener.

She watched him, stooped and wounded, and her heart was stirred. She didn't like seeing him like this. He was a good man, and truth be told, a very good father. He was always there for his children. He was particularly supportive of her—showing up at her soccer and lacrosse games, escorting her to the father-daughter dances at school, providing the funds for her to go abroad twice in high school, once as a sophomore and again in this her senior year. He was a prince, really, and she loved him very much. She truly didn't understand why he wasn't able to get along with her mother anymore, and it was beginning to frighten her.

Joe Delgado sat down again, pointed to the two bottles of Michelob in front of him, and looked at his daughter and said, "I'd offer you one of these, but frankly, I need them more than you."

Theresa Marie Delgado smiled, and her father beamed with delight. She wasn't beautiful, he conceded, but she was nonetheless an unusually poised young lady with an extremely attractive manner. "Kitten, I don't suppose you'd cut me in on the charges that have been submitted to the grand jury?"

His daughter looked down and started to cry, "Oh, Daddy, it's awful. It's awful. I'm scared."

Joe put the bottle down and moved his chair next to his daughter's, draping his arm around her shoulders. "Kitten, what's awful? What is frightening you? Tell me, please."

Theresa Delgado wiped her face with both her hands and looked at her father, "Daddy, Mom says we have to go live with Granddad and Grandmom—and Daddy, I don't want to. None of us do. Please don't make us go, Daddy. Please."

Joe felt an anvil drop somewhere in the pit of his stomach. He knew, somewhere in the recesses of his mind what this meant, but he couldn't quite piece it together. Why was Fran telling the children she was leaving him? Why was she uprooting the family, his family, and running off without so much as an explanation? "Terry, look at me. Stop crying. I need you to tell me what your mother said to you. Tell me. Now!"

Her father's harsh tone only frightened the child more, and she again began to cry and move her body further away from his in her chair.

He tried a different approach. "Kitten, has Daddy ever lied to you? Have I ever done anything to betray your trust?"

His daughter shook her head through her tears. "Then let me just tell you this," he said quietly but firmly. "Whatever your mother told you I did, I didn't do. OK? Your mother, Terry . . . has, ah . . . she has a problem. And sometimes she can think I've done something that I haven't done. She may even believe it—but that doesn't make it true—am I making any sense, Kitten?"

Theresa Delgado stopped crying and hugged her father. "Thank you, Daddy. I knew it wasn't true. I knew it, Daddy. I really did."

Joe hugged her, pulled her head close to his chest, and gently stroked her hair. "Thank you, Kitten. I need your trust right now. Please promise me you'll always trust me. And I promise you, I will never do anything—anything—to betray that trust."

His daughter put her arms around his neck and kissed him on the cheek. "I love you, Daddy."

Nearly an hour after walking in his own front door, Joe Delgado was beginning to feel a sense of peace. "Kitten, did your mother tell you what she thought I did?"

He felt rather than saw his daughter's head bob up and down on his chest. "What was it honey? What did she tell you?"

His daughter lifted her head slightly in order to be heard. "She said you were a 'whistleblower,' Daddy. She said you went to the *Philadelphia Chronicle* to rat out your own company. And that when your company found out, they would fire you and we would lose our house and . . . and everything. She said you promised her you wouldn't do it, but you went ahead and did it anyway because you really don't care about us. She said you only care about yourself."

Joe Delgado felt a panic he had not felt even when he was flying just above the tree line in the jungles of Vietnam. There were times when he was trying to maneuver his flying death machine, filled with gunners and spotters and all manner of heavy equipment out of harm's way, and it occurred to him that he might well be killed at any moment. But in those moments he had experienced a great peace that surprised and even puzzled him, and it allowed him to concentrate his mind on the task at hand—which was the taking and saving of lives. But in this moment, he felt no such peace. A cold chill swept over him, and he felt sick to his stomach. This can't be happening, he told himself. No one, absolutely no one, knew of his conversations with Sondra Lichtman and Roseanne Gilbert, other than the three of them. And there was no upside for either one of those women to leak it and blow the cover off a potential Pulitzer. The newspaper desperately craved another one, and he was its best bet. Even they would concede that. And yet, how else would his wife know that he did in fact contact the *Chronicle* and did in fact meet with two members of its editorial staff? It defied explanation.

"Daddy?" Theresa stirred in the silence and lifted her head from his chest, her eyes signaling a deep concern. "Daddy, you would never do anything like that to your company, or to us, would you?"

For the first time in a long time, Joe Delgado simply did not know what to say.

This provoked a deep angst in his daughter. "Daddy, please. Promise me you won't do something bad to lose your job and our house. I don't want to live with Granddad and Grandmom. Our whole lives will be ruined. We won't be a family anymore. We'll hardly ever see you. Please Daddy, don't do it. Promise me you won't do it."

He felt her looking at him, but he was unable to return her gaze. He was searching for an entry point from which he could explain the primacy of conscience, the accountability a man has to what is true and good, and what it meant to respond to the challenge of being a Christian in a secular age. But he could find no way to bridge those "goods" with the loss of family, the disruption of his children's dreams, and the loss of a daughter's trust.

In this moment, Joe Delgado sought a way to explain himself to his daughter and convince her that what he was doing, what he was resolved to do, was something she would come to see as an act of great courage—indeed something that would earn her enduring admiration.

But he could not find the words.

And so he didn't.

He turned to his eldest daughter, held her face in his hands, looked into her beautiful hazel eyes, and said, "I promise, Kitten."

She smiled, kissed him, and said, "I love you, Daddy."

He felt himself start to well up and squeezed her as he helped her off his lap. "I love you too, Kitten. Now how about you get yourself some sleep. I'm sure you have a very busy day tomorrow."

She smiled, turned, and left, and by the time she hit the doorway, she was singing.

Joe reached for the bottle opener on the other side of the table and cracked open another Michelob. He took a long slug and exhaled audibly. He felt peace. This night began badly, he acknowledged, but it ended well. He would call Sondra Lichtman in the morning and explain. He was sure she'd understand. And if she didn't . . . well, that was just too bad.

Father Sweeney was right after all. Nothing was more important to a man than his family.

71

The back table at Santa Chiara, just off the Piazza Panthe-one, was filling rapidly with large plates of cannelloni, bistecca, penne arrabbiata, calamari, pollo arrosto, and lasagna fiorno. Robust decanters of red and white wine were being passed back and forth. The conversation was high spirited, and at times even a bit raucous.

The priests from Philadelphia, far from mourning their last evening in Rome, were celebrating it. And why not? The combi-nation vacation and pilgrimage had exceeded expectations in every way. The weather was uniformly excellent, the cultural treasures awe-inducing, and the food otherworldly. The side trips to Assisi, Florence, and Siena were in some ways the highlight of the entire ten-day pilgrimage. And their time in Rome itself—in its cathe-drals and chapels, fountains and plazas—regenerated something within each of them that they did not know they'd lost. On this night, during this "last supper," they were celebrating that, too.

There was a long pause as the hungry men began devouring dishes that were just this side of divine. They'd completed their sightseeing by spending a considerable amount of time in two of their favorite Basilicas, Santa Maria Maggiore, founded in AD 332, and San Giovanni Laterano, founded in AD 337. Each dated its origin from the reign and patronage of Constantine the Great, who ushered in a new age of Christianity, going so far as to make a relatively new religion that was both despised and suppressed into the official state religion of the world's greatest power. This had presumably seemed like a good idea at the time.

Bob DiGregorio in particular loved Maggiore, which was a Renaissance masterpiece with exquisite marble floors and columns, larger-than-life canvas art, and breathtakingly ornate chapels. "You Irish would have taken twice as long and produced half as much," he whispered to Bill Bradford and Joe McManus as they walked past the main altar.

When they first entered the cavernous San Giovanni Laterano, which was far less ornate to the point of even being somewhat austere, DiGregorio whispered, "Now this one must have been built by the Irish. See how it reflects their spirituality."

Bill Bradford, who overheard, replied, "We can agree. I'm sure the only time the Italian workers were ever in a church was when they were getting paid to build it."

On this evening, the men in Santa Chiara were also celebrating their good fortune at having been born and baptized into a tradition where overwhelming gratitude to an all-merciful God was expressed in the awe-inducing beauty of timeless basilicas.

There was suddenly a lull in the conversation. Into the somewhat reduced decibel level Paul Krueger tiptoed. He put down his fork, looked around the table at his colleagues, and said, "What happened to us?"

This was greeted by silence. The other activity at the table—the eating and drinking, the talking and laughing, now ground to a halt. Krueger thought perhaps his friends hadn't heard the question, so he repeated it.

This time Bill Bradford answered, revealing as he did that he had misunderstood the question. "We got older, and became cynical," he said. "It's not like it hasn't happened to other men in other professions."

"Yeah, but we're not other men in other professions." Jim Cafano interrupted.

"That's not my question," Paul Krueger interjected. "I'm talking about our Church. What in hell happened? How did we go from this," he waved his glass in a circle above his head to indicate all of Rome and the once vibrant faith of an earlier Christianity, "to what we are today?"

"Do you mean today as in late twentieth century today?" Bob DiGregorio asked.

All eyes turned to Krueger, because in truth, as Bradford was to say later, not one of them knew what the hell he meant.

"I mean how did we go from the Church we grew up in, to the Church we're now the ministers of?"

The silence that greeted this clarification was of a different nature than the one that greeted the initial question. Krueger had, for all intents and purposes, just pointed his fork at the "elephant in the room." It was, they all understood, the elephant in every room in which serious Catholics gathered to discuss and mourn "first things." The elephant of catechetical illiteracy, the acculturation of the laity, the loss of identity of religious women, the loss of identity in Catholic higher education, the embrace of sexual promiscuity, microscopic attendance of Mass, acute vocational shortages, and impending episcopal and clerical scandal. That elephant. The one every priest at the table was now contemplating.

Silence. Tense, awkward, anxious silence.

"I think it goes back to the Council," Jim Cafano said, breaking it. "Just too much confusion. Who knows what we really stand for anymore?"

"I agree." It was Bob DiGregorio. "I remember even my parents wondering why the Church did away with mandatory meatless Fridays, the legion of decency, and the prayer to St. Michael at the end of Mass. I recall them saying that not asking St.

Michael to '. . . defend us in battle . . .' would open the door to all kinds of problems in the Church." He paused. "They were right."

"Too much, too soon," added Bob DiGregorio. "The Mass in the vernacular. The priest facing the people. The removal of the altar. Communion in the hand. The big push for ecumenism. I mean, pick any three, but not everything . . . not all at once."

"I don't think that's it, Bob. I really don't." It was Bill Bradford. "Look at the Church's history. There's always been a lot of confusion after these councils. There's more to it than that."

Jim Cafano said, "We got affluent. God becomes less important when you don't need things. Isn't that what Maslow said?"

"Maslow said the opposite," Joe McManus corrected. "He said once your primary physical needs are met, you begin addressing social needs until they're met, then intellectual needs, then metaphysical needs, and so on. But I think you make a good point about the Council; our people left the inner city and helped create a new suburbia that had a different aspiration. We followed them out, building churches, schools, and hospitals, but we didn't recapture enough of them for some reason."

"Money. I'm telling you, people forget God when they have money." It was Jim Cafano, and he was defending turf.

"I think it was more a case of the Council putting an end to the 'fortress mentality'," replied Joe McManus, who was now on the offensive. Among the "mediocre seven," only he had been singled out by the rector of the seminary and the archbishop as possessing the intellectual attributes to study in Rome—at the very North American College where they were now staying. This was where the best and brightest from the States were sent to complete their studies, and to network and otherwise prepare for the possibility of someday being consecrated bishops. McManus had declined the offer, wanting to stay close to an ailing mother who subsequently died of brain cancer.

"Whether or not they intended to do this, I don't know," he suggested. "But the immigrant Church of our grandparents and great-grandparents always saw Protestantism as the enemy. Their

Church, at least in their perception, partly defined itself in terms of what the Protestants were against—the Real Presence, the cult of the Virgin Mary, and papal infallibility. The Council, at least the way some interpreted it, demolished that wall in the same way the Berliners breached their wall. And our people saw it as a signal to mingle, to intermingle, and to assimilate. And they did."

"I just think we confused our people," Paul Krueger asserted. "When you change a lot of things people start thinking *everything* is in play. Then you have people in the Church telling them . . . pretty much everything is in play. I don't believe our people see a fundamental difference between us and other faiths now. One's as good as another. We all go to heaven . . . right?"

McManus smiled. "The richest doctrinal and intellectual tradition in the history of man vanishes in a single generation! Now that's some magic trick! You've got to hand it to him. The old boy's been very busy."

This was greeted by silence. Talk of the demonic was a vestige of another age. Even among themselves, priests avoided any reference to the devil. The Church had seemed to downgrade him after the Council. If she still had exorcists . . . even her priests didn't know who they were or how—and under what circumstances—to call them in for assistance.

John, who knew different, said nothing.

"What drove all of this, Joe?" Bob DiGregorio asked with what the others knew to be a pure innocence.

"Long, complicated story, Bob," McManus replied.

"How about the Cliffs Notes version?" suggested Bill Bradford wryly.

"An abridged version for those of us with short attention spans," added Paul Krueger laughing.

McManus eyed the table. He was not one to show off his erudition. His brothers, he decided, were sufficiently interested for him to continue. "Ok. Let me give you a massively truncated overview." He paused and took a gulp of wine.

"Joe . . . you can do this sober . . . if you want." John said this softly . . . as through a confessional screen. It brought immediate laughter and lightened the mood.

"Who'd know the difference," Bradford shouted to more laughter.

McManus took it good naturedly . . . knowing it was the price of having taken his course material more seriously than his confreres.

"OK. Two-thousand years in two minutes. Let's start at the beginning," he began with a broad smile. "Christ has risen, and ascended, and assumed his place at the right hand of God."

"Hey, not so fast . . ." Krueger interrupted to yet more laughter.

McManus ignored him. "The early Christians go underground. The Roman Empire views them as subversives. They are hunted down and fed to the lions. The blood of martyrs does what it is divinely intended to do. It gives rise to wider and deeper levels of faith. By the early fourth century, the Church—though still a minority and still persecuted—is flourishing. The emperor Constantine, under the influence of his mother, Helena, herself a devout Christian, decides to bring the Christians out of the catacombs. He does with the Edict of Milan in AD 313.

"He calls the first ecumenical council, Nicaea, and tells the bishops to get it down . . . meaning the faith . . . in writing. That they do. It's called the Nicene Creed. We say it every Sunday during Mass.

"He then declares Christianity the official state religion."

"So much for separation of church and state . . ." interrupted Cafano.

McManus turned to him and said, "Well, Jim, it's a case of being careful what you wish for . . ."

Cafano stared back unblinking.

"It generally worked out very well in the Byzantine East . . . until the Muslims took Constantinople in the middle of the fifteenth century. And it certainly produced some stunning achievements in the West, like the creation of Europe and the

510 / BRIAN J. GAIL

splendor of the Renaissance. But in some very important ways, it was the worst thing that could have happened to the Church," McManus continued. "She was now joined at the hip with the greatest secular power known to man. Millions get the message and convert . . . many for all the wrong reasons. And that thing about power corrupting . . . well, that turned out to be true of bishops and popes, too. Think Medicis.

"Anyway, once her interests are aligned with secular power, the Church loses her ability to be a voice for the powerless. The Gospel's 'preferential option' is given little more than lip service. Like every other power, she thinks only of self-perpetuation. She has enemies, and they must be vanquished. She expects her patron, the state, to assist her. One of those enemies, she thinks, is science. It appears to challenge belief. It puts her on the defensive. It demands answers she doesn't have. Think Galileo.

"This tends to undermine trust and spark a bit of restlessness among the natives. Her masses, however, are nothing if not long suffering. They are willing to suffer popes who have mistresses and sire children out of wedlock. They are willing to suffer bishops who buy and sell offices. They are even willing to suffer their own spiritual needs going largely unmet. The Faith is core to their identity after all. And, hey, we're all human, right? Even popes and bishops."

McManus paused for effect. "Then cometh a troublesome monk, a guy named Luther. He didn't think much of the corruption part, particularly the 'get out of jail' aspect of buying and selling indulgences. He posts his call for reform on a church door in Wittenberg, Germany in 1519. It detonates like an atomic bomb and leaves a mushroom cloud over the entire continent. When the dust settled, the Reformation was underway. All hell had broken loose."

"Literally?" Bob asked, wide-eyed.

This appeared to momentarily stump McManus. His eyes narrowed, his eyebrows arched, and his face seemed to contract slightly. "Well, Bob . . . in some sense I think . . . looking back . . .

we would have to say that statement is more than metaphorically true. Keep in mind, Luther's diagnosis was largely correct. It was his prescription that was incorrect. And, more to the point, the only reform that endures is reform within the Church. Proof of that, I suppose, is the reality of our now having tens of thousands of different Protestant sects. At the end of his life even Luther was stunned at all the splintering and disunity. No, I don't think that's what our Lord intended when He commissioned the Apostles to 'go forth and preach the Good News.' But clearly our Lord has proven Himself willing to work with whatever we give Him— however little it may be in any given age. And, we must confess, a good many of our non-Catholic brothers and sisters have proven to be better Christians than many of us."

There was silent assent around the table.

"Anyway, I'm off point. The Reformation led to hard choices for whole nations. With which Church, they asked, shall we align ourselves? Ultimately the choices led to wars. Though these wars were between nations, they were, in a real sense, civil wars. Christians fighting one another under the banner of nationalism. The wars proved ruinous. They destroyed the social fabric of a continent. Ultimately, in a tragic irony, they even destroyed the foundations of Christendom itself, which had midwifed their own civilization.

"Men of 'reason' . . . though not men of God . . . surfaced and called for an end to the senseless barbarism. They declared the Christian religion the sole source of the problem. Modern man must transcend the myth, they argued. Let us unbind ourselves from mindless and pernicious tradition and focus instead on what we all can see and touch and 'know.' Let us embrace science . . . the material world . . . for it alone is empirical. Religion is mere conjecture. Who can prove there was a Creator . . . or a risen Lord? Enough of this nonsense. As rational beings . . . let us agree to put an end to such destructive irrationality.

"These men had names . . . Voltaire and Rousseau and Kant and Descartes. They were regarded as great modern men of thought . . . a cadre of new philosophical geniuses. Their thought gave rise to what is commonly called the Age of Enlightenment."

He paused. He had their attention.

"Ideas have consequences. These ideas led to revolution. The one on the continent, the French Revolution, didn't work out so well. It promised 'equality, liberty, fraternity.' It delivered apostasy, anarchy, and tyranny—in a word, secularism. Its leaders made certain that the revolution itself was saturated in the blood of both the deeply despised clergy and their enablers, the aristocracy. France still hasn't recovered, nor has the rest of Europe for that matter. Look at the mess over here. The churches are empty. And because the churches are empty, the heads and hearts of the people are empty, too. Today, the European wants only accommodation. To what, he really doesn't care. Just don't bother me, he says. Let me live out my days in peace. These are the men C.S. Lewis had in mind when he wrote *The Abolition of Man*. These are his 'men without chests.'

"The American Revolution worked out better. The country was settled by Puritans who came to our shores in search of freedom—freedom *of* religion, not freedom *from* religion. This concept of religious freedom is in our DNA. Our framers regarded it as an immutable aspect of natural law. They understood it to be an inalienable right . . . as something granted by God, not men—and not by the states men formed. They formally declared this belief in the Declaration of Independence itself, then codified it about eleven years later in the Constitution. What they wanted, they got; limited government under God. For two hundred years it worked out pretty well. Now, as we are seeing, it's beginning to implode."

Silence. No one would contest the point.

Paul Krueger spoke for the others. "Why?"

McManus nodded. "America may have been discovered by a Catholic, but it was settled by Protestants. When the Catholics and Jews arrived, the social contract—a civil society's unwritten pact on how to live together in harmony—was covered by the

Decalogue. Who, other than atheists, had a problem with the Ten Commandments?

"Well, it turns out, over the past fifty years, America has produced a very aggressive community of atheists who prefer, of course, to call themselves 'secularists' or even 'progressives.' Somewhere along the way, their demands gave rise to a new civic virtue. A virtue that is not actually a virtue. It's called 'tolerance.' The secularists argued that since we don't all believe the same thing, it's not right for Christians to be imposing their beliefs on everyone else. So Christian laws, even the appeal to natural law, must be rejected. This 'God talk' must be driven from the public square—from our classrooms, our civic institutions, and especially from our courts.

"Now understand, this creates certain problems for a Church whose stated goals coming out of Vatican II were interior renewal and ecumenical outreach. How do you engage people who hate you, people who want to destroy you . . . and the very civilization you helped create? We've been a bit slow to see this. We are gradually being cowed into submission."

He paused reflectively. "I'll never forget the story of John Paul I asking a little boy in Rome if he loved his mother. The little boy said yes, he loved his mother. John Paul I then asked the boy if he would take care of his mother if she were sick. The boy said, yes, he would care for his mother if she were sick. The Holy Father then said, 'Well . . . the Church is a mother, too. And she's not well right now. Will you take care of her?' And the little boy said yes, he would take care of the Church until she was well again. Within days the pope was dead.

"This is what I think John Paul I saw in September of 1978. He saw his Church rocked by something of a perfect storm. He saw the confusion of a Church speaking with two different voices about what the Council really intended—and what its documents actually said. He saw a Church in the West yielding to centuries-old flawed and failed Enlightenment values, as her sons and daughters threw their faith overboard in a rush to be assimilated into toxic mainstream cultures. He saw a sexual revolution that raised questions about objective moral truth that his Church's bishops and priests did not feel entirely comfortable addressing . . . and therefore didn't.

"He saw a Church divided. He saw an indispensible voice stilled. He saw the people of God leaderless, sleepwalking into a valley of death, fearing no evil . . . because they had convinced themselves that evil no longer existed.

"This is what he saw. This and his own depleted physical reserves, and I believe it killed him."

Stunned silence.

For several moments no one spoke. Each man was alone with his thoughts. The small back room was bathed in a soft gauzy light. Nothing moved. There was no sound.

"We've been hollowed out." It was John, and he was as surprised as the others to hear the sound of his voice. The other men turned in his direction, hoping for an elaboration but not quite certain one would follow.

John cleared his throat and stifled a nervous cough, "Our generation has been seduced by the pornography we see in our living rooms. It started as soft porn, but it's getting more hard core with time. Sex is now an entitlement. And the Pill and all the other hormonal contraceptives, we think, make it anonymous. We've convinced ourselves there is no longer any consequence to having sex whenever we want . . . with whomever we want. So our kids hook up and cohabitate and contracept and abort and marry and divorce at the same rate as non–Catholics. We've said no to God . . . no to the sacred use of the most important gift he's given us. In saying no to Him, we've lost the power to say no to ourselves . . . even to our children. One generation depleting, then corrupting, the surviving remnant of another. This lack of restraint . . . this new hyper aggressiveness . . . is now present in every aspect of our lives—it's part of our culture, our politics, our business practices. If our technology permits us to do it, we 'just do it', as the ad says. We are a people without self mastery . . . without a moral impulse. We've lost our basic identity. We are a people who are now vulnerable to every conceivable evil."

The air left the room as though propelled by an invisible exhaust fan. The others looked at him as if to say, who are you channeling?

Another long silence ensued. John wondered if each man was asking himself the same question he was asking himself.

It was finally broken by Bill Bradford. "Are we saying the 'salt went flat' and that we are to blame?"

No one chose to answer the question.

"What about our bishops? Where have they been in all of this?" Paul Krueger asked in an attempt to divert blame.

Bradford jumped. "Exactly! They're down there in Washington, D.C. at the Bishops' Conference issuing all those oh-so-politically correct statements about nuclear disarmament and redistribution of wealth. What competency do they have in the area of public policy?"

"Yeah, where are the pastoral letters on abortion or contraception?" asked Jim Cafano. "Why are they so afraid to get out in front on the real life-and-death issues?"

"Because the Bishops' Conference has been sabotaged by the progressives," McManus said matter of factly. "Our progressives are the secularist's first cousins, though of course the secularists reject them at every opportunity. To the progressive mind . . . the Holy Grail is social justice. Moral truth is a distraction precisely because it involves absolutes and therefore is an embarrassment in a post-modern world. Our progressives reject these absolutes; they consider them pre-Vatican II."

"Then why do they stay in the Church, Joe?" asked Bob.

"For the same reason all dissenters stay in the Church. They know if they leave no one will pay any attention to them. They know they are only acknowledged by secular elites when they carry water for them, criticizing the Church about this and that from inside. They are of value to the secularists only to the degree they help the secularists marginalize—and ultimately silence—the

Church. The secularists of course are only too aware that it is the Catholic Church . . . and the Catholic Church alone . . . that stands between them and their ultimate goal, a godless utopian society."

"Don't our progressives get that?" Bill Bradford wanted to know.

"No. By rejecting moral truth and embracing heresy they have cut themselves off from sanctifying grace. They no longer understand the objective nature of moral truth. They are blind men, bouncing off one doctrinal wall after another. They have ended up on their butts, and they have now slid very far down a very slippery slope, and they need our prayers."

John thought the room now seemed ungodly hot. He wondered if the others noticed. If any did, they gave no indication. He decided to make an effort to drop the room temperature. "Well . . . this is the last time I'm going anywhere with you pathetic deadbeats."

Spontaneous, raucous laughter. A bit disproportionate, John thought. He decided to seize the moment and change the direction of the conversation. "I've got an idea," he said with uncharacteristic enthusiasm.

"Oh God! Somebody grab the check before Sweeney bolts with it," Bradford yelled.

McManus, noticing several waiters rushing in their direction, lifted a forefinger to his lips to quiet the table. All eyes turned back to John. He was surprised that he was now nervous. He was no longer sure of what he wanted to say. "Let's address the problems," he began a bit tentatively. "At least in our own parishes. Let's find these new evangelization apostolates and bring them in and let our people hear the truth. Let's pool our resources and share information and cost and talent. Think of the difference we could see in two or three years in our parishes. I'll bet we could double Mass attendance and triple the number of converts and get people going to confession again . . . and . . . " He was stammering he realized. He stopped cold. The blank expressions on the faces of the men around the table told him he hadn't excited much interest. This greatly puzzled him. The look on his own face apparently betrayed his sentiment.

"McDowell would transfer me in ninety days . . . maybe sixty," said Jim Cafano.

"I don't think old Roselli would go for it either," grunted Krueger.

Silence. John tried to hide his disappointment. He looked hopefully at the others. Bob DiGregorio brightened, "I think it's a great idea. How would we do it, John?"

John felt his heart quicken. "I think the first thing we do is get the Theology of the Body apostolates to come in and work with our Pre-Cana programs. Let our young people hear that their pope said the conjugal act itself is an icon of Trinitarian love . . . full and free, faithful and fruitful. That's astonishingly radical. Let the men hear that contraception objectifies the woman . . . denies the very gift of fertility that is a blessed part of her own identity. That it makes her less than an equal. Let them understand this is not only a lie . . . but a violation of simple justice . . . because the woman is always an equal partner in the sacred covenant in the eyes of God."

DiGregorio's eyes appeared to glaze over. He looked down and spoke softly into his chest—which John noticed, with affection, was stained with marinara sauce. "I don't think my kids will understand all that, John."

More silence. Then McManus, "My young couples would understand it. They just wouldn't accept it."

"Why not, Joe?" John asked in a borderline strident tone . . . which embarrassed him only slightly.

McManus turned to face him. "I just don't think they're ready to hear it, John," he said evenly.

"What can we do to get them ready to hear it?" John said patiently.

The others were now all ears. McManus was certainly no progressive, but he seemed dug in for reasons they didn't entirely understand. The tension slowly escalated. It was like watching two heavyweights rush together at the sound of the opening bell.

"Well, John . . . I'm not sure what we could do to pretend the last twenty-five years didn't happen."

"Clearly, I'm not suggesting we try."

"No . . . but what you're proposing would fail to address its reality."

"How?"

"By ignoring some or all of the following: these young people grew up in the homes of contracepting parents, went to Catholic schools and universities where they were taught that contraception was a matter of conscience, and live in a culture where contraception is universally practiced. Oh, and one more thing . . . most, if not all of them, are already cohabitating . . . and therefore contracepting."

"So what?" John knew he had to be careful. He did not want to lob a grenade into their . . . last supper . . . lest it truly be their last supper together. But he was simply unwilling to concede the point.

McManus appeared to throttle back slightly. He feared he would lose the good will of the others if he ran over one of their own in the open road. "John, I'm not arguing what you want to do is wrong; I'm merely suggesting it is . . . it may be . . . problematic . . . at least in the precipitous way you're suggesting we do it."

John tried to moderate his own tone. He didn't entirely succeed. "Joe, work with me here. We've spent the better part of the evening mourning the condition of the Church we love. As you yourself said, our young people are sleepwalking into the valley of death. How in God's holy name can we just stand by and do nothing?"

This pin prick appeared to irritate McManus. "Who is suggesting we do nothing, John?"

John Sweeney was not one to take a backward step in the face of even mild aggression. He was not unaware that this character trait occasionally complicated his life. "You seem to be . . . Joe."

Bob DiGregorio gasped audibly. "I don't think Joe is saying that John. I don't. Are you, Joe?"

"Of course not," McManus snapped glaring at John.

"Then what is it that you are saying, Joe? I'm not at all clear."

McManus was now struggling for control . . . of himself, the argument, and the room. "What I'm . . . clearly suggesting . . . is . . . we acknowledge reality. We didn't get into this mess overnight; we're not going to get out of it overnight. We've got to be thoughtful about this."

John believed he had him on the run. "OK. Let's be thoughtful," he said with barely disguised enthusiasm. "What do we think would be a thoughtful way to begin to address some of these problems?"

"Maybe put some of these materials in the back of the church in the bookracks," said Bill Bradford.

John looked at him to see if he really believed that was sufficient. To his dismay, it appeared he did. "Bob, we've all agreed that our young people don't come to church unless there's a wedding or funeral. How would we get these materials in their hands?"

"Their parents?" Jim Cafano asked hopefully.

"Jim . . . most of their parents don't come to church. That's part of the problem. We're down below 25 percent on Sunday." He looked at the others. He saw fear he didn't understand in their eyes. "OK, let's start with materials in the back of the church. Then what?"

"Maybe notices in the bulletins when the archdiocese is having events like the ones you're suggesting," Krueger offered.

"Paul, the archdiocese doesn't sponsor these kinds of things. You know that. We all know that. And we all know why."

"Why? I don't know why, John," Bob said.

John momentarily hesitated. He decided he was in deep enough already. *In for a penny, in for pound*, he told himself. "Because they think that it will cause a run on the bank. Word of it will spread and people will empty out of our churches. They'll be left trying to finance an infrastructure built for 75 percent Sunday Mass attendance with proceeds from about 10 percent. They've all been to Europe."

Silence. He had struck a nerve. He decided to advance. "My brothers. We will have to give an accounting for what we do when we go home. We all know that down deep. What are we going to do? I'm simply suggesting that doing nothing is not an option."

More silence. Then McManus, "Nobody's suggesting we are going home to do nothing, John. I think that's unfair, even uncharitable. All of us are trying to tell you just to slow it down. Let's fertilize the soil first. Let's not be casting seed indiscriminately on thorn bushes and rocky ground. After all, didn't the Master warn us about that?"

Something like scales lifted from John's eyes. He saw McManus in a bishop's miter with crosier in hand. The man knew what he knew. And what he knew would be put in service, not of his flock but of his grand design. He was a man with a plan.

He looked at the others. He saw them clearly. They were afraid. Afraid of their bosses. Afraid of their bishop. Afraid of their own people. Afraid . . . of themselves. Afraid of being unmasked if they were asked questions to which they did not have answers. He thought of John Paul II's very first words on the papal balcony to all of humanity. "Be not afraid," he had said. John now wondered if he was addressing his own Church.

Instead of revulsion or pity, which is what he expected to be feeling, he felt affection. He understood it to be grace. He remembered reading the great Spanish author Bernanos' *Diary of a Country Priest*. The last words of the novel were "all is grace." For the first time John understood the full mystery of those words. He now understood the ineffable mystical reality of grace—the reality of fallen man permitted an intimate sharing in the life of the Trinity.

He looked at the men around the table. They had not experienced his challenges. They had not been favored with a purgative *Dark Night* experience. They had not had a cup of coffee with a prelate . . . and breakfast with a pope . . . over the last two days . . . who had helped him understand the very purpose of priestly ministry. He would not, therefore, judge them. They were . . . him . . . before Maggie Kealey asked him if she could go on the Pill and still receive Holy Eucharist. They were him before Michael Burns, then Joe Delgado asked him if they had an obligation, as Catholics, to speak out against the engines of America's decline. No, he would not judge, lest he himself be judged.

Tomorrow they would board a plane for home. Within hours of landing, their shoulders would be under a very great weight of pastoral responsibility. The Church's mission would continue as it had for a hundred generations. It was, he understood, a work of the Holy Spirit through and around the cracks and crevices of deeply flawed men. He knew. He was one of those men.

"You're right, Joe. We've got to be careful where we throw that stuff. Especially me. As a pitcher, as you all remember, I had a few control problems."

The laughter that greeted his self-deprecatory retreat filled the room like a cleansing ocean breeze.

"When we played ball in the seminary, no one wanted to bat against you," Bill Bradford said with his head lifted high and his eyes sparkling. "We couldn't always tell if it was a case of your just being wild or if you were actually trying to hit us."

Gales of laughter.

"I have a confession to make," John said loudly over the laughter. "I was."

The sheer volume of the laughter that ensued brought patrons from other parts of the restaurant to the double doors of the room. They peered in and saw young men in dark clothing standing to embrace one another. They shoulder hugged and cupped the back of each other's heads and kissed each other lightly on cheeks aglow from too much wine.

To the onlookers they appeared as images of another group of men who stood around a similar table a very long time ago.

72

EPILOGUE

Michael Burns was tossing and turning—unable to sleep, unable to find the off switch for a restless, troubled mind. He rolled over and pressed the button on the top of his alarm to see what time it was. He groaned when the number flashed. It was 3:19 a.m.

It had been a traumatic day. Ron Zimmer summoned him at its conclusion to tell him that the Hal Ross agency lost the Cable Movie Network business. Burt Camfy called to say it was awarded to MMK&J, a large and well-respected agency whose chief executive officer wrote a screenplay that Richard Kloss produced and aired. The Hal Ross agency was the last of the four agencies to present, and what Michael found surprising was that the call had come within one hour of them returning to their offices. He asked Zimmer if such a swift decision was indeed unusual. "Not when the competition is a mere formality," he'd answered.

Michael had suspected as much when Ron Ashley, his nemesis, was dispatched to the agency, presumably by Camfy, to advise him and Zimmer that the CMN business case presentation that

Michael had spent a good three weeks building would not be presented before the new creative work was reviewed after all. CMN executives, he advised, saw them as two very different, even unrelated issues, and they regarded the new creative work as of paramount importance. *So much for Camfy falling on his plastic retractable sword*, Michael thought, as he exploded in rage. He directed his fury at Ashley, who went back to CMN's Midtown offices and claimed Michael had called him "the Antichrist," which Michael hadn't, but now wished he had.

Nelson Harmon's death from AIDS shocked and saddened all of them because he was universally loved within the agency, despite his having spent less than two weeks of his waning life there. He was a sweet and gentle soul and a very talented man, and his death had its greatest impact on his partner of twelve years—the inestimable Rebecca Peterman, whose creative output in the shadow of her partner's death became all too estimable.

Michael Burns was not particularly good at losing, largely because he didn't have sufficient experience. He had gotten quite used to winning in head-to-head sporting and business competitions, and when he lost he tended to personalize defeat and demonize those who unjustly inflicted it upon him. This of course was a massive and very personal defeat, and the news of its finality was devastating. He returned to his office and immediately called his wife. As she always did, she buoyed his spirits, if only momentarily. But she said something that even now, some twelve hours later, gave him comfort. "You did what you were called to do. Nothing more," she said. "Account yourself as nothing more than a 'useless servant,' and trust that God will repay you for putting Him before your career."

Despite his reasonably strong faith, Michael was not particularly good at trusting either. He did not like leaving things that related to his family and his career to anyone else—even the unseen God who had granted both. He was worried. Extremely worried. He had five children, a big mortgage, and he was unemployed. He also had another problem. Word of his run-in with

Kloss and the executives at CMN was already reverberating in the small, close-knit Madison Avenue community. He knew that. Rebecca Peterman said as much in the very questions she raised at her initial briefing. Given that, Michael knew it was extremely doubtful he would find work in New York, and perhaps anywhere else in the advertising industry. And the advertising business was really all he knew, he told himself. He couldn't very well just start over in another field and make the kind of money his growing family now needed.

He was trapped and saw no practical way out. And on this first night, he felt as though he might be suffering from a panic attack. He had a headache, his chest hurt, his thoughts were racing two beats ahead of his heart, he felt nauseated, and now he was perspiring. He had to do something, he realized. He jumped out of bed, and being careful not to wake Carol, he opened the door to the bedroom and closed it behind him. Quietly he made his way down the creaking one hundred-eighty-year-old steps of their Victorian farmhouse and into the study, where he sat down beside the fireplace. His head and heart were pounding, and he said a short prayer to the Virgin Mother, asking her to come to his assistance.

Out of the corner of his eye he saw a Bible lying on the coffee table and assumed his wife had, for some reason, brought it into the study from the living room, where she normally read from it before going to bed. He picked it up, something he never did—he was in many ways a typical Catholic and therefore almost completely deficient in matters biblical—and opened it randomly, hoping something might catch his eye and speak to him.

Something did. On the page before him, he saw a chapter heading in the New Testament, in the section entitled Revelation 3. It read, "To the Church of Philadelphia."

Michael went to get his reading glasses in the kitchen, where he left them only hours ago, and returned to the study, where he sat down again in the wing chair next to the fireplace and began to read. What he read he would remember for the rest of his life.

It filled him with the very hope and consolation he sought. And in his darkest moments in the years to come what he read on this night would remain lodged in his heart as a sign of God's love for him and his family.

This is what he read, "To the faithful Church of Philadelphia . . . I know of your weaknesses, but because you clung to me and did not abandon me . . . I will open a door for you which no one can close."

Michael Burns closed the Bible, shut his eyes, and said a prayer of thanksgiving. This passage, he chose to believe in this moment, was written some two thousand years ago expressly for him to discover in his wife's Bible, a Bible that was lying, not in the living room where it was normally found, but in his study, which became an unintended destination when the pain and torment of his own despair drove him from his own bed in the middle of a very dark night.

His God was speaking to him. He was touching him where he lived. And Michael Burns now understood that he was being given the very currency required for divine intervention—trust. He returned to his bed and slept the sleep of those who knew they'd been unfairly blessed.

. . .

Maggie Kealey thought about notifying Father Sweeney of Moia's death, but decided against it. She knew he would end his trip immediately and return home, something she absolutely, positively, did not want him to do. He gave every indication of badly needing this vacation and, God willing, he would find whatever it was he was searching for in Rome. Originally, it was her intention to delay the funeral until his return, but that was still seven days away, and she thought that too lengthy a postponement, given the outpouring of sympathy that her daughter's death summoned within the parish and beyond.

So she asked Monsignor Grogan to bless her decision to schedule the Mass and burial on the fourth day after Moia's death, which he did, and to say the funeral Mass, which he graciously consented to do. He also greatly unburdened her by promising to explain her decisions to Father Sweeney, and to handle all the inquiries from an overwhelming number of sympathizers.

This freed Maggie to tend to her distraught husband, whose needs all but drained her, and to her other children, who were traumatized by the shock and finality of their sister's sudden end. The younger ones were disoriented, almost literally walking into walls, and the older ones were drawn into reclusive shells that Maggie knew were unhealthy. She was well aware that her family would need counseling, particularly her husband, but she also knew that she couldn't worry about that now.

The morning of the funeral was gray and unseasonably cool. Slow-moving storm clouds hovered above the city, threatening to dump an unwanted dark and dank wetness. At the private wake for the family, two hours before Mass, Grace collapsed before the casket in anguish, and Maggie immediately regretted her decision to have it opened. The rest of the children would not approach it, and her husband, who did, was now off in a corner by himself, sullen and angry. Maggie dressed Moia in the dress she bought for her senior prom and never wore. When she knelt before the casket, she looked at her daughter and placed her hands on hers, which were cold to the touch, and said quietly, "Now my precious treasure, you have the mother you deserve, and she will do for you in heaven what I could not do for you on earth." Then she pulled from her pocketbook a fragment of a verse she'd written just before dawn that morning, and read it aloud to her still daughter, "Oh how we do miss thee, sweet child of anguished grace, pale rose amidst flawed thorns, spotless victim of our embrace." She then folded it, tucked it under her daughter's hands, and got up and left the room.

The Mass was an evocative masterpiece of beauty and consolation. A crowd of four hundred to five hundred people filled
the church, spilling out onto the steps and down to the sidewalks
and beyond. There were twelve priests on the altar, including
the cardinal who came, he said, to assure Maggie that Moia was
with God. He reminded her of what he'd told her a number of
years before—that Moia did not have sufficient command of her
faculties to commit sin. She was, he said, a "victim soul," whose
suffering greatly benefited many unseen souls. Maggie hugged
him, kissed him, and told him that he was a gift from God in her
family's hour of torment. This seemed to greatly please the older
man, which surprised Maggie, and she found herself wondering if
there was anyone who affirmed this lonely man in his own priestly
struggles.

Monsignor Grogan said a Mass that was simple and elegant
in its ritual and form. His sermon delivered a measure of the very
hope and consolation that Maggie long sought in her ten-year
battle with the dark forces that tormented her daughter. He also
confirmed something the cardinal had said earlier to her, a veritable lifeline that she now clung to in her grief and anguish, "Moia
Kealey was sick, and her illness was terminal," he told those assembled. "Some illnesses are not to be healed in this life. The God
who grants life is the same God who summons life, and He alone
wills purpose into a life. That Moia Kealey's life served a divine
purpose we can be certain, because brief though it was, she was
permitted to contend with mighty forces that were epic in scope
and biblical in nature. And the God who permitted her suffering
is a God who draws meaning from it—both for her who suffered
as well as for countless others."

Maggie arrived at the grave site numb with fatigue and
bowed by desolation at the harsh reality that her daughter was
now only moments away from fulfilling the dark prescriptions of
the prophetic prayer that was read at her casket when it was closed
for all eternity, "Thou art dust, man . . . and unto dust thou shalt
return." She stood now under a tent, her arm in Bill's, her family

beside her, their friends spilling out into a cold mid-day drizzle, opening umbrellas to partially shield themselves from the rain. As Monsignor Grogan began the final prayer, she caught sight of Jane Sammons, her husband's secretary, who was dressed from head to toe in black and was standing just inside the tent on the perimeter of a group that included Bill's family. Maggie suddenly realized the woman was looking directly at her husband, her eyes revealing a verboten intimacy that shocked her. And her husband, she now discovered, was looking directly at Jane. She felt a knife slice through her skin and sever the aorta on its way to penetrating and piercing her heart. A cold, clammy bloodlessness swept through her, plunging her into a dark abyss, not unlike the one that her own daughter was about to be lowered into. She closed her eyes and said a prayer to the Virgin Mother, asking for her assistance. When she opened them, she felt a resolve that calmed her and that no man, she vowed, from that day on would ever pry from her death grip. It was this resolve, born of generations of suffering ancestors who clung to their faith in even more difficult circumstances—and survived, faith intact—that she would transmit to her children. They too would know hard times, but she was determined that they would have their mother's example to draw upon when they thought they could not walk one more step. They would have that, and the faith upon which it rested.

Before he left for work the next morning, Bill Kealey awakened Maggie to say that he was leaving her to live with his secretary, whom he intended to marry in the spring.

As she struggled to make sense of what she was hearing, a door closing on a sacred covenant of some twenty-seven years, she looked up at her husband and was surprised at how slight a figure he now cast from above their marital bed. She saw what she thought may have been fear in his eyes, and if not fear, then certainly apprehension.

Suddenly she felt the venomous, metallic taste of bile in her throat. Something unknown released itself from her heart and momentarily jammed the switches in her mind.

She sat bolt upright. She opened her mouth to speak but immediately closed it. She thought of the children asleep in their beds. She knew if she opened her mouth again the sounds that she released from deep within her would ring in their ears long after they closed her casket and lowered it into the ground.

She fought herself . . . for them.

She looked at her husband and thought how true it is, as her mother was wont to say, that we really don't know anyone. How had this shrunken figure standing before her been hollowed out so . . . so thoroughly?

What happened?

Why did he give up?

Why had he turned his back on all they agreed was important in this life?

She remembered the early years when they would hold hands during long walks on quiet summer evenings and talk about the kind of family they wanted to raise. It would be large and devout and raucous, drawing all manner of others to their front door to breathe in the simple joy that filled its rooms.

It would be a family destination. A place in time where other children and even their parents, in search of something they wanted, would find instead something they needed.

This was one dream, she realized, that would indeed die hard.

Nevertheless, in this moment, she was surprised to feel . . . not anguish but peace. Not a sense of loss . . . but a sense of hope.

He would leave. She would survive.

There would be no discussion. The time for words had come and gone with the first, and last, lie.

She looked directly into the center of his eyes and said matter of factly: "OK, Bill. I understand. But there is something you must do first. Tonight you will gather the family and explain to them what you intend to do . . . and why."

Bill Kealey immediately felt a burning sensation in the area of his chest and dryness in the back of his throat. He began to fidget and squirm. He groped for words, but found none. He looked at his wife and found himself unsettled by the acceptance, more than resignation, he saw in her eyes. He had prepared himself for a loud and bitter departure. He now understood that far from being surprised, his wife had somehow anticipated this moment and had already come to terms with it. Indeed, it appeared she almost welcomed it.

He was overcome by a sudden need to somehow redeem himself, however partially, in her eyes. "Maggie, you can be certain I will be 100% faithful to my responsibility to provide for you and the children . . ."

She turned away and looked out a window across the room. The sun was rising just as she knew it would. She turned back, paused slightly, and said with a softness that surprised them both, "Faithful, Bill?"

Bill Kealey winced as the thrust penetrated the deepest recesses of his heart. He knew instinctively that he would never fully succeed in extricating this lance much less bind and close its mortal wound. He thought perhaps his heart had stopped. He could not speak.

So Bill Kealey simply turned his back on his wife and departed their room, departed their home, departed their family, and walked into the first day of his new life.

· · ·

Joe Delgado arrived home well after his children were in bed, and he found his wife in bed, too. He was not at all unhappy with this discovery because he did not have a particularly good day.

He awakened before dawn to a regret that tormented him, and that he was unable to shake from either his mind or heart. He worked fitfully—irritable and distracted, and not fully present to the men and women who depended on him for guidance on important matters that affected the work and lives of tens of thousands. He spent much of the day trying to determine who it was that informed his wife of his meeting with Roseanne Gilbert and Sondra Lichtman, and he concluded it must have been his own secretary, Helen Hurd. On this day she seemed somewhat remote, and she'd long been particularly close to Fran, having been a convent school classmate of hers. He knew there was no way of knowing for certain if it was in fact Helen who'd outted him. Just as there was no way of knowing how she'd come by her knowledge of his meeting with the *Chronicle's* managing editor and lead investigative reporter. What he did know, however, was that all the Pittman executive assistants developed intricate networks of informants and supplicants—said networks often overlapping in the line of duty. Someday he would figure it out, he told himself, but not now. He would let an appropriate amount of time pass, perhaps six months, maybe a year. Then he would begin to dig, and when he uncovered the source of his blown cover and present torment, he would exact his revenge. And if all worked out as he intended, the revenge would be exacted in full without the participants ever being able to detect his fingerprints. That was the mark of a true "c-level" executive, and he, Joe Delgado, was the real deal, as he vowed his betrayer would come to understand.

He decided to meet with Sondra Lichtman personally rather than break the news over the phone that he would not be going forward with the exposé. He figured he owed her that much. She did not take the news well. They met at a Center City watering hole about a block from South Street, which was a popular haven for the city's resident bohemians. She was late as usual and apologized profusely, and he did not interrupt her, knowing he would be doing the same within minutes.

When he broke the news, she started to cry, and it reminded him of what he already knew—just how important this story, his story, was to her career. It was clear she regarded it as a career-maker, and she was distraught at having lost it for reasons she was unable to fully grasp. She responded by graciously saying she understood his daughter Theresa's fear and his pledge to her last evening, but it was clear she didn't really understand it. And he knew she never would. She would always wonder how a man who professed to believe what he professed to believe could just walk away from what he knew was the right thing to do. Later in their brief conversation she asked him this twice, and each time he found his own reply wanting. How, she asked, could he put the momentary well-being of one woman ahead of the long-term well-being of countless millions of other women? He told her the only reason he could was "because that one woman is my daughter." She nodded and said that was "an" answer, but not "the" answer.

They departed on cordial terms, Joe promising to stay in touch in case something changed, but they each knew the chances of anything changing on a pledge between a father and a daughter was not very good. She would think about doing something with the story despite her managing editor's desire to see the whole thing simply go away, but she would ultimately decide against it. She no longer had any heart for it, believing it little more than conjecture without the Pittman files. Within six months, she would leave the newspaper and the field of journalism altogether to become a public relations executive for a cable television network. Joe watched her go, head down, shoulders hunched, and saw her now as some other man's daughter. He had broken her heart to avoid breaking the heart of his own daughter. It was not right, he felt more than thought. He had no right to do that to another father's daughter, and he felt deeply ashamed.

He returned to the office without dinner and tried to work through some alternative forecasts for the next fiscal year, but his real intention was to avoid going home. He did not want to see his wife. He resented her for emasculating him in front of his own children. He resented her for backing him into a corner and giving him no out before he was even prepared to defend himself. But most of all, he resented her for her sense of entitlement, for the ever-present threat of her taking his family and returning to her father's house, and for the baseless accusation always just below the surface that he was not the provider her father had been.

She was a fall-down drunk, he told himself, and she had now made his life a living hell. If he was not yet compromised at work, he knew he was only one mistake away in some unknown enemy's eyes. At home he was now on an even shorter leash. He was a school child in knickers. Whatever was done, whatever was said between them from this point on he knew—they both knew—love had died.

Joe Delgado took off his coat and hung it in the center hall closet. The house was quiet. He picked up a newspaper from the coffee table in the den—it was the *Philadelphia Chronicle*—and carried it with him into the kitchen, dropping it on the table. He opened the refrigerator and found . . . nothing. He walked into the garage and came back with three Michelobs. He sat down at the kitchen table and opened one. He took one very long slug, almost draining the bottle. It tasted good, very good. He chugged it empty and put the bottle on the table, opening the next beer.

On this night, Joe Delgado would drink seventeen bottles of beer. He would have consumed more if his wife hadn't taken four bottles to bed with her. In the morning he would discover he'd slept on three of those bottles—each of which was empty.

. . .

There was a spot in the sacristy where a celebrant could peer, unseen, into the church through a crack in the door and "count the house," as the saying went. On this Sunday morning, John Sweeney was doing just that, and he saw that St. Martha's Church was full. This was providential, he thought, because he had something he wanted to say to the people assembled, and he was glad there were many who would hear it.

Initially he thought it best to throttle back the engines, which had been idling roughly since the papal Mass. Best to let his people experience his transformation gradually, in carefully calibrated stages, lest they be overwhelmed and simply shut him off.

But ultimately he came to the conclusion he was simply incapable of doing so. The passion now blazing deep within him had a life of its own. His very soul had become a heart-seeking missile, and now before him sat its target . . . the people of God.

No, he decided, he would not throttle back. He would empty his heart. And if some, perhaps even many, complained to big Jim Grogan . . . well, so be it. He was prepared to risk incurring his people's displeasure in hopes of ultimately earning a deeper portion of their trust.

There were problems on the return flight from Rome and the plane was rerouted to Greenland for a "refueling," and, many passengers suspected, some unplanned maintenance. They did not land at Philadelphia International Airport until well after midnight, and it was close to 2:00 a.m. before John finally made it home and crawled into bed. He set his alarm for 8:30 to ensure he would be up in time for the 9:00 Mass, but it did not go off for some reason, and he was awakened at 8:40 by Jim Grogan, who seemed uncharacteristically anxious and preoccupied. The walk to the Upper Church was but a matter of steps through a covered walkway from the second floor of the rectory, and John, after shaving and showering, arrived early to greet the lector and altar servers. He was vested by 8:55.

He peered through the crack again, now looking for Maggie. He found her with the children in her accustomed pew, eyes shut and head bowed in prayer, but he did not see Bill, and this puzzled him. He looked for the Delgados and saw Fran and the girls but not Joe, and that too puzzled him. These couples had come to Mass together every Sunday for years and years, and he found himself growing concerned at the absence of the two men. He found the Burns family, which pleased him. It was a three-day weekend, and he knew they normally returned home to visit family on three-day weekends. He was eager to catch up with Michael to see how the family was doing, to tell him about his experiences in Rome, and to see how he was faring in his struggle with the powers who ruled the airwaves. He made a mental note to get all three couples together, maybe for a dinner at the rectory. He next looked for the John Paulistas and, as he expected, couldn't find any of them. He smiled. It would be interesting to see just how quickly word reached them about Father Sweeney.

At precisely nine o'clock the choir began to sing the entrance hymn, and John processed from the sacristy behind the altar servers and the lector. He smiled at Rose O'Rourke in the first pew, and at Bridget Murray, who was sitting next to her. At ninety-two Bridget Murray was perhaps the holiest woman in the parish. He ascended the steps to the altar, quietly intoning the old Latin prayer he learned as an altar boy, "*Introibo ad altare Dei*—I will go to the altar of God." At the top of the altar he bowed deeply and reverently before the tabernacle, which held the Most Blessed Sacrament, then turned to the congregation and said, "No truth to the rumor that I ran off to become a cloistered monk." The sound of laughter filling the church felt like warm sun falling upon his face. "I'm sure I have Monsignor Grogan to thank for that one." More laughter. He paused until the last echoes faded and said, "Let us begin as one humble family filled with gratitude to an all-loving and merciful Father . . . In the name of the Father, and of the Son, and of the Holy Spirit."

The first reading was from Sirach, one of the Wisdom books, and it was one of his favorites. It read, in part, "Some [God] blesses and makes great, some he sanctifies and draws to himself." John Sweeney hoped to help the people in the pews be among the latter.

The second reading was another favorite of his, from St. Paul to the Romans. "What will separate us from the love of Christ? . . . I am convinced that neither death, nor life, nor angels, nor principalities, nor present things, nor future things, nor powers, . . . nor any other creature will be able to separate us from the love of God in Christ Jesus, our Lord." John Sweeney was about to put that to the test.

The Gospel reading on this bright blue Sunday morning was from John 6, the famous Bread of Life Discourse where Christ says to a large crowd of his disciples, "Whoever eats my flesh and drinks my blood has eternal life, and I will raise him on the last day." Sacred Scripture reported that Christ said this after "taking pity" on the large crowd and feeding roughly five thousand of them with five barley loaves and two fish. Nonetheless, many apparently still did not believe, and as the evangelist notes, they grumbled among themselves, saying, "This saying is hard: who can accept it?" Our Lord, rather than back off or in any way attempt to soften what He knew to be truth, called them on it, saying, "It is the spirit that gives life, while the flesh is of no avail."

They found this no less difficult to accept, and as Scripture says, "As a result of this, many of his disciples . . . no longer walked with him." Again, Jesus refused to retreat from this "hard saying," turning instead to the Apostles and asking, "Do you also want to leave me?" It was Peter, His rock, who spoke for the twelve when he answered, "Master, to whom shall we go? You have the words of everlasting life."

The last time these readings were read at a Mass he'd celebrated in this church, John ruminated, he'd risen to speak and had punted. Today, it would be different.

He paused until the congregation settled in their seats. His eyes swept the church—left to right, front to back—looking for fixed points where he would focus his message. Maggie was at nine o'clock on his compass. Bridget Murray was at six o'clock. The people in the first several pews said later they saw his lips move briefly. He was saying a silent aspiration to the Blessed Virgin, "Entrust and trust." For John Sweeney it was code, and it meant, "I entrust what I am about to say to your Immaculate Heart, O heavenly Mother—and I trust that you will see to it that it bears fruit that will last in accordance with your divine Son's will."

Then he began, "Today our Blessed Lord is asking you and me the same question He asked Peter nearly two thousand years ago. He's asking us this, 'Will you leave me too over a hard saying?'

"Our first impulse is to say, 'Never, Lord. We believe your Flesh is real food and your Blood is real drink, and we believe that if we eat and drink in faith, you will raise us up on the last day, too.'"

He paused and swept the congregation. "But suppose our Lord said to us, 'Yes, I know you believe my Body is real food, and my Blood is real drink, but some of you eat and drink unworthily because you have not heard . . . or have heard but not accepted my "hard sayings."' You must know that nothing grieves me more. I have said these "hard sayings" through my Vicar, the pope, and the bishops who teach and preach in union with him throughout the ages. These men are the successors to my Apostles, and in my Church they speak for me; like my beloved Apostles they have not turned away from me because of "hard truths" that call men not to a self love, but to a higher love.

'And so I ask you today as I asked my disciples then, if you hear these "hard sayings," will you too turn away from me, or will you remain faithful as my Apostles did, even to the shedding of blood?'"

He had their attention. The silence in the church was unsettling. No one knew where John Sweeney was going with this, but they knew it was somewhere he'd never gone before.

"What are those 'hard sayings' in our age?" he continued. "What has our pope, Christ's Vicar, said to us that we wish he hadn't? What are the things that lead many to leave our Blessed Lord in this age? What are those things I don't want to preach, and you don't want to hear?"

He paused for effect. Then he launched.

"If I were a young boy, I wouldn't want to hear that reading pornographic magazines or watching adult videos is serious sin. I wouldn't want to hear that I couldn't receive Holy Communion until I went to confession. I wouldn't want to hear that pornography is immoral because it makes objects of women, and women are not objects—they are God's masterpiece."

Another pause. "If I were an adolescent, I wouldn't want to hear that if I went out on a Friday night and got high or drunk or had sex that I was committing serious sin—because I was profaning my body, which is a gift from God and a temple of the Holy Spirit by virtue of my baptism and confirmation. I would not want to hear that I could not receive Holy Communion worthily without first going to confession and receiving absolution. I wouldn't want to hear any of that. This is indeed a hard saying when you are young and many of your friends are doing these things."

Pause. "If I were a young married couple and did not yet have children, or a couple who was married and already had several children, I wouldn't want to hear that I could not use contraception to avoid having children. I would not want to hear that the lie of contraception enslaves us to a synthetic, conditional form of love. Christ came to liberate us for an authentic, unconditional love. I would also not want to hear that oral contraceptives act as abortifacients and kill many more babies in the womb than surgical procedures."

Longer pause. "If I were a couple approaching middle age having not yet been blessed with children, I would not want to hear that I could not use in vitro fertilization to have children. I would not want to hear that in vitro fertilization artificially creates life in a manner that relegates God to the role of an absentee landlord. I would not want to hear that this same God does not want man to undertake the creation of human life in ways that are independent of the conjugal act, which He has inscribed as the means by which the transmission of life is to proceed. I would not want to hear that to make use of *in vitro* fertilization is gravely wrong, and that I could not eat or drink worthily of the cup of salvation until I confessed this sin, repented from my heart, and received absolution.

"If I were a married man, I would not want to hear that every time I encouraged or permitted my wife to use some form of contraception I was objectifying her, denying her equality in the

marital embrace, and using her for my own selfish physical gratification. And that this is always wrong—on so many levels—and
is always a serious sin requiring absolution for worthy reception
of Holy Communion, because both Sacraments are essential in
restoring us to lives of grace and virtue."

He stopped to feel the disquiet in the church. He plodded
on, despite it. With an even heightened sense of urgency he said,
"Please understand me on this point. Our Holy Father has said that
a society that doesn't get the primordial gift of marital intimacy
right will not have the moral energy to confront the great civili-
zational challenges that await it.

"This makes the contracepting of the next generation literally life-and-death important, not just to families, but to whole
nations."

He paused again, now both hearing and seeing a growing
amount of uncomfortable shifting going on in the pews.

He continued.

"If I were a divorced and remarried man or woman, I wouldn't
want to hear that any prior marriage recognized by the Church
must be annulled before I can live with another as husband and
wife, and drink worthily of the cup of salvation.

"If I were a soccer or hockey mom, I wouldn't want to hear
that my child's practice or game schedule was not a legitimate
excuse to miss Mass on Sunday—not for me, not for him, and not
for her. And I certainly would not want to hear that missing Mass
on Sunday without a legitimate reason was a serious sin because
it dishonors our Creator . . . and that unless I confessed it, I too
could not receive Holy Communion worthily.

"If I were a businessman and complicit in the exploitation of
labor—treating men and women who worked for me as 'objects,'
and not as 'subjects,' in order to maximize my profit, I wouldn't
want to hear that this, too, was gravely wrong in the eyes of God.
I would not want to hear that God wants the laborer to have a
say in how his work is ordered, and to receive a just portion of

the rewards from his labor. I would not want to hear that God demands this simple economic justice from those who provide the capital, the owners of the business. And that, if this does not happen, a grave injustice has been done in His eyes.

"If I was a politician and I voted in favor of things the Vicar of Christ said and the Church has always taught were great evils, like abortion, I wouldn't want to hear that I was giving scandal, and that this was a serious sin. I would not want to hear that I could not receive Holy Eucharist in communion with true believers unless and until I confessed this sin and promised to amend my life.

"If I were old, sick, and suffering, with no hope of recovery, I would not want to hear that I could *not* ask the doctor to end my life. And if I were a child of a parent who was suffering from a terminal illness, I wouldn't want to hear that I must continue to provide food and water to the natural end of my father's or mother's life. I would not want to hear that to deny food and water, thereby ending that life, was not an act of compassion, but a gravely immoral act requiring absolution."

John Sweeney paused to let some of the coughing, shifting, head turning, sideways glances and foot shuffling, and small children now gazing up at their parents sudden rigid features, subside a bit.

Then he continued.

"And finally . . . if I were a priest, I wouldn't want to hear that if I did not preach what I knew to be true, calling my parishioners to the demands of an authentic Christian love; a love characterized by self-donation rather than self-assertion—and chose not do this, because I did not trust the people of God—because I was afraid my parishioners would turn against me—I would not want to hear that God would hold *me* responsible for their sins. And not just those sins! That He would also hold me accountable for every time one of my parishioners, after committing one of these serious sins, ate and drank unworthily—lacerating His sacred Body all over again. I wouldn't want to hear that, and I wouldn't want to hear that I would personally have to pay for those sins—either here or in purgatory—because though God is surely all-merciful in this life . . . He is just as surely all-just in the next."

Long pause. Absolute stillness.

"My friends, I wouldn't want to hear any of that. And I sure wouldn't want to preach it. But I have heard it, so I must preach it. And because I have preached it, now you have heard it, too. So the question our Lord asks of me and of you this morning is this, 'Now that you have heard a hard saying, will you leave me as many others have—or will you remain with me—indeed in me—as have so many of your parents and their parents before them?'"

John stopped and waited for that question to settle. He was in no hurry to continue. After several extended moments, the waiting bordered on the awkward. Only then did he begin to conclude.

"My brothers and sisters in Christ, there can be only one answer to the question our dear Lord asks each of us this morning." He paused, then thundered, "It is the answer St. Paul provided in the second reading, 'Nothing will separate us from the love of Christ!'" He said this with such force and such conviction that he could see the jaws of both Rose O'Rourke and Bridget Murray in the first pew actually dropping—and Bridget Murray's upper plate appearing to either loosen or fall out. "Nothing!" he thundered anew. "Not life or death! Not angels or powers or principalities! Not present things or future things! And not any creature . . ." he paused again for effect "not any creature, human or diabolical!"

He paused one final time for effect, then lowered and modulated his voice, "In the first reading this morning Sirach tells us that 'Some [God] blesses and makes great, some, he sanctifies and draws to himself.'

"Let us each vow that together we who are gathered here this morning will keep faith with our Lord and each other, and the generations who have gone before us. Let us vow to embrace the 'hard sayings' we have heard, and allow the Source of all life, all love, and all truth to sanctify us and draw us unto Himself, that we too may eat and drink worthily of the cup of salvation, and be raised up on the last day."

Father John Sweeney turned and walked up the steps to the altar and took his seat in front of the tabernacle. He closed his eyes and prayed. He gave praise and thanksgiving to his Lord for the people of God who were assembled before him. He asked his heavenly mother, the Blessed Virgin, to petition her Son's forgiveness for his many failings as a priest and as an assistant pastor in the service of her Son's people. He asked her to beseech her Son to forgive their sins—to regard them as his sins. He asked that she show him how he might personally reparate this sin, which he now claimed as his own. He prayed for their liberation, their deliverance from evil in all its manifest forms, for their God to grant them a clean slate in their spiritual journey. And he prayed for the courage, the wisdom, and the virtue to embody the very holiness that he now understood he was to summon from them in Christ's holy name—a holiness that was their eternal destiny from before the beginning of time.

Then he stood and led the congregation in the Creed.

After Mass, John Sweeney stood on the top of the steps outside the church, greeting his parishioners as they came out the front door. He was not at all surprised to discover he'd played to mixed reviews. What surprised him was that some of those he suspected would reject the message instead seemed to embrace it; while those he thought would be receptive seemed distant. The dead giveaway for those people was their asking him about his trip to Rome, and glancing down and to the left or right, avoiding eye contact.

More than a few people, however, did lean in while he was hugging or chatting up another parishioner or couple and say, "Thank you Father. We needed to hear that," or "That was powerful, Father. Thank you." One middle-aged couple approached and asked, "Father, we haven't heard anything like that in years. Do you have a copy? We'd love to read it again and share it with some of our friends."

But what most humbled John Sweeney was a young couple he did not know who appeared to be in their late twenties approaching him after many of the others had gone. They were waiting at the bottom of the steps until he was alone, and now they were making their way back up the steps with three small children in tow. It was the woman, the mother, who spoke first. "Father Sweeney, we've been having . . . some problems," and as she said this she glanced at her husband, who nodded in silent affirmation. "And we were wondering if we could come see you?"

John's heart quickened and he began to well up in the presence of such pure goodness. He was surprised to discover his tears did not embarrass him. An overwhelming sentiment of gratitude surged within him, and he silently gave thanks to the Blessed Virgin for her intercession. He'd been given a second chance. Its confirmation now stood before him in the form of family—that communion of love through which man most decisively images the likeness of the triune God.

"Yes," he responded quietly. "Just call me, and we'll set a time that works for you."

"Father, thank you." It was the husband, and he was smiling, which John noted made him look even younger. "You'll never know how much this means to us."

John looked at both of them and said simply, "You'll never know how much your family means to me."

As they turned to leave, John turned to go back into church and change. Two stragglers were slowly making their way up the aisle after what John assumed was an extended prayer of thanksgiving after Mass. They were old, one very old, and the brightness of the late morning sun made it difficult to determine who they were. John walked into the vestibule to get a better look and saw that it was Rose O'Rourke helping Bridget Murray, who was shuffling behind a walker. As they approached, the older woman mumbled something and looked up to see John's response. He hadn't heard her. It appeared she was without both her upper and lower plates, and was gumming a sound that was indecipherable.

John looked at Rose O'Rourke and asked, "Rose, what's Bridget saying?"

Rose O'Rourke bent low next to Bridget Murray's ear and said loudly and slowly, "Bridget, Father wants to know what you are saying?"

The old woman turned her head and mumbled something into Rose O'Rourke's ear, which made her smile. She lifted her head, turned to John, and said, "Father, Bridget says, 'That's the last time we'll be sending you to Rome . . . Father John Sweeney.'"

ACKNOWLEDGMENTS

Books, even novels, are collective endeavors. The research-ing, conceptualizing, writing, re-writing, editing, re-edit-ing, reviewing, designing, marketing, and most impor-tantly in this particular endeavor . . . the praying, are the work of many heads and hearts and hands.

I'm immensely grateful to the special souls below without whom this project would not have been initiated much less brought to completion:

- To my blessed wife, Joan, and our treasure, Kelly Ann, Jennifer, Michelle, Kate, Joan, Patrick, and Brian.
- To my brothers, Barry and Kevin, and my sister, Eileen.
- To my brother Knights of the Immaculate, Sean, Bud, John, Brian, and Anthony.
- To my friends Matt Pinto, Mike Fontecchio, Mike Flickinger, Devin Schadt, Meredith Fielding, Meredith Wilson, and Sue Allen.
- And, finally, two spirits from the Angelic Cohort whose earthly names are Tom and Emily.

God love you one and all.

Brian J. Gail is a former college and semi-pro athlete, Madison Avenue ad-man, Fortune 500 senior executive, entrepreneur, and CEO. He is currently an educator and author. Mr. Gail has served on numerous civic boards in his hometown of Philadelphia, including The World Affairs Conference, the National Adoption Center, the William Booth Society, St. Charles Borromeo Seminary, and the Regina Academies. He is a husband, father of seven, and grandfather of five. He and his wife of 40 years, Joan M. Gail, live in Villanova, Pennsylvania.

Fatherless is the first of a three volume narrative entitled *The American Tragedy in Trilogy*. It has been translated into several languages and is now selling in Europe and Australia. *Motherless* is the second volume in the series, and *Childless, the final volume, is scheduled to be published in the Fall of 2011.*